"Stand by!"

Curtis swung the starboard release wheel and held his breath. Overhead he could hear the steady beat of engines on the enemy dock.

"Charge gone!"

Curtis looked wildly around the control room as he heard a grating sound on the hull. The sub shivered and settled in the water.

"Jesus!" Duncan shouted. "They're lowering the dock! We'll be pinned underneath and go up with the charges!"

DIVE IN THE SUN

DOUGLAS REEMAN

DIVE IN THE SUN
DOUGLAS REEMAN

A BERKLEY BOOK
Published by G.P. Putnam's Sons
Distributed by Berkley Publishing Corporation

The Secretary of the Admiralty regrets to announce the loss of H.M. Midget Submarine *XE.51* whilst taking part in an offensive operation against enemy coast installations. Next of kin have been informed.

ADMIRALTY COMMUNIQUE

Chapter 1

THE NIGHT WAS moonless and very dark, and the black heaving water of the Adriatic moved uneasily in an oily, sullen swell. Occasionally the ebony water reflected a tiny pinprick of light from one of the small stars, which seemed very high and aloof from the sea beneath, while from the invisible Italian coastline a small, hot breeze clawed weakly across the dull surface.

A watcher, had there been one, would have caught the briefest glimpse of a slender, stick-like object which rose rapidly out of the depths, throwing up a tiny feather of white spray as it cut through the water, like the antennae of a forgotten sea-monster.

The periscope vanished, as suddenly as it appeared, and for a short while the sea was again empty and desolate, then, with a surge of foam and spray, the sea was churned into a frightened torment, and the hard, streaming shape of the submarine rose gracelessly into view, the pressurised air hissing in a subdued roar, as water was forced from the ballast tanks, and the disturbed waves cascaded across the canting steel hull.

Within seconds, the confined space of the bridge above the conning-tower was filled with silent, purposeful figures, as the

1

lookouts carefully scanned every inch of the surrounding area with their night-glasses, while on the casing below, the gun's crew stood huddled around their weapon, their hands reaching for the prepared shells, and smoothing away the dampness from the controls.

The Officer-of-the-Watch relaxed slightly, as each man reported his horizon clear, and concentrated instead on adjusting the towel around his neck as a protection against the spray which drifted lazily over the squat bridge each time that the stem cut deep into the resisting waves. The electric motors died away, and were replaced instantly by the muffled thud, thud, thud of the powerful diesels, and he felt the air being sucked down into the open hatch behind him; air to feed the engines, which, in turn, would feed the starved batteries. In his mind's eye he could picture the too-familiar scene beneath his feet. The relaxing grins of the seamen, as they prepared to enjoy that first cigarette after surfacing. The watchful eye of the First Lieutenant, as he studied the compass, and passed his curt orders to the coxswain. The metallic clatter of countless pieces of intricate machinery, and the gleam of subdued lighting reflecting against the brass dials and greased periscopes. He stiffened automatically as another figure clambered over the hatch coaming and took his place beside him.

The captain glanced perfunctorily through his glasses, and checked the lookouts, before he squinted at the luminous dial of his watch.

'Just about time, Pilot,' he said at length. 'She'll be popping up any second now!'

They trained their glasses over the rear of the bridge, their eyes straining against the darkness, and trying to peer beyond the green and blue phosphorescence which danced crazily around the submarine's wake.

There was a strange air of tension on the bridge, and as the seconds ticked past, each man felt a rising edge of alarm.

Then, as they waited, the dark water took on a more definite shape, and slowly and painfully, the blurred outline of another craft rose quietly above the white track of their wake.

Occasionally the tow-line tautened and whipped angrily above the wave-crests, and the other craft would veer round unhappily before being brought under control by its hidden helmsman.

The captain chuckled quietly. 'Well, there she is! Our midget submarine is still with us!'

He spoke lightly, but the other officer had watched him closely during the last six days and had seen all too clearly the immense strain on his captain's thin face. Six days of bitter anxiety as they had towed the tiny submarine and its deadly cargo across the war-torn Mediterranean, from Malta around the "heel" of Italy, and steadily northwards up the hostile waters of the narrow Adriatic.

And now, nearly four hundred miles along the Italian coast-line, his responsibility was practically over. It would soon be time to drop the two and leave the little, fifty-foot miniature of his own boat to carry on with its dangerous mission.

He paused at the top of the hatch. 'Call me the second you sight anything,' he said unnecessarily, 'and watch the tow-line. We don't want anything to go wrong now!'

He clattered down the shiny ladder to the control-room, brushing past the next group of lookouts, who stood, their eyes covered with dark glasses, and smoking beneath the hatch, like a collection of blind men, and walked tiredly across to his First Lieutenant.

'All clear, Number One,' he nodded. 'The midget has sur-faced quite well, and I'll be taking off the passage-crew any minute now. I'll just have a word with her operational crew before they take over, and go over the details again with her skipper.'

'I'd rather them than me, sir! People think *this* job is bad enough, but at least there's room enough to stand up!'

The captain yawned and stretched his cramped shoulders, his eyes resting momentarily on the pale, tired faces of his men, and his nose taking in the sour odour of oil and sweat, of damp clothing and stale food.

'It's a long war,' he remarked indifferently, 'and I'll never forgive Their Lordships for passing this towing job on to me. I've had to pass up several good targets because of it!' He frowned as he thought of his silent torpedoes lying peacefully in their tubes, and of the merchant ships which had crossed his sights during the last few days. But his orders had left him in no doubt. He was to tow the midget submarine, *XE.51*, to a point thirty miles east of Rimini, and do nothing to arouse the enemy's suspicion, or give them cause to suspect any hostile activity in what was practically "untried ground".

'D'you think they'll have any luck, sir?'

The captain paused in his stride by the chart table and leaned the faded elbows of his stained jacket on the chart. He checked the wavering pencilled line of their course and the small cross which marked the end of the journey.

'They must!' It was a flat statement. 'In twenty-four hours' time Italy will be invaded from the south and south-west by our chaps and the Yanks, and all hell will be let loose.' He tapped the chart with a pair of brass dividers. 'Here, the port of Vigoria— not much to look at, is it? But Intelligence and R.A.F. Recce have reported that the Jerries have got their biggest floating dock moored there. If the Allied invasion gets started all right in the south it'll be their *only* floating dock which is big enough to handle their big stuff—cruisers and the like. If they got one whiff of what we're up to they'd tow the blessed thing across the Adriatic to Split, and could do all their repairs there. It could make a big difference to their surface forces.' He shrugged again. 'So, Number One, our little friend is going to take care of it!'

They stood looking at the chart in silence, visualizing the harbour defences, patrol boats, mines, and the inevitable uncertainty of Intelligance reports.

'We'll rendezvous with them afterwards, as arranged, and tow 'em back. Simple, eh, Number One?'

A shadow darkened the chart table, and they turned to face the giant of a man who stood loosely beside them. All of six feet tall, he was powerfully built to the extent of clumsiness, but there was nothing awkward or slow in his square, unshaven face and cool, grey eyes, nor in the hard set of his jaw which jutted forward in a half-humorous, half-mocking grin. On the shoulder of his battledress blouse he carried the word "Australia".

Lieutenant "Steve" Duncan, R.A.N.V.R., First Lieutenant of *XE.51*, eyed the two officers calmly, his big, square hands resting on his hips. He was most people's idea of the typical Australian, outspoken, tough, and seemingly larger than life. When he spoke, his voice was surprisingly low and well-modulated, and his hard, Queensland drawl made an incongruous note in the humid control-room.

'I've just been listening to you chaps,' he remarked slowly, 'and I'd like to point out that you're talking the sort of complete drivel which I'm beginning to believe is typical of everything in this war that I hate most!' He smiled gently, as if amused at the cold hostility in the submarine commander's eyes or by the look of alarm shown by the other officer, as he darted a quick glance at his captain's faded gold lace, which proclaimed him not only a regular officer, but two ranks senior to the Australian lieutenant.

The captain smiled thinly and pressed the palms of his hands against the edge of the chart table.

'What is ailing our Colonial friend now?' He had got used to his imperturbable passenger during the slow passage, and had somehow avoided any definite argument, but on several occasions it had been a near thing. The trip was almost over. He felt he could now afford the luxury of tearing the man's arguments to shreds.

'Well.' Duncan rubbed his bristled chin pensively, his clear eyes staring hard at the dripping side of the hull, as if penetrating the metal, and already staring at his nearing objective. 'I think this is a duff trip! I reckon it won't matter a tinker's damn if we go after the dock or let it stay where it is!' He returned his steady gaze to each of the others in turn. 'Furthermore, I guess that if the Allied invasion of Italy depended on the sinking of a blessed dock, it'd be a pretty crook effort! No,' he shook his head slowly, 'it's just another small, crackpot scheme that some joker has had in London or someplace, and it's snowballed into a "must", something that everyone now thinks is essential.' He guffawed deeply. 'Only thing is, they forgot it's going to be damn dangerous for some poor suckers to carry out!'

'You mean, you don't think you're capable?' The tone was cutting.

'Capable? Well, isn't that typical again? Just because some poor, ignorant Aussie has the effrontery to question the realism of his orders, you immediately take it as a personal insult!' He shook his head sadly, but the deep crowsfeet at the sides of his eyes revealed the hidden humour he was finding so enjoyable. 'We can do it all right! I've been in tougher spots than this before.' He waved his hands vaguely. 'All over the joint! Norway, up the Channel, and even down at Taranto. But those efforts were almost worth the sweat! No, we can do it all right, but I'm sick to death of being told to be a good boy, an' die for my country. Whose country, for Chrissake?'

'Now, look here——' began the other officer angrily, but the

captain stopped him with a jerk of his head.

'All right, so you're capable. What does your skipper think about it? Does he think it's a waste of time, too?'

'Ralph Curtis? He's different.' A faraway look crept into his eyes. 'He's a natural, a born skipper. He can take a midget sub through the saloon bar of the "Royal George" an' no one would spot him. I've been on every operation with him right from the start. I'd not go with another. In fact, we've always been a team, up to the last job, when we lost our diver. But me an' the skipper, an' old George Taylor, the E.R.A., we've hung together like dung on a blanket!' He grinned broadly. 'Still, we've got a new diver for this job.' He looked at the captain cheerfully. 'A brand new sub-lieutenant, and the only regular officer in the crew. Still he doesn't seem a bad cove for all that!'

There was a pregnant silence, and the shipboard noises seemed to move in on them. The clatter of a pump and the crackle of morse from the radio room, and in the far distance the sound of a plaintive mouth-organ.

A short, wiry petty officer, his body tightly encased in padded buoyant trousers and battledress blouse, with a pistol hanging from his hip, padded quietly down the control-room. He tried to side-step the three officers, but Duncan pulled him into the group with as little effort as a man picking up a dog.

'Say, George,' he said casually, 'the captain here says we're on to a real good thing! Isn't he just a smart one?'

Petty Officer George Taylor sighed deeply. He had been through all this before, in a dozen ports, with a dozen different kinds of results. Always Duncan had dragged him into one argument after another, seemingly for the pleasure of seeing the displeasure on the other officers' faces at having a ranker drawn into an intimate conversation.

Taylor was a Londoner, born and reared in Hackney, and until the war had called him had served happily, if not ambitiously, in a large garage and service station in Mare Street. Nothing had mattered much in those days, and the outside world had been something either to avoid or to ignore. He had contented himself with "nights out" with the boys, beer and chips at the old Hackney Empire, and a good scrap at the Fascist meetings over in Dalston on a Saturday night. If anyone had told him that one day he'd be sweating in an engine-room of a midget submarine, a space with less room to move about than the back of an Austin Seven, while it slid silently under a watchful German warship, or played tag among the minefields, he would have told him to "'ave 'is 'ead tested!'" He was a quiet, unimaginative man, but like so many of his breed, completely fearless and difficult to shock.

'I just bin with the blokes in the P.O.'s Mess 'ere,' he commented, as if he hadn't heard Duncan's remarks. 'Real nice little place it is, too, when there ain't so many blokes in it.' He cocked his head on one side. 'You called the skipper yet?'

'Nope. I aim to let him get all the sleep he can.' He turned to the submarine's captain. 'You ready to get rid of us yet?'

The man smiled. 'More than I can tell you.'

At that moment the loose green curtain across the tiny wardroom entrance jerked to one side and a slim, dark-haired figure yawned and stretched hugely in the opening. In his new battledress and spotless white sweater, Sub-Lieutenant Ian Jervis looked little more than a boy, and at nineteen his round, youthful face and smooth pink cheeks gave the impression that he was merely playing at some new game and was obviously enjoying every minute of it.

'Aha, our wayward diver!' grated Duncan. 'An' about time, too! All ready to leave this palatial scow, Ian?'

Jervis smiled readily, although he always felt uneasy and slightly nervous with this great Australian. After his Dartmouth training, and coming from a family which had boasted several admirals, including his father, he had never quite been able to accept the atmosphere of unreality and casual indifference which seemed to pervade the men of the newest arm of the Service. He was, as Duncan had pointed out, the only regular in the crew, and he couldn't help feeling that he didn't quite belong. Whether it was as simple as that, or whether it was because he was only a new replacement for the other diver who had been killed, he couldn't quite decide, but it was there all right. Then there was the skipper, Lieutenant Curtis. He remembered so vividly his first interview with him at Gibraltar when he had reported for duty.

The skipper had been sitting in his cabin on the submarine depot ship, apparently staring into space. Before Jervis could introduce himself, Curtis had sprung to his feet, his face white, his eyes suddenly alive and bright. He had stared for seconds at the startled Jervis, and then shaken him briefly by the hand and muttered something about being "in a daze", and had been quite friendly. But several times since then, and especially on the towing trip in the submarine, he had caught Curtis staring at him bleakly, his eyes dark.

He had tried to tackle Duncan on the subject, but he had been unhelpful and had joked at his boyish fancies. Or had he just been evasive?

He had wanted to ask Taylor, who seemed to be a pretty level-headed sort of chap. But there was always the question of rank, and his own unwillingness to start something he couldn't finish.

He wrote regularly to his mother, and occasionally to his father, who, much to his own annoyance, was in charge of a shore-establishment, and had tried to describe his job and his companions. Duncan was an easy character to put in a letter, with his peculiar sayings, which for the most part were quite above Jervis and seemed vaguely crude, and his rebellious attitude to the Service in general and regular officers in particular. But Curtis was different, and each time he tried to explain the man to his parents he realized that his words bordered on the most juvenile hero-worship that he would hardly have believed possible of himself.

He had heard about him when he had been under training as a diver for midget submarines. About the escapades in Norway, when he had won the Distinguished Service Cross and about his daring and cool courage in pressing home his attacks to lay his two-ton explosive charges beneath the unsuspecting enemy. But it was more than the hearsay; it was the man himself. Tall and slim, his shoulders slightly stooped from the constant cramping confinement of the tiny hulls, he had a strange dedicated hardness in his otherwise calm face, which made him older than his twenty-six years. He had a friendly smile, and had always shown willingness to overlook Jervis's early discomfort, but in his eyes he seemed to hold a reserve, a strange barrier, as if he was watching, waiting for something to happen. It was obviously something new, because he had heard Duncan asking Taylor, the E.R.A., if he thought "the skipper was goin' round the bend"?

He ran his fingers through his short wavy hair and grinned. 'I'm ready and willing!'

Duncan jabbed him in the ribs and leered. 'Don't talk like

that in front of these two jokers; you know what they say about submariners!'

Jervis coloured and glanced anxiously at the captain. The latter had turned his back on them, however, and was staring at the chart.

'Shall I call the skipper, Steve?' Jervis asked hurriedly.

The captain suddenly stood up from the table. 'Yes, call him,' he said curtly. 'Tell him I'm going to put over the rubber dinghy to take off the passage crew.'

'Poor chaps,' chuckled Duncan. 'The towing crew have had the job of looking after the midget all the way here, an' now we take over for the best part!'

The captain eyed him coldly, a glint in his red-rimmed eyes. 'It's a pity it's all a waste of time then, isn't it?'

Lieutenant Ralph Curtis lay fully clothed on a bunk in the submarine's wardroom, his hands knitted behind his head, his eyes wide and sleepless, staring at the curved metal hull which rose over his body like the side of a tomb. The curtain which he had drawn along the length of the bunk allowed the harsh wardroom light to filter eerily across his tanned face and fair, sun-bleached hair, and beyond it he heard Duncan's booming laugh and the subdued mutter of conversation. On the other side of the steel plating he imagined he could hear the swish of the Adriatic against the saddle tanks as the submarine forged her way through the night, her small charge wallowing behind her like a calf following its mother. He pressed his eyes shut for the hundredth time, but although sleep had eluded him for days, he felt the nervous tension running through him like an electric current, making his heart and body throb with something like pain.

What had happened? What had changed his life from a breath-taking adventure to a living nightmare?

He sighed deeply, and tried to stop himself from going over it all again.

He gingerly allowed his mind to explore the future, and felt himself pulling back, his stomach contracting violently. He touched his forehead dazedly, feeling the cold layer of sweat which chilled his face into a tight mask. He shuddered violently. Fear. Ice-cold fear. He could almost see his father's steady, unwavering gaze across the wide, littered desk.

'No guts, my lad! That's what's wrong with your generation!'
Then there would be a pause. 'Now, look at me. A self-made
man. Built up this business from nothing, just to give you the
chance I never had!' His father, even across the miles of invisible
ocean, his words, his very soul reached out to taunt and torture
him.

Curtis thought of his father, probably sitting behind that
same desk, dealing with new orders for light machinery—or
whatever he was making now—drumming into his employees
how important it was to help the war effort, and, of course, to
enlarge the business.

Beyond the curtain Duncan laughed again, and for a brief
instant Curtis felt the tinge of jealousy. Duncan, with his indom-
itable spirit and unwavering strength. He had served with him
long enough to know him better than anyone he had ever met,
and he had pictured so often the huge Australian astride his
pony on his vast farm, trotting through the dust, exchanging
jests with his father or his three brothers, and planning, always
planning some new improvement which in itself would entail
fresh labour and sweat before anything would show on the
shimmering dust-blown wastes of his untamed country.

And Taylor, the E.R.A., did he envy him, too? He twisted his
head on the coarse pillow as if to banish the nagging fears in his
brain. Taylor, the personification of the British working class.
Hard, shrewd, but gentle, and with a strange contentment which
left Curtis baffled.

Before it hadn't mattered. They had all been the closely-knit
crew of a midget submarine, the most lonely and the most
dangerous section of any navy in the world.

His mind ground remorselessly on. That had been before
Roberts had been killed.

His lips framed the unspoken words. "Before *I* killed him!"

He opened his eyes suddenly, his whole body trembling, and
stared hard at the shining deckhead. He remembered that day on
the depot ship, only a month ago, when young Jervis had arrived
to replace Roberts. It had seemed impossible at the time, the
cruellest stroke which fate could possibly have played. As the
boy had stepped into his cabin, with the bright sun behind him, it
was as if Roberts had come back from the dead.

He had questioned Duncan casually about the frightening
likeness, but he had shrugged indifferently and said that there

might be some likeness, but not so that you'd notice.

Curtis clenched his jaw tightly, his eyes watering. Some likeness! Were they blind? Or was he going mad?

A bell clanged in the engine-room and the beat of the engines slackened. It would be soon now. Soon he and the other three would be sealed in their little craft, and it would be too late.

He rolled over on to his side, biting at the pillow. Fear, when did it come to him? When did he first notice that the blood of courage had begun to freeze within him?

Soon it would be too late. The words beat like tiny engines in his skull.

This was the most dangerous escapade that they had attempted, and the most useless.

Before, it had been a mad, hit-and-run game, with no time to think, and the wild ecstasy of success to follow. But now, a floating dock in the middle of a hostile coastline, with little chance of survival however the attack turned out, and in addition, he was afraid. Desperately afraid—from his shaking hands, to the dry, bitter taste in his throat. He would refuse to go, and tell himself it was for the others' sakes and not for his own.

His father appeared again, mocking him with his smooth, shining face and well-clipped moustache. He knew what he would say all right. He remembered how he had fought desperately against the steady succession of planned moves which his father had called "your future with the company". The good school, mixing with boys whose only right to any future had been their birth, while he had had his bought in hard-earned money. Boys like Jervis, he thought suddenly, quiet, confident, decent chaps, who never spoke of money or business.

The war had been a blessing for Curtis, and he had fled from the factory and the board meetings, and the hard, probing tongue of his father, with something like relief.

It was that compelling urge to escape from his past of frustration and lack of purpose which had made him volunteer for midget submarines, and which had led him eventually to his own command.

He had looked then to his father for some small sign of faith, if not actual pride, but he had only written to complain of the time Curtis was wasting in the Service, time which the factory could not forgive or overlook.

When he had been awarded the D.S.C. after the Norwegian operations his father merely observed, 'Well, it might look all right on the company's notepaper, I suppose!'

That had been the last straw. Curtis had driven himself unmercifully, taking each operation with cold, calculated calm, and drawing closer to Duncan and the others for the comfort which had been denied him elsewhere.

Then it had happened, without warning, and like a stab in the heart. At Taranto, whilst attempting to lay the deadly charges beneath an Italian supply ship, they had become entangled in an anti-submarine net of a new, unknown pattern, which wrapped itself around the little submarine like a shroud.

Roberts, the diver, had given them a shaky grin and slithered into the Wet and Dry compartment and out through the hastily flooded hatch, and within seconds he was hard at work with the cutters, sawing his way through the slime-covered mesh of the net. Curtis watched him through the periscope, and saw his dim shape, with the pale blob for a face, twisting and turning, back and forth across the hull, barely visible in the dark gloom of forty feet of water. The patrol boat had found them just as the last strand was cut, and they heard the sharp ping of the submarine-detector echo against the hull as the invisible boat moved into the attack.

They had done this thing many times before, in many parts of the enemy's waters, but this time the diver was practically exhausted and had hardly the strength to pull himself back to the safety of the hatch.

Nearer and nearer thundered the racing engine of the attacking boat, and his scalp had tingled with the agony of suspense as he imagined the depth charges waiting to plummet down on to a trapped, unmoving target.

It was then that his last reserve had snapped and he gave Duncan the order to go ahead.

The midget submarine moved reluctantly from the pile of severed mesh, the ragged, knife-like ends clawing scratchily along the hull, screeching and moaning. Or perhaps it was Roberts crying out as the strands of wire ripped open his suit and carried his writhing body down to the bottom of the harbour.

The submarine had escaped, the supply ship blew up, and Curtis and the others were commended.

But somewhere at the bottom of that far-off-harbour, between the twisted metal of the sunken supply ship and the tattered diving suit, Curtis's courage and confidence lay as surely as dead men.

There was a dull, metallic thud overhead, as the deck party prepared to lever the rubber dinghy out of the opened hatch, and Curtis heard the muffled bark of orders, and knew that at any second he would be required to show himself to the others.

As if in answer to his racing thoughts the curtain twitched to one side, and Jervis, his pink face gleaming with excitement, looked over the side of the bunk.

'All ready to go, sir,' his voice shook breathlessly. 'The captain says he's ready to put us across to our midget!'

Curtis swallowed hard and pressed his lips into a thin line in an effort to remove the loose feeling from his mouth. He tried not to stare at the boy's eager face, and instead began to fumble with his clothing and boots.

'Very good. I . . . I'll come at once.'

He watched Jervis's retreating back, and heavily lowered his body on to the deck. His legs shook, and he put his hand on the littered table to steady himself.

Fool, fool! He cursed desperately and silently, the hidden words welling up within him like a bursting flood. Go ahead and tell them you can't go! You're washed up—finished!

He looked round wildly and unseeing at the deserted wardroom with its abandoned belongings, garish pin-ups, and dirty crockery. Even that place seemed like a sanctuary.

The towing submarine's commander peered round the door, his eyes watching Curtis bleakly.

'All set? Anything I can do to help?' His tired voice was friendly, and Curtis pulled himself together with a tremendous effort.

'Thank you, I'm ready,' he heard himself answer. 'I'll leave now.'

As he followed the other officer across the gleaming control-room, he caught vague and disjointed glimpses of the silent seamen at their stations, the First Lieutenant beside the coxswain, and friendly, unspoken messages which were passed by their sleep-starved eyes.

He glanced round blankly. 'Where's my Number One and the others?'

'Already on deck by the dinghy.' The submarine commander's answer was short, and Curtis detected the urgency in his tone.

Wants to get rid of us, he thought bitterly. It was no joke for the other man to have his ship lying on the surface, with its main hatch open and unable to dive. He wanted to get down again, and sneak away from the coast.

Curtis lifted one foot to the bottom rung of the long brass ladder, which snaked straight up the tunnel of the dark conning-tower. His legs felt like lead, and the knuckles of his hands gleamed pale as he gripped the ladder with sudden desperation.

He lifted his head and stared up at the tiny oval sky and the few stars which swam back and forth across the gently rolling conning-tower. He wanted to cry out, to die—anything; but instead he just stared at the faint stars, realizing at that instant that everything had suddenly become hopeless.

'Are you all right, old man?' The voice was practically in his ear.

Curtis didn't turn his head. He dare not meet the other man's eyes. He nodded dumbly and began to climb.

The stench of diesel fumes faded, and the salt air bit across his face as he hauled himself on to the bridge.

He began to climb down the side of the salt-caked conning-tower on to the casing, where a huddled group of figures wrestled with the rubber dinghy.

'See you at the rendezvous! Good hunting!' The submarine commander's voice was distant and already belonged to another world.

Duncan's teeth gleamed in the darkness. 'Well, here we go again, Ralph! Four against the flamin' world!'

'Our gear has been sent across in the dinghy, Skipper.' Jervis was already slithering into the little rubber boat. 'I'm really bucked to be going back to our little midget again!' He laughed and jumped down into the boat.

Taylor followed him silently and with casual ease, his feet hardly touching the lapping water.

Duncan gripped Curtis's sleeve in the darkness. 'I'll tell you now, Ralph, I think this deal is crook! But as it's you I'm goin' with, well...' he shrugged expressively, 'I'm not too worried!'

Curtis followed him over the side, his body hunched and loose in the bottom of the dinghy. He hardly noticed their short journey, hand over hand along the tow-rope, and when he stared up at the small, slime-covered hull of his command, he shuddered, his mind still unwilling to accept the fact that he was beaten.

They scrambled up on to the tiny casing, pausing only for brief handshakes with the three members of the passage-crew who had steered the little boat behind its big sister during the crossing, and then squeezed themselves through the circular hatch into their familiar surroundings.

Curtis remained on deck, and waited until the dinghy had been hauled aboard the other boat, and then slipped the towing wire. He heard the hatch shut, and then the thud of feet as the gun's crew ran below. With a roar like a sounding whale, the air hissed out of the big submarine's tanks as the hungry water surged in.

Curtis strained his eyes through the gloom, trying to capture the picture of the diving, black hull. A gleam of phosphorescence danced along her jumping wire and played briefly around the dripping gun muzzle, and then she was gone. Not one ripple or tremor remained to mark her passage, not even the probing periscope showed itself to ease the ache of his loneliness and fear.

He staggered as a roller lifted the little boat under his feet, and he groped his way towards the after hatch. As he lowered himself down he allowed his gaze to fasten on the forward hatch. The diver's entrance and exit. In his mind's eye he saw again the twisting figure and the distorted face which he had watched through his periscope. It was the same hatch, and this is the same boat, he told himself. Only I am different.

The hatch thudded over his head. They had started.

Chapter 2

DUNCAN WHISTLED SOFTLY to himself as he groped his way with practised caution through the maze of equipment of the midget submarine's tiny control-room and ducked his head tightly into his shoulders to avoid the low, curving deckhead, which was already streaming with condensation, the rough paintwork glistening with a thousand tiny rivers. Once aboard, some of his gnawing irritation and pessimism had dropped away, and for a few moments he busied himself checking the pumping system and hydroplane controls, his movements and observations automatic and thorough. He eased his powerful frame into his seat at the rear of the control-room, and allowed his eyes to wander for a while over the small boat's nerve-centre, pondering on the fates and the perversity of his own nature which had made him take such bitter discomfort in exchange for the rolling freedom of his father's farm.

Taylor was already seated forward, his hands resting lightly on the shining wheel, apparently studying the smooth dial of the gyro compass. Heaven alone knew what he was thinking about. Duncan could only see the back of his small head, but he could well imagine the man's quiet, secret smile and dark eyes, as he sat waiting to steer the submarine on its mission.

Jervis was grim-faced, his unformed features set in a determined stamp as he leaned uncomfortably across the chart table, dealing with his additional duty of navigator.

Behind his back, Duncan sensed, rather than heard, the soft purr of the main motor as it sent little pulse-beats throbbing through the toughened plating.

Forward of the control-room, and separated by a water-tight door, was the tiny, cramped compartment known as the "Wet and Dry", in which and from where, the diver left and entered the hull.

Duncan watched Jervis's tight lips musingly, and wondered how he would measure up to the job under actual working conditions. It would be a bit different from the training depot.

Beyond the "W and D" compartment there was one further space, where the batteries were housed, and where one man could sleep in comparative comfort. Not much of a ship, he thought, but with two-ton amatol charges which were slung on either side of the hull, like saddlebags on a mule, she was a match for the biggest units of any navy, as the *Tirpitz* had discovered to her cost.

The hatch clanged shut as Curtis slithered down on to the deck and rammed home the clips.

Duncan watched him through narrowed eyes as he leafed quickly through the rough log left behind by the passage crew.

Thank God old Ralph's aboard anyway, he mused. He smiled inwardly as Curtis ducked under the small periscope dome in the deckhead, the only place in the boat where a man could stand practically upright. The familiar, automatic motions took some of the edge from his mind, and made even the present risk seem almost commonplace.

Curtis caught his eye and smiled quickly, the corners of his mouth flicking upwards in a tight grimace. He's edgy, too, then. Or was that other business still worrying him? Duncan eyed his captain coolly.

'Here we go again,' he drawled. 'Another flamin' lesson in tactics!'

'Everything checked?' Curtis stared at him for several seconds as if weighing up his First Lieutenant's words to find some hidden meaning.

'Sure, Ralph, everything's all set. Let's go an' hunt for that little floating dock!'

Jervis twisted round at the chart table. 'Do *you* think it's all a waste of time, Skipper? I mean about our going after the dock and everything. Steve says it's too late in the campaign to matter!'

Curtis spun round suddenly, his eyes blazing. 'For God's sake keep your crazy ideas to yourself, Number One! There'll be enough for all of us to do as it is, without you preaching about how the damned war should be won!'

The sudden flare of rage seemed to drag the energy from his taut body, and he staggered slightly to the boat's uneasy roll.

Duncan shrugged and stared woodenly at the deckhead. 'Sorry, Ralph, I didn't know you felt so strongly about it. Forget it!' He grinned, but inwardly the nagging feeling that Curtis had changed came back more strongly than before. So he *was* jittery. I'll have to keep an eye on him for a bit, he thought.

Curtis nodded vaguely, already thinking of something else. 'Right, let's get started!' His voice was dull.

He stared round the control-room, as if seeing it for the first time, and for a moment Duncan thought he was going to falter. When their eyes met again he saw that some of the old light had returned and the gaze was steady and resolved.

'Dive, dive, dive. Thirty feet. Eight-five-oh revolutions.' The orders rolled off his tongue as he stood in the centre of their little private world. They all depended on him from that moment until they reached safety again—or died.

'Check the trim, Steve. Let me know when you're quite satisfied.'

Duncan relaxed in his chair, his grin wider. 'Aye, aye, sir!'

He wrestled with the hydroplane control as Taylor eased open the main vent valves and allowed the water to surge into the tanks, forcing out the air with a subdued roar.

Jervis started, and then crouched down again across his chart, and as Curtis looked across at Duncan he nodded silently.

Duncan winked back. 'He'll do, Skipper,' he said cheerfully.

The Australian's big hands grappled again with the pumping controls until at length he was satisfied that the boat was perfectly trimmed and the tell-tale bubble of the inclinometer rested quiet and motionless. Until that operation was complete nothing could be attempted or carried out in safety by any of them.

'Craft trimmed for diving,' he said at length.

'Right. Take her back to periscope depth, Number One.' The

boat rose easily and unhurriedly, and Curtis raised the slim periscope and tested it in every direction.

As he pressed his forehead against the cool pad, his eye projected over and across the black, silent wave-tops, he wondered how he had managed to get through the last few minutes. Minutes? It was like a lifetime.

It had been a near thing when Duncan had started to needle him, and what at any other time would have seemed the normal pre-operational banter had suddenly developed into something terribly important and infuriating. Supposing Jervis had been panicked by Duncan's words? Suppose it started to prey on his mind, as it was on his own? He felt a rivulet of sweat trickle down his neck, and he gripped the periscope-guide with sudden fear. The boy must be scared enough anyway, he thought, without being sparked into doing something foolish at the wrong moment.

He squeezed the button of the periscope hoist-switch and the thin tube hissed down into its well. He must keep going now. Must keep his mind on the present.

'Ninety feet, Number One.' He cleared his throat to disguise the harshness which had unwittingly crept into his tone. 'Steer three-five-oh.'

Taylor spun the wheel easily and watched the compass ticking round its case. 'Course three-five-oh, sir!'

Curtis leaned across the table at Jervis's side. He could feel the warmth of his body against his arm, and shuddered at the thought of his groping through the dark water in his skin-tight diving suit. He picked up the dividers and concentrated on the wavering pencilled lines and the craggy, uneven outline of the Italian mainland.

'Three hours to daylight,' he murmured, half to himself. 'We'll surface then and get our last good fix.'

'Where shall we hide up while we're waiting, Skipper?' Jervis's voice was also low, as if the enormity of their task had humbled him.

'Well, as you can see, the coastline up to the harbour approaches and main channel are pretty shallow, so I think we'll settle on the bottom about here.' He indicated a huddle of tiny figures on the chart. 'There's a sort of valley just there, carved out of the sandy bottom by the fast current which sweeps round the headland. The locals apparently call it *"il dietro del ca-*

mello", the "camel's back". It's a good sixteen fathoms deep, so we should be fairly snug there until nightfall, when we shall make our first run-in.'

He felt Jervis shiver, and he glanced at him sharply. 'D'you feel all right about cutting the nets?' He tried to keep the fierceness from his voice, and added suddenly, 'We shall at least have surprise on our side.' And not much else, he thought bitterly.

Jervis smiled quickly, his face pale against the glare of the chart-light. 'I'm quite looking forward to it, Skipper! I was afraid the war would be over before I'd even finished my training. It all seems worth while now!'

Duncan groaned loudly behind them. 'For Chrissake! The war'll go on for ever! Years an' years! Don't you fret, son, you'll have plenty of time to be a ruddy hero!'

Jervis laughed uncomfortably and looked at Curtis, his eyes grave. 'Well, you know what I mean, Skipper. My father has always impressed it upon me that it's vitally important for an officer to have war experience. It's such a terrific help in later years,' he finished lamely.

Curtis looked away. It was amazing to think of this boy discussing the war so dispassionately and calmly, and to think that it might only be an interlude in his naval career, when in fact they were crammed together in this little steel shell, nosing through enemy waters with four tons of high explosive to keep them company.

His father, he thought . . . so he, too, had a father driving him on. Suppose the war did allow them all to survive? He almost groaned at the idea of such a possibility. But just suppose. What would happen to them? Duncan would be all right, and probably Taylor would be quick enough to adapt himself, but would Jervis really be able to settle down to the rigours of a peace-time Navy? And as for me, he thought, suddenly angry . . . what would I do? Go back to my father's company, or try to break away on my own?

He remembered the last and only time he had tried to do just that. He had, through a few dubious contacts, managed to entangle himself with a group of young people in Chelsea. It had all seemed so different and vaguely daring. The loose talk, and midnight pyjama parties, and a few unsatisfactory meetings with trousered, overpowering girls who described themselves as either art students or models. It had been new, and for him, a glimpse of another life. But although they had been willing to accept his company, and had made him welcome, he had never been quite one of them. Always, behind him, lurked his father, and his background. In desperation he made the fatal mistake of trying to buy his popularity, and he still felt the quiver of complete shame he had experienced when one of the girls had said, 'Does you dear daddy know you're out so late, spending his cash?' He had driven home like a maniac, their laughter still in his ears.

He realized that Jervis had asked him a question, and the boy prodded the chart with his finger.

'... I mean, shall we leave the harbour the same way as we enter?'

'We'll have to wait and see what the exact situation is before I can answer that. According to reports there are at least two nets to get through. Then we'll have to creep right across the harbour, and that'll mean dodging the harbour traffic and hardly using the periscope at all, and then I'll try to get up alongside the main loading jetty.' He rubbed his chin slowly. 'The dock is apparently right alongside, and we should be able to duck underneath and drop the charges.'

'Here, Ian, come an' wipe down the flamin' boat!' Duncan's voice cut across their conversation like a saw. 'She's runnin' already!'

Jervis seized the big roll of old towelling and began to mop the streaming plates free of condensation. The air was still fresh, but the damp chill was already making itself felt, and they were all grateful for their extra clothing.

Curtis was glad to be left alone. He felt that by turning his body to the chart he could blot out the others, and by concentrating on his proposed attack he struggled to shut out their bantering conversation.

He tried to picture his boat as she must look to the fish. A small, whale-shaped object, thrusting her blunt nose through the dark water; blind, but for her instruments; helpless and lost, but for his calculations. Strangely enough, he felt a little calmer, but he had drained away so much of his energy that he found it difficult to decide whether or not that was a sign of hope or of resignation. He reached for his notebook and started again.

They would lie on the bottom for the following day and start to move in on the harbour defences just before nightfall. They ought to be at the first net before dusk, to allow Jervis a bit of practice before his real job started. If all went well they should be clear of the harbour and on their way out to the open sea by five in the morning. The charges would be set to explode beneath the dock at six, so they should be well clear before the pursuit started. Then rendezvous with the towing submarine the following night. He began to sweat again. That was less than forty-eight hours away! Yet it was a life's span, an eternity!

He forced himself to think of the Allied armies crouching on the Sicilian shores, waiting to make their spring across on to the Italian coast. What would they be thinking? Not about this ruddy dock, he thought fiercely.

''Ere, can one of you gentlemen give me a break on the wheel?' Taylor glanced over his shoulder, his dark eyes gleaming. 'An' I'll get a nice cup of char goin'.'

'Sure. Take over, Ian. Old George'll show you how to mix a good brew.' Duncan laughed lazily. 'Perhaps that'll be some use to you in your career, too.'

Jervis grinned and slid into Taylor's seat, his hands gripping the brass spokes of the wheel. He was used to Duncan's humour, but somehow he couldn't bring himself to react to Taylor's casual acceptance of his companions. If they had all been officers it might have been different, he told himself, but each time Duncan shared a joke with the petty officer, at his expense, he felt a needle of resentment prodding him. I'll get used to it, he thought; we're just four men. He glanced quickly across at Curtis's shoulders, stooped over the table. Perhaps we're only three men, and a leader of men! He smiled at his own reflection in the compass, embarrassed by the complicated depth of his own thoughts. Must be going off my chump. He spun the spokes and started to hum to himself.

The electric kettle began to whistle shrilly and Taylor deftly busied himself with the tea.

He had never quite got used to the process of preparing food or drink on board. He always wanted to laugh at his own antics as he crawled and ducked about the tiny stove going through the ritual which his mother had called, "Wettin' the bed!"

Poor old Mum. It couldn't be much fun for her, with the old man away at the docks most of the time, or bending his elbow in the Bricklayer's Arms, and spending most of her nights in the shelter at the end of the road. He remembered the shock he had received on his last leave, when he had turned the familiar corner and stood stock-still to gape at the savage gaps in the shabby terraced houses. He had never really thought much about the air raids before. When it had been mentioned in the petty officers' mess the others had groused and grumbled about the "bleedin' civvies", or had pointed out that the Jerries were getting a bit in repayment. But standing there on the corner, where he had grown up, had played about with the girls, and cheeked the coppers who came running and puffing after the street book-makers, it had suddenly seemed very real, and very personal.

After that he had given his soul to the midget submarine's engines, and moulded himself into the framework of the small company. He smiled as he thought of Jervis's expression when he had first been introduced. Poor little bugger, he didn't seem to know whether to shake his hand or to put him in the rattle for not saluting!

He handed a mug of tea to Duncan, and for a second their eyes met. Good old Steve. Maybe I'll go out to his country after this lot's over. Mum'd probably kick up a fuss about leaving "the street", but it'd do her good. It'd be a new chance for all of them.

He refilled the kettle methodically. We're all stark, bleedin' mad, he thought—drinkin' tea on the bottom of the bloody ocean, an' me dreamin' of home!

Duncan raised his mug. It looked like an egg-cup in his huge fist. 'Here's to yer! What a life!'

Taylor smiled his secret smile. 'Shouldn't 'ave joined if you can't take a joke,' he answered automatically.

Curtis took his mug of tea and lowered himself carefully into his metal seat, and cursed softly as a trickle of condensation found his neck. He sipped the tea slowly, and noticed that already it had attained the bitter taste which seemed to pervade the whole boat after it had been submerged for any time at all. He stared bleakly at the curved steel side and the quivering depth gauges. Somewhere beyond the toughened metal and the silent water lay the quiet, sleeping coastline, and he wondered vaguely what sort of a life the Italians would lead once the invasion had started, and which way their loyalties would lie. It was unlikely that their German masters would allow them much choice in the matter, he decided.

If only we could get on with the attack, and get it over, one way or the other. The waiting, and the probing, the constant watch over depth and speed, course and distance, only added to the constant worry and the twisting agony of fear.

He attempted to remember his reactions before his last operation, but he only succeeded in obtaining a few distorted images of the past. Like a flashback in an old film. He found he was squeezing the mug savagely, so he carefully stood it on the corticene deck covering, where it vibrated in mocking defiance to the tune of the motor.

It was with something like relief that he saw the hands of the brass bulkhead clock creep round, and he began to shift about in his seat in anticipation of doing something. Anything was better than listening to the others talking, and watching the instruments ticking and winking at him from each direction that he turned his sleep-starved eyes.

No orders were given, but each man moved quietly to his allotted place and sat waiting.

Curtis ran his hand slowly across the coarse material of his battledress, and felt the hard pressure of his stomach muscles. He had the overpowering urge to yawn and keep on yawning. With grim determination he gritted his teeth together and stared at the lowered periscope. He knew only too well that the urge to yawn was the most significant symptom of all. It was the open sign of fear.

He pulled himself together with a jerk, aware that Duncan was watching him and that they were all waiting for him to set the wheels in motion.

'I'm going up to have a look.' His voice was clipped but quite calm. 'How's the trim?'

'Craft trimmed for diving.' Duncan squinted at his gauges and juggled with the controls. 'Steady as a rock.'

'Right. Two-five-oh revolutions. Periscope depth.'

There was the barest tilt to the deck as the craft swam towards the waiting sun, and Curtis screwed his body into a ball, forcing himself down low against the deck, ready to use the periscope at the first opportunity.

'Nine feet, Skipper.'

He held his breath, and pressed the button of the periscope-hoist. He checked it slowly as it hissed out of the well, and then, with his face against the eyepiece, he continued to raise it until the bottom of the slender tube was just under two feet from the deck.

He watched, cold and fascinated, as the picture changed from a dark green, distorted jumble, to a sudden blinding light, as the lens broke the surface and cleared the friendly, glittering water. Scraping his knees, and heedless of the objects about him, he swung the periscope in a complete circle, from horizon to horizon and back again.

It was as if the stuffy, streaming control-room no longer existed. His body was still with the others, but his sight and his soul were free, and moving slowly and lazily across the clear green water.

He sniffed and licked his lips involuntarily, half expecting to taste the scent of the clean sea. But the oil and mustiness remained to remind him of reality.

After the darkness and the anxiety of transferring from the towing submarine, the waiting and the growing fear, the sight of the calm, deserted sea was breathtaking and somehow unreal.

He licked his dry lips, catching a brief glimpse as he did so of Jervis's face watching him questioningly.

He swore inwardly, and forced everything from his mind. Everything but the winding strip of white sand and green trees which formed the full length of his vision. A few white buildings shimmered in the bright morning light, and across a sand-bar of a small cove he could just make out the shapes of some beached fishing boats. The periscope halted in its search as he fixed his eye on a tall, crumbling lighthouse.

He snapped the fingers of his free hand, and spoke from the side of his mouth, in short, brittle sentences.

'Ian, look on the chart. Viserba lighthouse. Has it got a sort of domed roof, like an observatory? If it has, stand by to take a fix!'

He felt the pad pressing against his damp forehead, and wanted to shout at Jervis to get a move on. Instead he peered quickly round at the open sea behind him. Still empty. Not even a white-capped wave to mar the glossy sheen of green glass.

'Yes, sir. Viserba lighthouse it is!' Jervis sounded excited.

He felt a surge of relief flood through him. They were at least on course and running to time. They had passed Rimini in the darkness, and somewhere over the shoulder of that green headland lay Vigoria, and the dock.

The handle of the periscope slithered under the sweat in his palm and a tremor of cramp explored his thighs, but he hardly noticed. His brain worked rapidly and coolly, and for a moment the sickness of his stomach subsided.

'Take a fix.' He watched the lighthouse drift across his sight. 'Lighthouse bears Red one-four-five. The stone beacon on the headland bears Red one-oh. Got it?'

'Ship's head three-five-oh,' chanted Taylor from behind the compass.

'Give me a fresh course for the next leg, Ian. We'll alter course in five minutes from the time of the fix.'

Duncan's slow voice broke in on his racing thoughts.

'Say, Ralph, aren't you keeping the stick up for a bit too long? I mean, some joker may be having a look-see with some mighty powerful glasses.'

Curtis bit his lip. He knew that Duncan was right. It was almost the first lesson he had learned, but something twisted inside him, making him keep the periscope fixed on the shore.

'You attend to your job, Number One, and then I can do mine.'

The words were an implied insult to Duncan's ability to keep the boat steady, but the voice still drawled across the control-room, slow and unperturbed.

'Just thought you ought to be reminded, that's all.'

'New course, three-five-nine.' Jervis's voice had gone suddenly quiet and troubled.

Curtis wanted to scream at them, to drive his fist into Duncan's face, anything to shut up their stupid voices once and for all.

The lighthouse passed out of his vision as he viciously jerked the handle round.

A tiny bird glinted in the sun's light and dipped towards him. The sea was lighter now, and he could imagine the first hint of the warmth to come. He shivered miserably. Soon the little cottages would be alive with people, and the narrow tracks down to the white beaches would be filled with chatter and laughter. It was a different world, where a man could live and be free, could love and find happiness. While he. . . . He shuddered again, and swung the periscope to search for the lonely sea-bird.

The whole lens suddenly filled, and he stared in chilled horror at the wide, silver wings and the flashing arcs of the twin propellers. The periscope hissed down into its well, and he stared blindly at the depth gauge.

'Dive, dive, dive! One hundred and twenty feet! Hard a-starboard!'

He listened helplessly to the water surging into the tanks, and felt the deck cant and stagger beneath his feet.

In a strange, harsh voice he said, 'Enemy aircraft overhead. Coming straight for us!'

He tried to shut out the picture which filled his aching mind, of the aircraft's bombs plummeting down into the crystal-clear water, of the one short moment of horror before their broken hull sank swiftly to the bottom.

You fool! You damned, bloody fool! He ground his teeth together to stem the anguish which was tormenting him, and tried to concentrate on the swinging compass.

'Meet her, steer oh-nine-oh!'

Still nothing happened. Perhaps the plane hadn't seen them. Perhaps it had been moving too fast and too close to the surface to spot the short shadow of the midget submarine.

'Captain, sir!' Jervis's strangled voice was shaking with emotion. 'Maximum depth here is one hundred feet!'

The words struck his mind like an ice-pick, and he swung round to stare at the boy's white face, the edge of the chart crumpled under his fist. Then, reading the despair on his face, he wrenched his eyes to the gleaming dial of the depth gauge.

The long, slender needle crept remorselessly round. Eighty-five feet. Ninety feet. The boat plunged steadily towards the bottom.

'Hold her, Steve! Hold her!'

He saw Duncan's body stiffen as the man wrenched urgently at the controls.

The next few seconds lasted a lifetime. It was a race between the emergency air supply roaring into the tanks, and the deadly, wavering depth needle.

Some of the angle lessened in the deck, and the dive gradually slowed its pace. Then with a sickening lurch, which flung Curtis in a heap on the deck, the hull struck the first sand-bar. Like a mad porpoise she bounded across it, and struck again, the toughened metal scraping and jolting in protest. Curtis tried to regain his feet, and saw Jervis clinging desperately to the lockers, his eyes closed, his lips pressed into a thin line.

The lights flickered and then recovered, as the boat bumped and heaved across the bottom.

Duncan's face was wet with sweat, and his normally calm eyes were wild. 'I'm holdin' her! Come on, old girl, steady now!' Another bump made him curse, and stagger in his seat.

Curtis's voice was flat and without emotion as he took over control once more, and with the blood pounding in his ears he settled the boat slowly on the bottom. The unbroken purr of the electric motor died away, and the shaken vibration of the hull settled into a pregnant stillness.

For a while no one spoke. The condensation began to drip heavily across their heads, yet nobody moved. They were like four stricken corpses.

Duncan slowly recovered and released his hands from the controls. He seemed to prise his fingers free, and as he drew in a long intake of breath the others began to move from their carved positions.

Curtis felt the weakness flooding through his trembling body, and wanted to vomit.

He said suddenly, 'Sorry, chaps. I'm afraid I made a muck of that.'

Taylor turned gingerly in his seat, as if afraid that any small movement would start the submarine on its mad capering once more. 'Bit er bad luck that! Just as well you spotted the bastard, sir!'

Duncan laughed softly. 'Yes, Ralph. A bit of luck.'

Curtis looked at him dully, aware of the stillness and the tension, but mostly aware of the contempt in Duncan's cold eyes.

Taylor glanced anxiously from one to the other. He sensed that something worse was about to happen. Something more dangerous and impossible than anything that the enemy could do. He must do something and damned quick. The captain had lost his nerve at the time, possibly. Didn't we all? And old Steve was looking a bit nasty, too, but something must be done before it got any worse and the strong link of their friendship and loyalty was broken.

'Er, d'you reckon they saw us, sir?' Taylor's voice was unnaturally casual. 'Will it make much difference to us if they did?'

Curtis fumbled blindly with the chart, his eyes misty. 'I don't know. Perhaps they didn't.'

'No, maybe they thought we was a whale.' Duncan crossed his legs carefully. 'Don't kid yourself, George. They saw us.

They've probably got every damned Eye-tie alerted from here to
the Vatican! It'll be a really good do now! Too right it will!' He
spat angrily on the deck.

Jervis ran his fingers across his damp face. 'Well, we knew it
would be a risk coming up here at all.' There was a pathetic
defiance in his voice, and Duncan's hard stare softened.

'Sure, kid. But we don't have to waddle about the surface like
flamin' ducks, do we?'

Curtis turned wearily towards the forward door. The bunk in
the tiny battery compartment seemed the only place to hide from
the implied insults.

'We shall carry on as arranged.' He stared at each of them in
turn, his eyes burning in their sockets with the effort. 'Try and
get some sleep; we'll need all we can get. We'll start our run-in at
eighteen hundred.' He looked lastly at Duncan, half hoping that
the old, lop-sided grin would come back. But the Australian's
eyes were indifferent, and without waiting for Curtis to say
more, he yawned and began to search for the electric kettle.

In the stinking darkness of the battery compartment Curtis
laid wide-eyed and stiff on the narrow bunk, each muscle and
nerve stretched and taut.

He heard Duncan's laugh and Taylor's tuneless whistle, and
as he laid staring at nothing he felt already excluded from their
world, and so sudden and terrifying had been his complete
collapse that even then he was unable to grasp the magnitude of
the disaster.

As the rim of the sun dipped towards the edge of the hidden
horizon the midget submarine encountered the first net. Although the speed of the boat was only a little above one knot,
and even though they had all been tensely waiting for just such a
moment, each man recoiled with the sudden shock, and waited
breathlessly for the motor to slow even more and the harsh
grating of the groping mesh to quieten sullenly as it sagged
against the craft's blunt bows.

Jervis was already dressed in his tight diving suit, and sat
uncomfortably in the "W and D" compartment, his face white
against the dark skin of the shining costume.

It had been terrible, waiting on the bottom for the coming of
darkness, with his imagination torturing his thoughts and pre-
venting the sleep which he craved so desperately. Coupled with

that, the brittle atmosphere within the boat and unusual silence between his companions built up a fresh uneasiness, which the promise of action did little to dispel.

He grinned lamely as Duncan craned his body round to squint at him through the narrow watertight door.

'All set? Ready to have a go, kid?'

Jervis nodded stiffly, the suit already dragging on his body. 'Shan't be sorry to get out and stretch my legs!'

Curtis scrambled across the control-room, his face tight and grim. His eyes darted from the diving suit to the depth gauge, which stood steady at thirty feet. The slow turning screw of the boat kept her solidly against the net in the exact position required for her to burst through, as soon as the tough mesh had been cut.

Without speaking, Curtis connected the oxygen supply and gently fixed the boy's nose-clip in position. For a moment his blue, troubled eyes rested on Jervis's face, and a brief smile of encouragement softened his hard expression. He gripped his hand tightly, the only part of his body to be left uncovered, and when he spoke his voice was quiet but surprisingly strong and steady.

'Take it easy, Ian. If you find you can't manage it alone, one of us'll come out and give you a hand.' The grip of Jervis's hand tightened. 'Promise me you won't do anything crazy. We've got plenty of time for this job, and there's no need for heroics.'

Jervis nodded, and moistened his lips. 'I'll be careful, Skipper.'

Taylor, sitting straddle-legged at the wheel, called hoarsely, 'Good luck! Don't take too long outside!'

Curtis snapped the circular face-piece in position and clipped it tight.

Jervis watched the preparations, suddenly aware of the great silence and feeling of loneliness.

Without another glance Curtis closed the watertight door, and the diver was quite alone.

He perched his body carefully on the edge of the "heads", and began to breathe in regular, steady gulps of canned air. The compartment was so small that it always reminded him of the cupboard under the stairs at school, where he had nearly suffocated when locked in for a prank. The sides brushed his shoulders and his head was only inches beneath the curved deckhead.

Shutting out the urge to panic, he reached out and twisted the valve which would flood his tiny compartment and enable him to escape to the outside.

The pump started, and within seconds he felt the water swirling across his feet in an angry torment. Up and up, pressing the suit against his legs in a cool embrace, the water was soon lapping his buttocks and exploring his thighs. Nervously he plunged his hands deep, to accustom them to its temperature and to be ready for the work outside the hull. It was warmer than he had expected, and he placed them on his knees and watched them sink into the rising water like two pink crabs. Over his chest, around his neck, and with a sudden flurry, over his head. He was completely submerged. He waited a moment longer, and then, satisfied that the pump had ceased and conscious of the pounding of his heart, he allowed one arm to swim upwards to release the clips on the hatch. Holding carefully to the rim of the hatch, Jervis rose smoothly through the circular opening.

Once clear, he twisted his body round, his limbs turning lazily to the pull of the water, until he faced the night-periscope, where he knew the skipper would be watching him, and gave the thumbs-up sign. A cloud of tiny silver air-bubbles, released from the folds on his suit, scattered towards the surface, and he lifted his face to watch them disappear above him. Already his fears were beginning to die, and in their place came the usual feeling of exhilaration which the very sensation of diving seemed to bring. He watched, wide eyed, the strange ceiling of the sea, less than thirty feet over his head, a vast, undulating sheet of green glass, speckled and spanned with long gold braids from the setting sun. Occasionally little groups of fish darted towards him, only to halt quivering in their flight before hurrying nervously away from the strange creature before them.

Jervis moved slowly and leisurely along the dark casing of the hull, fascinated by the huge, towering shape of the net which wavered towards the boat like a spider's web grappling with a fly. He released the powerful wire-cutter from its pocket inside the casing and gingerly took hold of the nearest mesh. Beneath him the submarine was poised and still but for the faint tremor of the slow-turning screw and the ribbons of weed which danced lazily from the hydroplanes.

Jervis felt almost sorry for his companions cooped up in their steel shell, and wondered briefly what they were talking about.

He checked the cutter and then laid the knife-edge on the first thick strand. Slowly and methodically he began to cut away the wire, snipping and sawing out the sections of the net in the shape of a giant inverted "V", leaving the apex intact against the boat's snout. It began to get darker, the water above and around him changing to a dark, mottled blue, and he lost all sense of time. His life and his thoughts were concentrated on the net and the cutter, which grew heavier and stiffer in his aching grasp. The muscles in his back protested at every move, and his hands felt raw and ice-cold. Once, in order to grip the cutter with two hands, he lost his footing on the net, and the weight of the heavy instrument dragged him downwards past the boat, before he could pull himself against the rough wire and drag himself painfully back to the widening hole, his blood pumping in his skull.

Somehow he finished, and with a savage gulp at his air-supply, he hacked away the last strand. With a tired shudder the panel of wire folded over away from the boat, and their way was clear. He felt the boat begin to move, and slipping and sliding along the hull, he guided her through, holding the savage, torn wires clear of the hull until the net suddenly vanished astern in the gathering gloom.

He returned the cutter and wearily groped his way into the open hatch.

So weak was he by that time that he had to make several attempts to clamp down the hatch, and as he lowered his body on to the "heads", he made the last effort and turned down the valve-handle.

Mesmerized, he watched dully as the water began to fall away and some of the pressure on his chest started to subside.

Still dazed, he saw the watertight door open and felt Curtis opening and removing his face-piece. He couldn't hold the cup of tea which was offered him, but sat, shaking like a child, as Curtis held it to his lips.

'Well done, Ian! Very well done!' Curtis sank back on his haunches as if removed from some terrible doubt.

The others called from the control-room, and Jervis gave a slow grin. 'Boy, it's damp outside!' was all he managed to say.

The next minutes dragged by as the boat moved cautiously across the wide harbour approaches. Each man concentrated on his job except Jervis, who lay back limply in his wet suit, eyes closed, his thoughts resting not on the last net, but the one ahead.

Curtis checked his notebook once more and glanced at the clock.

'Take her up. Periscope depth.'

Duncan eyed him quickly before turning back to his instruments.

He thinks I'll do the same again, thought Curtis, a sudden spasm of white-hot rage coursing through him. Damn him!

He lifted the periscope slowly, squinting frantically to accustom his eyes to the dusk and the distorted movement of the low wave-tops. For a while he could see nothing. Then, as he swung the thin tube in a narrow arc, he caught his breath sharply. The high side of a ship loomed darkly to one side, a mooring-buoy nodding gently at its stem. He lowered the periscope and waited until they had passed the silent ship. Probably a merchantman moored in readiness to leave by daylight.

The motor whined steadily, and at a painful crawl they moved deeper and further into the harbour. When he raised the periscope again he caught a glimpse of a tall, white tower shimmering eerily on the end of a long breakwater. He measured the distance and bearing rapidly, and waited for his next look before making a decision.

'Just coming up to the main entrance,' he spoke tersely. 'Steer oh-one-five! Keep her steady at periscope depth, the bottom's fallen to only five fathoms hereabouts!'

He raised the periscope once more and watched the white tower fading into the distance. A small, dark shape rounded the end of the breakwater, and the steady beat of her powerful diesels throbbed through the submarine's hull, making them stiffen into a fresh alertness.

Narrowly Curtis watched the boat swinging towards him. The white finger of a searchlight stabbed once, twice, and three times, casting quick, furtive beams across the still hulls of sleeping ships alongside the tangle of jetties and wharves.

'Patrol boat,' he said softly. 'Probably hasn't got any Asdic——' He bit his lip, as a sharp, metallic ping echoed along the hull. The submarine turned like a boxer to parry the thrust, so that her narrow beam was in the path of the probing detector.

The patrol boat's engines faded away across the harbour, and Curtis took another look. The traffic was getting thicker. Two small launches putt-putted across his vision, and a lumbering coaster glided past towards the harbour mouth, a low plume of black smoke darkening the night sky.

Twice more they ducked to avoid anchored ships, and once they sweated painfully as the hull scraped against a mooring-buoy.

The lens of the periscope suddenly filled with red light as a lamp stabbed out ahead. Then, as he watched, the long shape of a destroyer began to slide across the main harbour towards another ship, the one which had flashed the light.

Curtis paused to dash the sweat from his eyes. This was a bit of unexpected luck. They must be getting near the next net, and the outward bound destroyer was having the gate opened for her.

'Get ready to give me full speed! As soon as the gate's opened, I'm going to make a dash for it!'

Jervis sat up immediately, his eyes searching. 'Won't they pick up our motor, at full revs?'

Curtis was pressing the hoist-switch again and shook his head briefly. 'No, the big chap'll drown ours!'

Suppose we can't make it before the boom-gate vessel closes the gap? A cold chill ran across his neck. We *have* to make it!

The destroyer's engines thundered through the boat, making the instruments chatter and vibrate like mad things. Curtis saw the long, grey shape slide past, the froth already mounting at her stem.

'Full ahead! Steer oh-two-oh!'

He had said it. They were suddenly moving more rapidly towards the narrow opening in the gate. The buoys which supported the nets bobbed darkly, like the heads of tired swimmers, and the boom-vessel grew larger and sharper in detail. He could see her long, spindley funnel and the bulky shapes of her winches and hoisting gear. He heard clearly the thud of her engine as she began to draw the buoys together again.

We're not going to make it! He watched in rising anguish, as the gap became narrower and more distorted.

He could see the rust-dappled sides of the ship, and caught the glow of a cigarette from her narrow bridge. Thirty feet, fifteen feet, there seemed to be no entrance any more.

He saw the high, jagged stem rising over him like an axe, and wanted to hide his eyes from the impenetrable wall of metal which loomed across their path in a solid barrier.

'Hard a-starboard!' His voice was a sob.

He saw the vessel sheer away, and heard the grate of metal along the hull, as the casing ground against one of the buoys. A final jerk, which made Taylor gasp and cling more fiercely to the wheel, and then they were curving round, away from the net. They were through.

'In!' said Curtis. He couldn't trust his voice for more.

Duncan spoke from between his teeth, 'Well, there's no turning back now, is there?'

'Was there ever?' Jervis was massaging his raw hands and watching Duncan curiously.

Duncan laughed shortly. 'Could be, Ian. Could be.'

At minimum speed the boat prowled across the harbour, while Curtis hurriedly checked the chart and measured the distances between the piers and jetties. Jervis knelt at his side, studying Curtis's quick, skilful movements.

'You did that for *me,* didn't you, Skipper? You didn't want me to go out and cut another net?' He spoke very quietly and saw Curtis stiffen.

Curtis turned his face so that they were only inches apart. 'Questions! Nothing but damn questions! For Christ's sake shut up and let me get on with my job!'

Jervis coloured, and lowered himself shakily to the deck. Duncan glanced casually at him and shrugged. 'A hard life, ain't it?'

Curtis twisted a pencil between his strong fingers and closed his eyes tightly, forcing his reeling thoughts to grapple with the attack. Jervis, the young fool! Did he really think I wanted to make it easier for him? Hadn't it occurred to him that I can't stand the suspense of waiting any longer? Steve knew. He sees right through me. He knows I can't hold out much longer.

He crawled back to the periscope and raised it cautiously, thinking as he did so how quiet it seemed in the boat.

The long grey finger of the loading jetty lay before him, its sharp outline broken in places by the bulky shapes of moored vessels. They passed softly down the side of a high freighter, a dim arc-lamp giving him a quick view of some army lorries lashed across her decks. The lamplight filtered across the water in a pale silver sheen, too weak to endanger the tiny black stick which moved so purposefully through the uneasy, lapping wavelets.

They don't seem to be very worried about the blackout here, he thought absently; perhaps the Allied invasion has been delayed. Surely something must be happening in the south by now. 'Damn!' He pressed the button as another patrol boat chugged slowly amongst the ships. Some uniformed figures squatted around a small gun on the boat's foredeck, their uniform buttons glinting under the arc-lamp.

He listened to the engine fading away, and Taylor began to whistle softly between his teeth.

Curtis took another quick look and edged the boat even closer to the nearest merchantman.

The submarine sank like a sounding whale, and dipped under the ship's fat bilge, scraping the sand and muck on the harbour bottom, and once, with a sharp metallic screech, actually colliding with the stonework of the jetty.

Silently the boat settled on the bottom and the engine died away.

'We there?' Duncan sat back heavily in his small seat.

'The dock is about fifty feet ahead of us.'

Curtis's words dropped like pebbles in a still pool. He waited while each of the crew digested them.

'What'll we do, Skipper?' Jervis suddenly checked himself, afraid that Curtis would turn on him again. But his captain merely looked at him unseeingly and bit his lip.

'There doesn't seem to be much water here.' Duncan spoke slowly, as if he, too, were being cautious. 'If that flamin' dock is a bit low in the water, we might find it a bit of a squeeze!'

'We're going in now! We've got to drop a charge at each end of the target, to make quite sure!' He turned to Jervis. 'Get into the "W and D", Ian; you might have to go out and assist things in a minute.'

The submarine moved forward once more. Curtis counted off the seconds, visualizing the giant, factory-shaped floating dock towering over them. There was a sharp metallic clang, and the control-room rocked violently.

'We're underneath,' he announced flatly.

'Christ, they must be bloody deaf up there!' The words were forced from Taylor's twisted lips. His whole face looked sunken and shone with sweat.

The boat stopped.

Curtis checked the fuse-settings of the charges and began to wind the big basket-wheel on the port side. They heard the charge fall away, and each man imagined the deadly shape falling like a giant leaf, to settle practically alongside the hull.

They began to bump their way along the bottom of the dock, Curtis checking the time and trying to estimate when they had covered about three hundred feet.

'Stand by!'

Curtis swung the starboard release wheel and held his breath. Overhead he could hear the steady beat of several engines, probably generators on the dock, or maybe some repairs being carried out.

'Charge gone!'

Curtis looked wildly around the control-room as a fresh grating on the hull cut the words from his mouth. The boat shivered and settled down again. There was a strange groan from the metal overhead.

Duncan sat bolt upright. 'Jesus! They're floodin' the dock! We'll be pinned underneath an' go up with the charges!'

Curtis pulled desperately at his jacket, as if stifling to death. 'Full ahead!' He tapped Taylor sharply on the arm, so that the man jumped in his seat. 'Use the wheel all you can to free us!'

The motor whined and shuddered on its bed, and as the sturdy little hull twisted under power and rudder they heard the clinging pressure of the massive dock on their casing, as it tried to hold and destroy its own killer.

Through the glass ports in the periscope dome Curtis saw a break in the black wall of disturbed mud and overhanging shadows. One more thrust. We've *got* to get clear!

Over his shoulder he said, 'Watch it, Steve! Don't let her break surface and give the whole game away!'

'Hark who's talking!' Duncan's voice sounded breathless with the effort of controlling the boat's savage motion. 'I guess I'm not in the mood for a ruddy sermon!' he added jerkily.

Curtis momentarily forgot the danger and the grinding of metal against the hull. A wave of sickness coursed through his taut limbs, and he stared wildly at the other man's intent and angry face.

'What did you mean by that?' He had to hold his stooped

body close to the periscope to prevent himself from falling. 'What the hell are you implying?'

'Forget it till later!'

'Damn you! I'm asking you now!' His voice rose to a shout, and Taylor wrenched his eyes from the compass to stare miserably from one to the other.

Curtis reached out and gripped Duncan's shoulder. 'Come on, spit it out while you've got the chance! Tell me what you've been thinking all this time! Now's your chance to get it off your ruddy chest!' He glared round the boat, seeing only a misty picture of the wet, glistening plates and Taylor's bent shoulders at the wheel. Of Jervis's white face framed in the open door, and lastly Duncan's tight lips and lowered head. As the Australian remained silent, Curtis shook his shoulder and shouted even louder. 'You think I'm scared, lost my nerve, is that it? Or are you afraid to tell me that I'm a murderer, too?' He fell back weakly, his blue eyes suddenly dead.

Duncan's hands were rigid. 'I said forget it, Ralph. For Christ's sake get a hold of yourself.' His tone had changed and he sounded uneasy. 'Right now, I guess we have a job to finish. The rest'll keep.'

At that moment the submarine cleared the overhanging end of the dock and moved awkwardly towards the center of the harbour.

Duncan licked his lips. 'Looks as if the Eye-ties didn't get a tip that we were comin' after all,' he said slowly. 'I guess we're all born lucky.'

Curtis ran his palm along the periscope, heedless of the thick grease which clung to his skin. You finally did it, he told himself. You finally cracked. It was almost a relief. He was dimly aware of Jervis's quiet voice behind him, talking to Taylor.

'Steer one-five-five. We should be clear of the main jetties in about ten minutes.'

'Aye, aye, sir.' Taylor's answer was automatic and subdued. All the life seemed to have gone from him.

Curtis eyed them moodily. They already think I'm redundant, something to be tolerated until we get back. He watched Jervis moving uncomfortably by the chart table, his shining diver's suit hanging on him like an obscene skin.

'I'll give the necessary orders, thank you.' His flat voice made Jervis start and move clumsily towards the diving compartment.

'When I've got the boat back to the rendezvous you can all do what you like. Until then,' he paused wearily, 'you'll obey orders. All of you!'

The boat slid silently through the water, and no roar of engines overhead, or the sudden crashing detonation of depth charges, pursued their slow and cautious passage. It had been a perfect attack. Curtis almost groaned aloud at the mockery of his thoughts.

As if reading his mind, Duncan stirred his cramped body. 'Pretty smooth, Ralph. I'd say there's not much wrong with your touch that a good rest won't cure. We've all been overdoin' things a bit.'

'Periscope depth!' Curtis fiddled impatiently with the switch and ignored Duncan's words. He felt strangely calm and resigned; it was a feeling which his self-made loneliness only helped to strengthen as he glared bleakly at the crouched figures grouped about him. Each man was wrapped in his own private thoughts.

The periscope hissed slowly upwards.

He searched the harbour eagerly, a feeling of crazy reckless-ness making his head swim. He saw a small motor boat moving like a shadow towards the top of the anchorage. With childish defiance he kept the periscope raised and looked back at the fading shape of the dock.

But for you everything might have been different. But the lie died in his brain as his eye turned back across the black water and fastened on a small bobbing float. He stared at it blankly, forcing himself to concentrate once more and aware of some rising sense of warning.

A thin grey streak probed faintly across the sky, and the outlines of the distant ships became harsher. Soon a new day would dawn in Vigoria, and with it would come disaster when the charges exploded. He watched the float bobbing towards him. We're on the right course for a quick exit. We should be up to the nets soon, but not as quickly as this. Then he saw another group of floats. He chilled. It must be another net.

'Thirty feet! Another net!'

The deck tilted obediently, but at the same instant they heard the clatter of wire across the hull. He realized he was still holding the periscope switch in his hand and he pressed it frantically. Even as the tube hissed down he heard the sharp groan of metal, and a thin trickle of water ran across his wrist. He stared at it for some moments before he could bring himself to realize that the periscope had been caught in the net. The scraping of the wire ceased and the boat skimmed under the net.

'Only an anti-torpedo net,' said Taylor quietly. 'Luck's still with us!'

Curtis wrenched desperately at the hoist. The periscope was jammed solid, and the water still seeped threateningly down the greased tube.

'Take her up. Surface!' He stood upright under the dome, his hair pressed against the rough metal.

Duncan eyed him strangely.

'Surface,' he repeated heavily. 'We're blind. We'll have to run out on the surface!'

He opened the hatch, gasping as the salt air struck him in the face and a stream of spray broke over the coaming. Heavily he climbed up on to the casing, leaving the others behind in the darkened control-room. Wearily he strapped himself to the twisted periscope standard and braced his feet on the slippery deck. He bent his head until his lips brushed against the speaking tube, his eyes on the white tower of the harbour entrance.

Why not just step over the edge? Finish the whole damned business once and for all? What was the point of trying to escape now? As soon as the dock blew up, every destroyer and aircraft for miles around would be looking for them.

The first line of net buoys loomed ahead, and he conned the boat round until the shape of the boom-vessel was lost in the gloom. The boat moved smoothly between the first two nodding buoys, while Curtis gritted his teeth and waited for the net to grip them. They passed cleanly over the top of the sagging net and he breathed again. It was a race now. The next net must be reached before it became any lighter. Already the sky had brightened alarmingly, and somewhere across the harbour he heard the scream of a train whistle.

He spoke carefully down the pipe. 'Give me full revs!' He was amazed at the calmness in his voice. 'Once over the next net we should be O.K.'

'We over a net already then?' Taylor's voice rattled tinnily up the tube. 'Cor, fancy that!'

He heard Taylor pass the information to the others, and without warning he began to tremble violently. He knew then that he couldn't desert them whatever he had done, or whatever they thought of him.

They passed over the last net, within two hundred yards of a sleeping destroyer, and turned for the open sea.

Chapter 3

CURTIS LOCKED HIS fingers tightly behind his head and lay back uncomfortably on the small bunk across the chart table. He tried to relax his body and concentrate on the steady, monotonous pulse-beat of the motor.

The shaded light in the control-room seemed to have lost some of its brilliance and shed a yellow, sickly glow across the instruments and dials, and twisted Duncan's intent face into a mass of shadows, from which his cold eyes stared fixedly at the depth gauge and the clock.

Taylor was still at the wheel, while Jervis was trying to find sleep in the forward battery compartment.

Curtis again resisted the temptation to look at the brass clock. It must be nearly six, he thought. Soon the charges would explode and turn the peaceful harbour into a raging hell. He swallowed hard, tasting the bitter coating of oil and grime in his throat.

The submarine had dived as soon as it had cleared the harbour approaches, and as the sun rose above the horizon like a solid gold ball they had groped their way down to a depth of thirty feet and steered purposefully across the open bay.

He pressed his eyes shut and tried to calculate the situation more clearly. They would have to lie on the bottom soon and rest. As soon as the charges exploded he knew from past experience that every craft and plane would be alerted, and their slightest movement in the shallow coastal waters would invite attention and attack. He heard the wheel creak, and he was reminded of his new worry. The gyro compass had started to play up. Both he and Duncan had carried out the usual check, but the rapid alteration and sudden deviation pointed to one thing. The severe grinding which the boat had received beneath the floating dock had caused more damage than any of them was prepared to admit. He bit his lip hard. The boat was blind, and with a faulty compass as well, the possibility of making a rendezvous with the towing submarine in the middle of the night seemed hopeless. Apart from that, he knew that by taking his time over his approach to the rendezvous, and by keeping the other, larger craft helpless on the surface, he was doubling the risk to their lives, as well as those of his own crew.

His aching mind shied away from the obvious solution, from which there was no real alternative. We shall have to ditch the boat, he told himself, and try to make it overland. He had heard of other crews doing the selfsame thing in the past. But that was in Norway, an occupied country, not in Italy. He shuddered.

'Damn!' Taylor spun the spokes again, and craned forward over the compass. 'She's not answerin', Steve!'

Duncan waited a moment before replying. 'Bring the cow round to due east again. Then ease 'er off to your course slowly. We've got to keep goin' for a bit, just to put a few miles between us an' the big bang.'

The wheel creaked, and Curtis felt his heart beginning to thud painfully against his ribs. Duncan knows, he thought. He knows we're going to ditch.

'Course steady on oh-nine-oh.' There was a pause. 'Oh, sod it! She's payin' off again!'

Curtis forced his eyes open and slowly eased his legs down to the deck.

'Keep trying,' he said quietly. 'I'm going to set her down on the bottom shortly. But keep trying for a bit longer.'

Duncan looked up, his eyes searching. 'Feelin' better, Ralph?'

Curtis nodded vaguely.

'Good. I reckon I was right about this bein' a crook deal.'

Curtis stiffened, but the other man shook his head briefly, a small smile breaking through his dirty, stubbled face.

'*We* were all right, Ralph. It was the job which was stupid! I reckon you did real well to get us out like that, and on the surface, too!' His grin broadened. 'I thought we was all goin' at each other's throats for a bit, eh?'

Curtis felt a tremor of emotion coursing behind his eyes, and he looked away.

'Sorry about that, Steve. It's all been playing on my mind a bit.' He groped for the right words. 'I've never forgotten how young Roberts died. It was my fault. I killed him as surely as if I'd shot him.' He found that the relief of confiding in someone was almost more than his mind could stand, and he slumped heavily against the useless periscope. 'And now all this happening.' He waved one hand around the boat. 'I don't mind telling you, we're in a jam.'

'You mean we're goin' to let the old boat go, is that it?' Duncan eyed him calmly. 'Reckon it's all we can do under the circs!'

A great tidal wave of sound engulfed the hull, a sullen, angry roar, like the crumbling of a distant dam. Together they looked at the clock, while Jervis scrambled through the open door, his eyes wide and enquiring. It was two minutes past six.

Silently Duncan reached across and gripped Curtis's hand. 'Well done, Skipper. You blew the bastard's bottom off! You got us in, and you got us out!'

They all shook hands, and Curtis wanted to cry out as each man looked him in the face and smiled. Jervis rubbed his hands across his pale face and looked from one to the other, as if amazed by the calmness of these experienced seamen, while Taylor turned back to the compass, a small secret smile of private satisfaction on his tight-lipped mouth.

'Shall we be able to pick up the towing sub all right?' Jervis seemed to suddenly come to life.

Duncan shot a quick glance at Curtis and rubbed his chin slowly. 'We'll be makin' the trip on foot, that is unless we can whip a boat off some damned Eye-tie!'

Curtis hardly noticed the look of dismay on the boy's face; he was already reaching for the chart. Of course, that was the answer. Steal a boat and move down the coast by night. They should be able to find some sort of hide-out during the daylight, and if the Allied invasion had got into full swing they ought to be able to contact their own people within a week, maybe less, if all went well. He ran his eye across the chart, his mind picturing again that quiet fishing village he had seen through the periscope. His finger paused over the markings on the roughened chart. Was that only yesterday? He shook his head wonderingly.

The towing submarine would wait at the appointed place, and then return to base. Signals would be made, and in due course the dreaded telegrams would be received in four homes. Four homes, separated not only by distance, but by completely different ways of life.

A small moment of cruel pleasure flickered through his mind as he thought of his father. No doubt he would even make capital out of his bereavement, he thought bitterly.

Jervis looked even paler, and Duncan reached out with his foot to kick him chidingly in the ankle.

''Ere, snap out of it, Ian. It'll do us good to stretch our legs.'

Jervis still stared straight at the side of the hull, his eyes dull. 'What would they do to us if they caught us? Would we be treated as prisoners-of-war and everything?'

Curtis eyed him levelly. 'They say they're going to hang every midget submariner, frogman, commando, charioteer, and what-have-you that they can catch, Ian. The German High Command say we're all saboteurs, and must be treated as such. So get it through your head—we're not going to be caught!'

'No, that's right, sport!' Duncan laughed only with his mouth. 'We're goin' to see that you get home to your dad, the Admiral, just so that you can tell 'im what a lot of scruffy jokers we all are in this outfit!'

Duncan turned back to Curtis, a look of careless ease on his face. Curtis's sharp words had somehow struck new life into him, and even Taylor looked more relaxed. 'Where you settin' us down, Ralph?'

'I'll go back to this deep underwater valley, you remember, "il dietro del camello", and as soon as it's dawn tomorrow, we'll slip ashore. We can sink the boat in deep water then.'

'What'll we take with us, Ralph? I guess we won't want to lug too much ashore, especially if we've got to swim for a bit!'

Curtis pulled the chart closer to the light.

'The beaches are pretty shallow for a long way out. I think it'll be more of a wade than a swim. We'll need the emergency pack and a good water container.' He rested his hand almost gingerly on the holster which hung on his hip. 'We shall need these as well. Although I don't aim to have to use them.'

'I wouldn't mind too much.' Duncan eased his depth controls, his eyes distant. 'You should see my old man. He can knock the eye out of a jack-rabbit at a hundred yards with a pistol.' He shook his head, marvelling at his own memories. 'He sure is quite a guy.'

'What did he say when you came over and joined the Royal Navy?' Curtis was suddenly curious about Duncan's father, although he had heard so much about him he sometimes felt he knew him better than his own.

Duncan gave his slow smile. 'We was out checkin' the wire one day, when we ran into old Dick Masters, the constable. He told us he'd just got the griff about the boys pullin' back to Dunkirk. I was so worked up about the mess the Pommies were makin' of it I said I wanted to make for Cairns and join up. My old man didn't even bat an eyelid.' Duncan grinned affectionately. 'He just waved his fist across our land—an' we've got quite a piece—and he said, "I built this up from nothing! I've worked hard all me life, an' I've seen drought, famine, death, good times, an' bad, an' I've made something for a man to be proud of. But d'you know, boy, the thing that still stands out most in my memory is the morning that me an' my cobbers hit the beach on the Dardanelles. So I'm not goin' to stand in *your* way now!"'

'He must be a fine man,' said Curtis quietly.

Duncan nodded. 'He's a bloodthirsty old bastard, that's for sure!'

Jervis was peering at the chart, his mind confused by the casual conversation. 'It's a long way from that village to the south coast. I wonder if we shall be able to contact the army all right.'

'I got a brother in the Eighth Army,' said Duncan slowly. 'Reckon we should spot him soon enough.'

'I didn't know that, Steve.' Taylor's voice showed rare surprise at the secret.

'Well, I didn't want you to think I'm always boastin'; I'm a modest guy, y'know!'

As the clock turned down the hours, Curtis found that the preparations for leaving the boat helped to settle his nerves, and now that he had made his decision he felt a new feeling of relief overriding his other fears.

The compass got steadily worse, and once he surfaced the boat for the briefest period possible to try to fix his position.

He opened the hatch, half blinded by the dazzling sunlight, and more than apprehensive about what he might find.

The horizon was clear but for the thin white line of the distant headland. They were well off course, as he had feared, but still close enough inshore to pick out the twisted point marking the curve of the coast. Somewhere behind that line he knew he would find the village. As he swung his binoculars in a wide arc he saw a tell-tale wisp of smoke on the horizon, and even as he watched he saw three slim grey hulls scudding in a tight formation across the sparkling water. The sun beat down on his neck, warming his limbs and driving the stale, chilled cramp from his bones. Destroyers, and moving in fast. The hunt had started. In the far distance he could faintly hear the heavy drone of aircraft, probably taking off from the aerodrome at the rear of Vigoria.

The hatch clanged shut over his head, and the boat began to dive once more.

Duncan licked his lips. 'Man, did you smell that air, George? I just can't wait to get out of this can!'

Taylor nodded, and watched the compass closely. Outwardly calm, he was vaguely troubled by the new turn of events and the fact that he didn't feel the security he had hoped for. He had thought that the only thing that mattered was to get the skipper and Steve together again. They seemed to be hitting it off all right, and the skipper appeared to be something like his old self again, but—he fidgeted in his seat—there was something else. The danger? He scoffed at himself with disgust. What was danger anyway? You couldn't see it; you couldn't feel it; so what the hell!

I hope we get back soon, he thought desperately. I don't want Mum all worked up worrying about me. He sighed deeply, suddenly feeling his weariness. Everybody worrying about somebody else. Makes you sick! The compass swung lazily, mocking him, and he muttered obscenely under his breath.

'Want me to take over?' Jervis sounded strange, too.

'No, I'm not dead yet!' he answered shortly. Bloody regular officers, he reflected with sudden anger. Nice as pie when things were going wrong, but once out of a jam and they were trying to ram rank down your throat.

Jervis sank down on the deck, feeling lost and at the same time in the way. He sat heavily on the coaming of the diving compartment watching the other three as if he was looking in from outside the boat and their world. The cold excitement of leaving the boat and cutting the net, followed by the nerve-stretching attack on the dock, left him weak and limp, and what might have been the greatest moment in his life, and the conclusion to a great episode in his career, had suddenly widened into something frightening and unreal. He watched Curtis searching through the lockers, a lock of his fair hair falling across his grimy face as he tossed unwanted articles aside with little grunts of impatient irritation and built up a small pile of equipment beside him on the oil-smeared deck.

Duncan stared woodenly at his controls, his hands and shoulders moving slightly at each perverse swing on the little boat, but from the faraway expression in his eyes Jervis could tell that he was already scheming and plotting over the next few hours, which might well decide whether they would live or die.

Jervis shook his head jerkily as a wave of fatigue brought the damp ache into his bones to replace his fading energy. He stared round at the unheeded and dripping hull, all at once realizing just how important the tiny boat was to all of them. It was not just a weapon of war, another machine of destruction, but the very breath of their existence. Take it away, or just abandon it, and they were all naked and out of their element. He wanted desperately to burst out with his ideas to the others, but something akin to a hidden pride checked him, and he sat staring from one face to the other, and tried to fathom out the exact course which events might take.

He had considered most possibilities in the past, but all his ideas had included the Navy and everything that went with it. He had always been surrounded and protected by it, and had been brought up to rely on the strange tradition and comradeship of the Service, which was more like a religion. Everywhere he had been he had always been surrounded by others of his own mould, and he had imagined himself after this operation, stepping ashore in Malta or Alexandria, and finding himself right back amongst the safety of the only life he understood. He could not bring himself to realize, even partly, just what it would be like suddenly to find himself washed ashore on some unknown beach, like a piece of flotsam discarded by the sea, and to find a way through a country which hitherto had been merely a collection of superior holiday resorts in his own experience, and was now a sullen, alien territory, with every sort of danger and hazard to keep him and his companions from reaching safety.

He nearly screamed aloud when Duncan started to talk about his father, and Curtis had begun to question the Australian about his farm and that distant life. It was crazy and unreal, and as if they were two strangers passing the time on a long-distance train journey, especially when, a short time previously, the skipper had been almost on the point of striking Duncan while the enemy dock had groaned threateningly overhead. And what was all that about murdering the previous diver? Jervis looked carefully at Curtis's set face and cold eyes as if he might find the answer there.

Curtis paused in his search and glanced up quickly, scanning the boy's face questioningly. 'Get out of that diving suit, Ian,' he snapped, 'and start smashing it up, and all the other diving gear. Got it?'

Jervis coloured and dropped his eyes, as if caught out in his thoughts, and began to struggle out of his suit. So there was no chance of a change of plans. It was all decided, and they were going to abandon the boat. He had held on to the forlorn hope that perhaps the damage wasn't quite so serious, and that there might still be a chance of making for the rendezvous.

As if in answer, Taylor let free a stream of curses as the campass danced madly in its case.

Jervis thought of the towing submarine's cosy wardroom and the smell of closely-packed, friendly bodies, and the buzz of casual but steadying conversation, which spelled safety and hope. He bent over his task, his eyes stinging with tears and loneliness.

Curtis sighed and sat back on his haunches to survey the pile of gear beside him.

'I think that's about all,' he was thinking aloud. 'Tinned food and chocolate. A torch, two escape maps, and a couple of grenades.'

Duncan smiled bleakly. 'Not exactly a campin' outfit, is it? Still, I daresay we'll get by.'

Curtis eyed him, his blue eyes troubled. 'I'm not looking forward to it myself, you know!'

He was amazed that he was able to think so clearly again, and that the ache of fear only lurked in his heart and not in his limbs. Perhaps it was because something outside his own will had taken over command of his actions, or maybe it was just the inevitability of disaster.

'Matter of fact,' continued Duncan calmly, 'I'm thinkin' it might be quite amusin'!' He released one hand from a lever to wave down the obvious protest. 'No, quite seriously, it'll be a sort of change for us.' He looked around the control-room, taking in the dirt and disorder, and the crumpled figures of the others. 'It's time we got shot of this for a bit. We ought to find the trip back quite interestin'!' He laughed impetuously. 'Say, Ralph, what a lark it'd be if we captured Mussolini or somethin' like that!' He chuckled and rolled his eyes. 'Might even latch on to some little Eye-tie senorita, too! They say the sheilas round here are quite somethin'!'

He looked across at Jervis's stooped head, and his eyes crinkled into narrow slits. 'Why, the boy he'd be really learnin' a few things!'

Jervis smiled weakly, but didn't answer.

'See? He's thinkin' about it already.'

Jervis licked his dry lips. 'I was just wondering about the strength of the enemy around this part of the coast,' he said at length, his voice quiet and unsteady.

'Strength of the beer more like! Christ, what wouldn't I give for a dirty great pint of Tooths' beer right now!' Duncan smacked his lips noisily.

Curtis was watching Jervis with sudden interest, and waved the Australian into silence. The boy had changed. He looked as he himself had felt such a short time ago. And with Taylor already showing signs of strain, it was cutting down their slim chances even more.

'How d'you mean, Ian?' he asked casually. 'What have you got in mind?'

Jervis swallowed hard, his face pale. 'What I mean is, Skipper, do you think there'll be many German troops around here, or will the Italians be in control?'

'It doesn't make a lot of difference, surely? We have to avoid them all, that's the only certainty we have. Don't imagine that the Eye-ties are soft, because they're not, and remember, it's their country we're messing about.'

'That's right,' said Duncan brightly. 'So long as they only outnumber you twenty to one, you'll find 'em pretty tough!'

Jervis looked across at Curtis with something like pleading on his round face. 'We're not cut out for this sort of thing, Skipper! We're sailors, not soldiers! We haven't got a clue about getting across open country and all that sort of thing, and living off the land!' The words poured from him like a flood.

'You speak for yourself!' Duncan wriggled in his seat. 'I've done it all me life till I was stupid enough to get mixed up with this caper!'

Curtis's mouth tightened and his eyes looked like twin pieces of blue glass. 'Look here, Ian. Lots of our blokes have had to ditch before now, and have made it! In Norway, for example, when the country was deep in snow and England across the other side of the sea. You must have heard or been told about it?'

'But, Skipper,' Jervis had committed himself, and seemed incapable of reading the warning in Curtis's face, 'that was a country where the people were all for the British——'

Curtis cut him short. 'Whereas, this country is warm and full of food and God knows what else, *and* with a bit of luck the army are waiting for us at the other end by now! If you weren't up to this sort of risk, you should have got your father to wangle you into something safer!'

He knew that his words were cutting the boy in half, but he knew, too, that everything depended on the others being ready to back him up when the time came. Without another word he crawled through the diving compartment and into the battery room, his mind already busy with his hazy plan.

Duncan breathed out slowly. 'Well, Ian, I'm not the one to brag, but I could have told you that would happen!'

'I—I'm not afraid! It's just, it's just . . .' he faltered helplessly, all his defences down, 'I've never experienced anything like this before.'

'Hmm. It's not exactly the kind of affair we want to dabble in every day, is it?' He leaned over and banged the boy's shoulder. 'Cheer up, cobber! D'you want to live forever?'

When eventually the motor died away, and the midget submarine settled on the soft sandy sea-bed, the Adriatic was dark and still and allowed the boat and her crew peace and time to dwell on their thoughts for the morning which was yet to come. A destroyer cruised seawards looking for the unknown marauder which had left its mark painted in the sky over distant Vigoria—a sullen, flickering red glow which refused to be quelled.

Somewhere in the darkness, beyond the destroyer and her consorts, the towing submarine's commander watched the glow in his periscope. 'There'll be no rendezvous after all, I'm thinking,' he said softly.

The thick, damp air of the control-room was tense and expectant as the small boat moved slowly and carefully towards the surface. Each of the four men stooped across the controls was thinking the same thoughts, and wondering what was awaiting them in the world above their heads.

The hands of the brass clock pointed at four o'clock, and even in the boat's confined space Curtis seemed to feel the chill of the dawn mingling with the foul, fume-laden air. He stole a quick searching glance at the others, noting their bulging pockets and rumpled battledress blouses. They had all discarded their waterproof clothing to give them some semblance of uniform should they run straight into an enemy patrol. Curtis shivered, in spite of his taut muscles. He had heard that the Germans had a quick way with suspected saboteurs.

We should be about a quarter of a mile offshore, he pondered; that'll enable us to sink the boat in deep water and still make it possible to swim to the beach fairly easily. He pictured the details on the chart which seemed burned into his brain, and wondered if they could make the trip to the small hill at the side of the village without being seen.

Duncan looked up from his controls, his face suddenly alert and strained.

Curtis tensed automatically, and bent his head as if expecting to hear the sound of engines overhead, but Duncan frowned and shook his head briefly.

'No, Ralph, it's not that,' he said slowly. 'The motion—d'you feel it? We're jerkin' a bit too much!'

Curtis bit his lip. Duncan was right; the boat was rolling far too much, and as the depth gauge crept backwards and the boat swam persistently upwards, the motion of the hull, normally steady and calm until the actual moment of surfacing, was extremely uneasy. That could only mean that the weather had deteriorated during the night, and one of the brief Adriatic gales had materialized to make their task even harder.

Taylor spun the spokes carefully and shifted in his seat. 'Bit of roughers!' he muttered. 'Just our bleedin' luck!'

'It'll make us more difficult to spot, if there's anyone watching.' Curtis kept his voice even. 'We shall have to make it quick though.'

The boat lurched, and he put out his hand to stop himself falling. The heavy automatic against his hip reminded him again of the uncertainty, and for an instant a tremor of panic coursed through him. He cursed himself. No second thoughts now. This was another point of no return.

'Ten feet, Skipper!'

Curtis was grimly reminded that this would normally have been approaching periscope depth before he had blinded the boat with his stupidity. He wondered vaguely if Duncan was thinking the same.

He slipped the clips on the main hatch and braced his shoulders beneath it. The motion was much worse and the whole control-room was swinging through a crazy arc, throwing pieces of loose gear from side to side, and making the hunched occupants cling on to the controls, or anything else, to prevent serious injury.

'Surfaced!' Curtis spat the word from between his clenched teeth, and heaved open the hatch. For a moment the blast of cold air which lashed him across the face made him gasp, but the sight of the high grey waves which seemed to dwarf the casing of the boat forced all other thoughts from his mind. Gasping painfully, he dragged himself over the coaming and crouched on the small, wave-swept deck. He had to cling to the broken periscope with all his strength to prevent himself from being tossed into the swirling, white-capped water, and with his eyes half-blinded by spray he peered anxiously towards the shore, or where it should have been. Overhead the scudding black clouds tried to disguise the feeble efforts of the dawn to break through, and he knew that unless he acted at once, daylight might surprise them helplessly tossing on the surface. As the boat lifted sluggishly beneath him he caught sight of a dull grey hump and a thin strip of beach. It looked miles away, and as the boat fell heavily into a trough he realised that it was going to be a difficult trip, and they would be in poor shape when they reached the protection of the shore. *If we make it*, he thought wildly.

A long, low roller, its jagged crest laced with blown spray, pushed the boat on to its side and sent a stream of water plunging through the half-open hatch. The boat felt heavier and was not answering to the helm. It could not be long now.

Curtis choked as his head ducked under the clawing seas, and leaned into the control room. Water surged about confined space, and already a necklace of blue sparks danced across the switchboard.

'Come on!' He had to yell to make his voice heard above the thunder of the breakers. 'Bale out!'

Taylor appeared beside him, his slight body distorted by his life-jacket, his unruly hair plastered across his tanned face. As he scrambled up beside Curtis he looked at the sea and swore.

'Christ! Look at that bleedin' lot!' He forced a grin. 'Feel jus' ready for a swim!'

Curtis nodded and helped to pull Jervis over the coaming. The boy looked as white as death, and as a curtain of spray rose over the pitching hull he cried out and hung on to Curtis's arm.

'All got your life-jackets fixed?' He had already checked, but anything was better than just sitting in silence as the water pounded across their sodden bodies.

Duncan pulled himself up beside them, panting heavily. 'She's goin', Ralph!' The water streamed across his thick hair, adding to his wild appearance. 'No need to open the vents!'

'Right, lads!' Curtis spoke jerkily. 'Make for that hill and try to keep together! If we get parted, get there anyway, and watch out!'

Taylor stood up, his legs splayed on the slimy metal. ''Ere we go, blokes!' There was no humour in his eyes, as with a deep breath he stepped clear of the casing. In a second he was well away from the boat, his body buffeted by the waves, and his dark head and orange life-jacket showing only briefly over the surging water.

Duncan followed, making a huge splash as his seaboots kicked out behind him. 'Keep goin', George, I——' his words were drowned by the roar of the rollers cascading across the midget submarine's stricken hull.

Curtis gripped Jervis's arm savagely, so that their faces touched. 'Keep going, and don't look back!' It was suddenly terribly important that the boy should be safe. 'I'll be behind you. Now jump!'

Jervis stared mesmerized at the sea and sobbed, his face puckered up with fear.

The boat plunged again, but didn't seem to be answering her buoyancy tanks.

She's going, Curtis thought desperately. For a moment a twinge of regret crossed his mind. The plunging, water-logged hull beneath his slipping feet had lost its power to kill and maim, it was somehow pathetic as it tried to lift above the waves yet fell each time deeper into their cruel embrace. The bull-ring lifted momentarily in defiance and then he felt her begin to slide from under him.

'Jump, man!' He thrust his hand under Jervis's life-jacket and pushed. Together they fell spluttering and gasping into the spray. Curtis felt his ears sing, and tasted the bile in his stomach as he was sucked under. He emerged, choking and gasping, and turned, treading water, to watch *XE.51's* propeller turning slowly in the air, as the small, cigar-shaped hull pointed skywards like a memorial. To us, he thought, with sudden fear.

Then it vanished, and with a groan he started to strike out towards the beach, all thoughts banished from his mind but for the cruel necessity to keep swimming, and not give in to the desire to let himself be dragged after his command.

Of the others there was no sign, but he did not seem to worry any more. Nothing mattered but to keep swimming. To keep swimming.

Chapter 4

THE SHORT, STEEP waves pounded along the beach, whipped into fierce breakers by the blustery wind. As the sky brightened, their colour began to change from a dirty grey to a deep, cold green, and their anger and strength seemed to mount, as if to vent their full fury upon the white sands before the sun rose to drive their passion back into the langour of a late Adriatic summer.

Duncan had lost sense of time, and until he felt the sand grate against his leaden boots he had begun to feel that his sense of direction had gone, too.

The water within two hundred yards of the tempting safety of the beach was shallow, and half swimming and half crawling, he made a slow and painful progress. Each time he tried to rise up to his feet in the waist-high water a breaker would smash him down from behind, and he felt the strong undertow pulling at his sodden clothes, and the treacherous sand sliding and sucking at his boots. The life-jacket was more hindrance than help, and several times he tried to slip from the harness, but each time he had to give his full strength to a fresh tussle with the waves, which dealt him unwavering body blows from every direction at once.

As he reeled once more to his feet, he half turned and saw a yawning crest bearing down on him, and wearily he kicked forward to save himself. He had a blurred impression of being hurled forward like a twig on a mill-stream, then his face and chest were crashing and scraping on the smooth sand, and he waited for his lungs to burst. He laid where he had been flung, vaguely conscious of the heaviness of his limbs and the receding roar of the water. Gingerly he opened his eyes and winced. His eyes and mouth were seemingly filled with grit, but he realized that he was firmly on the beach, and a feeling of urgency drove his aching body to its knees and he crawled clumsily up the shelving sand, the sea creeping and hissing up to his heels, to claw and pluck in one final effort to claim him.

The buttons had been ripped from his blouse, and his trousers dragged at his hips as if anchored to the ground. His hair was matted across his streaming forehead, and he was aware of the grit burning in his left eye and the painful beat of his heart. He sat on his haunches in the puddled sand, glaring round with one eye, a wild, gaunt figure, dark against the lightening sky. The beach was empty, and not even a sea bird challenged the disturbed fury of the water.

Suddenly his glance steadied on a small blue hump which ebbed and rolled across the other side of the sand spit.

With hidden energy Duncan staggered to his feet, and half shambling, half running, he hurried towards it. He kept shaking his head to clear the water and the deafness from his ears, and he held his face to one side to give his good eye a clearer view.

Taylor's body was limp, and in Duncan's hands it already seemed to have the frailty of death.

He pulled the man's head clear of the waves and began to drag him up the beach. Taylor's feet bobbed and nodded with each effort, and his heels cut two pathetic furrows in the virgin sand. As he laid him down, the water began to pour from his open mouth, and Duncan's heart bounded as he heard him begin to retch. Taylor vomited and groaned, and hit out feebly at the air. As his torn fingers touched Duncan's arm, they clutched tightly to the wet cloth and stayed motionless, while the remnants of his mind tried to convey the sense of safety to his half-drowned body. His eyes fluttered open, and Duncan gently wiped the sand and salt from his face.

'All right, cobber? Take it easy.' Duncan smiled sadly.

Taylor stared at him in a mixture of fear and disbelief. 'Steve? Steve?' he croaked vacantly. 'What you doin' 'ere?'

Duncan grinned broadly. 'Waitin' for a bus! What d'you think?'

He propped him carefully against a hillock of soft sand and peered round quickly with his awful, one-eyed stare. 'You stop here, chum, I've got to get after the others!'

Taylor groaned and lay back obediently. 'The others? Oh yes, the others!' He gingerly felt the firm ground under him, and suddenly smiled. 'Christ, that was close!'

Duncan moved down to the water's edge, his mind working furiously. He could now see the other side of the small cove quite clearly and the hill for which he had battled so painfully. Must look for the others, he thought, can't just take George and leave them to rot.

He broke into a run, his boots slipping and sliding, and his stinging eye making him stagger into the water in a drunken, zigzag course.

He halted, sniffing the air, some sense of warning flooding through him. In front of him was a small broken cliff, where one of the hills around the village had fallen into the sea. He heard a voice and then a few short footsteps.

He craned his head and fumbled for his pistol. His groping fingers found only an empty holster, and without even giving it further thought he doubled his huge fists and stepped slowly to the edge of the rocks.

A feeling of relief changed his caution to one of abandon as he saw Curtis swaying in the water knee-deep and staring out to sea. 'Ralph! You son-of-a-bitch! Am I glad to see you!' He reached him in a bound and gripped him by the arm.

Curtis shook at his hold, in a feeble, pre-occupied effort to free himself, never taking his eyes from the sea, and it seemed to Duncan that he was trying to walk back into the waves.

'Ralph! What's up? Have you seen somethin'?' He glared painfully over the water, but saw only the empty tossing whitecaps.

Curtis took another step and mumbled half to himself in a low, broken voice.

'I've let him go, too! I'm going back for him!'

'Who? Ian?' Duncan swung him round to study his face with sudden anxiety. 'I found old George; he's coughin' his heart up on the beach, but he's dinkum otherwise!'

Curtis didn't seem to hear. 'I let him down. He needed me, and I let him go!'

A thin watery beam of yellow light lit up their bruised faces, and Duncan trembled with suppressed urgency.

'Come on, Ralph! There's nothin' you can do. If he's gone, he's gone, an' that's that!'

Curtis turned drunkenly on the soft sand, his eyes blazing. 'I've killed him, too! Damn you, let me go! I'm going after him!'

Duncan looked back up the beach. Taylor might try to find him and get lost. The skipper was obviously done in, and in no condition to make decisions about Jervis or anything else.

'Ralph, come on, boy,' he spoke with deceptive gentleness. 'We've got to hit cover, but quick!'

'Must go and find him.' Curtis staggered weakly and started to wade into the water.

Duncan patted him on the shoulder, and as Curtis turned impatiently towards him, he drove his fist upwards in a short, vicious uppercut. Curtis didn't even touch the sand, as he was pitched across the other man's broad shoulder.

Breathing hard, Duncan plodded along the beach until he met Taylor swaying unsteadily by the hillock where he had left him.

'Cripes! Is the skipper dead? 'As 'e bought it?' Taylor trotted to meet them, his face strained and suddenly old.

'Nope! He's passed out!' Duncan measured up the distance to the hill and took in the mass of bushes which crowned its summit like a green wig. 'C'mon, we got to move, George, and get ourselves bedded down.'

The climb upwards was slow and painful. Every minute of the journey made Duncan's breath wheeze and sob, and each second he expected to hear a challenge or the crash of a shot. Taylor trotted beside him, muttering and cursing, oblivious to danger and still only half aware that he had survived.

They found a thick clump of bush and bracken on a small overhanging shelf of sandstone, and Duncan laid his burden thankfully under the shade of the leaves. 'Sit down, George,' he said patiently, as Taylor stood dazedly on the edge of their hideaway, 'you're a bit too old for shooting!' He sighed as Taylor slumped heavily beside him like a puppet which had had the strings cut from it, and peered over the top of the coarse grass at the side of the ledge. The village was smaller than he had imagined. Tiny, whitewashed, single-storied cottages scattered carelessly in the deep cleft between the hills and lining the rough track which led down to the beach. He could just see the line of brightly painted fishing boats pulled up on the far end of the sand spit, and licked his lips. One of those might do, he thought.

A dog barked, and he saw the shadows cast by the cottages begin to harden and darken as the sun filtered through the cloud, which already seemed to be fading.

Several of the dwellings had smoke drifting upwards from their chimneys, and Duncan was aware that he was ravenously hungry. The smoke was going straight up, he realized bitterly. The wind had gone as suddenly as a bad dream. But for its visit, their suffering might have been saved, and Ian might have been with them. A figure stepped from one of the doors, small and indistinct. It stretched, and Duncan imagined him yawning to greet the morning. It was peaceful and unreal. Untouched and all the more terrifying because of it.

Duncan sighed and rolled on to his side, feeling the water drain from his boots. A little of the sun's rays touched his cheek, and he felt very tired. He turned to speak to Taylor, but he was already asleep, sprawled on his back where he had fallen in the effort of pulling off his sodden jacket.

With a groan he turned on to his back and laced his fingers beneath his hair and felt the coarse mixture of sand and salt which it had collected.

His mind wandered aimlessly back to the midget submarine, and he imagined their control-room already being explored by the fish. It was to be hoped that too much oil had not seeped to the surface, he decided, it might make things more awkward. He heard a long intake of breath, and craned his head to watch as Curtis sat up slowly, rubbing his jaw. The blue eyes moved vaguely around the bushes and the clear ceiling of the sky before they eventually settled on Duncan.

'Sorry about the poke, Ralph.' Duncan spoke guardedly. 'I guess it was 'bout all I could do.'

Curtis frowned as if trying to piece together what had happened, and then his eyes clouded and he drew up his knees to his chin, his arms wrapped round them.

'I was going after him.' It was more of a question than a

statement. 'I remember him calling.' He shook his head. 'Perhaps I only imagined that I heard him.' He sat up with a jerk. 'Hell! Where the devil are we?'

Duncan grinned, and allowed his bunched muscles to relax slightly. 'On the goddamned hill! Right where you wanted us!'

Curtis raised himself on his knees, still rubbing his chin. 'You can still land a punch,' he commented, as he surveyed the village beneath them.

'No hard feelings, Ralph?'

'Not to you.'

'D'you want to go over what happened?' Duncan saw the crouched shoulders stiffen, and wished he could see his eyes.

'He was drowned,' he said flatly. 'What else is there to realize?'

Duncan sighed, and tried to open his left eye. 'What else, as you say. What a bit of damned bad luck.' He decided it would be prudent to change the subject. 'What now exactly?'

Curtis sat back on his haunches, the clean outline of his face turned towards the sun. 'We must wait until it's dark, and then have a scout round.' He eyed the fishing boats narrowly. 'Of course, if that lot shove off for the day, we might slip out during the day and get the lay of the land. We'll have to get some grub. We don't seem to have much left.' He pulled out his wet pockets. 'I've only got a grenade and this tin of meat.'

'I know which I'll have!'

Curtis smiled for the first time. 'Thanks, Steve,' he said simply.

He looked at Duncan's eye. 'Here, let me have a go.' He cut the tail off his shirt with his diver's knife, and after drying it in the warm air he began to dab the grit from the inflamed eyeball.

Every so often they watched the houses, waiting for some sign of what to expect.

A woman in a bright red dress left one of the nearer cottages and walked slowly towards the beach. The two officers stared at her curiously. She was short and fat, and her long black hair gleamed dully in the sunlight. She was a woman, nevertheless, and one of the potential enemy.

'What a bird!' Duncan blinked his eye and smiled happily. 'I feel ready for anythin' now. Even her!'

Some men and women had gathered at the top of the track,

and Duncan's heart gave a leap as he saw the fishing nets that some of the men were dragging down the path. 'They're goin' out, I guess.'

'Good. There don't seem too many of 'em, do there?'

Duncan hissed sharply, 'Hold it, there's a car or somethin' comin'!'

Taylor groaned and suddenly appeared beside them, scratching his stomach absently.

'Get down, George!' Duncan snapped. 'The big picture's just startin'!'

The villagers had nearly reached the sand spit, and they could hear their voices quite clearly as they chattered and laughed and stuffed their pockets with food which the women were carrying. They, too, were suddenly aware of the noise of the car engine. They all halted, and several more faces appeared at some of the doorways.

Curtis frowned. 'They're not used to cars here either, apparently!'

'Not surprised.' Taylor was watching the people as if he had never seen any before. 'What wiv them bleedin' roads I'm surprised they see anythink!'

'Nuts! I've driven over worse'n this,' began Duncan, but Curtis's frozen expression halted him.

A small, sandy-coloured scout car came labouring around the side of the end houses, and with its fat tires skidding over the dirt track, drove straight for the centre of the village.

They gazed at the man who stepped from the back seat and stood tapping his boot impatiently until the villagers started to hurry towards him.

Duncan dug his fingers into the sand. It was not quite as he had expected it would be, and the man, rather than he and his companions, seemed out of place.

I've been fighting them for four years, he thought slowly, and this is the first proper German I've seen.

He had seen plenty of prisoners, but they were quite different. Sullen, beaten, they bore no resemblance to the slim, impatient figure who leaned negligently against the side of the car. He could see the pistol at his belt, and the long-peaked Afrika Korps cap with its silver eagle.

Curtis wasn't looking at the man any more. He stared fixedly at the bright orange life-jacket which the German officer had just pulled from the car and flung at the feet of the fisherman.

'D'you see that, Ralph?' Duncan whispered excitedly. 'The bastard's got Ian's jacket! What d'you think it means?'

Curtis shook his head, his eyes puzzled. 'Ian might have slipped out of it and the thing's been washed up somewhere, or,' he added harshly, 'Ian might have been in it when they found it.'

Duncan seemed even more excited. 'The wind, Ralph, don't you remember? It was agin us! He wouldn't have been washed up yet. He must have made it on his own!'

Curtis appeared to Duncan to grow in stature. 'Steve, you may be right!' They both turned their eyes to the German. 'But where the hell is he? I wish to God I could hear what that Jerry's saying.'

'They don't seem to like what he's said, anyway.'

Duncan was right. The villagers bowed their heads, and some started to shout from the crowd in high, protesting voices. But the officer raised his hand so that his watch glittered in the sun, and at the same time tapped his holster.

Then he turned his back and climbed into the car, and within seconds only a cloud of yellow dust remained to mark his visit.

'Well, what d'you make of that?' Duncan peered at the fishermen who were dispersing towards the boats.

There was no shouting or laughter any more, and Curtis saw one elderly woman dabbing her eyes with her black skirt.

'I imagine that Jerry has made some sort of threat.' Curtis spoke musingly. 'After the dock blowing up, and then finding a British life-jacket, they've come to the conclusion that there's a saboteur of some sort hiding in the vicinity. He must have warned 'em to keep their eyes peeled—or else! That makes it even more important that we should find Ian before someone else does.'

'I'll go,' said Duncan woodenly.

'We'll both go, separately,' said Curtis. 'George must stay here, just in case Ian shows up later on.'

Taylor screwed his face into a grimace. 'Wot, leave me all on me jack? Can't I come too?'

'No. Don't talk so wet.' Duncan eyed him cheerfully. 'You must keep the welcome mat down for us!'

They settled down to wait, watching the boats being warped down the white sand and into the calm water. There were a few waves and only a few shouts, and then the boats were moving slowly away, their tan-coloured sails hanging limp and the ancient diesel engines thumping noisily on the clean air.

The women and a few old men watched the boats depart, and then they moved back to the village and stood in small huddled groups, their hands and arms jerking expressively as they loitered together, apparently unwilling to be left alone.

Taylor produced a watertight packet of chocolate, and they ate it in quick, hungry gulps. They were all feeling the pains of thirst very badly, and when Duncan saw an old villager carrying a long-necked bottle into a cottage he ground his teeth angrily.

'Jesus! Just look at that joker! I'll go down an' have some of that if he waves it about any more!'

Curtis looked down at the empty beach. Empty but for a torn fishing net and a few nodding gulls. The boats were well clear now, small coloured smudges on the green sea.

'I'll work down along the beach, Steve, and try to get beyond the cove, where you found me last night,' he added with a thin smile. 'I think your best bet is to skirt the houses and try to find where the road leads. No tricks, and no risks. Got it?'

Duncan saluted with a coarse gesture and grinned, his teeth white against the stubble of his chin. 'Right! How long shall we all be?'

'Not too long. 'Bout an hour at the most.'

'Blimey! An hour?' Taylor scrambled up protestingly. 'What am I supposed to do then?'

Duncan forced him down again. 'Steady, George. Just sit tight and keep yer eyes peeled!'

Taylor huddled miserably under a bush and watched the two figures disappear round the side of the hill. It was bloody to be left alone. His eye fell on the sand-covered grenade which Curtis had left behind. The mechanic's brain took over from his fears, and with quick, deft movements he began to dismantle and clean the bomb, his face set in concentration.

Once down the hill and across the open sand spit, Curtis realized just how inadequate his plans were. He felt completely naked and unprotected as he pressed himself against the rocks and stones at the foot of the small cliff and stared wildly about him, as if he was already being hunted.

He had repeatedly put off thinking about the actual method and time of escape, and the admission of his failure to make some definite plan worried him. The thought of Jervis made him leave the cover of the rocks and hurry further along the side of the cove. It reminded him of Cornwall, with its deserted beach and impressive silence. But the suspense and the constant fear of discovery made him concentrate on each piece of cover in advance and stop to listen at every few steps.

Once he looked back for the hill, but it had vanished from his vision. That made him feel even more alone, and he had to force himself to move forward again until he reached the end of the cove where the hills and the beach met, and the only way forward was to climb. He studied the hills carefully and slowly. Sparse green grass, yellowed by the heat and the salt air, and some small clumps of trees. Here and there were a few haphazard plots or gardens cut into the hillside, as if the villagers had half-heartedly tried to cultivate the land and had given it up as a bad job.

Suppose I had come ashore at this point? he thought. Where would I go? The hill for the rendezvous was invisible, and with the sea at my back there was only the open sand of the cove or this range of hills.

He thrust his hands into his pockets. They were dry and stiff, and his fingers felt the familiar shape of his pipe. He had neither his pouch nor any matches, but the feel of the pipe gave him confidence. It was like an old friend, and he stuck it between his teeth, the salt taste reminding him of his thirst.

Suppose I meet someone? What do I do? Shoot him, or her, and just walk on? He felt the pistol suddenly heavy at his hip. This is madness. I must think of something. He found that he had started to climb the smooth side of the hill.

He froze as a dog barked shrilly in the distance, and he wondered how Duncan was getting on. Duncan would be better at this sort of thing, he thought bitterly. He was good at everything. If he had been in command none of this would have happened.

He looked back at the open sea. It was no longer hostile. It was home and refuge all in one. He was, as Jervis had said, out of place ashore. The sea shimmered and seemed to mock him.

A dark shape moved in the corner of his eye, and even as he turned, he saw the forepart of a ship begin to move slowly round the headland. For a moment panic gripped him. It was as if the ship was looking for him and had already moved round to trap him from behind. He calmed slightly when he considered that he must be invisible as he stood on the grassy slope, and as the ship slowly took shape the very idea of pursuit seemed ridiculous.

She was an old coastal schooner, and had once been very beautiful. Her slim hull still bore traces of white paint, and her long raked bowsprit and two lofty masts added to her appearance of past craftsmanship. Her dirty sails were furled, the canvas hanging from the yards in uneven, careless bundles. A blue cloud of exhaust gas hovered around her high counter, and he could clearly hear the rasping cough of an old engine.

There were plenty of similar craft plying their trade up and down the Adriatic, and the Germans had made full use of them for carrying supplies and troops, and thereby relieved the overworked railways and roads. A few figures were on her littered deck, but only one man appeared to be in uniform. The sun flashed on a white cap and drill tunic as a tall figure strode from one side of the poop to the other.

Instead of going about and making for the open sea, she altered course towards the cove, and he saw a group of figures gathering in the bows around the anchor.

Must know the water pretty well, thought Curtis, as he watched the ship feeling her way between the dark patches of the shallows. He remembered well enough how little depth there was outside the cove, and wondered if the little schooner was permanently based here.

He watched narrowly as a dinghy was lowered over the ship's side and bobbed reluctantly against the hull, while the vessel continued to move slowly towards the shore.

He heard a faint shout, and saw the splash under the bowsprit as the anchor plummeted down.

A moment later the little schooner swung lazily at her hawser, and the engine, after a few rasping coughs, fell silent.

Curtis sat in the grass, biting on the stem of his pipe and feeling the warmth of the forenoon sun coursing through his whole body. A tiny sea-breeze fanned his face, and he jerked back his head to shake away his dry, salt-caked hair.

He found that he was able to concentrate more fully and his mind had stopped jumping from one possibility to another. Somehow, he knew that this schooner was the answer to his prayer, the avenue of escape.

Thinking of the others brought his mind back to Jervis. They had to find him before they could do anything else, before they could contemplate any movement at all.

Then there was the problem of finding out about the Allied invasion. Suppose it had been called off? That would mean a complete alteration of plans.

He leaned forward as the dinghy shoved off from the schooner's side. Two roughly dressed seamen pulled at the oars, while two other men sat in the stern.

Curtis snuggled down deep in the grass and made a small opening to watch the boat's leisurely approach.

One of the passengers was a short fat Italian in a faded red shirt, and a greasy peaked cap tilted over his eyes. Flabby and middle-aged, he had only the cap to show his authority. Must be the captain, thought Curtis. Yet the other man, who sat stiffly on the thwart, was obviously no mere seaman.

The boat grated ashore and the fat Italian stood up and stepped easily over the gunwale on to the firm sand. As he stepped clear of the dinghy he revealed his slightly-built companion, whose white drill jacket and well-creased trousers clashed with the rough appearance of the other men. Curtis's heart quickened as the second passenger stepped carelessly on to the beach and, after a brief word with the Italian, started to walk up the cove, practically on the same track which Curtis had just taken. As he walked he swung his uniform cap in his hand, his fair hair tilted to the sun and tanned skin dark against the white drill.

The sun also reflected on the glittering shoulder straps of his tunic. As he drew nearer Curtis realized what he had first feared, that the man was a German naval officer, the two bright bars of gold lace proclaiming him to be a lieutenant.

Must be in command of the schooner, he thought. It was common practice for the Germans to put their own officers in charge of the normal Italian crews.

The German was practically below him, and Curtis caught his breath as he stopped to examine the deep footmarks in the sand. Curtis's own footprints. But after a cursory glance round, the lieutenant carried on his way towards the end of the cove.

Curtis lost sight of him for a few minutes, and then saw that the German was climbing up the hill by a small narrow path, his legs moving in long rhythmical strides and his head thrown back like an athlete.

He waited until the other man had passed over the rim of the hill, and then, very slowly, his mouth dry, and not only from thirst, Curtis started to follow him.

The house which confronted him on the other side of the ridge was a surprise in itself. Two-storied and spacious, it stood in the middle of a vast, diamond-shaped flower garden. Small stone walls separated the various colourful sections from the wide circular drive which surrounded the house, and several large ornamental ponds, with gentle fountains playing on the dark water, were placed at intervals around the gardens.

The house, white-painted and cool, seemed to be all windows, and as he watched he saw the German run lightly up the steps to the deep, sun-shadowed porch and disappear into the house.

In the drive stood three cars—two large Fiats, and the dusty scout car which Curtis had seen earlier.

He licked his cracked lips as the sound of the hissing fountains penetrated his racing thoughts. He cursed himself for his weakness, and tried to peer round the small wall nearest him to see the other corner of the building. Probably a German officers' mess of some sort, he decided. Although a more un-military place would be hard to imagine. He glanced at his watch. Ought to be getting back soon. Taylor will wonder what the devil's happened to me.

There was a sudden grinding of gears and the sound of a labouring engine beyond the line of trees which framed the house, and then a long-muzzled armoured car, the black crosses clearly painted on the turret, drove into view and parked beside the scout car. After a few moments three soldiers in field-grey uniforms tumbled out of their vehicle and sat on the grass under one of the trees. He could hear their laughter, and watched enviously as one man, a corporal's chevron on his sleeve, held a chianti bottle high over his head and tried to catch the liquid with his open mouth as it splashed redly across the front of his tunic.

Curtis tore his eyes away and began to retrace his steps. Once clear of the ridge he started to run down the hill towards the beach, conscious of the need to get under cover and discuss his discoveries with the others.

He paused wearily at the foot of the small cliff and mopped his streaming face with his sleeve. As he lowered his arm he froze, and stared fixedly at the horse and rider which were cantering slowly and easily towards him.

At any other time the girl and her chestnut horse would have been a sight to make any man stand and gasp, but at that moment, as she turned easily in the saddle and shaded her eyes to watch the anchored schooner, Curtis was rooted to the spot with the sudden danger and menace which she represented. She was clad in a bright green shirt and well-cut jodphurs, and her hair, which was woven into a long single plait, hung across her slim shoulders like a blue-black snake that rippled and shone each time her body jerked to the horse's motion.

A sudden desperate idea came to Curtis as he watched her drawing nearer and nearer to his position. The schooner was obviously a regular visitor to the cove, as was the German officer, so why shouldn't this girl take him for a German from the ship?

He already had his battledress trousers tucked into the top of his leather sea-boots, and with his fair, sun-bleached hair and blue eyes he looked more like the popular conception of the typical Aryan than did either of the officers Curtis had already seen.

The horse saw him and stopped, its huge liquid eyes watching him anxiously, while the front hooves pawed the sand in quick, agitated movements.

The girl swung around in the saddle, a look of brief annoyance flitting across her dark face. Then she saw Curtis, and her full red mouth tilted at the corners in surprise, and for a moment Curtis thought she would speak.

With his heart pounding against his ribs, Curtis nodded to her, his head bobbing forward in a neat motion which helped to hide his face from hers.

Keeping his eyes hard and cold, he allowed his mouth to smile briefly. *'Guten Tag, Fraulein!'* And then he had passed her.

He forced his eyes to stare dead ahead at the wavy line between sand and sea, and waited breathlessly for the girl to call after him, or hear her challenge his appearance on the lonely beach.

After a while he stopped and bent down to remove his boot. As he tipped an imaginary stone from it, he glanced quickly back up the beach. He was just in time to see the sun's reflection across a piece of green shirt and the horse's chestnut flank before both horse and rider vanished over the Ridge towards the hidden house.

A shiver ran through him, and he looked down at his filthy battledress and salt-whitened boots. His face felt rough and bruised, and his whole being throbbed with weariness and sudden frustration. His father's voice seemed to boom in his ears, probing, chiding, and sarcastic. All at once Curtis began to realize just what his present position really meant. He was little better than a hunted animal. As a person he no longer existed. He thought of the proud girl on her horse, the look of surprise and contempt on her face. No doubt the mistress of one of the Germans, he thought, and he suddenly felt the old hatred begin to mount within him. It was as if his father had forced him to hate once more, had even provided the goading force to make him act. He ran blindly along the beach, only half aware of the rocks which he ducked around and the stunted bushes which afforded him cover.

He was breathless when he eventually reached the top of the hill, and fell gasping beside Taylor and Duncan, who eyed him with alarm.

'O.K., Ralph? Did you find anything?'

Curtis lay propped on his sore elbows, his chest heaving painfully. For a few moments he could not speak, but he stared unbelievingly at the flask of water which Duncan proffered him. He grasped the slim, straw-bound bottle and lifted the neck to his lips. They watched him as he swallowed a mouthful of water and closed his eyes in silent ecstasy.

'Well, Ralph?' Duncan rubbed his hands together impatiently.

Curtis nodded slowly. He could still feel the water in his throat. It was like the fountains around the silent house. 'I saw some more soldiers,' he answered flatly. 'And the ship!'

A light gleamed in Duncan's eye. 'The ship? Ah, yes. We are thinking the same things, eh?' He grinned recklessly.

'Where did you get the water?' asked Curtis sharply, the bottle again catching his eye. It was like a piece of another world.

'Christ, never mind the bottle!' Taylor exploded, his face drawn. 'What about the bleedin' Jerries?'

Duncan ignored the outburst. 'Found the bottle outside a hut, and then tumbled on a stream. But, Ralph,' he leaned forward, his face urgent. 'I found out a few things, too! I think Jerry is movin' up troops all over the place, and look at this!' He handed Curtis a crumpled sheet of newspaper. On the front page was a printed map showing the southern half of Italy. The whole southern coastline was stabbed with huge arrows, each marked with a Union Jack. Curtis stared at it blankly, the glaring Italian headlines dancing before him like a weird code. 'Don't you see, Ralph, it's on! The boys have landed!' Duncan's voice was dangerously loud. 'The invasion's under way!'

Curtis handled the scrap of paper as if it was a precious document.

'Today's date on the paper,' he said at length, 'so they must have been fighting for a couple of days already.'

'Does that mean we're going to pinch a boat?' Taylor looked anxiously from one to the other.

Duncan eyed the schooner, which swung at her anchor like a small white toy, the distance masking her scars and adding to her graceful beauty. 'Too goddamned right we'll pinch a boat! Eh, Ralph?' He rubbed his hands together like sandpaper. 'There's only a Jerry officer an' a handful of flamin' dagos aboard! We can get aboard her easy, an' with the grenade and our two pistols we can take care of them easy!'

His jubilation and wild excitement was infectious, and Curtis rolled over to stare at the ship, his blue eyes cold and hard.

'We might, at that,' he said softly. 'We shall have to do it when she's due to sail, and not before.'

Duncan shrugged. 'Hmmm, I guess so. It wouldn't do to give anything away to the locals. I don't reckon that old engine'd take us far enough before the high-fly boys came after us.' His eyes took on a dreamy look. 'Just think, George, a coupla days and we'd be reportin' to Admiral Cunningham in person. One flamin' dock blown up, and one little Eye-tie schooner for a bit of yachtin'!'

Taylor looked unconvinced. 'It's a long way,' he muttered.

Duncan slapped him across the shoulder. 'Yeh! An' it's a damned long way to walk, too!'

Curtis was thinking hard; a plan was coming at last. All they had to do was find out when the ship was leaving, and be ready. He sighed, *and* find Jervis. He suddenly remembered the Italian girl. She had been beautiful, and he tried to picture her face, but he could only see her red mouth and the arrogant tilt of her head.

'Bitch!' he said savagely.

'How's that again?'

Curtis shook his head, irritated with himself for allowing the girl to intrude on his plan. 'Nothing. But I was just thinking, we'll have to get ourselves cleaned up a bit.'

Duncan's jaw dropped. 'We aimin' to go callin' on the local parson?'

'We may have to look like Germans,' answered Curtis slowly.

'Us?' Taylor was looking worse. 'We'd never get away wiv it!'

'I already have!'

He turned back to the ship. She was suddenly inviting and beautiful, like a lonely woman. He sighed wearily and rested his head on his hands. Where the hell was Jervis?

As if reading his thoughts, Duncan said quietly, 'If the boat's ready an' we haven't found Ian,' he paused, 'well, are we leavin'?'

'What d'you think?' He kept his eyes averted.

'I think we shall have to go. After all, he may have bought it already.' He shrugged. 'Still, you're the skipper.'

Curtis felt desperately tired. 'Yes, *I'm* the skipper,' he answered bitterly.

Taylor shifted uncomfortably in the sand. 'The crew of the boat ain't come ashore yet. Maybe they're shoven' off sooner than we think?'

'Nope. They've not taken on fresh water yet.' Duncan's voice was patient. 'I saw some of the locals gettin' the water cart filled, so they'll be in for tonight, I reckon.'

'Did you see her captain?' Curtis turned his mind back to the plan.

'What, the fat little bloke with the cap? Yeh, I saw him. He was gabbin' about the water, I think. He didn't look so hot, did he?'

It all seemed suddenly clear and urgent, and Curtis sat up with a quick, nervous movement.

'Look here, Steve, this is how I see it.' His voice was crisp, and Duncan eyed him with evident surprise.

'We'll get down to the village this evening, when it's nice and dark, and have another poke round for Ian. At the same time we'll get a wash and tidy up, so that we don't stand out as bloody scarecrows if we want to show ourselves. I think the Jerries will be worried at having a saboteur hanging around the place, and sooner or later they'll start putting the heat on the villagers.

That's what our friend was doing this morning, I imagine. Right so far?'

Duncan nodded thoughtfully. 'Yeh, I think so. D'you think Jerry is worried about his gallant allies? I mean, d'you suppose he's wonderin' which way the cat'll jump when our fellas get a bit closer?'

'Well, wouldn't you?' Curtis smiled grimly. 'I'd like to get my hands on some of the bastards!'

'What in hell's got into you, Ralph? I'd have thought you'd done your share of blowin' 'em up!'

Curtis shrugged vaguely. He wondered at himself and why he was feeling so bitter again. Was it the girl's expression? Was it that she had seen him for what he was? He shook his head angrily to clear it of these stupid fancies.

'How's the other pistol?'

'S'okay,' said Taylor. 'I give it to Steve. 'E's more 'andy wiv it.' He held up the grenade with something like pride. 'This'll do me!'

'Right. Well, hang on to it.' Curtis surveyed them bleakly. 'It'll be quite something if we pull this off!'

Duncan tossed the pistol and caught it lightly in the air. 'We'll give the little Jerry lootenant something to write home about!' He tossed the gun again, his mouth set in a hard smile. 'I hope he's enjoying himself with the local sheilas tonight!'

Taylor looked across. 'Why, for Pete's sake?'

The gun landed with a sharp smack in Duncan's palm and pointed unwaveringly at the sea. ''Cause I don't think he'll get another chance, that's why!'

They settled down to watch and sleep by relays, each man taking a turn in the vigil over the dusty village and the little glimmering ship.

Each man saw them differently. Duncan watched the white cottages and followed the movements of the villagers narrowly, with the eyes of a hunter. He didn't feel either beaten or subdued, just the vague urge to get to grips with the future, and as soon as possible. A young girl walked down the path to the sea, leading a goat on a cord. He smiled secretly. A girl under the sun, with her mouth against your ear, and her body close to yours. That would be more like it.

Taylor saw only houses and vague shapes of people moving near them. They were all hostile and alien to him, and each untoward movement made him duck his head and curse the stupidity of leaving the submarine. Somehow he didn't feel it likely that he was going to live much longer, and the more he thought about it, the more the shadows seemed to close in.

Curtis saw many things, although few of them were there to see. Once the girl's face was there, shimmering in the sand, mocking him, like the girl in Chelsea. And then he began to sweat as he saw the twisting, distorted face of Roberts in the severed net. But as his body got nearer, Curtis saw that the face was different; this time it was Jervis, and the face was changing. It was no longer distorted and swollen, but sad and reproachful, and the dead lips said silently, "I trusted you, and you failed me"!

Curtis ground his teeth and mopped the sweat from his eyes. The sun smote his neck like a fiery sword, and he groaned aloud with the thoughts which tortured him. Was that why he wanted action? To free himself from his guilt? He tried to concentrate on the schooner, which seemed to quiver in the heat-haze. Tomorrow. What would happen then, and how many of them would be left?

He glanced back at his companions, who were sleeping in the shade of the bushes—Taylor with his mouth open and his breath rough and uneven; Duncan sprawled like a dead man in the sand, the pistol protruding from his belt like a wicked steel eye.

Which of us will be next? He reached wearily for the flask, and remembered the house on the hill. She would be there. Cool, soft dress, and slim brown hands stroking that long plait of hair. Damn her! And all the others! But the strange yearning in his chest persisted and kept him company throughout his watch.

The sun crossed its summit and began to move graciously over the flat sea. Some of its rays fell on the schooner, and some lighted the sails of the returning fishing boats. And some caressed the dark green trough which hid the flooded submarine, where it lay empty and harmless, like a dead shark.

Chapter 5

SUB-LIEUTENANT IAN JERVIS opened his eyes slowly and stared vacantly at the roughly-timbered roof above his head. For several long moments he lay quite still, as if waiting for life to re-start and events to fall into their proper perspective. He was aware instead of the throbbing pain which burned across his head like a branding iron, and the great feeling of weakness which made him groan again and move his head dazedly from side to side.

As his cheek brushed against the rough, dirty pillow under his head, he chilled, as the complete strangeness of the silent room brought the terrifying memories flooding back to him in a series of wavering pictures. Most of all, he remembered the sea. The great, black towering waves which dragged and beat at his body until he no longer held the breath to call out, and which filled his eyes until he could no longer look for the help which he knew could never come. He tried to wrinkle his brow, as if that might help to clear his brain, but the stabbing pain across his head made him cry out, and his eyes clouded with tears. Vaguely he could remember the beach rushing towards and then beneath him, as a wave lifted him up and flung him like a rag doll on the shore. Then the blow, a second of flashing light which exploded in his skull, and then . . . he stared round . . . and then what?

Slowly the picture of his refuge became complete, as with short, painful twists of his neck he examined each section of the room. It was only about ten feet by ten, and appeared to be some sort of hut. The floor was bare, stamped earth, and the bright sunlight which filtered around the sides of the strips of sacking which covered each of the two tiny windows displayed, amongst other things, a pile of old, sea-washed bottles and a torn net, while against the broken brick grate was stacked a mass of old driftwood, a navigation lamp, and a stinking bundle of rags. A movement in the grate made him gasp, and he lowered his gaze to meet the curious, unwinking stare of a large grey rat, which sat perched on an upended tin can, slowly and methodically cleaning its whiskers.

'G'on! Scat!' Jervis tried to shout, but his voice was a mere croak, and he let his head fall back on to the sacking of his pillow. He tried to think and keep back the tide of misery which threatened to engulf him with each new discovery.

As he moved his head, his palm touched the warm skin of his thigh, and with quick nervous movements he found that beneath the evil-smelling blanket he was quite naked. The shock made him struggle up on to his elbows, and the realization of his nakedness brought the feeling back to his limbs. The roughness of the blanket against his skin, the pain in his head, and the fact that he was alone in some strange hut, told him that at least he was still free. But who had put him there, and where his rescuer had gone, was quite another thing. And where were his clothes? A cold chill ran down his spine. Suppose someone had found him, and hidden his clothes while he fetched the police or the soldiers? He struggled with the blanket, suddenly frantic. Must get out. Must get away. The messages hammered in his head as he scrambled over the side of the battered couch. As his bare feet took his weight, the hut seemed to swim around him in a mad whirlpool, and he reeled against the wall, trying to fight off the dizziness and the pain, his hands scrabbling weakly for support. The rat scuttled amongst the old bottles and vanished, and Jervis stood with his legs astride, as if on the deck of a heaving ship.

Another movement caught his eye from across the couch, and for a moment he was almost too frightened and sick to look.

It was a long strip of cracked and scored glass, probably taken from an equally old wardrobe, and as Jervis stared at his own distorted reflection he hardly noticed the bruises on his sunburned skin, or even the crude bandage which entangled his skull like a turban. As the blood pounded through his veins, and his fingers gripped the wall behind him, he found that he was staring, not at a proud, dependable officer, but at a shaking, frightened boy.

With a sob he leaned back against the warm stonework and closed his eyes. He was suddenly both ashamed and completely without hope. To be found like this.... He looked down at himself in despair. It was the final stab of failure.

Where were Curtis and the others, he wondered. Most likely dead, as he himself might have been but for all this.

He sensed that there was someone or something watching him, and he had to force his head round to look. The room was still and empty, the sun glinting on the old bottles and making his limbs shine against the filthy couch, like a statue. His eyes reached the heavy door and stopped. It was just the same as before, but for the cracks in the unplaned woodwork. They no longer allowed the sunlight to enter like little gold spears; they were black, covered from outside.

So they've come. He felt his limbs go slack, and a bitter resignation held him quite still and limp as he stood and watched the door. A small spark of defiance dared to lighten some of the blackness in his mind, and he tried to pull himself together, to get ready for whatever was to come.

The door opened with surprising quickness, and the strange figure stood black against the sunlight and the green hills, like a gaunt scarecrow.

The man stepped inside the hut with a queer, loping gait, and shut the door behind him. For a moment he leaned back against the door and stared fixedly at Jervis as the rat had done, without speaking or moving.

Jervis clenched his fists and gazed, wide-eyed. The man was dressed in a greasy, ragged smock which hung almost to his knees, and from under which his thin bent legs protruded like sticks. His feet were encased in a dirty pair of sandals, and the skin of his bare feet was thick with grime and filth.

Jervis could only stare at his face. It could have been any age between twenty or fifty, encircled with a mass of wild, straggly black hair and a thick beard, which left only the large, vacant brown eyes and a patch of sun-wrinkled skin uncovered. It was his mouth which drew Jervis's fascinated eyes. It was wide and slack, and moved loosely with restless abandon, as if its owner neither possessed the will nor the wish to control it. Even as he watched, the creature's tongue lolled wetly across the rim of his beard and an unheeded stream of spittle ran downwards across the tattered smock. As Jervis stood against the wall he saw that the man was carrying what appeared to be his uniform, rolled in a tight ball, the boots and pistol belt protruding from the middle.

'I . . .' began Jervis slowly, his voice shattering the silence of the room. 'I must thank you . . .' he stopped. The man only rolled his eyes wildly and allowed his mouth to slip into a lopsided grin.

God, he groaned inwardly, a raving lunatic! A crazy hermit or beachcomber who had stumbled across his body by accident, and who was going to torment him even more. He held out his hands for his clothes, and waited for the man to snatch them away.

Instead, the grin faded, and for a brief moment he looked almost solemn, and then, with great care, he handed the bundle to Jervis.

Keeping one eye on the figure by the door, Jervis began to struggle into his crumpled uniform. It was a tremendous effort, and once he would have fallen but for a clawlike hand which darted out and held his elbow like a vice until the weakness had passed.

Eventually he had finished dressing, and only the pistol belt lay between them on the floor. As he bent to pick it up a look of indescribable pain crossed the other man's face, and he cowered back against the wall.

Jervis stood up, the heavy belt gripped uncertainly in his hand. For a moment he forgot his own pain and misery, and his heart filled with pity for the human wreck who had rescued him, bandaged his head, put him to bed, and dried his soaked clothing, and who now cowered with fear at the sight of the gun.

He tossed it on to the couch and grinned shakily. 'See?' He pointed at the gun. 'See? Friends, yes?' He stopped. It had sounded so ridiculous, and apart from the change of expression on the creature's face it was obviously useless trying to speak English. As Jervis watched, the grin reappeared, and the man nodded violently, his thick tangled hair falling across his forehead like a mane. From his mouth came a queer, spine-chilling gurgle, as if he was choking, and then more nods.

Jervis sat down weakly on the couch and followed the man's movements with his eyes, as he darted around the hut, searching and scratching amongst the piles of flotsam and junk.

An idea crossed his mind, and he waited until the man had his back turned, and then, mustering his strength, he called sharply across the room.

'Here, you! Stand to attention when you're addressing an officer! What's your blasted name?' He fell back on the couch, laughing uncontrollably and with something like hysteria.

What else can happen now? A deaf-and-dumb madman for company, and I don't even know where I am! He jumped as he felt a prod in the thigh. The man was holding a cracked cup out to him.

Jervis held it to his lips. It was strange that he felt no thirst, but this poor creature had probably been pouring water down his throat while he was unconscious. He sipped the brackish water slowly, aware that the brown eyes were watching him eagerly.

He handed the cup back, and received some fresh tomatoes in return. He offered some of them back, but immediately the man shrank away, and shook his head decidedly.

'All right, my friend, I'll eat, and I only wish I could tell you just how I feel about being rescued, and about your kindness.'

The tomatoes were delicious, and he handed back the empty plate, a smile of satisfaction on his lips. He hoped that would make up for the lack of words, and he was rewarded by the lopsided grin and a low grunting.

Jervis wondered what would happen next, and stood up to look from one of the windows.

The effect was instantaneous. He felt the clawlike hands on his arms, and as helplessly as a baby he was dragged back to the couch. The wild figure shook his head and waved his arms about in a frenzy, and once, stood against the window, crucified by the sunlight, and shook his head so violently that Jervis thought he was having a fit.

Jervis nodded slowly and tried to smile. 'All right,' he murmured softly, 'I get it. You're trying to tell me it's not safe to go out. So what'll we do? Stop here till the war's over?' He lay back on the blanket, the throbbing in his head again taking control.

Can't think about it any more. Must rest. Must get my strength back. He watched through half-closed lids as his weird companion capered around the hut, his shadow looming and fading like a huge bat. He felt the strong fingers pulling off his battledress blouse and lifting his feet on to the couch, but he didn't care any more. In some strange way he felt safe, and allowed some of his defencelessness to fall more as a mantle than a scourge.

When he awoke the sun had moved from the windows, and the squalid interior of the hut was deep in shadows. Jervis yawned and moved his aching head gingerly from side to side. He was once more alone, and for one instant he thought the meeting with the pathetic hermit had been part of a dream, but the stench of rags and the surrounding heaps of rubbish brought back his memory and made him wonder where his protector had gone.

His legs felt a little stronger, and after taking a few cautious steps around the hut, he went to one of the windows and peered through the cracked and grime-tinted glass.

He found that the hut was situated on the side of a gently sloping hill, which ran down to a wide span of beach, and which appeared to be completely deserted by both dwellings and trees alike. As he pressed his cheek against the blistered frame, he could just see the edge of a small village, two or three little white houses, slumbering against the grassy slopes of the neighbouring hills, their low walls bathed in deep blue shadows, as the sun passed slowly towards the horizon.

It must be late afternoon, he decided, as he gazed first at the sky and then at the strip of lighter skin across his wrist, where his watch had once been. I wonder if any of the others are safe, and whether he, or they, are waiting on the hill? He shook his head to clear away the throbbing pain. I must do something, or I'll go as mad as that other poor devil.

He pulled the pistol belt from under the blanket and gingerly drew the automatic from its holster. He weighed the weapon in his palm, and remembered the little red-faced petty officer who had instructed him and the rest of his class by the side of a Scottish loch.

'Now, gentlemen! All you 'as to do is point at 'is belly, an' squeeze the trigger! Got it?'

It had seemed so remote and vaguely theatrical at the time that probably none of the young officers had really considered

the true implications. But now Jervis pulled back the slide and
heard the top bullet in the clip snap into the breech. He applied
the safety catch, and once more stared out of the window. What
should he do first, he wondered?

I'll wait until my friend comes back and then try to make for
the rendezvous. Suppose it's empty? He shivered at the thought.
He would be no better off than before. In fact, here at least he
was safely hidden. But suppose one of the others *had* survived,
and lay injured or sick somewhere out there on the beach, or up
in the hills? His mouth tightened, and he slipped the gun into his
trouser pocket. He knew he had to go. It might be the skipper.
The thought of Curtis, and how he had surfaced the submarine
to save him the agony of cutting another net, decided him.

A lorry revved its engine in the distance, and a flock of
sleeping gulls rose in a white cloud from the beach, screeching
and mewing.

Jervis crossed quickly to the door and pressed his eye against
one of the wide cracks.

He found that he could see right along the edge of the village
and across the winding track which led away from the sea, and
from which came the sound of yet another engine. As he
watched, he saw the front of a heavy diesel lorry heave itself
around the side of the hill, spewing thick dust and sand from
under its fat tires, and grind down the middle of the road.
Another followed, and after a brief interval, two more. They
were giants, their sides caked with old mud and their high canvas
canopies torn and dirty. The engines whirred into silence, and
from the cabs he saw the figures of uniformed drivers, they, too,
dust-covered and worn, climb down and gather around their
vehicles.

Italian soldiers, he thought, as he watched one stubble-
chinned driver relieving himself at the side of the road. Didn't
look like a search party. They had obviously driven a long way,
and looked anything but warlike.

Jervis watched them keenly, his eye watering against the
crack, but oblivious to his cramp or the pain in his head. This
was the enemy, and he felt neither elated nor frightened. The
little grubby soldiers were as he had always imagined them to be
when he had heard and read of them surrendering by the
thousands to the Eighth Army in the desert, in the first, far-off
flush of victory.

A few of the villagers had started to move up the track towards the lorries, but the drivers waved them back, and one of them even unslung a machine carbine from his shoulder, as if to emphasize the point.

The villagers, mainly fishermen and their wives, hung back in a curious, chattering group, while from between the packed bodies a few children squeezed through and gazed wide-eyed at the visitors. One of the drivers, a tubby little man with a short pointed beard, walked slowly towards the rear of one of the lorries, and on tiptoes shouting at someone inside, and occasionally shook his head. The crowd was silent now, and Jervis could feel the tension rising like a wave. The Italian soldier, he appeared to be a corporal, stamped his foot and angrily turned his back on the lorry, and strutted back to his men, who were watching disinterestedly from the side of the road. They all seemed to be waiting for something, or somebody. An officer probably, Jervis decided.

There was a sudden flurry of movement from the first lorry, and before any one of the soldiers could move a pair of legs slithered over the tail-board, and a man staggered out into the dying sunlight. There was a gasp from the crowd, and the corporal stepped angrily forward.

Jervis had gone cold, and he could feel the hair rising on his neck as he stared at the lone figure which stood swaying in the dust, his eyes blinking and staring round at the watching Italians. His khaki battledress was torn and stained with long patches of dried blood, and one arm was completely hidden under a great wad of dressings and rough bandages. His young red face was racked with pain and anger, and he shook his unruly hair from his eyes and swallowed hard.

'Fer Christ's sake,' his voice rose in a high cracked sound, 'are yer just goin' ter stand there?' He waved his uninjured arm at the lorries, his face torn apart with sudden desperation. 'My mates is in there! Some of 'em's dyin'!' The corporal had reached him by this time and pushed him roughly towards the lorry. A murmur of sympathy rose from the watching fishermen. The British soldier staggered against the tail-board, the fight already draining from his face. 'They're wounded! Don' you understand, you Wop bastards? Fer Christ's sake give us a drink of water!' But the corporal seized him by the belt and jerked him over the tail-board, and followed him into the hidden interior.

Jervis sank back, stunned and sick. Hearing that pain-racked Cockney voice, and seeing the misery of the man's face, had swept away his previous feelings and fears like a cold wind. He beat the dirt floor with his fist in impotent rage. A few yards from the hut were four lorries crammed with British wounded, and *he* had been worrying about his own plight. They must have been captured in the south, he thought wildly, and they had probably been driven non-stop, two hundred miles or so, to this miserable place. The swine! There were tears of rage running unheeded down his chin, as he thought of the horror such a drive would entail to wounded men fresh from the firing line. What were they doing here anyway? There had been no hospital marked on the submarine's chart, just a godforsaken fishing village. Sobbing with rage, he pressed his eye back to the crack. A small khaki scout car had arrived, and the Italian soldiers had pulled themselves into some semblance of attention.

Jervis stared with sudden hatred at the slim, dapper officer in the polished boots and Afrika Korps cap who stood listening to the excited explanations from the corporal.

The German nodded briefly and glared round at the soldiers and the villagers. He pointed at the lorries and waved his arm angrily over the village. Still nobody moved, until with a sudden crash the officer banged his fist on to the bonnet of his car. With a jerk everyone started moving at once, and Jervis saw the women passing jugs of water and fruit to the soldiers, who in turn carried them into the lorries.

It was at that moment that Jervis saw his new companion trotting vaguely along the side of the hill towards the hut. In the fading light, and set against the background of bustling villagers, he looked even stranger than before. But Jervis closed his eyes and groaned aloud, as he saw the German officer pause impatiently in the middle of his orders, to glance sharply at the passing figure. The strange, capering scarecrow was the same as before but for one thing. Over his smock he now wore Jervis's blue battledress blouse, the gold lace shoulder straps glinting and reflecting in the dying light.

The German frowned and turned as if to continue with his task, and none of the villagers seemed to take any notice of what was obviously a familiar figure, until with a jerk the officer flung up his arm and pointed excitedly, while his mouth struggled with the right words of Italian.

For a moment the soldiers gaped at him, but as the officer pointed again, they ran after the slow-moving figure, their boots clashing on the loose stones, and their faces both angry and mystified.

Within twenty yards of the hut, one of the soldiers overtook their quarry and pulled roughly at the man's arm. He and the soldier skidded to a breathless halt and stood staring uncertainly at each other. Jervis watched wildly as the German, followed by his own driver, came slowly up the hill to the waiting group, while the idiot gave his lopsided grin and stood beaming at each man in turn. The German pointed to the tunic with an impatient gesture, and one of the Italians reached out to pull it from the gaunt shoulders. Impatiently he shook the groping hand free and clutched the tunic more closely to his body with childish defiance. His eyes were screwed up with anxiety, but the grin remained, as if its owner was unwilling to believe that anyone could want to deprive him of his new possession.

The officer was obviously getting completely exasperated. Now that he was so close, Jervis could see the sharp, pointed features beneath the long-peaked cap, and the lines of irritation about the man's thin mouth.

He spoke sharply to his driver, a slow-moving giant of a man in grey tunic and dusty jackboots, who stepped forward with casual ease and drove his fist into the idiot's face. Like a puppet, he fell on his back, while the big German trooper bent laboriously over him and stripped off Jervis's jacket, as if he was undressing a stubborn child.

He handed it to the officer, who searched rapidly through the pockets and examined the shoulder straps eagerly, while the other soldiers looked from him to the still figure on the ground and shuffled their feet uneasily.

The Italian corporal shouted from the bottom of the hill and pointed to the hut.

Jervis chilled, as all the eyes turned up towards his hiding place. It was as if they could already see him through the crack in the door.

The officer tossed the tunic to the ground and slipped open the top of his long leather holster. Ignoring the Italians, and never taking his cold eyes from the hut, he jerked out his Luger and pointed it towards the door.

'*Guck mal, of da noch jemand drin ist!*' he ordered, the

sharpness of his voice falling on the human air like a knife. His driver snatched the machine carbine from the Italian corporal, and started slowly towards the door.

Jervis's eyes widened as he saw the man walking calmly, yet with obvious alertness, towards him. The grey uniform blotted out the other faces, and as he drew even nearer Jervis could see his fat, heavy face quite clearly, and the little beads of sweat which trickled from beneath the grey forage cap.

He shivered violently and groped for his own pistol. He stood back from the door and raised the gun slowly in front of his body. It seemed to be of terrible weight, and his hand shook, until he gripped the butt with such force that his wrist ached and his knuckles were white against his tanned skin.

Nothing happened, and he ground his teeth together to stop himself from shivering. He could feel the sweat running down the small of his back and was conscious of the great stillness which seemed to hang over the hut and beyond.

The crash of glass which shattered the silence made his body leap, and the sour taste of vomit pause in his throat as he spun round on the floor, his eyes seeking blindly, the pistol waving from side to side. He felt all the strain of the past day exploding in his brain, as he looked at the long black muzzle which lay across the sill of the small window.

'*Hände hoch!*' The fat German gestured with the carbine towards Jervis's pistol. A smile played across the fat lips with something like pity, but the eyes which peered through the broken glass were hard and devoid of all compassion.

Almost unconsciously, Jervis let the gun fall from his nerveless fingers and immediately hated himself for giving in so easily. As if reading his thoughts, the German pointed the carbine unwaveringly at the boy's stomach, and shook his head briefly.

'Still! Stand still!' The clumsy words were filled with menace.

The door jerked back on its hinges as a well-delivered kick brought the sunlight pouring into the hut, lighting the scene, and seeming to lay bare Jervis's shame.

The officer nodded curtly to the face at the window, and picked up Jervis's pistol. He tossed it to someone outside the door, and regarded Jervis with cold curiosity.

'You are a British officer?' The voice was as hard as the eyes, but the accent was almost flawless.

Jervis shrugged. 'Yes. Sub-Lieutenant Jervis, Royal Navy!'

As he answered, he lifted his head and looked the other man straight in the face. A feeling of pride or despair made him draw himself to attention and lift his chin defiantly.

'Please spare me the heroics! You will need all those later!' He waved the pistol sharply. 'Outside! And do not be tempted to do anything stupid!'

Jervis blundered out into the sunlight and blinked at the circle of watching faces. At the bottom of the hill the soldiers raised their rifles threateningly, and drove the villagers away from the road and clear of the lorries.

Jervis walked down the hill to where the scout car stood, and where the idiot sat in the dust, rubbing his chin and moaning gently. Jervis stopped dead at the sight of him, and turned back to the officer. 'That man there,' he pointed, and the idiot caught his eye and smiled pitifully, 'he knows nothing about me. He's deaf and dumb!'

The German eyed him thoughtfully, his face in shadow. 'Then he will be no loss, will be?' He barked an order, and the Italian corporal sprang to attention, his little beard pointing out at a ridiculous angle, but his eyes fixed on the seated prisoner.

'He's mad!' continued Jervis, suddenly frantic. He had seen the look of hatred on the corporal's face. It was as if the man had been looking for someone to vent his temper on, and to clear the air of his own humiliation.

The German smiled. 'He was assisting you to escape. What does it matter who or what he is?' The smile faded. 'An example must be made; these people are swine, without backbone, they have to be taught a lesson!' He pushed Jervis's shoulder. 'Now, into the car, we have a journey to make!'

The driver slid into his seat without even a glance at his prisoner, and waited for his orders. Jervis gripped the armoured side of the car, and turned back to the hut. Over the officer's shoulder he saw the corporal beating at a writhing shape on the ground, whose wordless mouth twisted and mouthed in horrible contortions as the soldier stood astride him, a heavy steel rod in his fat hands. The other soldiers laughed and jeered, and one of them tore the old smock from the broken body, and waved it like a flag over his head. The movements ceased with awful suddenness, and the corporal looked down at the German, his streaming face split in an ingratiating smile. Jervis stumbled blindly into the car, heedless of the watching soldiers, and conscious only of the pathetic ragged heap at the corporal's feet.

The German officer nodded to his driver and the car began to move. 'Carrion!' he said, half to himself, and then settled down comfortably in his seat, the Luger resting in his lap.

Jervis drew his legs together and bunched himself into a tight ball in the corner of the open car. The very idea of bodily contact with the officer who sat so calmly at his side seemed at that moment to be unclean, and he felt his tight limbs trembling with helpless rage, and a new feeling, previously unbeknown to him, but which he now recognized as hatred.

He only half noticed the last of the white cottages slide past in a cloud of dust, and the crouching hills close in to blot out the laughing sea. He kept remembering his strange friend and helper, and seeing his awful silent pleas for kindness and mercy. And the British wounded; his mind vaulted painfully back to the sun-baked lorries and their loads of human suffering. What would happen to them? He forced himself to look sideways at his captor. He saw that the man was watching him quietly, his eyes darkened by the soft peak of his cap.

'You are no doubt wondering where we are going? What is going to happen to you, *ja?*'

Jervis shrugged with an indifference he no longer enjoyed. 'I suppose you intend to shoot me, isn't that the general idea?'

The German frowned, and then sighed with mock sadness. 'You are a prisoner, you will be treated accordingly. However, if you intend to co-operate with my superior officer, I have little doubt that you might be given more,' he paused significantly, 'preferential treatment!'

Jervis clenched his fists. 'Why did you let your men kill that poor creature? He didn't know or understand anything!' The words burst from him. 'Now I understand what is meant by German cruelty!'

'Silence! How can you understand anything?' His face was tight with rage. 'You are a mere boy, masquerading as an officer! I suppose you are going to tell me that when you blew up the dock at Vigoria, you did not know you blew up many innocent persons also, is that not so?' His mouth twisted into a bitter smile. 'Civilians, dockyard workers, all blown to hell!'

'The dock was a military objective, it was part of the war!' Jervis leaned forward until the muzzle of the Luger rested against his side.

'War! Of course it was war, and so was that business back in the village, so do not try to make black white!'

They both glared angrily at each other in silence, and Jervis became aware that the driver was whistling softly, his massive head sunk indifferently into his shoulders.

'What will happen to those wounded?' Jervis's voice was quiet and flat, the angry outburst had sapped away his strength.

'The wounded?' He appeared to ponder on the matter, but he, too, seemed to be regretting his sudden flare of temper. 'They will be looked after. At the moment we are a little short of medical staff, but never fear, they will be cared for. The Third Reich never abandons those who have fought bravely!' There was an imperceptible sneer in his tone.

Jervis ignored the implication, and stared down at his knees. 'How is the battle going in the south?' He tried to appear calm, but his heart was pounding with sudden eagerness to hear news of the outer world, *his* world.

The German laughed shortly. 'It is being won.' For a moment a smile passed across his cold features, and the years seemed to drop away. 'No doubt I shall be able to find out for myself very soon.' He stared past Jervis at the green hills. 'For four years I have been fighting the British, and always people ask, how goes the battle! But it still goes on. France, Holland, Egypt, and now Italy.' He shrugged, irritable with himself. 'It will be over one day. That is all I can say!'

The car halted at the side of the main road, and their voices were drowned by the thunder of vehicles. Jervis watched as lorry after lorry rumbled past, each jammed with stony, set faces and nodding coal-scuttle helmets. More lorries carrying tanks and guns thundered along the narrow road, shepherded by military police on motorcycles. To Jervis it was like a film. This was part of the enemy war machine, and next to him was a German officer. It was more like a nightmare. He glanced up at the sun and back to the road. They were going south. To the front. A cold thrill ran through him, and he remembered the wounded in the village. How many of these German soldiers would live to see the sun rise in a few more days? He pressed his lips together in a tight line.

I hope you rot in hell! It was like a prayer.

The car started again and swung into a tiny narrow lane between two crumbling white gateposts.

A German soldier saluted, and then they were speeding up a long gravel drive towards a proud rambling house on the top of a slope. As the car swung past a pair of gentle fountains and topped the rise, Jervis swallowed and bit his lip. Beyond and below the house lay the sea. He wished he could not see it. Each diadem of glittering green light seemed to mock him, as the smooth surface caught the last brilliance of the sun.

I shall never see it again, he thought. The car had stopped in front of the house, and the officer pointed to the entrance. 'The end of the road, *ja*?'

As he climbed wearily up the side steps at the entrance to the house, the smell of fresh flowers and the cool cleanliness of the dark interior only added to the feeling of unreality, and he stood uncertainly in the majestic, marble-pillared hallway, only half taking in the ornate, gilt-encrusted decorations and the single chandelier, which hung like a huge ear-ring from the domed ceiling.

Tall doors of dark seasoned wood opened off from each side of the hall, and he stepped back involuntarily as two soldiers, hatless and with their sleeves rolled above their elbows, staggered past him, panting beneath the weight of a large metal trunk. He noticed, as his eyes became accustomed to the gloom, that the place seemed littered with pieces of luggage and packed equipment, and on a magnificently carved chest he saw an upended steel helmet and a pair of goggles perched incongruously alongside a tall, flower-filled vase.

The German officer grunted, and tapped Jervis under the elbow. 'Wait here. I will inform the colonel of your arrival.'

Jervis watched the thin, brisk figure cross the polished floor, his high boots clicking on the wood blocks, and pass through one of the doors. Jervis did not have to turn his head to know that the driver was standing close beside him, and he felt his spirit draining from him, leaving him in a daze of miserable uncertainty.

Somewhere in the house a telephone buzzed like a trapped fly, while from the sun-dappled drive came the staccato roar of motor cycles. The two soldiers returned and picked up more of the baggage from the floor.

One of them, a short, red-faced man, stopped for a moment and stared at Jervis in surprise. For a moment, a slow smile crossed his face, but immediately it vanished, and he hurried away with his burden, as the officer returned.

He stopped directly in front of Jervis and ran his eyes sharply over his crumpled trousers and stained jersey, as if he was carrying out an inspection.

Jervis coloured. 'Satisfied?' he asked with sudden anger. 'I'm afraid I didn't find time to change!'

The German's face remained impassive. 'The colonel will see you now. He has not much time. The regiment is leaving immediately.' He rubbed his sharp chin, his eyes thoughtful. 'The colonel speaks no English. I will translate the information you have to give.' He turned on his heel before Jervis could answer, but as he opened the door he said softly over his shoulder, 'Do not irritate the colonel, he is not in the mood for insolence!'

Jervis followed the officer into the wide, comfortable room, his heart pounding painfully, and his fingers clenched tightly against his sides. His captor halted, his boots coming together with a sharp click, which jerked Jervis's racing thoughts into readiness in spite of his misery, and made him glance round with chilled anticipation.

The long windows which looked out across the lawns to where the sea sparkled so invitingly covered the complete side of the room, while the other walls were lined with books and hung with large military maps.

The desk which dominated the room was also littered with maps, and several field telephones, which hung in their leather cases, ugly and out-of-place.

A tall, stooped officer stood behind the desk, whilst to one side, and sitting with his legs crossed in a comfortable chair, was a dapper, quietly dressed civilian.

The colonel straightened his back slowly, as if it was both an effort to tear his eyes from the maps and to find time for this interruption.

He listened to the short, barking sentences from Jervis's captor, his pale eyes moving restlessly around the room, and his long slender fingers beating a gentle tattoo on the top of the desk. Jervis wanted to scream as the voice droned on, while the colonel listened, and the civilian's head nodded slowly in either agreement or understanding.

The colonel held up his hand, his voice, which was surprisingly low and soft, was directed to the officer, although the pale eyes were now fixed on Jervis in a flat, unwavering stare.

'Herr Colonel wishes to know how your raid was carried out. Answer please!'

Jervis swallowed hard, and met the colonel's eyes. 'I am not obliged to answer. According to the Geneva Convention, I——' he got no further.

The colonel slammed his fist on to the desk, so that a pencil rattled noisily across the floor, and his voice, although still under control, was harsh.

'Herr Colonel says that you are not to be stubborn. You are not making it easy for yourself!'

The civilian spoke for the first time, and Jervis wrenched his gaze from the tall figure by the desk to the other man, who nodded encouragingly, his grey, clipped hair catching the reflections from the dying sun.

'I am Guilio Zecchi.' He dropped his dark eyes to study the pointed toe of his shoe. 'I am the Mayor and political liaison officer to the colonel here. Please do not disregard the colonel's warning, he is a dangerous man, and,' he shrugged eloquently, 'he has much to do!' He wriggled his plump shoulders more comfortably into the chair, and smiled gently. 'We know that you were responsible for the crime in Vigoria.' He waved a well-manicured hand, as if dismissing the whole incident as some unfortunate lapse of sanity. 'The Colonel wishes to know how you did it. Tell him!'

Jervis was thinking furiously. They had not caught Curtis or the others. They did not know about the submarine. He spread his hands in a movement of resignation.

'I was landed by submarine some days ago.' The lie came easily. 'I placed the charges beneath the dock, and went back to rendezvous with the boat before the explosion was due. My rubber dinghy sank, and I had to swim ashore. I struck my head. . . .'

At this point the colonel pointed to Jervis's bandage, and barked a question.

'The Colonel asks how you managed to treat your injury?' The officer's voice sounded strained.

Without turning his head, Jervis spoke from between his clenched teeth. 'Tell him about the poor wretch who helped me, and how your gallant soldiers taught these gutless Italians a lesson!' He darted a glance at the mayor, and was gratified to see a brief look of anger darken the smooth face.

The colonel looked from one to the other, and then at his watch. As if to add to the urgency of the proceedings, one of the telephones whirred impatiently.

The colonel spoke sharply into the mouthpiece, his eyes searching across one of the maps. With a grunt, he slipped the telephone into its case and bundled the maps together into a flat folder. He lifted his eyes quickly and stared at Jervis, his face tired and suddenly old.

'The Colonel says that you will be detained here for the night. Tomorrow you will be shot!'

Jervis staggered as if he had received a blow in the heart. He couldn't speak or even move his mouth, which had suddenly gone quite dry.

The colonel walked slowly around the desk, his eyes sweeping the room as if to ensure he had left nothing behind. He halted between Jervis and the door, and his tone was quiet, almost gentle. Then he nodded to the mayor who still sat in his chair, and marched briskly from the room.

Jervis turned to see the door close, and met the cold stare of the other officer. The man's face was expressionless as he said, 'Herr Colonel said it is better to die a brave man, than to be interrogated by the Gestapo!' His shoulders seemed to sag. 'He is right. Be thankful.' He gestured with the pistol. 'March! I will take you to your quarters.'

Jervis faltered, knowing that his face was ashen, but still he forced himself to speak to the mayor.

'There are British wounded in the village. What can you do for them? You must do something to help!'

'You do not think of yourself? That is good.' He studied Jervis closely. 'You are brave. Never fear, the wounded are being taken care of. They will go north by sea. The roads are filled with, er, military traffic. There is no room for anyone going the other way, I fear!'

Jervis tore his eyes away, and looked once more at the sea. I must hang on, can't break down now! His lip trembled.

'Thank you, sir. I feel better now!'

He crossed to the door, the German behind him.

There was a roar of engines, and he heard several vehicles crunching down the drive. He noticed that the luggage was missing from the hall, and only one soldier stood by the entrance.

He glanced involuntarily at the chest. The helmet and goggles had also gone. He walked blindly down a white-walled passage, the colonel's words ringing in his brain. Tomorrow you will be shot.

They reached an open door to one side of the long passage, and involuntarily Jervis stopped and drew back, the bare, stone-walled room which confronted him brought home the hopeless-ness and complete collapse of his final position.

The German's voice was crisp and alert, as if he, too, sensed the awful finality of the forbidding room.

'Inside,' he snapped, 'it would be stupid to resist!'

Jervis's shoulders slumped, and he walked slowly through the door. It had once been a storeroom of some kind, and the rough walls were lined with wooden shelves, empty but for scraps of old straw and torn paper.

A camp bed stood in readiness in one corner, and a crude bucket in the other.

Jervis stared round unbelievingly, his trapped gaze taking in the bareness of the room, the lack of even a window, and the armed sentry who now stood watchfully behind the officer.

'Food will be brought shortly. I would advise you to eat, then try to sleep.' The German's tone was almost matter-of-fact. 'The sentry does not speak English, and he has been told to shoot, should you try to escape! Is there anything you wish to say?' One eyebrow lifted slightly.

Jervis clenched and unclenched his fists, and tried to clear his brain. 'How... I mean when will it be?' His voice was hoarse, and in the confined space of the room his breathing sounded fast and uneven.

'First light. Five o'clock, I think.'

'I see.'

How unimportant he seemed to be to these people. He was already dead in their eyes. He remembered how the colonel had been impatient to leave with the regiment, the blowing up of the dock no longer important. Those details could be left to some-one else to worry about.

The German looked at his watch and sighed. 'I am going. I wish you luck!' He smiled briefly. 'Perhaps I, too, shall be joining you soon!'

'I thought perhaps you might be staying to...' Jervis faltered.

'I am a soldier—not an executioner! I will follow my regiment, and see how goes the battle.'

He spoke sharply to the sentry, who stood stiffly to attention, his eyes fixed on Jervis, his lips moving slightly as if repeating his officer's orders.

The officer paused in the doorway. 'Good-bye, *Herr Leutnant*, be brave!' With those words, he stamped away down the passage, his boots echoing mockingly back into the room.

Jervis looked at the sentry, who stood stiffly by the open door, his Schmeisser automatic pistol cradled across his forearm, its barrel moving slightly in time with the soldier's breathing.

He was little more than a boy, tall and gawky. His ungainly limbs were distorted by the huge boots and the heavy steel helmet which seemed to make his narrow face even more insignificant.

Younger than I am, he thought, and just hoping that I'll make a run for it. Almost without thinking, he stepped halfway towards the door. The Schmeisser rose a couple of inches, until it was level with Jervis's chest. The soldier's thin mouth split into a wide grin, and bared teeth giving him a slightly crazy look. 'Bang!' he said, and laughed delightedly at his joke.

Jervis turned his back, and forced himself to lie down on the bed. By twisting his head to the wall he was able to blot out the sentry, who still chuckled in the open doorway, and as he concentrated his aching eyes on the rows of uneven bricks, he thought again of the way in which he had already been forgotten. He rubbed the palms of his hands angrily across his eyes until the pain forced back the tears which threatened to lay bare his misery and fear to the watching soldier. God, why this way? Why didn't I fight it out in the hut? His tortured thoughts ran on in their haphazard groping for an answer, but only bricks were there to mock him.

The house seemed very silent, and he decided that it must be nearly dark outside. He darted a glance at the door. The gun was still rigid and unwavering. Perhaps he'll be one of the firing squad. Or maybe they don't do it that way. Wait until I fall asleep, and then . . . a trickle of sweat ran coldly across his cheek, as he remembered the sentry's gun.

By an almost physical effort, he thought of his father, and the sun slanting across his mother's grey hair as she pruned the roses. His father had always seemed to be rather a forbidding man, but as Jervis closed his eyes to try to picture him more clearly, he could only see the kindness in the old man's face.

But of course, he thought dully, they think I'm dead already. The submarine will have been reported missing and I shall be merely remembered, as I am remembering them. The cold finality of it seemed to sober him, and he lay wide eyed, staring at the flaking ceiling. His breathing became calmer, and his limbs started to relax.

It's funny how death doesn't seem half so terrible, once you know it's inevitable, he thought, and I must make sure that I don't let myself down when the moment comes. The corners of his mouth drooped, and for an instant the sickness began to mount again inside him, so he turned his thoughts back again, it was useless anyway to look forward.

He stiffened, as the sounds of voices drifted down the passage. One, a woman's voice, called out sharply in Italian, and the other was swallowed up by the banging of a door.

The sentry drew his feet together, as the first voice drew nearer. It changed suddenly into fluent German, and the soldier nodded violently, his helmet jerking forward over his admiring eyes. Jervis stared at her coldly, a feeling of resentment and anger changing the girl who now stood inside the room, from a creature of beauty to another part of a scheme to mock and degrade him.

She stood quite still, looking down at him, her bare brown arms silky beneath the naked light bulb. She was wearing a plain, dark green dress with a leather belt, the tightness of which helped to accentuate the rich curves of her body.

Her dark eyes were almost black with the contempt and hatred which she directed at Jervis, and her wide mouth trembled as she spoke softly over her shoulder in German. The sentry, who was peering round the edge of the door, tittered, and settled down comfortably to watch, as the girl moved slowly across the room, stooping slightly, as if to make quite sure she took in every detail of Jervis's face.

He sat up slowly, and was about to rise to his feet, when the Schmeisser motioned him to remain seated.

So that she can mock me to her heart's content, he thought bitterly. He stared fixedly at her slim, bare legs, and was half tempted to throw himself at her. Only a few feet separated them. He tingled at the idea. It would be one last gesture.

He went suddenly rigid. The girl continued pacing the floor, but her sneering voice had changed to English. He looked up, startled, and her eyes flashed with anxiety and sudden urgency.

'Keep your head down! There is little time, so do as I say, and I might be able to help you!'

For a moment his eyes held hers. She was no longer sneering, her mouth was trembling with desperation, and he lowered his head, so that neither she nor the sentry should see the faint hope in his eyes.

She breathed deeply, and carried on with her pacing. As she spoke, the sentry tittered happily, quite convinced that she was continuing her attack in English.

'Listen to me, I will help you to escape, if you will tell me where your friends are!'

Jervis's hope changed into a sudden cold wariness, and he sat forward on the edge of the bed, his eyes following her feet, but his mind again on guard.

'I know you lied to the colonel. I saw one of your friends on the beach this morning. Tell me where I can find them, and I will fetch them to you.'

Jervis shook his head. 'I am alone. I don't know what you are talking about.'

She darted her hand beneath his chin and jerked up his head so that her eyes held his in a silent plea. 'Please! I tell the truth, I saw one of them today!'

The shock of her smooth skin against his neck made him search her face with new interest. 'Describe the man you saw.'

She stamped her foot, but there was frustration not anger in her eyes. 'There is no time!' She saw his obstinate mouth, and she darted a quick glance at the door. 'He was tall and fair. He had two stripes on his shoulder, and and he was carrying a pistol! Now do you believe me?'

Jervis struggled with his emotions. It could be a trap to draw the others into the net. That must have been Curtis she saw. A little breath of warmth moved within him, but he forced himself to consider the girl's words. 'Why didn't you tell the colonel about this?'

'I cannot tell you that. You must trust me. Please!'

She stood over him, her hands clenched and her body trembling with emotion.

'It could be a trap.' Jervis watched her eyes, and saw the

despair which followed his words. He knew that he was going to tell her, and he knew, too, that by so doing, he was risking more than just his own life, and the few hours left until dawn.

'The hill at the end of the beach. By the fishing boats. They might be there. I don't know.' As the short sentences jerked from him, he instantly regretted his outburst, and looked up at her with sudden fear.

But for a moment her wide eyes softened, and she nodded quickly. 'I will go, before someone suspects. I am going to hit you now, I am sorry!' With that, she struck Jervis a ringing blow on the cheek, and as he reeled back across the bed, she stepped quickly from the room.

He sat up, gingerly feeling his face. The blow had somehow cleared away his doubts about her, and he felt a tremor of excitement run through his body, which even the jeering laugh of the sentry did nothing to dispel.

He met the sentry's stare calmly. You wait, my lad. If the skipper comes you'll laugh the other side of your face.

He lay back on the bed and closed his eyes. The girl had been a link, no matter how frail, with the outside. And from the outside, help would come, he was sure of that. He had to be. It was all he had left.

Chapter 6

CURTIS SETTLED HIS elbows more comfortably in the grass, and craned his head as high as he dared to watch the first of the lorries as it trundled awkwardly down the track and on to the beach. As the front wheels tested the strength of the sand, the driver revved his engine impatiently, the blue diesel fumes hanging listlessly on the still air. The villagers followed the lorry in an anxious, silent crowd, occasionally pointing either at the beach or the lorry, but mostly watching the uniformed figures who waved at the driver, or shouted urgently whenever the wheels threatened to leave the narrow track.

Curtis had been on watch when he had heard the lorries halt at the top of the village, and after waking his exhausted companions, had fretted impatiently, and constantly changed his position to try to see what was happening. He had seen some of the returning fishermen run with their women up the track, ignoring their nets and showing an indifference to their boats which was completely alien to their kind anywhere.

'Somethin's up, Ralph.' Duncan had come completely awake, his eyes narrowed against the sun. 'Reckon it's a search party?'

They had felt for their scanty weapons, and Curtis had placed Taylor at the rear approach to the hill to watch for any new activity, but after what seemed like an eternity, a few uniformed Italians had sauntered down to the beach accompanied by the captain of the schooner. And now, the first of the lorries had started to move towards the sea.

'They're goin' to load some gear on to the ship,' said Duncan. 'Looks like they might be sailin' soon, eh?' He smiled slowly, the leathery skin about his eyes bunching into broad crowsfeet. 'We still goin' through with our plan, Ralph?'

Curtis studied the lorry, noting the travel stains across its broad bonnet.

'We'll take her whatever happens. Unless they're embarking a regiment of troops!' He smiled slightly, but inwardly he was already considering that such a possibility would smash his flimsy plans to nothing.

'Another truck on the way,' announced Duncan suddenly. 'An' there's some behind that!'

The dust rose in a thick cloud as the four lorries manoeuvred into a ragged line on the edge of the soft sand and halted. The fishermen were listening to a tall officer in a dove grey uniform, who was waving a stick vaguely towards the boats and then at the schooner. The fishermen walked back to their boats and stood in a silent group, while the officer held up his stick like a sword and pointed at the lorries. He was smiling, his teeth gleaming whitely beneath a neat black moustache. He was apparently shouting some sort of a joke to the onlookers, but until the soldiers laughed, none of the villagers moved or spoke, and the tension could be felt by the three sun-baked figures at the top of the hill.

The tail-boards of the lorries fell with a series of dull thuds, and some of the soldiers climbed up inside the tall vehicles.

Curtis swore and squinted fixedly at the scene, wishing that they would finish their job, whatever it was, and leave the beach empty once more.

'Bloody Eye-ties!' Duncan rolled his tongue across his lips. 'Always make such a shindy over everything, I shouldn't be surprised if——' He stopped, and Curtis felt his fingers dig into his arm.

Neither spoke as the first khaki figure half fell, half staggered down on to the sand. He stood swaying dazedly from side to side, feebly trying to support himself on a piece of boxwood. One of his feet was encased in a great wad of bandage, and he tried to hold it clear of the ground by leaning on the little piece of wood. His bent swaying shape threw a queer twisted shadow across the white sand, like a caricature of a man.

Another soldier climbed down and cannoned into him, and for a moment they swayed together, in a frantic embrace. This man was whole, but for the bandage across his eyes and most of his face. His hands gripped the other man and held on desperately, as the cripple fought to hold his balance and at the same time pacify his blinded comrade.

One of the drivers laughed and kicked away the wooden prop, and both of the tattered figures rolled over in the dust. Curtis drove his fingers into the grass until they were buried in the coarse dirt, the heat of his rage and anguish almost blinding him, as one by one the ragged, khaki scarecrows fell, or were dragged from the four lorries.

Duncan was crouched by a bush, his thick arms rigid, like a runner waiting for the gun, and his jaw moving silently as he cursed and swore under his breath in a savage chant.

There were altogether about thirty wounded men on the beach. Some sat dejectedly in the sand, their heads hanging practically to their knees, while others clung together for support, their bandages stained either with dirt, or by the bright red patches which marked the pattern of their combined suffering.

Some just laid where they had fallen, crumpled shabby forms, which had once been British soldiers.

A driver shouted hoarsely, and some of his comrades climbed back into one of the lorries and dragged two more figures down over the tail-board.

The officer shouted angrily and waved his stick, but the driver merely shrugged and prodded one of the bodies with his foot.

A figure suddenly detached itself from the khaki huddle and limped stiffly towards the officer. He carried one arm in a sling and only one eye was visible from beneath the massive dressing about his head. No one moved to intercept him, as with his good arm swinging in almost military precision, he marched up to the Italian officer, who stood swinging his stick idly against his polished boot, as if he had been hoping for and expecting just such an encounter.

The soldier halted, his head twisted on one side so that he could see the other man. A set of sergeant's stripes hung loosely from his sleeve, and as Curtis watched with sick horror, he could see the glint of campaign ribbons on the soldier's chest.

The sergeant pointed stiffly at his companions and then at his own injuries. His mouth opened and closed slowly, as if he was trying to explain his requirements in that peculiar pidgin English which British troops use when confronted with a foreigner.

The officer yawned elaborately, and in obedience, some of his men laughed. The sergeant's red face seemed to get redder, but he brushed the sweat away from his face and continued to speak and gesticulate. The officer was evidently getting bored, for he called to the men by the boats and turned on his heel.

The sergeant dragged himself painfully after him, anxiety giving him sudden energy.

'Christ! The poor devils are dyin'!' Duncan's voice shook as the words were dragged from him. 'That stinkin' bastard's makin' the guy crawl!' He half rose to his feet, one hand groping for his pistol.

Curtis dragged him down beside him, his face set in a bitter mask. 'Get down, Steve! We can't do anything for them yet!'

'Yet? You mean we're goin' down to have a crack at those yellow apes?'

Curtis nodded, his throat clogged, as the wounded men began to stagger to their feet. 'We'll help them, if it's the last thing we do!' He slammed his hands together. 'Look at them! God, why doesn't someone give them a hand?'

The officer walked away towards the sea, and one of his men pushed the sergeant towards the boats.

Duncan ran his fingers through his hair and pulled at his jacket, as if he could no longer breathe. 'All those blokes bein' packed into that one crummy ship? How long'll they be aboard for Chrissakes? They need medical attention, and quick!'

Curtis narrowed his eyes, as he looked towards the still forms which lay by the lorries. 'Not them,' he said softly. 'They're out of it.'

One of the watching women was crying into her apron, and Duncan looked down at her, his face hard.

'Yes, cry, you bitch! When the Eighth Army comes through here, you'll remember all this!'

The boats pushed off from the beach, but as one of them

bumped against a sandbank, weighted down with its heavy load, one of the khaki shapes half rose from his seat, and the silence was split by a terrible cry of pain.

In the bows of another boat a stocky figure scrambled precariously on to the gunwale, his head bandages gold in the sun. Curtis groaned aloud; it was the sergeant again. His groan faded into a sob as the sergeant's cracked voice floated across the painted water.

'Bless 'em all, bless 'em all! The long an' the short an' the tall!'

The schooner's captain waded after the nearest boat and climbed clumsily over the stern, while behind him, alone on the beach, the officer danced up and down with rage, screaming and waving his stick at the sergeant, *'Silenzio! Silenzio!'*

An old fisherman standing by his cottage door saluted with sudden gravity, and a woman pulled her child closer to her skirt.

Curtis watched the boats bump alongside the schooner, their shapes blurred and indistinct.

'We'll board her tonight,' he said quietly. 'Whatever happens now, we have to take that ship!'

Duncan stared down at the officer, his face tired and heavy. 'I hope he's around, when we go!'

They looked at each other, both aware of the new implication and the coldness which had enclosed them like a shroud.

They waited until the bodies had been removed from the beach, and the lorries had departed, and then settled down to wait for the darkness. The waiting had been made easier by the hatred which waited upon each of them with persistent greed.

The grass around the hilltop rustled uneasily as the cold breeze from the north tested its strength momentarily on the side of the slope, before passing on with mounting strength to fan out across the bay and bring the dark water alive with dancing whitecaps. Occasionally the moon showed itself in a feeble silver crescent, and tinged the edges of the black racing clouds with its fading brilliance, so that they looked angry and solid as they scudded purposefully across the late evening sky. As the moon darted an occasional ray upon the shoreline, the distorted shapes of the cottages shone like large lumps of sugar, before fading away into the blackness of the surrounding hills, and the sand spit seemed to rise from the sea in an effort to hold the passing light, before it, too, joined the shadows and the unsettled noises left by the wind.

Curtis stood up and stamped his boots in the dust, while he

attempted to study the luminous dial of his watch.

Taylor stood at his side, his face an indistinct blob against the sky. He was buttoning his jacket, and carefully going through his pockets.

'We makin' a move soon, Skipper? There don't seem to be anybody about.'

'Yes, soon.'

Curtis stared towards where the schooner lay, but against the constant movement of the water and the rearing and falling of the short, white-crested waves, he could no longer see the vessel's hull. The nagging doubts persisted, and he had only half heard Taylor's question.

Suppose the ship pulled out without warning, and without waiting for the German officer to rejoin her? Until the last of the daylight had passed with the sun behind the headland, he had watched the movements in the village, and had waited coldly for the ship to show some sign of departing. Fresh water had been rowed out to the schooner's side, the operation being carried out in several laborious trips by the fishermen in their boats, but still nothing happened. Like the others, Curtis had expected that a doctor would arrive to attend to the wounded, but the village had gradually quietened, and the ship had become more and more indistinct in the gathering darkness. Perhaps they had a medical officer on board, he thought, and dismissed the idea as unlikely, the gnawing anxiety he felt for the wounded soldiers only adding to the uncertainty of his next move.

A stick cracked, and both men went stiff. They heard Duncan curse briefly from the ground below them, and Curtis moved to meet him.

'See anything?' His voice was low, but the urgency was clear in his question.

Duncan shook his head, and held up the water bottle. 'Just filled this in the stream, an' came straight back up. All quiet in the village though. 'Cept for a couple of Eye-ties on motor bikes.' He jerked his thumb towards the main road. 'Police, I guess.'

Curtis pulled his belt tighter, and adjusted his holster with sudden care. 'Might as well get started then.'

'Yep.' Duncan handed over the bottle, its crude neck cold and wet. 'Pity about Ian,' he said slowly. 'But there's more to think about now.'

Curtis drank without feeling. 'Yes.'

Taylor shifted his feet and took the bottle with sudden eagerness. He drank deeply and wiped his mouth with his sleeve. 'Well, shall we go? I'm fair gettin' the wind up, standing about up 'ere!'

Curtis peered at their dark shapes, and wished that he could see their faces. 'Well, here goes.' His stomach contracted and he swallowed hard. 'We'll go down now and get one of the boats away. I'll just go over the drill again.' He looked at Taylor. 'You go straight to the poop, by the mainmast. I think the engine-room hatch is about there, so you'll be ready to get things started if we carry things the way we want them. Here,' he handed the pistol to him, 'take this. If anyone tries to enter or leave the engine-room, show him this.'

'S'pose he won't stop, what then?'

'Kill him!' Curtis was surprised by the chill in his own voice.

'I reckon there'll be about ten to a dozen in the crew, an' there are about three soldiers or coppers on board that we know of as well.' Duncan's hand rasped across his chin. 'We might be able to enlist a bit of support from the Tommies, too, eh?'

'Maybe.' Curtis hurried on. Now that he had shown his hand, he wanted desperately to get started. 'You, Steve, will stay with me. We'll make for the after hatch, the one behind the wheel, as I think the captain'll be in there. Once we've got him safe, well, we'll see.' He paused. 'Any ideas?'

'They only seem to have a short cable down, Ralph. We can slip the anchor completely, and get clear without any fuss at all, provided there's no bloody noise!' Duncan flexed his shoulders. 'If we can get out of this blessed place, we can be sixty miles clear by dawn!'

Curtis frowned. So many ifs, but there was no other way.

''Ere, wot a lark if we made it O.K.!' Taylor chuckled with something like his old humour. 'Won't the blokes be surprised, eh?'

Curtis gripped his arm tightly. 'We'll have a go, George. We'll feel more at home out there anyway.'

Curtis looked up warily, as Duncan's hand rose like a white glove.

'Don't move, blokes!' His voice was almost conversational. 'But I think we've got company!'

They all stood transfixed in attitudes of surprised watchfulness, each man straining his ears and eyes without moving his head.

Curtis was conscious again of his heart pounding with mounting persistence. 'Jervis? D'you think it's Jervis?' His voice was a mere hiss of breath.

Duncan's head turned slightly, and as the moon peeped over a cloud, his bared teeth gleamed like those of a cornered animal. 'No, it's not him,' he said slowly. Curtis saw him move his hand, and heard the metallic click of a safety catch. 'Stay 'ere!' Duncan sounded preoccupied and strange. 'I'm a bit more used to this sort of caper. I'll head the bastard off, whoever it is. Got yer knife, Ralph?'

Curtis nodded and slipped it from inside his blouse. It was still warm from contact with his own body, and he suddenly regretted giving his gun to Taylor.

'Now keep still. Give me time to get clear. P'raps he won't come up here, an' we won't have to do anythin'. But if he *does*...' He left the rest unsaid, and as the others watched, his huge bulk seemed to melt into the bushes with hardly a sound.

Curtis leaned forward, his mouth half open, his eyes wide with concentrated effort. Then he heard it for the first time. The uneven swish of grass, and the soft crunch of sand, as cautious footsteps groped their way along the side of the hill.

He heard, too, the rasp of Taylor's breath, and the soft moan of the wind across the top of the bushes.

With the wind in his ears, Curtis repeatedly lost the direction of the footsteps, but with each lull he heard the sounds getting steadily louder and nearer, and he gripped the knife with sudden determination. Nothing must interfere with the plan now. Nothing and nobody.

If only he knew where Duncan had gone. He held his breath, realizing that the sounds had stopped.

Curtis raised his foot with elaborate care and stepped nearer to the bushes. His sleeve brushed against Taylor's taut body, and he moved his mouth against the man's cold ear.

'Right below us,' he whispered. 'Think I can hear his feet on those stones!'

'Let's get 'im fer Gawd's sake!' Taylor's voice shook with suppressed despair. 'I can't stand much more!'

Curtis nodded briefly and held the knife before him like a rapier. He tucked his chin into his chest and waited, eyes on the edge of the slope.

It was even darker and, but for the distant whitecaps, there was no division between land and sky, sand or sea.

Curtis took half a step forward as another twig cracked, and the footsteps started again.

From the corner of his eye he saw a slight hardening to the outline of the ledge and as he turned, the pale oval of a face rose cautiously over the long grass.

His feet moved with sudden fury and he flung himself down the slope, the knife lifting above his head, as with a sob he reached out for the wavering shape, which had halted, trapped on the loose edge of the final slope.

With a thud their bodies met, but even as they crashed down on to the ground, Curtis's fingers had found the throat, and savagely he forced backwards into the grass, the knife held poised and ready.

Taylor slithered down beside him with a grunt. 'Got 'im! Well done, Skipper!' he panted.

A cloud parted, and as their spreadeagled forms were bathed in the unearthly light, Curtis trembled, and allowed the choking throat beneath his fingers to relax.

Two terrified eyes stared up at him like black pools, and he felt the long hair across the back of his hand as the girl moved her head and retched weakly.

One bare leg was pinned beneath him, and the other was crooked against his chest in a pitiful defence, while from her parted lips her sobbing breath jerked in quick, painful gasps.

Duncan rose from the ground like a shadow, the moonlight giving his touseled hair a wild halo. 'All clear below!' he jerked. 'Nobody else followin'.' He motioned to the knife which still hovered uncertainly in the air. 'O.K., Ralph, finish him off!' He dropped to his knees and gasped with amazement. 'Jesus! A dame! That's all we needed!' He continued to stare as Curtis sat back on his haunches and slipped the knife into his belt. 'What the hell's she doin' up here, eh?' He rubbed his arm angrily. 'Better finish her off anyway. Can't risk an alarm now!'

Before the moon disappeared, Curtis saw the girl's hand move gingerly to her throat, and for a moment there was a strained silence as she coughed and tried to speak.

'It's the girl I saw this morning on the horse,' Curtis said, and he reached out to touch the thick braid of hair. 'I didn't expect to see *her* again!'

'Please! Please listen to me!' Her voice was husky and

strained, and the three men watched her with mixed emotions, caught off guard by the sound of their own tongue. It was a soft voice, yet full of strength and without fear.

'I was looking for you. I knew that you were here on the hill.' She broke off and coughed painfully for a few moments. 'I thought you were going to kill me,' she continued, the words directed at Curtis's dim shape, 'the . . . the knife was ver' close!'

Curtis drew his hand away from her hair and stood up abruptly. 'How did you know where to find us?' His voice was flat and impersonal, as if he had not heard the tremor in her tone.

'Your friend, the young officer. He told me!'

There was another short silence. The wind moved amongst the leaves, and Duncan knelt closer to the girl, as if unsure of his hearing. It was Curtis who acted first, and with such speed that the others jumped back in surprise.

He reached down and seized her wrist, dragging her to her feet, until her face was almost against his, her teeth bared with pain.

'What did you say? *Who* told you?' His blood was pounding madly in his brain, and he was unconscious of her cry of protest, as he twisted her wrist savagely. 'Now be careful what you say, for if you're lying, I'll kill you with less feeling than stamping on a beetle!' His voice was dangerously calm, but the force of his words made her twisting body go suddenly limp and still.

'It is true! He told me! You must see that I speak the truth. He is a prisoner at my father's house. He was caught by the soldiers this afternoon.'

Curtis felt her body tremble, but he held his grip, and nodded curtly. 'Well, go on! What else?'

She dropped her face, and seemed all at once to shrink before him. 'They will shoot him at daybreak'—she cried out sharply as he twisted her arm further—'unless, unless we do something to rescue him!'

'*We?* What's this then? Have you changed sides all of a sudden?'

'Steady on, Ralph!' Duncan was on his feet, his words casual. 'She may be trying to help. She didn't have to come here, did she?'

'It's a trap.' Curtis stared down at her bowed head, as if to penetrate her defences and find the truth. 'They've made Ian talk, and have sent her out as the bait!'

'It is not so! I want to help him, and you!'

'Let's hear her story, Ralph.' The voice was more insistent. 'Can't do any harm.'

Curtis released her wrist with a jerk and she shrank away from him, rubbing the bare skin with her hand.

'All right. Talk. And make it quick!' Curtis turned his back and stared out to sea, breathing quickly.

She turned to the others, her hands outspread. 'We can go to the house,' she began eagerly, 'he is in a small storeroom at the side of the kitchen, you could——' She halted as Duncan waved his hand to interrupt. He still held the pistol, and the steel gleamed dully as it passed over her head.

'Hold on, sister. One thing at a time. Who are you anyway?'

'I am Carla Zecchi; my father is the mayor here and of the neighboring villages.' There was a touch of pride in her voice.

'Big stuff, eh, George?' Duncan spoke thoughtfully, his eyes resting on her slim figure. 'Where does your father come in to all this?'

She shrugged. 'Your armies have invaded my country, and the Germans are already worried about our government. They think we might not wish to remain their ally when it is inevitable that the country will be destroyed by continuing the fight. My father does not know I am here. No one does, except for your friend.' Her shoulders lifted slightly. '*He* trusted me!'

'He didn't have much choice maybe?' Duncan rubbed his chin, then irritably thrust the gun into his holster. 'How is he? Is he all right?'

'He is well. But time is short, we must act now!'

Curtis spoke sharply over his shoulder. 'Ask her why she is doing this!'

'Well? Wnat's the answer to that?' asked Duncan.

'My father will be one of the first to be arrested if the Badoglio government tries to parley with your army commanders. He has supported the régime right from the start, and the Germans would try to make an example of him.' She shuddered. 'That must not happen. If I can help you now, perhaps you will be able to help my father to escape with you!'

'How exactly?'

'I know a house to the south of here, where you could hide, and when your army reaches that place, you can tell them how my father helped you to escape. They would not be ungrateful.'

She stopped, breathing jerkily, her hand rubbing at her throat.

'Does he know about all this?' Duncan looked quickly towards Curtis, but his figure was unmoved.

'No! He would never agree. He is a patriot. He does not think our government will ask for an armistice. He is loyal only to them.' She tossed her head angrily. 'He is mistaken. I know it!'

'You could be right there!' He turned again to Curtis. 'Well, Ralph, what d'you think?'

Curtis jerked his head. 'Keep an eye on her, George, Steve and I will have a little yarn about this.'

She watched them quietly, her legs gleaming in the pale moonlight. 'I thought the British were kinder to their prisoners than this.' She said it with neither bitterness nor anger, and Taylor raised his hand anxiously.

'Quiet! D'you want to upset the skipper again!'

'So he is the captain? He is a hard and cruel man, I think!'

Taylor eyed her furiously. 'We seen some of your bloody Wop soljers behavin' like gents this afternoon, I don't bloody well think! You jus' keep nice an' quiet, an' maybe things'll work out as you say. O.K.?'

Curtis and Duncan stood side by side on the far edge of the hill.

'I think she's telling the truth anyway, Ralph. In fact, I'd stake my life on it!'

'You may have to!' Curtis shook his head impatiently. 'I believe her story up to a point. But there's a lot she's not told us yet. Still, the idea's all right. It's given me a new lease on life!'

'You mean we're goin' to this flamin' house and hide out till the pongoes arrive?' Duncan was incredulous. 'What about the ship? And the poor bloody soldiers aboard?'

'Shut up! Keep your voice down!' Curtis glared at him through the darkness. 'Of course my plan still goes. But there's no need to tell her about it. We'll make for her father's house now. I've already had a good look at it, I believe, and get Ian away. If that works, we'll get on to phase two, that suit you?'

Duncan gripped his arm. 'Sure, Ralph, you certainly are a crafty cove! You were a bit tough on her though. I thought you were goin' to bite her head off!'

'I've no time for any of them.' Curtis stared across at the two dark figures. 'But come on, we've got to pump her some more yet!'

The girl watched him apprehensively. 'You decide?'

'How many troops at the house?' Curtis ignored her angry intake of breath. 'Is that armoured car still there?' He watched her reaction to his words with cold satisfaction.

'German soldiers nearly all gone. Six are left in the house as guards, but most troops had gone by this afternoon. They have gone to the fighting in the south,' she added.

'I see. Nobody else then?'

'There are the local Carabinieri, but they are stationed at the other side of the village. Their officer is at the house, too, and of course Heinz...' she faltered, 'I mean that *Leutnant* Beck is there also.'

'Heinz is it?' Curtis laughed softly. 'That's the German officer from the schooner, I take it?'

'Yes.' The answer was guarded.

'How long will he be there? He might upset things if we arrive unexpectedly.'

She shook her head. 'No, that is impossible. He is leaving on the ship at midnight. He is sailing with the wounded soldiers.'

'Midnight, eh?' Curtis answered casually, but he knew that Duncan had followed his train of thought.

'Right, you lead on, *signorina*, we'll get into position by the house now and spy out the land.'

Duncan was looking at his watch. 'Nearly nine o'clock. Things are gettin' interestin'! By the by, Ralph, how do we aim to spring Ian from this place?'

They all looked at the girl.

'He has one guard. You will be able to silence him, yes? The other soldiers are in a small lodge on the other side of the estate. It will be safe.'

'And the policeman? That *gentleman* we saw on the beach today?' Curtis eyed her bleakly.

'He will be going to the schooner. Some of his men are already aboard.'

'Well, well.' Duncan rubbed his hands together, and Curtis looked at him warningly, but the Australian merely smiled and continued to rasp his hands together.

'Let's go,' snapped Curtis suddenly, and with the girl's slim shadow ahead of them, they scrambled in single file down to the deserted beach.

Curtis glanced sideways as Duncan tapped him on the shoulder. 'Good about Ian, eh, Ralph? I know how you felt about leavin' without bein' sure!'

He nodded. 'I only hope he *is* still safe!'

They hurried on in silence, occasionally stumbling across a hillock or mound of sand, or halting to listen for any sounds from the village.

The sea seemed angrier now, and the water sloshed and gurgled into little runnels across the beach, whilst in the bay the waves crowded together in a disturbed fury of noise.

Curtis watched the girl narrowly as she twisted and turned along the edge of the beach, towards the steep hill at the end of the cove.

He felt no fatigue or weariness of any kind, all the anguish and pain of the last days dropping away like a cloak, and walked like a man possessed of some cold, terrible force which drove him forward, calm, and dedicated to the task in hand. It was like the old days, he thought, no time for regrets or hopes. Just the uncertain objective ahead.

They climbed the long, curving track, the girl's feet beginning to lag and falter with the effort of the pace. Once she stopped and looked back at him. 'Can we rest for a moment?'

He gestured sharply. 'Keep going! You said yourself that there's little time!'

Taylor sighed with astonishment when they reached the first of the fountains in the dark garden.

'Cor! Like 'Ampton Court!' His voice was normal, and Curtis was again grateful for the supreme standard of toughness required in the submarine service.

The house was totally dark, the blacked-out windows shining in the moonlight like great blind eyes.

They lay in a line behind a flower bed, the girl between Curtis and Taylor. Her breath was painful, and she seemed near to collapse. Curtis tapped her on the arm, suddenly conscious of her smooth skin, cool beneath his fingers.

'Which way do we go in?'

She raised herself with an effort and pointed. 'That is the side where the kitchen is. The room where your friend is lies next to that archway.'

'Right, this is what I want done.' Their heads crowded together expectantly. 'Steve, get round to the rear of the house, that'll put you between it and the lodge where the guards are. Take one grenade with you, in case we're rushed!' He turned to the girl. 'George and I'll come in with you at the front. Can the sentry see us from his position?'

'No. But we are too soon yet! The other two are still there!' Her eyes flashed with alarm.

'Maybe they'll be with your father, eh?' He smiled calmly. 'O.K., Steve, you get going!' Duncan slid away over the flower bed and vanished.

She gripped his sleeve with sudden alarm. 'What are you doing? You said you would wait until they had gone to the ship!'

'*You* said that!'

She shook his arm, her voice frightened and angry. 'But, but it will be dangerous! They are too many for you!'

Curtis handed the remaining grenade to Taylor, and took the pistol in exchange. 'Come on!'

She still clung to him, pulling him down. 'You cannot do this, he will fight you! It will be a disaster!'

He dragged her to her feet. 'Who? Heinz? If he's sensible, he'll do as he's told! As *you* tell him!' He let the words sink in.

'You swine! You... You...!' She stood trembling with frustration and fury, but Curtis waved the pistol towards the house.

'Remember what I said earlier, and there's your father to think of now!'

The gravel sounded terribly loud as they crossed the drive and passed along the side of the house.

They reached a long french window, and Curtis pulled the girl to his side. 'What's this?' he whispered.

'The library.' She sounded lifeless and beaten.

From behind the drawn curtains they could hear the sound of voices and the soft purr of an Italian orchestra.

'Good, listening to the radio. Your father?'

She again nodded.

'Who's the other one? The German?'

'Yes.' It was only a whisper.

They moved on to the deep porch, and Curtis saw her hand rest hesitatingly on the door handle. He turned to Taylor. 'Keep close, and watch out for the other chap!'

Taylor showed his teeth. 'Right!'

The air which fanned their faces as the door opened was warm and scented with flowers, and Curtis glanced quickly from the dim hall-light to the long passage which curved away from the far end. All was quiet, and very still.

She crossed the dark floor to a pair of wide doors, her small feet making no sound. She paused and looked at Curtis's face imploringly. 'Please?'

But Curtis looked past her and moved the gun sharply. His heart seemed to have stopped, and he could feel Taylor's body crowding behind him in the doorway.

Taylor's unshaven face was drawn and wary, his grubby hand clutching the grenade in front of him like some kind of offering.

'Open!' Curtis hissed the words between his teeth.

The doors opened wide to reveal the soft lighted room, with its deep chairs and rows of leather-bound books, but Curtis had eyes only for the plump, unsmiling man who lay back in his chair, his fingers pressed together, his brow creased in a frown of concentration. He saw, too, the gleaming white uniform of the officer he had seen on the beach. In that split second he saw it all, and when they turned to look at the girl, Curtis thrust her to one side, the gun steady in his fist.

'Tell them to stay where they are, and keep still!' The words were harsh and without feeling, the impact of his voice and his sudden appearance making the two men freeze into positions of shocked dismay.

'My father understands.' She spoke hoarsely, and then continued in German. The young officer half rose from his chair, his expression slowly changing to one of fury.

Curtis smiled unpleasantly. 'Tell him to be sensible. I'd hate to dirty that uniform!'

The mayor gripped the arms of his chair and levered himself forward, his face pale but surprisingly calm. 'If you have harmed my daughter in any way I shall see that you suffer for it!' His dark eyes flashed defiantly, and Curtis shrugged his shoulders and pointed to the girl.

'She is well. See for yourself. Now,' his tone became sharper, 'where is the police officer?'

She ran to her father's side and dropped to her knees, while the German stared stonily at her and then back to Curtis. The mayor ran his fingers over her hair, as if to reassure himself, but said nothing.

'Tell him, Papa!' She looked up at her father, her eyes grave. 'It will be for the best!' She said something in German, her voice soft and pleading, but the lieutenant still stared in front of him with dulled eyes.

'He is in the room upstairs, *signore*. The one at the top of the stairway.'

Curtis hesitated. It had been easy so far, and he knew the danger of resting on his laurels. His eyes darted around the room, but he could see no further weapons.

'All right, George,' he said mildly, 'christen the Jerry.'

Taylor frowned uneasily, and then his dirty face split into a grin. 'I gotcha, Skipper!' And he walked briskly across the room towards the bookcase. As he passed behind the German's chair, he suddenly raised the grenade and brought it down viciously on the man's skull. The girl choked back a cry, and sat with her hands wrapped across her open mouth, her eyes on Curtis's face.

Taylor watched the man slump to the floor, and wiped the grenade on his sleeve.

'Well done, George!' To the two pairs of eyes across the room he said, 'He will be safer there. He might have been tempted.'

He beckoned the girl. 'We'll pay a visit upstairs.'

She kept away from him as they mounted the soft stair carpet. Curtis, his eyes watchful, halted in front of the bedroom door. He looked at her with tired gravity, suddenly realizing that he hadn't really seen her before in the light.

She was very beautiful, and with her eyes black with anger and fear she possessed the perfection of a wild animal. He shut his mind, and thought of Jervis. It was impossible to believe that he was somewhere on the floor below.

His finger gripped the door handle. 'Wait here. Don't move.' He opened the door slightly and peered through the brightly lit crack into the soft-scented bedroom.

The Italian officer sat pensively on the edge of the bed, slowly pulling on his boots. His jacket hung open, and on his shining mane of greased hair he was wearing a hair-net. He whistled softly, and stood up to look at himself in the mirror.

Curtis remembered the limping, battered British sergeant on the beach, and felt the pity drain out of him.

He stepped across the carpet and rammed the gun into his spine. Their eyes met in the dressing table mirror. The blue ones hard and uncompromising; the others popping out with sheer terror.

They left the room together, the Italian not even noticing the girl, and walking with exaggerated eagerness to show he was willing to co-operate.

Once inside the library again, Curtis tossed the Italian's small automatic to Taylor. 'They're all yours, George!' He grinned, but the sweat was pouring down his spine in a steady stream, while his stomach felt as if it was full of lead. 'So far, so good. Now for Ian!'

He walked to the door, but the girl held up her hand. 'I will go first, as I said I would.'

'I thought you had perhaps changed your mind?'

'We do not all break our promises, *Capitano*!' She spat the words at him.

They stood in the silence of the hall, she slim and defiant, and Curtis beginning to feel the first reaction of exhaustion.

He cursed inwardly. No time for that now. This is going to be the worst bit of all.

She brushed past him and walked confidently into the passage. Curtis waited a few seconds, then looked slowly around the curve of the wall.

Immediately, he saw the sentry. A young boy in German uniform, his small eyes fixed on the approaching girl. A shaft of light poured through an open door beside him, and Curtis licked his lips worriedly. It would be a close thing, he thought, and measured the distance along the passage.

She halted, and Curtis watched her hips move provocatively, as she casually leaned against the doorpost. She spoke loudly to someone inside the room, her voice filled with scorn, yet the words making Curtis raise his pistol and point wildly at the sentry.

'Hey, Englishman! Wake up! I have brought a friend, but do nothing yet! I will tell you when to do something!' She laughed, and Curtis saw the soldier's thin face split into a foolish grin.

Curtis breathed out slowly. What a chance the girl was taking, he thought, as he watched the wavering snout of the man's Schmeisser.

She turned lazily away from the room, so that she faced Curtis, her hands pressed against the wall behind her. Her breasts moved quickly beneath the soft green dress, and Curtis could well imagine the effect she was having on the sentry.

The man faltered, and for a brief instant Curtis felt almost sorry for him. The oldest trick in the world, he reflected.

Then, as the sentry's gun wavered, she reached forward and flung her arms around his neck. The next few seconds were filled with terror and hate, as Curtis jumped along the passage in a few bounds and pulled the man's steel helmet backwards from his head. The thick leather chinstrap bit into the soldier's throat, and he dropped his gun with a clatter, as he scrabbled furiously with clawing fingers to save himself.

Curtis was only half aware of what he was doing. There was so much to see and understand. Jervis's pink, wildly excited face danced to meet him, while over the soldier's writhing shoulder the girl leaned weakly against the wall, her eyes closed.

'Skipper! Oh, Skipper! You came back! You're here!' Jervis babbled incoherently.

The body gave a final gasp and slithered to the floor.

Curtis clapped his hand across the boy's shoulder. 'Good to see you, Ian,' he muttered. 'Now pick up that Schmeisser and let's get organized!'

Jervis looked at the girl, his high spirits giving way to concern. He touched her arm gently, and she opened her eyes to stare at him, her expression dazed and bewildered.

'Thanks!' Jervis faltered, unsure of himself. 'You were wonderful!'

Curtis glanced at them sharply, his mind already seething with the urgency of his scheme, and fully alive to the increasing danger. 'Get the clothes off him!' He jabbed his foot into the crumpled body at his feet.

Jervis tore his eyes from the girl and looked at the dead soldier's empurpled face with sick revulsion. 'What for, Skipper?' he asked in a low voice. 'Do we need the uniform?'

'No. But I want it to look as if you killed the guard and escaped in his clothes. We'll carry them down to the beach and bury 'em in the sand.' He jerked his head impatiently. 'Get your clothes off as well, and chuck them on the floor!'

Jervis coloured. 'But what do I wear if——'

'Just do as you're told, Ian. I'll have some other things ready for you by the time you're finished. Now for God's sake get a move on!'

He gripped the girl's elbow and guided her forcefully along the passage. He glanced back to see Jervis tearing with frantic haste at the soldier's uniform, his face averted from what he was doing.

'What are you doing? What is it that you are planning?' She twisted in his grip, her voice bitter.

'We're leaving. I told you!'

Curtis pushed into the library, to where the two Italians and Taylor sat facing each other in uneasy stances of watchfulness.

'Is 'e all right, Skipper? You found 'im?'

'He's fine, George. Now listen. Strip the uniform off the Jerry here, and take it along to Ian. Tell him to get it on immediately. It should be just his size.'

He watched as Taylor stooped over the unconscious officer, his eyes burning with sudden fatigue. 'What time was our friend due to leave for the schooner?' He directed the question to the girl without turning his head.

'About eleven. I told you they were sailing at midnight.'

'They still are.'

Curtis eyed the well-muscled body of the German stripped to his underclothes, as Taylor gathered up the white uniform and ran from the room. A tough customer, he thought. Just as well we laid him out for a bit.

The Italian police officer who, Curtis noticed, had removed his hair-net, was sitting bolt upright on the edge of his seat, his pop-eyes fixed on Curtis's pistol. 'Plis, *signore*,' his words were slurred with fear, 'what you do? I not soldier! I give no trouble!'

Curtis eyed him coldly. 'You will leave for the ship as arranged, with one of my officers, d'you understand?' The Italian nodded with pathetic eagerness. 'Right, you behave yourself, and you might be allowed to live!'

The mayor had recovered his bland composure, outwardly at least, and frowned at Curtis's last words.

'What do you hope to do? You are playing a dangerous game!'

He eyed his daughter, his face suddenly grave. 'What made you act as you did, Carla?'

She shrugged defiantly, her tanned, heart-shaped face controlled and calm. 'I thought this officer would help you to go away from here.' She spoke in careful English, the words directed as much at Curtis as her father. 'You know what will happen if our government sues for peace. You have always known it!' The mayor did not interrupt her, but his eyes were sad and he stared vacantly at his hands. 'We would have been safe then. We could have waited in peace for a while!'

'I understand,' he said quietly, 'but I do not think that this officer will permit such an arrangement.' He lifted his eyebrows questioningly, and looked up at Curtis.

'We are all going in the ship!' Curtis stared at him, coldly angry. He ignored the gasp from the girl, and the flash of hatred in her eyes. 'We will sail tonight at the time which has been arranged. I cannot leave you here, obviously, so you will have to keep us company. I must warn you again, that as I have no choice in what I am doing, you will be advised to do as I say, or I will not answer for the consequences!'

Taylor spoke from the door. 'Right! I've done that, Skipper. What next?'

'Go and fetch Steve.' He glanced at the ornate clock over the fireplace. Ten to eleven. 'Keep your eyes peeled, George!'

'I must admire the way you are dealing with a difficult situation.' The mayor smiled thinly. 'You are a man of many parts, *signore.*'

The girl murmured beneath her breath, her eyes on Curtis.

'You must not think too badly of him, Carla. He will die if he is captured. He is desperate.'

'He is a cheat, and a liar!' She swung her shoulders round, her face hidden.

Her father smiled again and spread his hands defensively. 'You will not get far, *signore*, I am afraid. The sea will be alive with our ships!'

'Whose? Yours or the Germans?'

'What matter? We are allies!'

I wonder for how long, Curtis thought. He jerked round, startled, his gun swinging towards the door.

Jervis grinned with embarrassment, and held out his hands awkwardly. The uniform fitted well. 'Steady on! I'm on your side!'

Curtis smiled. 'Go with this yound lady, and get all the first aid gear you can lay your hands on—bandages, lint, anything. Be back here in five minutes!' He addressed the girl. 'Help him, please, and bring a small bag for your own things. *One* bag,' he added.

Duncan shouldered his way into the room, the light playing across his wild, unshaven face and crumpled uniform. 'Dinkum, Ralph? Good!' He nodded to the mayor and fastened his gaze on the other Italian. 'I thought we'd meet again,' he growled.

'Later!' snapped Curtis, his eye again on the clock. 'Did you see anything?'

Duncan dropped his voice. 'Don't tell Ian this, but I found something out in the field by the guardhouse. There was a nice new post driven into the ground, complete with ropes! And nearby there was a neat little open grave!'

Curtis looked grim. 'Near thing, eh?'

Duncan stared round the room. 'Sure thing. Say, didn't young Ian look a peach in his new outfit? What's the idea? When I met him with our girl friend just now, I thought the game was up!'

The German on the floor groaned, but remained motionless, and Curtis pointed at him briskly. 'Tie him up, Steve. You'll probably have to carry him to the ship, so make a good job of it.'

Duncan shook his head in admiration. 'You're a marvel, Ralph. I just don't know what's keepin' you on your feet, let alone holdin' your brain together!' He cut the silk cord from the curtains with his knife and knelt across the German.

The clock began to chime, and Curtis peered through a gap in the curtain. All was quiet, although the moon was much brighter and turned the hedges and buildings to patterns of blue and silver.

Jervis returned carrying a sack and a large case. 'A few personal things,' he explained defensively as Curtis's eye fell on the case. 'I've got a few bandages as well.'

'Right. You, Ian, go down to the beach now, and wait at the end of the sand spit. If anyone from the village speaks to you, just wave the Schmeisser at them. They won't stop to argue.' He indicated the police officer. 'Take him with you. When you leave by the front door, make sure that you hold it ajar for a minute or two. There's a sentry on the main gate, I understand, and I want to be sure that he sees you both leave. Everything must look quite normal.' He turned to Taylor. 'You take the mayor and his daughter and go out the back way. Keep to the path we came by, but keep out of sight. Make certain there's no trouble,' he added harshly.

Taylor licked his lips. 'Ready, mate?'

The mayor stood up and took the case from Jervis. He linked his arm through the girl's and followed Taylor through the door.

Jervis clicked his heels and smiled shakily. 'Gosh, it's like a miracle, seeing you both again!'

Glass clinked from the oak sideboard as Duncan slipped two bottles inside his blouse. 'Get crackin', Ian, an' keep an eye on this joker! I want to have a word or two with him later!' He looked threateningly at the shaking Italian.

Jervis put on the German cap, tucking his rough bandage under the rim. 'Lucky he's got a big head!' he grinned, as the German groaned again and twitched violently.

He slipped the machine pistol under his arm and beckoned to the police officer. 'Come on then. We're going home!'

Curtis and Duncan watched the two figures stand momentarily under the light from inside the porch and then stride across the drive and down towards the cliff path. In a few seconds they were out of sight. The house was suddenly quiet, and Curtis looked at Duncan wearily, his face grey with concentration and effort.

'Let's follow George, eh? We can leave this place now.'

Duncan smiled cheerfully and hoisted the German across his shoulder. 'I'm glad you decided to listen to the girl, Ralph. She'll be good company!'

'We're not in the ship yet, or out at sea either!' Curtis was instantly ashamed of the snap in his voice. 'Sorry, Steve, I'm about done in.' But he knew that the girl was the real cause of his irritation.

'Not bloody well surprised! Wait till we get back to Alex. I'll get you something to put you right!'

They crossed the lawn and started down the narrow track. Curtis stopped only once, and looked back at the deserted house. There'll be quite a panic in there shortly, he thought grimly.

Chapter 7

THE WIND WAS veering rapidly to the east, and some of its force could be felt on the beach, as the short rollers plunged unevenly along its length, throwing tongues of spray and spume across the moist sand.

Curtis peered at his watch and then across the dark, pitching water to where he judged the schooner was riding.

Duncan dumped the German's body on the ground and stretched his arms with relief. Curtis could hear the German biting and choking on his gag, but did not even spare the man a glance; he concentrated instead on the sea, and Jervis's white figure which stood stark against the black backcloth like a ghost.

He was dimly aware of the other figures huddled behind him in the overhanging shadow of the hill, and of the girl's lowered voice as she spoke to her father. Taylor was standing a little apart from the rest, his head turned towards the hidden village.

He saw Jervis raise his arm, and imagined that he could see the flash of his torch as he gave the awaited signal to the ship.

'It'd be a real joke if the perishers have shoved off without waitin' for the Jerry and his mate, eh?' Duncan chuckled without humour. 'We'd look a right lot of mugs then!'

'Signor Zecchi has informed me that this is the correct time for the schooner's departure, and he has also explained the signal that is normally given.' Curtis spoke shortly. 'I don't think we need disbelieve him at this stage.'

'Thank you.' There was a trace of sarcasm in the mayor's reply. 'I am honoured that you trust me so!'

Curtis moved his shoulders in a quick nervous gesture. 'I think you know better than to play games!'

They fell into an uneasy silence once more, and Curtis wondered what Jervis was thinking as he stood on the edge of the water with the tall Italian. Now that the first wave of violence and fury had passed from him, he felt a vague prickle of resentment and disappointment which he could not begin to understand. Coupled with the feeling of emptiness, he knew that in some way he was still blaming himself for everything which had happened.

He stiffened, and cocked his head on one side. Faintly at first, and then more persistently, came the squeak of oars and the slap of a boat in the trough of the waves.

'Ready?' He was awake again, and momentarily his fears moved into second place. 'George, watch this lot. Steve, you and I'll go down to the boat as soon as it beaches.'

'I'm with you!' Duncan blew into his cupped hands. 'Quite a lively sea for movin' about, I must say!'

They saw the boat slide sluggishly over a white-capped roller and slew carelessly across the shingle. Two humped figures bent over the oars, and their faces gleamed white in the moonlight, as Curtis and Duncan ran down into the water.

Curtis laid his hands on the gunwale and spoke slowly to the police officer, his words plucked from his mouth by the wind. 'Tell them that there are extra passengers,' he said. 'You can tell them that we are members of the German Navy if you wish!'

The officer's eyes rolled from Curtis to Duncan, who was standing with casual watchfulness behind him, one hand beneath his jacket, and then in quick, excited sentences, he spoke to the oarsmen. One of them shrugged obediently, while the other merely stared indifferently at the water which sloshed across the boat's bottom-boards.

Duncan steadied the boat as Taylor shepherded the mayor and his daughter down the beach.

The girl turned as if to make one last protest to Curtis, but as she stared at his set, shadowed face, she sighed and stepped lightly into the boat. Taylor followed them, his lips pursed in a silent whistle and, at a nod from Curtis, Duncan ran up the beach for the German.

One of the oarsmen looked up, startled, as the body was dumped behind them in the bottom, but Duncan glared and growled unintelligibly under his breath, and the man bent uneasily across his oar.

Jervis sat upright in the stern, his shoulders squared and his face shaded by the cap.

Before pushing the boat into deep water, Curtis examined the placing of everyone in it with silent care. He nodded to Jervis, satisfied that he was sitting in the most conspicuous position, and where any lookout was bound to see the German uniform, before realizing that anything unusual was happening.

He had done all he could, and with a grunt he pushed the boat clear.

The oars rose and fell, and the boat rose and plunged across the waves. With its extra load it was sluggish and unsteady, and the bottom was soon filled with water, which moved across their feet and splashed persistently along the worn gunwale. The land seemed to fade almost at once, and but for the glint of the moon along the sand spit and the dim hump of the hill, it had already lost its identity.

They saw the schooner's hull first, her smooth white side pitching angrily, as she tugged at the anchor cable, and then, as the boat moved slowly under her high stern, the tall, circling masts and the flapping, carelessly-furled sails loomed over their heads.

Across the stern Curtis could just see the vessel's name, *Ametisa*, scrawled in wide gilt lettering, which had once, no doubt, been the pride of her owner or captain.

The bow oarsman opened his mouth as if to hail the deck, but Duncan punched him in the arm and shook his head.

The boat scraped alongside and Curtis stood up, his limbs suddenly light, and reached for the schooner's rail. He heaved himself up and over in one quick movement, his boots skidding on the wet deck.

He glared round, his eyes searching desperately amongst the unfamiliar shapes and shadows of the darkened ship.

Duncan stood beside him, and then Jervis. Taylor's small

figure rose and fell in the boat alongside, his shoulders stooped like a small idol, as he sat quietly watching the others in the boat, his pistol in his hand.

What the oarsmen thought, Curtis neither knew nor cared, and he rested momentarily against the scored gunwale of the ship, unsure of what to do next.

At that very moment, a figure seemed to rise out of the deck between the masts, his uniform buttons glinting in the circle of light which followed him through the opened hatch.

Duncan stepped easily forward and waited for the man to climb on to the deck. As he bent to refasten the hatch, Duncan drove his boot into the lowered head, and then caught his body before he could fall on to the wet planking.

'One less,' he said calmly, and pulled a pistol from the man's belt. Still holding the limp figure, he tossed the gun over the ship's side.

Curtis spoke quietly over the gunwale: 'Signor Zecchi! Up here quickly!' Turning to Duncan, who was busy tying up the policeman with his belt, he whispered: 'We'll grab the skipper now!'

The mayor arrived on deck, his eyes blinking around him.

'Come on,' snapped Curtis. 'Steve, stay on deck!'

He propelled the mayor to the after hatch, aware that Jervis was following behind, the Schmeisser pointing dangerously at his legs. He slid back the hatch and almost fell down the steep ladder beyond, and ducked beneath a swinging oil lamp, which cast an uncertain glow along the short passage with its three closed doors. Curtis paused uncertainly, the mayor pressed against him, and Jervis's white legs still on the ladder.

As if in response to his unspoken question, a door opened, and the fat stomach of the captain appeared in the passage. He was still wearing the greasy cap which Curtis had seen earlier, and his round, unshaven jowls dropped even lower as he stared at Curtis's gun and then at his face.

He opened his mouth to speak, his breath fanning across Curtis in a curtain of sour wine and tobacco, but the mayor shook his head authoritatively and held up his hand.

'Stay still, *Capitano*,' he commanded quietly. 'This is a British officer!' He waited patiently, but the Italian sailor merely goggled at Curtis, his throat moving and bobbing above his red shirt. 'He is taking your ship!'

'Do you speak English?' Curtis spoke sharply, aware of the

time all this explanation was taking.

'*Si!* Ver' good English!' He glanced round desperately. 'Where you come from? I not understand what is happening!'

'Get on deck and call your men! And be quick about it!' Curtis stared at the fat, sweating face in exasperation. 'You are sailing at once!'

'But, *signore*——' he spread his palms appealingly.

The gun moved lower. 'Call them!'

Jervis squeezed back to allow him to pass, then ran up the ladder after him.

The captain peered worriedly at Jervis and shook his head, before reaching up to the bell, which hung on a bracket on the mast.

Duncan uncoiled himself from the rail, his eyes on the captain. 'He O.K., Ralph?'

'We'll see! Any sign of the others?'

Duncan laughed shortly. 'They're up in the fo'c'sle, playin' dice, by the sound of it.'

'Where are the wounded?'

Duncan shrugged. 'Not a sign of 'em yet.'

The bell jangled loudly, and Duncan loped across the deck to halt beside the narrow door leading into the fo'c'sle.

Light spewed across the ship as the door swung open, and a blue cloud of tobacco smoke billowed up between the legs of the six men who stamped irritably into the cold air.

Three of them were uniformed Carabinieri and the others seamen, their ragged jerseys and dirty duck trousers clashing with the smart boots and belts of their companions.

There was an exclamation of surprise, and one of the police-men dived backwards to the door, which, just as suddenly, slammed hard into his face. He reeled back, his hand clamped across his bleeding mouth, as Duncan stepped from behind the door, the gun balanced in his hand like a toy.

'Stand still, you jokers! Unless you want to step off!' He grinned savagely at each of them and gestured towards the trussed figure on the deck. 'One of yer mates! See?'

They stared round the deck, drawing together as if for sup-port, while Curtis spoke rapidly to the captain.

'Where are the rest? You should have a bigger crew than this!'

Counting the two oarsmen still in the dinghy, there were only five seamen.

'I am trying to tell you,' began the captain, his voice resigned and tired. 'These are all I have! My other boys desert, two...three days ago, I forget! They get worried 'bout the invasion, they wanna get home to their families! Me? I got no family, justa this boat!' He clenched his thick fists in sudden despair. 'Now you gonna take her away from me!'

'Where are the soldiers who were brought aboard?' Curtis made an effort to control his rising temper. 'Come on, man! Where have you put them?'

'They below, in the hold,' he answered sulkily. 'I was told to put 'em there!'

Curtis stared at him in disbelief. 'Wounded men? In the hold?' He seized the man savagely by the front of his shirt, and thrust his face forward. 'By God, you bloody Wops sicken me! If any more of them die, I swear you'll regret you were born!' He felt the fat body quiver. 'Now, prepare to get under way, just as you were ordered!'

'I do my best.' He moved his hands vacantly, his face twisting worriedly. 'Is a ver' difficult channel!'

Duncan's voice grated across the deck. 'You'll get us clear though, won't you, Captain? Just for us?'

The captain glanced at the hard mocking eyes and swallowed unhappily. Then he jerked his hands at the stunned sailors and pointed to the capstan. One of the men started towards the hatch over the small engine-room, but Curtis shook his head.

'Come up, George, and get the engine started.'

Signor Zecchi coughed. 'You leave little to chance, I see.'

Curtis ignored him, his aching brain groped for possible flaws in his plan, and he tried to keep his mind away from the silent wounded below his feet, at least until they were clear of the anchorage. He watched dully, as the girl appeared on the deck and stood shivering beside her suitcase. The two sailors heaved the wriggling German after her, and then towed the dinghy round to the davits aft.

Curtis turned to the police officer. 'Get your men in a line, quick!' To Duncan: 'Search them, and make sure they're well locked up!'

Surprisingly, the captain said over his shoulder, 'There is a good storeroom down there.' He pointed to another hatch. 'They will be safe in there.'

When Duncan had herded the Carabinieri away, and the German had been dragged after them, Curtis eyed the captain thoughtfully. 'Aren't they friends of yours then?'

The captain shrugged and spat over the gunwale. '*Facisti!* They stink.'

The deck quivered, and there was a dull roar from the engine-room, but after a few coughing protests, the motor settled down to a confident rumble.

The captain spat on his hands and took the wheel, whilst from forward came the clink of cable as the capstan heaved in the anchor.

He leaned comfortably on the wheel and pouted his thick lips expressively. 'We won't get far, *signore*! Patrol boats! Bombers! No, we won't get far!'

He spun the wheel and peered at the compass, which danced loosely in its ancient brass binnacle. A thin spindley lever at his side protested as he pushed his bulk against it, until it squeaked level with a worn plate stating *"Velocita massima!"*, and as the propeller churned a cheerful white froth beneath her counter, the *Ametisa* swung drunkenly into the wind and thrust her sharp stem over the first long roller.

Curtis watched for a few minutes, then beckoned to Jervis. 'You stay here on the poop, and watch the deck. Nobody is to go below until Steve has searched all the crew's quarters.' He glanced at the captain's squat shape, his fat straddled legs braced behind the wheel, and raising his voice, he added, 'And if we go aground, shoot him!'

He turned away from Jervis before he could answer, and stood for a moment against the rail, his hands resting heavily on its worn and grooved surface. The sudden realization that the ship was his—brought home to him by the steady beat of the engines and the swish of foam against the pitching hull—seemed to bring all conscious thought to an end. The weight of his body grew heavier on his arms, and his head sagged forward over the rail. He was shivering, and had to clench his teeth to withstand his weakness, which felt like real pain.

'*Signore?*' The mayor moved quietly at his elbow. 'May we go below now?'

Curtis levered himself away from the rail, his fingers slipping reluctantly from its support. He peered at the mayor through half-closed eyes, and nodded wearily.

The girl's voice was cold and unforgiving. 'Perhaps he wishes us to be locked in the store with the others!'

He stumbled past her and led the way down the steep ladder to the cabin flat. The lamp swung more jerkily than before, and the narrow passage leaped and staggered with the ship's lively movements. The hissing roar of the sea was muffled, and the air was thick and stale. He pushed open the first door and glared at the bare cabin, with its neat bunk and newly-painted sides. Another lantern swung crazily from a deck beam, casting strange shadows across the cabin's clinical bareness and the framed portrait of Adolf Hitler. A small safe was bolted to the bulkhead, but apart from a narrow wardrobe containing some more items of German uniform, there was nothing dangerous in sight.

'You can have this one, *signorina*. It was evidently your friend's cabin, so it's bound to be fairly clean!'

She looked at him without speaking, her slim body swaying to the motion of the ship. She placed the suitcase on the bunk, and with her eyes still on his face, she slowly ran her fingers along the black plait across her shoulder.

Curtis took the mayor's arm impatiently, and led him to the other cabin.

It was completely the opposite to the other. The captain's possessions were scattered across the bunk and on the deck, while on the rickety table stood two empty *vino* bottles and a half eaten sandwich. Over the bunk a series of voluptuous pin-ups smiled and reclined in crude abandon.

There was a pistol in one of the desk drawers, and a mountain of old letters and papers.

'Stay here!' he ordered curtly. 'I think you now understand our position well enough?'

The mayor inclined his head gravely, but Curtis had the impression that he was secretly amused.

'Don't touch anything. Go to bed, if you like.'

He lurched for the door, the air suddenly beginning to stifle him. More than anything else he wanted to lie down, and the sight of that filthy bunk tempted him more than anything he could remember. He paused for a second in the doorway and looked back at the plump, dignified Italian.

'I am sorry you have been caused all this inconvenience, and I appreciate your daughter's courage, whatever her reasons,' he faltered, and the mayor stared at him, his black eyes expressionless. 'Perhaps it will all turn out for the best for you, too.' He stopped, angry with himself, and ran up the ladder.

Duncan greeted him with an easy smile. 'All quiet, Ralph. I think the captain here has cottoned on to the general idea. I don't reckon his boys'll give any trouble now.'

'Good,' Curtis answered vaguely. 'Now for God's sake let's have a look at those poor devils below!'

Two seamen rolled back the hatch, their eyes on Duncan, and Curtis bent carefully over the high coaming, a feeling of nausea rising within him as the stench of closely packed bodies, sweat, and something worse hit him across the face.

The light in the hold was poor, but good enough to see in an instant the twin lines of crumpled figures which ran along both sides of the hold. Some of the soldiers lay on pieces of sacking in positions of sleep or even death, while others dragged themselves aimlessly between the lines muttering encouragement, or cursing each other as either a wounded limb or a careless boot started off another frenzied convulsion of pain.

Duncan followed close behind him, two lanterns adding to the picture of misery. His face was a mask, but the cold light in his eyes dimmed as he stared over Curtis's back.

One of the soldiers rolled wildly on to his back, his fingers hooked into his sacking. 'Water! For God's sake give me a drink!' A chorus of cracked voices joined his plea in a terrible cry, whilst from the far end of the hold Curtis saw the red-faced sergeant stagger to his feet, his good eye darting around his men. 'Easy there, lads. Be all right soon.' He sounded tired, and his voice was no longer jaunty.

He peered down the dim hold, watching the two figures on the ladder. 'Come on, lads,' he pleaded. 'Don't let the bloody Eye-ties see you're done in!'

A lump filled Curtis's throat, and he gripped the ladder fiercely. 'For Christ's sake,' he groaned, 'they'd have died down here! Look at them!' He swayed, and Duncan gripped his arm savagely.

His voice, close against Curtis's ear, was steady and very quiet. 'Come on, Ralph! Give 'em the shock of their lives!' He squeezed more insistently. 'You can do it! You know you can!'

Curtis tore his eyes from the hold and met Duncan's stare. The awful strength from the man's eyes seemed to run through his blood like brandy, and he bit his lip with sudden determination.

He stepped slowly down into the hold, his hands at his sides, and the light glittering and swaying across his fair hair and the tarnished gold lace on his shoulders.

He halted, praying that his voice would not let him down. He need not have worried, his words, amplified by the sides of the hold, and cutting through the sudden silence, were clear, and full of confidence.

'All right, you lazy lot! The convalescence is over!' He paused, his hands on his hips, his unshaven chin jutting forward. 'The Navy's here!' He stopped, unable to continue, and stared blindly back at Duncan, who nodded his huge head and grinned.

The effect of his words was instantaneous and electric.

The sergeant ran towards him, his arm-sling jerking and bobbing, as with his other groping hand he prodded the startled men and shouted with wild excitement.

'Hear that, Ginger? It's the bloody Navy! What did I tell you, Bert? It's them! It's all right!'

Curtis was stunned by the shouts and the pathetic capers of the sergeant, and could only stand in the middle of the whooping, hopping soldiers.

The blinded soldier sat bolt upright on the pile of rags in one corner, shaking urgently at the arm of the man next to him. His mouth moved in a white crescent beneath his bandages. 'Wake up, Ralph! We've been rescued!' He stopped tugging, and sat back, suddenly lost and silent, his fingers still holding on to his friend's tunic.

The soldier, Ralph, lay where he was, unmoved and indifferent, his glazed, unblinking eyes staring at the deckhead.

Curtis watched, suddenly cold. It was not only the feeling of loss which he seemed to share with the blind soldier; it was also that the dead man had been called Ralph.

He pointed desperately, and calmed the sergeant's excited shouts. 'Help him, Steve,' he called, 'and get some of the sailors down here quickly!'

The sergeant was speaking again, his boots together with something like his old smartness. 'Sarnt Dunwoody, sir! First Batallion, Middlesex Light Infantry!'

He stared at Curtis as if still unable to believe what he saw. 'By God, sir, I don't know 'ow you got 'ere, but by heaven it's a bleedin' miracle!' His face seemed to crumple, and he fidgeted with his sling. 'I don't think we coulda managed much longer!'

Curtis nodded dumbly, aware that Duncan and three of the more able soldiers were passing round great mugs of fresh water.

'The buggers wouldn't give us anything to drink. Kep' sayin' we'd have to wait!' continued the sergeant with abrupt fierceness, as he relived the whole nightmare over again. 'Wait! After bein' blown to 'ell an' then bein' cut about in a Jerry dressin' station, to say nothin' of twenty-four hours in a bleedin' lorry!' He stared round at his men with something like paternal pride. 'But they didn't give in!'

'You've been in charge all the time?' The question was a mere whisper, but the sergeant smiled sadly.

'Yessir. Y'see, our last officer died before we was patched up. 'E was a good kid, too!'

Curtis saw the campaign medals on the old soldier's chest. A generation and another war apart.

'I'll see that you're not forgotten either, Sergeant.' He swung round to follow Duncan, afraid that the sergeant might see his face.

Duncan's voice seemed to come from every direction at once. 'Come on, sport! Get this down you! It's only water, I'm afraid, but I've got those goddamned Eye-ties cookin' a month's rations up for you as fast as they can move their little selves!'

He bent over the blind soldier. 'Come on, young un, give me a hand with this water.' The soldier shrank away, but Duncan pulled him to his feet and thrust the big water jug into his hands. Then leading him slowly between the men, he manoeuvred him away from the other silent figure.

He caught Curtis's dull stare and winked. 'Think I'll join the army, eh, Skipper?'

Curtis smiled. It was the first time Duncan had avoided using his Christian name. So he had noticed, too.

He caught sight of the stocky little soldier whom the sergeant had called Ginger. He was staring at the Italian seamen with undisguised hatred, his mouth quivering.

'Here, you!' Curtis beckoned across a prostrate soldier. 'Come here a minute!'

The man came quickly, his eyes feverish but alert.

'Are you fairly fit?' Curtis studied the man's single bandage about his throat. 'I mean, d'you feel you can give me a hand?'

The soldier grinned, his whole expression changing to one of eagerness. 'Sir! Just give me the word! I'm so keyed up, I think

I'll go off my head if I can't do something!'

'Well listen, er, Ginger, go on deck will you? There's an officer there by the wheel dressed as a German. He's guarding, among other things, a pile of pistols we've taken off the guards. I want you to gather them up and pass them to any one of your chaps you think is fit enough to keep an eye on things. O.K.?'

'Yessir!' The man was already halfway up the ladder, his nailed boots clattering on the wooden rungs.

'And no reprisals!' Curtis called after him

He halted, level with the deck. 'They're not worth a bullet, sir!'

Curtis took a deep breath and sought out the sergeant once more. 'How are your men now!'

Dunwoody sighed worriedly. 'Not too bad considerin', sir. Four dead and ten pretty grim.' He brightened slightly. 'But the other twelve seem to 'ave taken new 'eart since you arrived, sir!' He glared admiringly. ''Ow did you get 'ere, sir?'

Curtis eyed him glassily. 'Too long a story for the moment. But I can tell you this, we're not even half out of the wood yet!' He forced a weak smile. 'But if you can carry on here for a bit, I'll be very grateful.'

'Jus' tell me what to do, sir.' He, too, seemed to have taken on a fresh strength.

'Any more N.C.O.'s?'

'Bert's pretty good,' he answered slowly. ''Ead wound, an' gets a bit dizzy, but 'e'll last out a bit longer, sir.'

'Right, put him on deck behind the wheel. Let him sit on something, and see that he's armed.' The soldier, Ginger, reappeared with the guns, his face pale but determined. 'He's to watch the crew and see that there's no funny business. You can carry on down here and serve out the food when it arrives. I'll see if we can get a good hot drink too, if that's possible!'

The sergeant loosened his belt. 'Leave it to us, sir.'

Curtis climbed the ladder to the deck, pausing on the top rung to let the salt air sting his face. His weariness still closed in with relentless persistence, but stubbornly he forced himself on to the darkened deck.

The moon had vanished altogether, and the weather was freshening. Overhead, the cloud banks scudded across the black sky like solid things, and the loose rigging moaned and creaked in monotonous liaison. A dim light flickered against the captain's fat face as he leaned over the compass bowl, and Jervis's white shape hurried to meet him.

'How are they, sir? Can I do anything?'

'There's a soldier coming to relieve you, Ian. I shall want——' He broke off as a thin corporal clambered unsteadily from the hold and peered at them from beneath his white bandages. He was wearing a khaki balaclava rolled over his dressing, and looked almost piratical. 'Ah, here he is! Know what to do, Corporal?'

'Yessir!' The man scrambled across the heaving deck and planted himself firmly on the after hatchway behind the wheel. He rested a small pistol on his knee, and began to rock to and fro, his arms folded in solemn concentration.

'Now,' continued Curtis, having seen that the captain had noted the new arrival, 'I shall want you to get cracking on the chart, if there is such a thing aboard, and there's a safe which might prove interesting, too.'

He crossed to the captain and glanced at the compass.

'Clear of the sandbanks?'

'*Si, signore*, we are almost abreast of the headland I think.'

'Stay on course, due east until we're well clear, and then I'll give you a fresh one. Got that?'

The man shrugged. 'We will not get far, I think that——'

Curtis bent closer, his eyes cold. 'I don't give a damn what you think. Just do as I tell you!'

'*Si, Tenente.*' His tone was subdued.

'Do you ever get challenged when you pass the headland?'

'Not unless a patrol boat comes. Then we sometimes speak.' He squared his thick shoulders with something like pride. 'But they know that I, Fausto Macchia, am always reliable. I know this coast like my own mouth!'

'Where are your charts?'

'There are two in my cabin. I do not need such things on my trips.'

'Our journey will be somewhat different, I think,' said Curtis with cold irony. 'I'm going to have a look at them now, so call me if you are worried about anything.'

The captain laughed bitterly. 'Worried? On such a fine night?' He cursed silently as Curtis disappeared down the hatch.

The mayor was sitting on the edge of the bunk, his eyes half closed. Curtis hardly spared him a glance, but hunted about the cabin until he found the charts beneath a pile of old magazines. He swept the bottles from the table with the back of his hand, his impatience mounting when he saw the grease and various stains which almost covered the markings on the charts.

He tossed one to one side and studied the other, his legs braced and his elbows planted on the edge of the table. He swore beneath his breath and pulled the lantern closer.

'Out of date, not corrected, and not been properly used for years, I should think! Here, Ian, get cracking.' He found an ordinary ruler in the desk and an old pencil. 'Try and lay off a course from here.' He tapped the chart with his finger. 'That's where I think we'll be in about an hour. I want you to lay off a course to take us approximately east south east from that position. By daylight we should be well clear of the coast, and then I'll decide what to do.'

He looked at his watch and stared fascinated at the hands opened to one o'clock. Fantastic, he thought, only an hour, yet we're at sea and away. He caught the mayor's eyes flickering in the lamplight, and turned his back. A ship full of disabled men, and smouldering Italians. What were *they* thinking about? How long would it take them to realize and assess the position of their new masters?

'Can you cope, Ian?' he asked abruptly.

'I'll try, Skipper. It's a bit of a mess.' He rubbed his nose ruefully. 'But I'll have a go!' He gestured towards the mayor. 'He'll be watching me!' The boy grinned, and Curtis's mouth tightened into a hard line.

He held up his watch so that both could see. 'In four or five hours it'll be daylight. He'd have been watching you then, no doubt, if we hadn't got away!'

He slammed the door behind him, and stood breathing heavily in the passageway. He was wrong to use the boy like that. What the hell was the matter with him? He half turned to re-enter the cabin, but a shaft of light fell across his arm as the other door opened quietly. She stood looking at him in silence, the edge of the door pressed against her breast. His eyes wavered, but he forced himself to remember how she had ensnared the sentry at the house.

'Well, *signorina*?' he asked levelly. 'Can I help you?'

'I was just wondering what was happening.' Her voice was soft, and seemed to act as a caress on his burning brain. 'Is it getting rougher?'

'A little.'

'You look like death, Lieutenant. It is a great strain for you.'

He still stared at her, his eyes heavy with fatigue. She looked lovely . . . and yet. He shook his head as if to clear it. Yet . . . there was something hidden behind her wide eyes.

'You capture the ship; you kill a man with your bare hands; and still you go on. You are a remarkable man!' Her full lower lip glistened momentarily, as she smiled gently. 'What makes you keep driving on?'

Suddenly he wanted to forget the ship, and everyone in it, and just be able to bury his aching head on her breast. Just to stand together, and feel the protection of her soft warmth.

He opened and shut his mouth, unable to find any more words.

'My father admires you, you know.' She tossed her head and sent the long black plait dancing across her shoulder. 'I think you are fighting *two* wars, yes?'

Duncan skidded down the ladder, followed by two soldiers. Curtis eyed him dully, and braced for another onslaught of questions. Duncan merely nodded calmly and glanced quickly from him to the girl. Then he jerked his thumb at the other men, who stood staring at the girl in dull surprise.

'I've come to fix that safe, Ralph. I thought you'd like these two blokes to watch this end of the ship.'

One soldier had both hands encased in huge dressings, but the other seemed complete but for grotesque strips of adhesive plaster across his cheeks and neck. They both grinned self-consciously and continued to look at the girl.

'All right,' said Curtis tonelessly. 'Think you can manage it?'

Duncan laughed and with over-elaborate courtesy he took the girl's forearm and slid past her into the cabin.

'This ain't a safe, it's a sardine tin.' Duncan rubbed his hands. 'Soon have the back off that.' He looked up. 'Some of those lads need fresh bandages quick, Ralph. I don't like the look of a couple of them.' He lowered his eyes. 'They'll not last till mornin'.'

'I see.' Curtis opened the cabin door behind him and looked at the soldiers. 'Make yourselves comfortable in there. The food'll be down soon.'

'I will go and help with the wounded soldiers.' The girl stepped into the passage, so that the rolling of the vessel brought her shoulder against his chest. 'I will be happy to serve them.'

Her eyes were dark and masked her thoughts from him.

'Very well.' He pressed his palms against his legs. 'Thank you.'

'Good girl, Carla! They'll sure get a kick out of that!' Duncan dropped to one knee, his hand on the safe, and Curtis felt a stab of resentment at the casual use of her name.

She smiled across at Duncan and then started up the ladder, her legs practically touching him.

He stared after her, until he realized that he was still looking at the empty swaying hatchway.

'We'll split into two watches, Steve,' he said vaguely. 'You and George first, and then I'll come on with Ian at dawn.'

'Lie down, Ralph,' commanded Duncan softly, 'before you bloody well fall down!' The safe dropped off its fastening, and Duncan examined the back intently. 'Huh, just tin, I'll soon fix that!' In the same tone he added, 'I can deal with things here, you're worn to a splinter!'

Curtis shook his head stubbornly. 'Lot to do. Must hang on a bit longer.'

'We'll need you more when it's daylight,' answered Duncan soberly, 'a whole lot more. Christ, man, we can manage now for a bit. What in hell's name are you tryin' to prove?'

Jervis looked round the door, his eyes watching Curtis unsurely. 'I've worked out the course, Skipper. What now?'

'Leave it with me, Ian,' Duncan said coolly. 'You an' the skipper are watch below for a bit.'

The boy looked at Curtis for confirmation, and he shrugged heavily. 'All right, Ian, hand over the watch. Get some sleep.'

Duncan's mouth twisted into a smile. 'That's it, Ian, get your head down while you've got the chance.'

Curtis looked at them as if he was going to add something more, but instead he pushed open the door of the captain's cabin, and blinked wearily at the small cluttered space, and at the two soldiers who squatted on the deck in one corner, one leafing through a tattered magazine, and the other leaning against the bulkhead, his eyes closed in sleep.

The soldier with the magazine grinned cheerfully. 'Everything O.K., sir, Jim here's having forty winks.'

Curtis steadied himself against the table. 'Let him sleep. Call me if you need anything.'

Signor Zecchi was curled up in the one decent chair, his hands thrust deep into the pockets of his grey suit, and his tie loosened across his chest. His heavy lids fluttered uneasily, and he watched Curtis stare at the empty bunk.

Curtis could feel the man's eyes upon him, but he was conscious of the desire to sleep more than anything else. I mustn't give in, he protested inwardly, but the bunk swept to meet him, as he sprawled with sudden and complete surrender on the crumpled blankets.

The soldier dropped his magazine and moved slowly around the cabin, the heavy boots sliding with each roll of the ship. Deftly he lifted Curtis's sprawled legs over the side of the bunk, and unfastened his belt.

Without a glance at the mayor, he slithered down again on to the deck and reached for his book.

The mayor cleared his throat. 'I do not think private soldiers in the Italian army watch over their officers so carefully.'

The man glanced at him sharply, but seeing the sadness in the mayor's eyes he grinned openly. 'Well, somebody's got to look after 'em, mate, and I reckon this one's worth it!'

Curtis groaned and dug his fingers into the pillow. The voices in the cabin were part of another world, and he did not even attempt to fathom out their meaning.

As the darkness closed over him, he could recall the girl's face and her voice saying: "You are fighting *two* wars". He rolled over on to his face and lay still.

Above the stuffy warmth of the cabin the wind sighed and moaned along the deserted deck, and as the ship lay momentarily to one side, a white sheet of spray hissed over the gunwale and broke angrily against the loose rigging.

Duncan prowled restlessly back and forth across the poop, his chin deep in his jacket collar, and his stomach burning contentedly with the whisky he had taken from the house.

The captain still lolled across the wheel, his thick legs braced and fluid as each wave lifted the poop behind him. Duncan smiled grimly and glanced quickly at the compass as he passed.

They were on their new course which, all being well, would carry them clear of the coast before dawn. Then, he halted as if to relish the thought, they could turn for the south. Two hundred and fifty miles at eight knots, that would be just over a day's streaming, and they should be within reach of some friendly forces.

It would be unlikely that the schooner would be missed for

two days, he pondered, and by that time, well, anything might have happened. Then there was the girl, Carla. He glanced at the darkened hatch across the hold. She was still down there with the troops. Lucky devils, but there was plenty of time for him, too, he decided.

In his side pocket he carried the contents of the German officer's safe. A small book of recognition signals and local patrol areas. Ralph would find that very useful, but it'll keep until first light. He met the captain's face across the compass, and the man's mouth opened as if to speak. Duncan glared at him fiercely, and continued his pacing.

At the weather rail he paused and grinned into the teeth of the wind. They were all frightened of him, he knew that, and enjoyed the feeling of power it gave him.

He thought of Curtis, and marvelled at his stamina and will to keep going. He's changed all right; more than I'd have thought possible. He looked down at the dark water, fighting his own tiredness with sheer brute force. 'We've all changed,' he spoke aloud, 'and I'm not sure if it's for the better!' He laughed harshly, and two Italian seamen who darted past carrying the empty food tins from the hold, stopped rigid in their tracks, like rabbits caught in the glare of headlights, and waited until Duncan had crossed to the other side of the deck before they scuttled towards the fo'c'sle.

The steady beat of the engine pulsed life into the ship, and with each turn of the pitted and scarred screw, drove her onward into the night, leaving the darkened shoreline to sink into the storm.

Taylor climbed heavily around the shuddering engine, his filthy hands moving with strange gentleness across the rusted controls, as if to coax and wheedle the best effort from the ill-used cylinders, which had carried the ship heaven knew where in the past, and upon which they all depended at this moment.

He sank back at last, his boots lolling and nodding within inches of the giant flywheel's gleaming teeth. He was happy in his own peculiar way, and watched the wheel spinning with the inner satisfaction of a born engineer.

The hatch was shut, the air thick with fumes and the stench of cheap diesel oil, but to him the tiny engine-room was a refuge, and something he could understand. If anything went wrong with the bellowing engine, he could deal with it. He glanced sleepily at the tools which he had arrayed on the deck in readiness, knowing just how much the others depended on him. His head rested against the pulsating bulkhead, and he closed his eyes, leaving his ears to follow and check the gyrations of his charge. It shut out the sound of the storm, and hid the misery of the wounded in the hold. He did not even have to worry about the behaviour of the skipper, or what made each of them act so differently, now that they had been given a new role to play. His head lolled, and a gentle snore drifted into the racing engine.

Twenty feet behind Taylor, beyond the bulkhead and lying uncomfortably in the narrow passage, Jervis still stared fixedly at the swinging lamp, his troubled eyes following the darting shadows as if mesmerized. Overhead came the measured tread of Duncan's boots, and he wanted to join him and pour out his heart to him there and then.

What was different? He tried to think of all that happened, but already the German colonel and the sneering sentry had lost their firm outlines of reality. He touched the bandage around his head, hoping that he might be able to see more clearly the eager, pitiful expression of his strange, mad saviour. It was no good. Each time he was reminded instead of the present, and the uncertainty which the dawn would bring.

He flinched as a trickle of water filtered through the hatch and splashed across his face.

Curtis had made him feel as he did, he knew that, but he was still reluctant to consider the cause of his behaviour.

When he had burst into the house and dropped the sentry's lifeless body carelessly on the floor, that should have been the greatest moment of Jervis's life. But as he closed his eyes, he could only think of the overriding disappointment which had shown in the skipper's eyes. It was almost as if Curtis had expected to find someone else in the cell, someone for whom he had been searching for a long time.

He pillowed his head on his arm and sighed. Perhaps I'm going off my head, he thought unhappily. A large wave punched the side of the hull with sullen force, and Jervis swore aloud, and was more surprised at his own words than the anger of the sea. Must be getting like Steve, he thought, and with a ghost of a smile on his lips, he fell asleep.

The *Ametisa* seemed eager to do battle with her common enemy, and as her raked stem dipped into each trough, the long bowsprit slashed downwards like a sword, until, with the water cascading over the bow, she lifted skywards again, victorious and trembling. One of the furled sails billowed with sudden fury, as the searching wind found its way into its folds and puffed it out from the yard in a flapping, ungainly pocket.

The captain looked up from the deck, his eyes squinting into the darkness as he searched the night sky for the new sound. He half reached for his bell, and then shrugged and continued to wrestle with the wheel, as if one more disaster was not even worth his consideration.

The schooner plunged on, alone in the tormented water. Of her passengers and crew, some slept the sleep of the exhausted and the beaten, while others still clung to the last shreds of watchfulness and human cunning.

Some wondered about the dawn, and a few prayed for the strength to meet it.

In a corner of the streaming deck, covered by canvas and firmly lashed in place, four soldiers lay together. They were neither thinking nor hoping, and for them the dawn would never come.

Chapter 8

DUNCAN CLATTERED NOISILY down the ladder, slamming the hatch behind him, and almost stepped on Jervis's sprawled form in the middle of the passage. He stood astride the curled body and yawned hugely, his raised fists brushing the low deckhead. With a grunt he stooped and shook Jervis's shoulder.

'C'mon then! Don't make a bloody meal of it!'

Jervis groaned and sat up blinking, his red-rimmed eyes staring round at first with shocked unfamiliarity and then with renewed weariness.

'Oh, it's you, Steve,' he answered dully. 'I wondered where the blazes I was.'

Duncan's eyes crinkled. 'Who the hell were you expectin'?' He gestured towards the girl's cabin. 'Or is that where you've been all night?'

'Steady on, Steve,' began Jervis hotly, his face flushing, 'you're wrong about her! She's a damned fine girl!' He struggled for words. 'Why, if it wasn't for her, I'd be dead right now, and you'd have sailed without me!'

Duncan smiled grimly. 'Well, that's got that off your chest, hasn't it? Now perhaps you'll call the skipper and tell him it's

nearly dawn, leastways it would be, but for the blasted clouds!'
He turned heavily on the ladder and reached for the hatch. '*I*
think she's dinkum, too, Ian, if that's of any interest to you.'

Jervis struggled to his feet and swayed against the door
frame. 'I know, Steve. It's just that I can't understand what's got
into the skipper. He keeps flaring up all the time. I just don't
know how to cope with him when he's like that.'

'Well, Ian, just put yourself in his place. How d'you reckon
you would have measured up to all this, eh?' He sighed and
rested his elbow on the ladder. 'It's just that we're not used to this
kind of war. Up till now it's been a pretty remote business for us.'

'How can you say that?' Jervis interrupted. 'Why you and he,
and Taylor have been right in the thick of it from the beginning!'

Duncan raised his hand patiently. 'Not in this way. As I said,
it's been sort of remote. This is the real war. Bein' able to see the
enemy for once as flesh and blood, not just a hunk of ruddy steel
in your periscope sights!' He opened and closed his hands, whilst
Jervis watched them as if fascinated by their power. 'Bein' able
to see how they work, and act! And knowin' what it's like to hunt
and be hunted!' He slammed back the hatch, and sniffed at the
air. 'By the way, Taylor's name is George. You might remember
that, Ian!' His body clambered over the coaming, and Jervis was
left staring at the closed hatch.

'Damn!' he said fiercely.

The ship lurched and he smoothed the rumpled uniform with
distaste. The German eagle on his right breast seemed to mock
him, and even the uniform made him feel more than ever a man
on the outside, looking in.

He wondered how it could all end, and whether the schooner
was in fact the real answer to their destinies, or merely a means
to their ultimate destruction.

He cleared his dry throat, and pushed his way into the stuffy
cabin. The lamp had burned lower, and he had to strain his eyes
to make out the distorted shape of Signor Zecchi sprawled
open-mouthed in the chair, his feet entangled with those of a
sleeping soldier whose bandaged hands stuck out in front of
him, their hidden suffering marked on the soldier's thin face.
The other soldier stared up at him, his eyes glassy, and forced a
grin.

Jervis crossed to the bunk and laid his hand on Curtis's arm,
which hung over the side of the bunk like a dead thing. He

jumped as Curtis immediately sat up, his eyes bright and searching. He looked up at Jervis, his face pale, almost grey in the lamplight, and for a few seconds seemed to have difficulty in collecting his wits.

'Lieutenent Duncan's respects, sir, and it's just on the dawn.' He paused, stupidly aware of the formal naval speech and how out of place it sounded under these circumstances.

Curtis rubbed his knuckles savagely into his eyes and coughed. 'Well, Ian, no one can say that your training hasn't been thorough!' He sat upright, his hair tousled across his forehead, but with a smile on his lips. 'We'd better go on deck and see what's what, hadn't we?'

Jervis smiled gratefully and followed Curtis from the cabin. He watched Curtis's shoulders stoop as if from the shock, as the keen air met them on deck, and waited with all the alertness he could muster, prepared to justify himself in front of Curtis and all the others if necessary.

Duncan's shadow broke from the rail. 'Mornin', Ralph! You're lookin' a bit better.'

Curtis smiled with his teeth. 'Feel like death! I don't see much light yet.'

A tiny flicker of silver lanced at the black line where the horizon should have been, and occasionally the clouds seemed to lose their power as a growing glimmer crept over the sea's edge.

'Angry!' commented Duncan, and then pointed up at the masts. 'But you can see the topmasts now!'

Curtis lifted his head and stared up at the quivering spars and the billowing ball of loose canvas. 'What about that?' His voice was hard as he turned to the captain, who still leaned heavily across the wheel.

'S'not important, *signore*. We never use him.' The voice was tired, almost disinterested.

'It might be later on! Get your men to work on it as soon as it's light!'

He looked down at the package which Duncan had thrust into his hand. 'What's this, Steve?'

'Baccy! Got it from forward. Thought it might interest you, seein' what a glutton you are for the old pipe!'

They watched as Curtis pulled out his pipe and slowly filled the bowl with rank Italian tobacco. It was a moment of peace, and nobody wanted to spoil it. It suddenly seemed terribly important that Curtis should have his smoke.

He ducked his head beneath the gunwale, and they heard the rasp of a match. He stood up, the reflection from the glowing bowl casting a small flush across his taut features. He blew out a cloud of smoke, and they watched it hover momentarily around his head, before being plucked away by the wind.

Curtis breathed deeply, his body balanced and relaxed on the wet deck.

'A forgotten ship,' he said slowly. 'No one knows where we are, or where we're making for!' He puffed out more smoke. 'Only *we* know anything! I only hope to God we're doing the right thing!' he ended fervently.

Duncan yawned. 'It's a right queer set-up all right. But I'll tell you now, Ralph, if we pull this off, it'll be really something. It may prove something different to each one of us,' he paused, his shadowed eyes on Curtis's face, 'but it'll be worthwhile!'

'I hope so!' Curtis looked across the tumbling water. 'Bed, Steve. I'll take her now.'

Duncan opened the engine-room hatch and peered into the foul interior.

'Good old George,' he chuckled. 'I'll leave him be!' He swayed across to the after hatch and yawned again. 'Just a couple of hours an' I'll be up again, lookin' for some grub.'

His head was level with the deck when Curtis called him.

'Yeah? What d'you want?' Duncan's voice was slurred. 'Thanks, Steve. Just thanks.'

They heard him laugh. 'Oh sure!' The hatch slammed.

Jervis trembled and checked his muscles angrily. 'I always thought it was warm in this part of the world, Skipper.' His voice was tinged with caution.

Curtis leaned back against the rail, his pipe jutting like an extension to his chin. 'A strange sea this,' he answered quietly, 'as unpredictable as a woman.'

'D'you think we shall see anything. I mean a ship or something like that?'

He shrugged. 'Hard to tell. Never has been a lot of enemy activity up here. It was a bit too remote for our ships to operate, except for submarines that is, and they don't like it either.' He shook his head slowly. 'No, we just can't be sure of anything yet. We must be on our toes the whole time.'

'I'll get some lookouts sorted out as soon as it's lighter,' began Jervis. 'The soldiers might be able to do that quite well.'

'Yes, the soldiers.' Curtis stared at the silent hump on the deck. 'We must bury those chaps, too. As soon as possible.'

He suddenly gripped Jervis's arm, and pointed across the sea. 'Look, Ian! D'you see that?'

He followed the pointing finger, half afraid of what he might discover. A pattern of gold light spilled across the horizon and splashed the distant waves to give them life and an angry splendour. The clouds above moved faster, as if to escape the full majesty of the dawn, which refused to give way to the storm and to the passing power of the night.

'It never fails to move me.' Curtis was quite sincere. 'It makes all this seem so fragile and unimportant.' He laughed, as if embarrassed. 'It's quite something, as Steve would say.'

Two seamen appeared on deck, scratching and yawning, and from the spindley funnel over the fo'c'sle a puff of smoke proclaimed that breakfast, of sorts, was on the way.

Curtis examined the long telescope which he had procured from the captain and tested it on the horizon.

'Not exactly a Zeiss, but it'll have to do,' he commented.

Jervis walked slowly across the sloping poop and stared back along the dim, uneven wake, following it until it was lost in the fading shadows and torn apart by the short, steep waves. Already the outlines of the individual white crests were becoming more clearly defined, whilst around him the ship seemed to grow larger, and more vulnerable.

He turned his back to the sea, and watched Curtis pacing briskly up and down across the poop. The wind ruffled his fair hair, and gave him back his boyish look, but the eyes which darted up to the masts, or scanned the lightening horizon, were neither young nor restful. Jervis sighed, and wished he understood what was going on behind those cold eyes, and whether any of Curtis's thoughts were directed at him.

There was a slight disturbance at the hold hatchway, and Sergeant Dunwoody stood swaying in the grey light. Seeing Curtis, he stamped aft and halted by the wheel. His hand swung up in a smart salute.

'Mornin', sir! What orders, sir?' His eye studied the tired naval officer with interest, but his expression was calm and respectful.

'We must bury those four chaps of yours.' Curtis pointed with his pipe stem. 'It won't do the rest of them any good to see them lying there.'

Sergeant Dunwoody fidgeted with his sling. 'Another gone in the night I'm afraid, sir. 'E was done for before 'e got on the boat.' His tone, although matter-of-fact, did not disguise his sadness.

Curtis looked at the compass, his eyes distant. 'I see. Very well, we'll get on with it now. Before there's anything else to worry us.'

The sergeant hurried back to the hold, beckoning as he did so to two seamen.

Curtis stared at Jervis. 'Give him a hand, Ian.'

Jervis stood by the lee rail as the seamen unlashed the bodies and laid them in readiness. The extra one was hurriedly wrapped in a length of worn canvas, and an old seaman, his face a mass of tiny wrinkles, like a piece of hardened leather, began to sew the ends together with twine.

A bar of gold light mounted the ship's rail and spilled on to the deck lighting the seaman's bent head and his thick mass of grey hair. There was little warmth in the gentle ray, yet already the decks had lost their coat of spume and spray, and even the sounds of the sea seemed lulled.

The sun glinted on the man's needle, as with a jerk he broke the thread and raised his eyes, their watery brilliance telling nothing to Jervis, who stared fascinated at the soldier's boots which still protruded from the end of the canvas.

He shook himself and looked quickly at the hold, aware that some of the soldiers had come on deck and were standing in a silent group by the hatchway, their bandages white against their sunburned faces, and their tattered khaki clothing clashing with the dark green and silver of the sea.

Sergeant Dunwoody glared round and nodded to Curtis. 'Ready, sir!'

Curtis stared in silence at the five bundles which had once been men.

'Have you a British flag aboard?' He faced the captain, suddenly angry.

'No, *signore*. We have just the usual signal flags.' He pointed at the locker by the mainmast. 'I am deeply sorry, but we have no use, you understand.'

Curtis walked quickly to the locker and wrenched open the

lid. He could feel all eyes on him as he pulled the untidy bundle of flags on to the deck in a tangled mass of colour.

He had intended to drop the soldiers over the side during the night, but now that he had seen the sergeant's face and those of the other wounded, he was glad he had waited. Whatever lay waiting for them in the path of the sun, and however wasted his efforts might be, he suddenly felt that this thing was terribly important. His fingers closed over the International Code flag V. It was a white flag with a bright red diagonal cross. That would have to do, he thought, and beckoned to Jervis.

'Spread this over them,' he said, 'it's all I can find.'

Over his shoulder he said curtly, 'Stop the engine!' He heard the long lever grate over, and seconds later, the engine coughed and died away.

The engine-room hatch banged open and Taylor's heat-reddened face appeared over the coaming.

''Ere, what the 'ell d'you think you're doin'?' He glared at the captain, who pointed quickly to Curtis and laid a fat finger across his lips. Taylor blinked wearily. 'Sorry, Skipper!' He then leaned across the coaming, his chin on his forearms, his eyes distant.

Curtis looked round the watching faces, and wondered what he was going to say. He had never seen a sea burial before, let alone conducted one.

A squeaking block distracted him, but when he turned angrily towards the sound, he saw the captain hauling the Italian tricolour to the position of half-mast. He had removed his greasy cap and his bald head gleamed in the sunlight like a brown egg.

His eyes fell on the girl and her father, who had also appeared on the poop. Signor Zecchi looked old and crumpled, but the girl at his side stood proudly against the stiff breeze, her thin dress pressed against her slender body, her gaze fixed upon Curtis. He noticed that her hair was loose, and some of the severity seemed to have left her, as with each breath of wind she put up her hand to brush the hair from her face.

Curtis tore his eyes away. The ship lolled heavily in each trough, and started off a fresh set of noises. Ropes creaked and blocks clattered as the rigging bit at the spiralling masts, while at the waterline the water gurgled impatiently, as if hungry for what was to come.

'We came together by accident,' began Curtis, his gaze fixed

on the wavering bowsprit, 'and I don't know these men as well as
you do. But I know that I am speaking for all of you when I give
them God's blessing.' He stopped. The words sounded foreign
and stilted, and he looked quickly at the men. Their faces were
set and grim, yet some of the tension seemed to have gone. 'We
will now commit their bodies to the deep.' He finished, his mind
empty. 'Carry on, Mr. Jervis!'

The planks were hoisted by the seamen, and Curtis set his
teeth, as one of the bodies began to slide towards the edge.

Suddenly the sergeant's voice crashed on his ears. ''A' Company, 'shun!'

The soldiers lurched to attention, and Curtis was thankful,
knowing that the sergeant and all the others had felt as he. They
did not need his words. They were saying good-bye in their own
way and tomorrow, if it came, they would speak with friendly
ease of these five men.

The seamen placed the planks carefully on the deck, and one
of them rolled up the flag. It was over.

'Thank you, Sergeant. You can carry on to breakfast now.'

'Sir.' He wheeled to leave and paused. 'A nice neat job, sir, if I
may say so.'

Curtis nodded to Taylor. 'Full throttle, George!' His head
vanished, and Curtis breathed with quiet relief as the engine
rumbled into life.

The captain had put another seaman on the wheel, and wiped
his hands across his trousers. 'I will see that my men carry out
your orders. You can trust me, *signore*. I have never liked
working for the Germans.' He spat accurately over the rail.
'They have no humour, you understand!'

Curtis smiled, and the captain spread his hands with obvious
delight. 'See, *signore*, you at least agree with me on that!' He
ambled forward, humming to himself.

Signor Zecchi turned up the collar of his thin jacket, and
glanced from Curtis to the empty sea.

'Where are we this morning?'

The girl interrupted with a soft laugh. 'Does it matter, Papa?
We are his prisoners!' She smiled sadly at Curtis, her teeth
gleaming through the dark veil of her blown hair.

Curtis shrugged. 'What difference indeed,' he answered. 'You
will be safe aboard this ship, but who knows what is happening
on the mainland by now. Perhaps the Germans have started to
shoot some of your countrymen by now!'

'Never! We hate war, but we are loyal to our allies!' But there was less conviction in his sunken eyes.

The girl shivered, and her father took her arm. 'Come below, Carla. There will be breakfast soon. You will become ill in this wind.'

Her eyes played across Curtis's face. 'I will wait a little longer, Papa. You go below now. I will watch the sun drive away the night.'

He sighed and left them together at the rail.

'I liked the way you spoke to your men, Lieutenant. It was a bad thing you had to do.'

'I've had to do worse. Thank God there weren't more of them.' He looked sideways at her firm chin and slender throat. 'If they had been left down there without attention, many more would have died.' He watched a small pulse beating beneath her throat. 'As it is, I can't be sure yet.' He left his fears unsaid.

'You have done what you thought you had to,' she said gravely. 'If you had followed my plan, you could have been safe in a good hiding place.'

'Then we could have waited with your father for the British Army; then he *and* his social position would be restored, is that it?'

She kept her face averted, but he saw her shoulders toss with impatience. 'Would you not do that for your own father?'

Curtis laughed aloud, and she stared at him in a mixture of rage and despair. 'You are mocking me, Lieutenant!'

He laid his hand on her shoulder and shook his head. 'I am sorry, *signorina*. I apologize for laughing, but I am afraid you do not know my father!'

He fell silent, and she lowered her eyes to his hand, which still rested across her shoulder. 'I think I will go below now.'

He dropped his hand, conscious of the warmth in his palm. 'Perhaps you will be good enough to help with the wounded again?'

'Is that what you really wanted to ask, Lieutenant?' She smiled at the discomfort on his face, and walked to the hatch. 'I will help.' With a wave to Jervis who hovered eagerly nearby, she ran lightly down the ladder.

'What a girl, Skipper! I've never seen anyone like her!' Jervis scratched his head, as if the right words would come from there. 'Why, she's lovely!'

Curtis examined his pipe and began to fill it. 'What would

your father have to say about her, I wonder?'

Jervis drew himself up and inserted one hand melodramatically into his jacket. 'Looking at girls, Ian? Disgustin'! What's her phone number?' Jervis stopped the imitation and grinned with embarrassment. 'Well, something like that anyway.'

Curtis stared at him in amazement. It was as if the boy had suddenly taken on a new personality, or a fresh lease of life. 'Well done, Ian!' he said, knowing that if he had treated him better he would have behaved like this before. 'I'm sure your old man would say nothing of the sort!'

He loosened his jacket and ran his fingers through his hair. The air was humid, in spite of the wind, and the clouds seemed to be holding the heat steady over the sea, while the sun dipped and wavered across its surface, plunging it into dark shadow for one minute, and opening up the rollers into barriers of green glass the next.

He felt his rough chin as he watched a seaman place a tray of coffee and hot sausage on the deck by the wheel.

'After that, I'm going to have a shave, Ian, *and* a bath if I can manage it.'

'Shall I call Steve to relieve you, Skipper?'

He smiled briefly at the boy's pink face. 'You're the navigator. You can manage by yourself, eh?'

Jervis grinned. 'I think so, in fact, yes, Skipper!'

The morning wore on, the schooner's course taking her further and further from the mainland, until it seemed to all aboard that they had been sailing purposefully towards the horizon for days instead of hours.

Curtis had stripped to his trousers, and was busy shaving with the captain's razor in the cabin. His skin, washed and briskly towelled with a sheet from the bunk, glowed pleasantly, and he smiled at his reflection in the small mirror as he remembered the captain's own towel. It was hardly the thing to touch, let alone use.

Duncan sprawled in the bunk, snoring with relaxed ease, and from across the passage he heard the girl talking to her father.

He paused with his shaving and rested his hand on his own shoulder. He met his own gaze in the mirror, as he remembered how she had looked at him.

An urgent tapping overhead on the glass skylight made him glance up, ashamed of being discovered with his thoughts. Jervis was stooping over the sill, squinting through the dirty glass.

'Skipper! Another ship! Fine on the starboard bow!'

Curtis dropped the razor and kicked at Duncan's outflung arm. All the peace and security which had lulled him during the dawn fell away in a second, and he felt that he and the ship had been laid bare and open by his weakness.

Duncan rolled off the bunk and landed lightly on his feet, reaching automatically for his pistol belt, and glancing up at Jervis's face as he did so.

'What's up? A riot or somethin'?'

'A ship, Steve!' Curtis threw his jacket across his bare shoulders and wrenched open the door. 'Keep down as we go on deck, and make sure all our people stay hidden!'

'D'you aim to fight it out?'

Curtis paused at the top of the ladder and looked downwards, his face a mask. 'Fight? With what?'

Duncan grunted and pulled the belt tight around his waist. 'Well, I don't aim to end up in any stinkin' grave, not without a scrap, anyroad!' He glared belligerently.

Curtis laid the telescope on the hatch coaming as Duncan squeezed past him, and dropped uncomfortably on to his knees. 'Remember the wounded, Steve!' He hissed the words after Duncan's bent shoulders. 'D'you want to get them shot up, too?'

Duncan did not answer but ran crabwise towards the hold.

Curtis sighed and steadied the telescope against the pitch of the ship. The wavetops loomed distortedly in the lens, and with difficulty he trained it round until he saw the sudden movement of the other vessel.

Silver-grey in the feeble sunlight, it moved purposefully across his line of sight, a white bow-wave slashing from either side of the high sharp stem as it cut into each roller and sheared the green water into a seething chaos of spray.

He watched the ship's silhouette with practised eye, his heart heavy. A *Dardo* class destroyer, he thought, and one shell from her battery of four-point-sevens would put a quick end to all his hopes with no effort at all.

She was still about two miles away, yet even as he watched she grew larger in the lens, until he could clearly discern the white caps on the high bridge, and the long, slender gun barrels on the fo'c'sle.

The captain padded up the ladder and paused uncertainly by

the wheel, his eyes following the other ship.

Curtis snapped the telescope shut and looked up at him. 'Have you seen her before?'

The captain shrugged vaguely. 'Maybe, *signore*. Who can say? We often meet the patrol ships, but I do not come as far south as this in normal times!'

Duncan crawled along the deck, keeping his powerful body hidden beneath the bulwark. He slithered to a halt opposite the wheel, and supported his chin in his hand.

'All snug an' quiet, Ralph. How's the visitor gettin' on?'

'She's moving in,' he answered slowly. 'She's bound to ask us who the hell we are.'

As he spoke, a light flickered from the destroyer's bridge, and some of the bow-wave dropped away, as the ship slowed down.

'She's flashing.' Curtis spoke in almost a whisper, his throat dry. 'Make your reply, Captain.'

Duncan tossed the small code book across the deck to land within Curtis's reach.

'It gives the recognition signals in there, Ralph, and all the right dates for this month.'

He pulled the long diver's knife from his belt and jabbed it into the deck. It quivered in the planking like an obscene crucifix, and Duncan smiled lazily at the watching captain.

'Make sure you give the right signal, sport! We don't want any accidents, do we?'

The captain tore his eyes from the knife and spoke quickly to the seaman at the wheel, who ran to the flag locker. He took over the wheel and jerked at the spokes uneasily, until two flags soared to the schooner's gaff and broke stiffly into the breeze.

Jervis stood in full view by the rail, his hands clasped behind his back, as if he was Officer of the Watch in a peace-time battleship. He stared fascinated at the graceful destroyer, feeling that each pair of binoculars was trained upon him, as it might well be, and tried to keep the appearance of bored irritation which he had already seen used by German officers.

A harsh metallic voice boomed across the water, the Italian words hardened and distorted by the loud-hailer, and the captain reached wretchedly for his battered megaphone.

'What's he saying?' Curtis barked, maddened by the stillness which had engulfed the schooner. 'What do they want to know?'

'They wish to know where we are bound. But I think they are otherwise satisfied!'

'Tell them we are making for Bari. To evacuate wounded personnel.'

He drummed his fingers on the deck as the captain yelled across the narrowing gap. It seemed fantastic that the patrol ship should be satisfied, and yet why not? He tried to put himself in the destroyer captain's place. No doubt they encountered count-less schooners and other coastal craft in these waters, and there was enough to worry about already, what with the invasion and the increased sea traffic, without bothering with a vessel so obviously under the control of the German Navy. He watched, holding his breath with relief as the other ship's screw whipped the sea into a fury, and drove her steadily on a diverging course.

Jervis stood stiffly at attention and saluted the tiny figures on her armoured bridge.

Duncan laughed. 'Well done, Ian! Proper little Nazi you are!'

Jervis looked down at Curtis and smiled shakily. 'Gosh, Skipper, that was a near thing!'

'We'll alter course as soon as the destroyer's hull down,' answered Curtis thoughtfully. 'She may report our position by radio, although I doubt it. But we can't afford to take chances. Get below, Ian, and start on your chart. I want to keep more to the eastward if possible, though it'll be a longer way round. We can't afford to cross swords with that sort of thing!'

Jervis watched the destroyer's shape shorten as she turned away, a soft plume of smoke drifting from her squat funnel. 'I wish we were in something like her, Skipper. Why, we might even——' He broke off, his eyes wide with alarm. 'Look out! Hold her, for God's sake!'

The girl burst through the hatch, her leg brushing away Curtis's hand, as he reached vainly to stop her. Before anyone could move to intercept her, she had reached the taffrail, and stood silhouetted against the sky, her long hair streaming behind her.

Even as Curtis hurled himself across the deck, she lifted her arms high and waved with wild desperation after the destroyer.

Curtis pinioned her arms to her sides and pulled her down to the deck, so that their faces were inches apart. He stared at her wild, blazing eyes and her lips parted yet soundless, as she met his gaze with all the fury and venom of a trapped animal.

'You little fool! What the devil are you trying to do?' He tightened his hold as she wriggled madly under his body. 'I should have realized that you'd try something like this!'

Duncan sprawled against one of the open wash ports, his eyes narrowed while he followed the other ship. He relaxed slightly and turned his head. 'She's still goin'. They didn't notice a damned thing!'

She suddenly went limp, and Curtis released his hold, his face a mixture of anger and weariness. 'Go below,' he ordered, 'I'll talk to you in a minute.'

She stepped slowly on to the ladder, her face turned towards the ship. It was already well clear, and its outline had begun to shimmer with indistinct beauty.

Curtis felt for his pipe, his thoughts racing angrily through his brain. It was his fault. He should have been more prepared for something like this. If only she'd speak. Anything would be better than the great emptiness which seemed to fill her dark eyes.

'I have my responsibility, *signorina*,' he said, his voice flat, 'just as you have yours.'

She looked at him with a long, calculating stare. 'You do not understand, Lieutenant. You are a hard man, yet,' she shrugged, as if dismissing him, 'you were not always so, I think. Why do you try to prove what is not there? Why must everyone suffer because you must satisfy your own soul?'

Curtis trembled. 'What the hell are you talking about? We are at war, in case you have forgotten, and I don't intend to sacrifice the men under my charge to please you or any other damned——' He broke off, angry with himself, and frustrated by the small smile on her lips.

'Because of any damned Eye-tie? Is that what you're trying to say?' Her smile vanished and she dashed the loose hair from her face. 'You are like the Germans! You delight in this war! As if it were some sort of game!'

Curtis saw the expression of agony on Jervis's face as he reached the girl's side in two strides.

'Don't you ever say that to me again, *signorina*!' She moved back against the hatch, as if expecting a blow. 'I'm sorry I trusted you, that's all! And if the Germans are relying on your people as allies, I'm sorry for them also!' His eyes blazed with suppressed emotion. 'Now get to your cabin, and keep out of my way! See that she and her father understand what I mean!' He glared at Jervis. 'And then carry on with the navigation!'

He walked stiffly to the rail, trying to shut out the sounds of her feet on the ladder.

Duncan stood up and sat on the rail facing him. 'That was quite a potful, Ralph! Still, I reckon you can't blame her exactly. How would you feel under the circumstances?'

'For God's sake stop it!' Curtis turned on him, his body trembling. 'I'm sick to bloody death of being told what I must do!'

Duncan took the weight of his body on his hands and leaned slightly forward. 'Take it easy, Ralph. I'm just sayin' that you can't blame the girl, that's all!'

'I'm not blaming her, or anyone else! I don't give a damn what she thinks, or how she feels, so long as she doesn't interfere with what we have to do!' Curtis's eyes swept furiously across the horizon. 'And if you want to start giving me lectures, you can think again!'

Duncan stood up, his face impassive. 'In that case, I'll leave you alone for a bit, an' go below. I'll be havin' a spot of shut-eye if you want me.'

He waited a while, watching Curtis's stiff shoulders black against the sun. He was about to add something more, but with a grimace, he lowered himself down the ladder.

What in hell's name is the matter with us? he pondered. It irritated him to feel this vague threat of discord between them, but it annoyed him still more that he was unable to root it out and destroy it.

All at once he wanted to be alone with his thoughts. Everywhere he looked in the ship he found either soldiers or seamen, and now as he entered the cabin, he found the mayor once more in the chair, sitting gloomily with his feet resting on a locker, his eyes staring into space. The two soldiers were asleep, and in the light which filtered through the skylight, their faces appeared grey with fatigue and shock.

Jervis looked up from the chart and smiled wanly. 'Hello, Steve. I've just laid off that course the skipper wanted.' He scratched his head with the ruler, his nose wrinkling with distaste. 'God alone knows if it's anywhere accurate. Even with the vaguest sort of dead reckoning it's pretty hopeless without any proper navigation instruments. I don't know how they've managed I'm sure.'

Duncan fell heavily on the bunk and sighed. 'Don't give it a thought, kid. We're zigzagging all over the flamin' ocean, so I don't suppose it makes a blind bit of difference whether it's accurate or not!' He sighed again, and pulled a bottle from his inside pocket.

'Is that whisky?' Jervis stared with surprise.

'Sure is. Our little friend here left it lyin' on the table when we left his house.' He held it up to the light and frowned. 'Not enough to keep a dog alive! Want a lick?'

Jervis shook his head. 'Couldn't we give some to the wounded?'

'I've already given 'em the other bottle, and some brandy I found in the crew's quarters. 'Sides, I don't reckon they ought to have too much till they've been seen again by a doctor.' He took a long sip from the bottle and let his head fall back on the pillow. His creased face seemed consumed by inner thought and worry, which was so unlike his normal demeanour, that Jervis squatted on the edge of the bunk and peered at him closely.

'What's the matter, Steve? Is there anything I can do?'

'I'm all right.' He glared over Jervis's shoulder at the silent figure in the chair, and lowered his voice. 'No, I'm damn well not all right! For once I'm out of my depth, and I don't feel . . . well . . . how shall I put it? . . . at home.'

'Everything's going well so far,' began Jervis cautiously, but was silenced by the gleam in the Australian's eyes.

'How can you talk like that, man? Anything might happen. Right now; this afternoon; or at midnight. Surely you realize that?'

'Yes, but that's a chance we have to take.'

Duncan gripped his wrist fiercely. 'Don't tell *me*! I know all that! I suppose it's this situation, and this flamin' ship. Before, it was better. Just the four of us.' He smiled with the nearest approach to sadness that Jervis had ever seen. 'Four against the world! That's how it was. Now look at us!' He snorted. 'All bits an' pieces hangin' together for mutual support. It's ragged, an' I don't like it. I like to be able to deal with anything I'm called on to meet. I'm useless at this sort of game.' He drank some more whisky and closed his eyes.

'What about the skipper?' Jervis asked cautiously. 'What

does he plan to do if we're spotted again?'

Duncan smiled sourly. 'Ralph? He's so twisted up inside that he doesn't know whether to spit, or have a haircut! What with him an' that girl, well, I give up!'

'She saved my life, Steve.'

'Sure, I know that.' Duncan sounded completely weary. 'But what's she up to? Blow hot, blow cold! One minute she's a little heroine helpin' us jokers, and the next she's yellin' for the Duce to come an' rescue her! Huh, women!'

'I don't know a lot about women, I'm afraid.' Jervis waited, half expecting Duncan to laugh at him, but he merely grunted, and lifted the bottle once more. 'But she's really lovely. I've never seen anybody like her.'

'Well, if that's how you feel, go an' have a yarn with her. It'll do you good.' He grinned crookedly. 'And it'll give me a chance to get some sleep!'

Jervis picked up the chart and moved quietly from the cabin. He paused outside the other door, then knocked.

She opened the door immediately and stared at him in surprise. 'Well? Have you come to taunt me?'

Jervis coloured and fumbled with the chart. She stood easily in the centre of the small cabin, her hands on her hips and her lips parted in an expression of smouldering resentment.

'I wanted to know if there's anything you need.' He swallowed and stumbled on. 'Please don't be upset about what has happened. I know how you feel. It's all such a beastly business.'

Her mouth softened and her slender body seemed to relax. 'Come and talk to me, Ian. You do not mind my using your first name?'

He lowered his face to hide his pleasure. 'No. No, of course not. Tell me what is worrying you.'

She shrugged and sat on the side of the bunk. Jervis's eyes strayed to her slim neck and the dark shadow at the top of her dress. She had not noticed, and seemed intent on watching a small beetle which explored the bulkhead opposite her.

'Well, Ian, I cannot tell you what happened to me. You will not believe me, because you are a man, but when I saw that ship, that Italian ship, I was so overcome that I acted without thought.'

'It was a dangerous thing to do, *signorina*.'

'For you, yes. I understand that well enough. And believe me,

Ian, I would not wish anything to happen to you. But,' her mouth quivered momentarily, 'what about my father and I? What will happen when you reach your friends?'

'You will be well looked after. I can promise you that! We shall say how you saved my life, and everything else you have done.'

She smiled sadly. 'You are a good person to know, Ian, but I am afraid that you have forgotten that we are enemies. My father is a Fascist and loyal to the régime. When our country is overrun, as it will be, for the Germans will not try to hold such difficult territory, there will be a new government, with different ideas. When my father is released, it will be like returning to a foreign country. No one will want to remember him, or what he has helped to do!'

'Could it have been any different?'

She walked to the bulkhead and watched the beetle scurry into a crack.

'If we had gone to the hiding place I told you about, it might well have been different. My father has friends and certain property, which would help considerably.' Her eyes lifted to his face, bright and warm. 'You do see that, don't you? Please tell me that you at least can understand!'

'I think I do.' Jervis felt suddenly humble. It was true what she had said. There would be little warmth left for a pro-Fascist when the old régime had fallen.

Her eyes were moist but she smiled across at him. 'Thank you. I could not bear to think that I brought all this on my father without any reason at all. It has been driving me mad! But I know that the Germans would have killed him, just as they would you. When someone is useless to them, they destroy him, like cutting off an infected limb!'

She began to plait her hair, her hands moving with new life.

'Come, you must take me to the wounded. I will change their dressings.'

Jervis looked at the chart, aware that Curtis was on deck waiting for him.

'I'll tell him what you're going to do.' He grinned sheepishly. 'He ordered you below, remember.'

She patted the plait into place and tossed it over her shoulder. Jervis thought that at the moment she looked like a child,

although he guessed that she must be at least four or five years
his senior.

'Yes, you tell him. I will look after those men, no matter what
he says! You go and tell him that, and I will tell my father that
you have said all will be well!'

She ran past him, and instinctively Jervis caught her wrist.
She halted, quivering like a doe in flight.

'Thank you for your confidence,' he said awkwardly.

Her look of surprise faded, and she regarded him gravely.
'You are good, Ian.' Rising on her toes, she kissed him briefly on
the cheek, then with a smile, she had left him.

For some moments he stood staring at the door, his hand on
his cheek. 'Carla,' he said softly, but only the beetle heard him.

He looked up anxiously as he heard Curtis call harshly from
the deck, 'Ian! What the hell's taking you so long?'

Jervis blinked as he arrived on the poop, aware of the sudden
change in the weather. Most of the cloud banks had broken, and
the heat rose from the baked deck to greet him, like steam from a
boiler. He turned his face from the sea, blinded by the millions of
shimmering lights which stabbed from every dancing wave and
from the white-hot stare of the sun.

Curtis studied the chart and compared the markings with
those in the German's notebook.

Jervis stood back, watching his engrossed face with fresh
curiosity. Remembering what Duncan had said, he felt a pang of
uneasiness as he studied the young-old face with the cold eyes.
Eyes which were now scanning the chart with fanatical eagerness, as if amongst the scrawled lines and symbols were the
answers to his secret fears.

'It's the best I can do, Skipper.' Jervis spoke warily. 'The gear
is pretty crude for this sort of thing.'

Curtis grunted and watched a wheeling gull, which like a lone
watcher, swooped and dived across the wake.

'The girl is going to attend to the soldiers,' added Jervis after
a long pause. 'Is that all right?'

Curtis nodded vaguely. 'Girl? Oh yes, of course.'

He squinted up at the masts and studied the uneven shape
squatting on the yard. A leg swung easily with the motion of the
ship, as the old Italian seaman scanned the horizon.

Jervis followed his gaze and gasped. 'Can he be trusted? I

mean, do we have to rely on his lookout?'

Curtis eyed him slowly. 'Who else d'you suggest? One of the wounded perhaps? Or yourself?' His tone was deceptively mild, but Jervis had now learned to recognize the danger signal.

'Sorry, Skipper. I expect he'll be fine for the job.'

'That's a comfort to know.'

Curtis watched the girl's shadow cross the deck as she hurried past, carrying a roll of freshly torn cloth. She kept her eyes averted, but there was the hint of a smile on her soft mouth.

Curtis waited until she had vanished into the hold, his expression watchful.

'Alter course. Steer due east.'

He followed the captain's plump hands as they spun the worn spokes over to port. A ruby ring flashed incongruously on one finger, and Curtis stared at it, as if fascinated.

'How long will it be before we make towards the land again?' Jervis saw the shutter drop again in Curtis's eyes, as he brought his mind to bear on the question.

'Soon, I hope. I can't delay too long.' For a moment Jervis thought he would open up a little more, but he merely added, 'The wounded need attention badly.'

Sergeant Dunwoody clattered noisily towards them. His red face was beaded with sweat, and he had discarded his jacket. Jervis noticed that his khaki shirt was spotted with blood.

Curtis stiffened. 'What's wrong, Sergeant?'

'That other chap, sir. Lake. He's dead I'm afraid. 'E 'adn't a chance anyway. But it's something else as well, sir. The dressin's are pretty bad, an' I'm a bit worried about it. The lads need seein' to quick, sir.' He watched Curtis, squinting his good eye and plucking nervously at his sling.

'I see. I'll do my best, Sergeant.' Curtis bit his lip and nodded. 'I'll do my best.'

'I'm sure you will, sir.' Dunwoody forced a smile and stared round the empty sea. 'Cor, like Ramsgate, ain't it?'

'Go with the sergeant, Ian. See what you can do to help. I'll have the hatch taken right off so that they get a bit more fresh air.'

Jervis faltered. 'It's not your fault, Skipper. You've done more than anyone could expect.' He stopped, aware that Curtis was not listening. The pale eyes were on the move again, searching the horizon, watching and calculating.

'Are you comin', sir?' The sergeant fidgeted at his elbow.

Jervis still hesitated, feeling that he should try to explain his thoughts to Curtis. 'Perhaps we shall find it easier to miss the patrols than we thought.'

Curtis seemed to jerk himself together with a great effort. He glanced briefly from Jervis to the sergeant, and gestured towards the hold. 'Get to it, Ian. There's a lot to do yet.'

Jervis sighed and followed Dunwoody's broad back into the deep recess of the hold.

The sunlight swayed back and forth through the wide hatchway like the beam of a drunken lantern, as the ship rolled uneasily from side to side. The sea, driven by the short gusts of wind, was furrowed into long, lazy rollers, and the schooner's course took her broadside along them, making the very masts groan in their sockets.

Jervis steeled himself for the job he had to do, as he met the sour stench which was trapped by the high sides of the hold, and carefully avoided the still body at the foot of the ladder, with its face covered by a piece of blanket.

The first wave of joy and enthusiasm which had greeted Curtis and Duncan when they had boarded the schooner had spent itself on the shock and misery which had now made itself felt in the hidden menace of the soiled bandages and discoloured skin.

A soldier rolled painfully on his side and tried to vomit into a basin. Each time he turned, his injured legs thudded helplessly on the deck, and he fell back, retching and exhausted. There was a flurry of movement, and the girl hurried to his side, her feet stepping and dodging the sprawled limbs and torn bandages. Even in his wretchedness, the soldier feebly tried to push her away, unwilling for her to see him in this pitiable state. She brushed her hands aside and knelt down on the deck, the man's head firmly pillowed on her knees.

Her voice was low and husky, as she smoothed away the hair from his damp face. 'Come on, Tommy. Gently now.'

Jervis turned away and went after the sergeant, who was stooping alongside another man and talking in low tones with the corporal, Bert.

He looked up as Jervis joined them, and shook his head worriedly. 'Look at this lot, sir. I don't quite know what to make of it.'

They had removed the bandage from the man's thigh, and Jervis swallowed hard, the spittle thick in his throat. What had once been a mere flesh wound in the man's leg, had blossomed angrily into a savage mass of discoloured and weeping tissue.

'Er, what is it? Can we clean it up a bit?'

The corporal sucked his teeth and sat back on his haunches. 'Gone rotten, that's what! He'll lose that leg, I'm thinking!'

''Is leg? 'Is bleedin' life, you mean!' hissed Dunwoody fiercely. ''E needs penicillin an' transfusions,' he added vaguely.

The man in question opened his eyes and stared glassily at Jervis's uniform. His thin body began to shake with silent laughter, and the corporal gingerly covered up the wound.

'Can't you stop this bloody ship rolling about, sir?' The man's voice was a mere whisper. 'It's making me feel numb all over. Can't feel my legs at all.'

Jervis forced a smile. 'Won't be long now. We'll have you home soon.'

The sergeant followed him as he moved along to the next man, and tugged gently at his sleeve.

'It's miles an' miles yet, ain't it, sir? What chance do we really 'ave? We can't go on kiddin' these chaps if they ain't got a chance!'

Jervis looked woodenly at the man at his feet. Naked, and flat on his stomach, he was quite still, but for his fingers which were curled into a blanket in a desperate grip. Two of his companions were engaged in removing a soiled dressing from the small of his back by gentle strokes of a rag soaked in warm water. The bowl they were using was already slopping over with bloodstained water and pieces of skin. The man groaned, his neck muscles bunching with effort, and one of his hands began to pound at the deck.

'Steady, mate. Keep yer 'air on!' The sweating soldier with the rag glanced up at Jervis and shook his head. Aloud he said, 'Old Jim 'ere is a real card! Swingin' the lead proper 'e is!' But there were tears in his eyes as he spoke, and he seemed to Jervis to be trying to tell him something more. That no matter how bad they all felt, they would back Curtis to the end.

He beckoned the sergeant away from the others. 'How long, Sergeant? Just how much time d'you think we have?'

Dunwoody stared round helplessly, and then seemed to come to a decision. 'We can hold on, sir. None of 'em wants to give in, but they're livin' on borrowed time, as from now, I reckon!'

Jervis ran his fingers through his hair and felt the sweat running over his scalp. If the ship turned for the coast now, and right now, there was a chance that these men might be saved. A military hospital could never refuse to help men in this state, be it Italian *or* German. Then they would be able to lie in safety until the Allied armies reached them. And us? He shuddered. There would be no mercy for himself and the others, he decided.

A shrill cry from the far end of the hold made his teeth grate, and helped to decide him on his next action.

'I think we should consider the state of the worst case, Sergeant, and act in his interest first.'

The sergeant didn't answer. He was unused to sharing confidences with an officer.

He walked to a patch of sunlight, where the girl was busy rolling another bandage. She looked up at him, her lips pale.

'You're doing wonders, Carla. I don't know how you're sticking it out.'

'They are so helpless. It is all so...so terrible for them.'

'I am going to tell the skipper just that.' Jervis watched her small hands manipulating the crude bandages. 'We must make for the shore now.'

Her eyes widened. 'But that is dangerous for you? You will surely be captured again?'

'We shall see.' He reached up for the ladder. 'Perhaps you will get your way in the end, *signorina*.'

She passed a hand across her brow, and picked up a basin. 'I must go to them, Ian. Be careful what you do. I am sure that your captain already has a plan. He may not be willing to give in to you.'

Jervis felt vaguely piqued by her remark. It was as if she did not consider him capable of making such a decision. He stuck out his chin and started up the ladder.

'I know what I'm doing, Carla!'

He found Curtis still by the wheel, as if he had never moved. His face turned towards him as he approached, and one eyebrow lifted questioningly.

'Well, how are they?'

Two seamen staggered from the fo'c'sle carrying a huge can of fresh water towards the hold, and Jervis waited until they had gone before answering.

He met Curtis's stare. 'I think they're in a damned bad way, sir. Some of the wounds are going septic.'

Curtis glanced towards the bowsprit and tapped his pipe into his palm. 'If we had not taken the ship, they would still be en route for Venice. By tonight they might have reached their destination, and from that time this ship will be missed and an alarm will go out. We will have to be very careful and make full use of the darkness. Tomorrow we might well be within close contact with our own forces, or the following night at least.'

Jervis quivered with exasperation. 'But, Skipper, half of them'll be dead by then!'

'If we hadn't arrived aboard, I expect most of them'd be dead by now.' There was no harshness in his voice. It was merely a plain statement of fact.

'How can you talk like that? Don't you care what happens? They're helpless, but so pathetically eager to prove their loyalty to *you*! Can't you do something for *them*?'

Curtis twisted the pipe between his fingers, his mouth tight. 'That's enough, Ian! I asked you to help the wounded, not start behaving like a child!' He stared angrily around the deck, his eyes blazing. 'Don't you think I know about all this? That's why I'm trying to get them back to their own people. I owe them that.'

'Or do you mean that *we* won't be captured?' Jervis let caution fly to the winds. 'Who are the more important? Us or them?'

Curtis let his arms fall limply to his sides, and Jervis thought he had given in. But his voice was calm and unhurried, as if he was speaking to a fractious schoolboy.

'I've given you your orders. Now kindly carry them out.'

Jervis stammered with anger. 'You won't turn for the coast then? You'll carry on with this scheme of yours?'

'I'll alter course when I'm ready. Not before. Now carry on, Mr. Jervis!'

'Aye, aye, *sir*!' Jervis was trembling with suppressed rage and emotion. 'I hope you're satisfied!'

As he blundered towards the hold, Curtis's cold voice halted him in his stride.

'And another thing, I'll trouble you to discuss these ideas with me before you start holding council with everybody else!'

Jervis almost fell down the ladder, and stood weakly on the bottom rung, breathing heavily.

'You spoke to him, Ian?' She crossed quickly to his side. 'What did he say?'

'He refuses to budge.' Jervis's eyes filled with tears of humiliation and bitterness. 'He's as hard as iron! I wouldn't have believed it!'

Carla Zecchi watched him thoughtfully. 'He may be right, Ian. He has had much experience perhaps?'

'Experience? Of what?' He winced as another cry floated along the hold. 'He seems immune to personal suffering! He's like a man possessed!'

The wounded man cried out once more and Carla plucked nervously at her thin dress. Its hem was stained where she had knelt in the soldier's blood, and there was a bruise on her arm to mark the place Curtis had gripped her as he pulled her to the deck.

'Come on, Ian, we must stop him shouting, before the others get more upset.'

He followed her, dragging his feet, casting quick, sickened glances at the suffering and pain which bordered the sides of the hold.

The cry from the tormented man even penetrated the thick bulkhead of the engine-room, and clashed with the persistent rumble of the diesel.

Taylor jerked out of his doze and lolled his tongue across his dry lips. The thick haze which hung over the engine hovered like a group of conversing spirits, which changed their hues and shapes as the shafts of sunlight filtered through the deck grill and danced across the revolving shaft.

Taylor groaned and eased his cramped body on to his knees. Listlessly he checked the gauges and the oil, and wondered what to do next. Overhead he knew that the sun was soaring to its noon zenith, and there would be little shade on the dried decks. Below it was stuffy and foul, but at least in the engine-room no one disturbed him. He had discarded his jacket and jersey, and sat bare to the waist, his spare body running with sweat, and his hair plastered against his forehead.

The skipper had peered down the hatch at him earlier, and had asked about the engine revolutions, but apart from brief, routine questions, he had seemed unwilling to talk.

That suited Taylor, who felt that by just concentrating on their jobs, they could somehow make the time pass more quickly, and with each turn of the shaft they would be thrust more speedily towards safety.

It was odd how the change of environment had altered them all. Without the hard shell of the midget submarine, with all its familiar pitfalls and discomfort, they seemed to move without purpose or confidence.

He felt disturbed and surprised at Duncan, who could always be relied upon for a jest or a bit of company. I expect he's more out of his depth than I am, he pondered.

There was little deck-space in the engine-room, merely a sort of planked catwalk which ran around the sides and provided a place for one engineer to watch over the diesel. Apart from that, the place was moulded into the hull, so that he could see the ribs of the ship running right down to the keel beneath and where the shaft vanished into its sleeve to join the thudding propeller.

He stared at the swilling and vibrating scum of bilge water, and watched it rippling around the ribs, to lap near the racing teeth of the giant flywheel. Once it reached that wheel, he knew he would be drenched, as it was picked up like a stream by a water mill. Never look after their bloody ships, he thought irritably, as he groped for the handle of the bilge-pump. I pumped the whole lot dry just after dawn, and here it is again. He cranked steadily and noisily, his breath wheezing in his throat.

Didn't join up to bugger about in this sort of floating ruin, he thought, as the ship rolled lazily, and forced him to put his hand on the hot exhaust pipe.

He pumped in an even, unhurried swing, his mind drifting wearily away from his task and the ship.

He thought of Madge, the girl who lived in the next street in Hackney. She was working on the buses now, and right good she looked in her uniform. He always went up to the garage by Hackney station when he was on leave, just in the hope he might be able to date her, before some other bloke got the chance. A grin split his grimed face. She was quite a girl! Kept changing the colour of her hair, but she was still smarter than all the little Yiddisher bits who hung around the town hall dances.

He yelped as a jet of slimy water cascaded out of the bilges and soaked his skin in a sheen of oil and filth. As he shrank to one side, the flywheel bit into the water and sent another small tidal wave sluicing up the side of the engine-room to cover him, and fall hissing on the engine casing.

He stopped pumping, his head cocked on one side. He shielded his eyes from the spray and peered down into the bilges. Instantly, his heart began to pound. There was no mistake, the lower rivets in the stout ribs were now covered completely, and he had been pumping all the time!

He forced himself to act calmly, and began to check the pump. It was working well and quite in order. The bilge-water was rising around the racing wheel in a steady stream now, and even as he watched, he saw the level rise over the engine bearers. Frantically, and fully awake, he began to pump with feverish haste.

Clank . . . clank . . . clank . . . he watched mesmerized, as the pump handle jerked back and forth, conscious only of the water which surged and hissed against him and the engine.

'Christ! We're sinkin'!' he gasped aloud. 'Can't keep this up fer long! Engine'll seize up in a second!' The sentences jerked from his twisted mouth, but, nevertheless, he stayed where he was, and glanced quickly at the level of the water.

Nearly a third of the flywheel was under water now, and the noise in the confined space seemed like a giant waterfall. He realized that he was in the lowest part of the ship, and the leak must be somewhere forward. He'd have to attract someone's attention, so that a search could be made. It was queer that no one had noticed anything, it must be quite a large leak.

He gasped painfully and turned to change hands on the pump handle. As he did so, a savage burst of water struck him full in the mouth, and he slipped, sputtering on the catwalk.

'Gawd blast yer!' he choked. 'I'm gettin' out! S'like tryin' to bale a battleship wiv a chamber-pot!'

He stopped and rubbed his hand across his wet mouth with sudden disbelief. There was no taste of salt at all, and apart from the usual tinge of oil, it was quite fresh and cool. He reached blankly for the handle, his sodden brain wrestling with the problem. It wasn't possible, and yet, he cursed aloud and bent over his task.

The sun, like a triumphant warrior, had succeeded in driving away the last of the clouds, and was able to concentrate its full strength on the lonely ship beneath. The deck-caulking, already in need of repair, gleamed wetly, and stuck to Curtis's boots as he moved restlessly about the shimmering deck.

The captain sat inert under the bulwark, his cap tilted across his eyes, and Curtis could not tell whether or not he was still awake; while the helmsman, a small wiry Sicilian, crouched across the spokes of the wheel, his scrawny neck protected by a length of faded bunting.

Curtis had to check himself from looking repeatedly at his watch and compass, and tried instead to concentrate on the bowsprit. He watched it rise sluggishly to point at the blue sky as the stem mounted a wave, and then as the schooner thrust her way forward, dip downward until it seemed to rest on the horizon like a pointer. He wished he had his cap, or something to help drive away the relentless throbbing in his head and neck.

A thin plume of smoke still rose from the galley funnel, as the huge pots of water were boiled for the business of cleaning wounds and dressings alike.

He had buried the last man to die before the heat had reached its maximum power, but apart from the sergeant and Giulio Zecchi, there had been few spectators this time.

He thought of Jervis and clenched his fists angrily. Young idiot. What the hell did he mean by getting so entangled with everything? He forced himself to relax. It was Jervis's first operational trip anyway, so perhaps this had to be expected. Still, his sort of reasoning was infectious. His predecessor, Roberts, would have acted differently, he thought, but immediately dismissed the idea. What was the use ... he was dead.

He squinted his eyes to look for the sea gull, but it had vanished, and in some way he felt saddened.

We're all dead really. Given up as lost by everyone but ourselves. His thoughts returned persistently to Jervis. Young fool. Couldn't see further than himself.

He watched the bowsprit and wondered about the night. It seemed so far off, that it took real effort to continue with his plan for altering course. If the schooner was reported missing before nightfall, it would be the end anyway. But—and his pulse quickened at the thought—if they could keep clear of patrols until they were hidden by the darkness, there was a chance, and a good one at that, he could get them all to safety.

He frowned as he listened to the clank of the bilge-pump. Poor Taylor was obviously suffering, too. He could imagine what this ordeal was doing to the E.R.A.'s strength of mind.

The mayor had left the deck, and Curtis was glad. The man's strange, haunted eyes troubled him, and already he seemed to have aged considerably.

A shout from forward made him look up startled. One of the seamen was shouting excitedly and waving an empty bucket.

The captain stood up with ponderous dignity, his eyes dark and grave.

'What's he yelling about?' Curtis asked. 'Tell him not to disturb the people below!'

The captain moved slowly across the poop, his hands feeling his pockets as if uncertain what to do next.

He faced Curtis with watchful calm. '*Signore*, he says that the fresh water is no more!' He waited for the impact to show on Curtis's taut features, and hurried on, 'That is impossible of course, for we take on a thousand gallons!' He shrugged helplessly. 'But if he says so, then it is true!'

Curtis's face was still blank, yet already the shock of the captain's words was working furiously on his mind. The seaman placed the bucket on the deck with a hollow clang, and stood quietly watching the two captains with patient interest.

Curtis heard the captain fire a series of questions at the man, but knew from the definite way he answered and the professional movement of his hands, that there could be no doubt about his findings.

The captain dropped his voice and moved still closer. 'It is very bad. The water has been allowed to drain away. The valve has been opened.' He met Curtis's eyes, suddenly enraged, as if he, too had been betrayed. 'It was no accident, *signore*!'

At that moment the engine-room hatch banged open and Taylor emerged, his skin running with sweat and oily water, his eyes blinking in the glare.

'Strewth! I thought we was done for! I've just pumped the 'ole bleedin' ship aht! Some clumsy twit must 'ave upset something!' He groaned wearily. 'An' I thought we was sinkin'!' he added reproachfully. He looked from one to the other, his quick mind already aware that his news held more impact than he had imagined.

'Where is the water valve?' Curtis's voice was calm, even distant.

'In the hold, *signore*. We use it when we drain the tank for cleaning.'

'I see.'

Curtis turned to Taylor. 'George, call Steve and the sergeant, I want all the people from the hold on deck. All those who have been fit enough to move about, and have had access to that part of the ship.'

'What's up then, Skipper?' Taylor scrambled towards the after hatch.

'We have a new enemy among us, George. It's too late to do anything useful about it, but I just want to meet the one concerned.'

The captain saw Curtis's face and shuddered.

Chapter 9

JERVIS TOOK A last look around the hold, noting the quiet which seemed to hang over the ship, and which surrounded the listless wounded men who lay in their various attitudes around him. Only two or three of the more capable soldiers remained to tend to their requirements as best they could, and Jervis felt his eyes straying to the large water-can which swung lazily from a deck beam. It was queer about the water giving out, he could not even begin to understand what had happened, and was almost too tired to contemplate it. Taylor had slithered down the ladder, his dark face angry, even sullen. He had muttered something about the water, and that the skipper wanted all the personnel from the hold on deck at once. Jervis had deliberately delayed his own departure after Carla, the sergeant and the others had left, partly because he wanted to make sure that the wounded were quiet and as comfortable as possible, and did not suspect that the sodden dressings on their wounds were the last they would expect, but mostly because he wanted to show Curtis that he, at least, was not impressed by this peremptory summons.

He sighed and climbed up to the deck. The sun hit him across the neck and seemed to sap the last energy from his body. He noticed that the group of assorted figures gathered around the poop were silent and watchful, and no one looked up as he walked aft and leaned heavily against the mainmast.

Curtis was standing apart from the group, his hair almost white in the glare, as he looked over the rail at the dancing wake.

Duncan and Taylor stood together by the hatch, the E.R.A.'s wiry body dwarfed by the other man's shoulders, as he leaned his elbows on the edge of the open door, his face dulled either by sleep or drink.

Curtis looked up, his eyes covering the group of weary figures and resting momentarily on Jervis. He cleared his throat, the sound drawing their attention to his face.

'You know that the fresh water has gone,' he began calmly, 'but you may not be aware of the cause, or,' he paused, his mouth hardening, 'the possible consequences.'

The girl moved closer to her father, who stared with passive eyes at the deck, the movement making Curtis turn briefly in her direction.

'Someone has deliberately opened the cock on the storage tank, while he, or she, was in the hold!' He waited while a babble of voices broke out on the poop.

Sergeant Dunwoody gestured fiercely with his hand, as if unable to find words. 'But sir,' he stammered, ''oo'd do a thing like that? I mean ter say, sir, we're bitched wivout water!' He glared with sudden suspicion at those nearest him and lapsed into silence.

Jervis watched the girl from beneath his lashes, conscious both of the meaning of Curtis's announcement and the sudden look of fear in Carla Zecchi's eyes. She had gone pale, and he could see her fingers twisting nervously into the back of her skirt. "Or she", Curtis had said, and Jervis was moved both by anger and pity. He remembered her coming into his prison and risking her life to entice the German sentry to his own death. It must have been her, it was all dropping into place now. He understood what she had meant by her hints about saving her father and getting Curtis to change his plan. No wonder she was unworried by Curtis's scheme to sail the schooner all the way to the south coast, while he himself had fumed and cursed at Curtis's hardness. She had known about this all the time; in fact, she probably got the idea from his own concern for the wounded. He forced himself to think and shut his ears to the protesting voices and distorted faces. What did it matter anyway? He had wanted the ship to turn for the coast, and now Curtis would have to alter course. The reason was unimportant. She had saved his life, and nothing else mattered any more.

Curtis held up his hand and the sounds died.

'Whoever is responsible for this stupid and dangerous act—and it is someone here right this minute—has committed himself and all the rest of us to one course of action only.' Jervis could see that Curtis was labouring to keep his voice under control. 'I shall have to turn immediately and try to find a way to the nearest port, where the wounded will be landed and handed over to the authority responsible for that area. Without treatment and proper care, clean dressings and all the rest of it, things were bad enough. Without water, and all that water means to injured men, there is no alternative but to give in.'

Duncan shook himself like a dog, and stared round with disbelief and amazement.

'Now listen, Ralph!' He moved his hands threateningly. 'You're not goin' to jag in without findin' out who did this are you?'

'Well, what d'you suggest?' Curtis sounded tired, almost distant.

'I've got ideas, by Christ I have!' He pointed suddenly at the girl. 'What about her? What's she been doin'?'

His eyes were slitted with fury, and Jervis forced himself to look at Carla, his suspicions immediately turned into reality as he saw her wide eyes dark with fear. She opened her mouth as if to speak, and Jervis stepped quietly in front of her.

They would shoot her or something, he thought desperately, the look on Duncan's face was enough to tell him that nothing Curtis would do or say could prevent it, even if he had wanted to.

He felt strangely calm, and his voice was almost conversational. 'As a matter of fact, *I* did it!'

The effect of his words was terrifying by its cool impact. Curtis stared down at him, his mouth quivering with shock. The others seemed to fade into indistinct shapes, and Jervis could only see Curtis's face and the utter disbelief which clouded his eyes, before the shutter dropped and his face became a cold, impersonal mask.

'Why?' One word, softly spoken, but as the ship lolled gently in a trough, it was like an axe falling on stone.

'Because... because it is useless to go on like this.' Jervis's elation had gone, he wanted to be free from the others and be left in peace. 'You wouldn't alter your mind. So I tried to do what is best for all of us!'

Carla Zecchi sobbed quietly, and Jervis shrugged with sudden impatience. What the hell anyway, they had been dead before. This was just the beginning of reality for them.

He reeled against the wheel, his head dancing with pain as a fist thudded into his cheek.

Duncan caught him by the arm and swung him round, his face twisted with fury.

'Why you dirty little gutless bastard! We pulled you out of the grave, and now you go and louse on us!' He raised his fist again. 'I'll make sure you don't do anything else! At least you're in the right bloody uniform!'

Jervis twisted free, feeling the salt taste of blood on his lips, and ran blindly across the hatch.

He saw Taylor's body jerk from the rail, and tried to dodge his foot as it shot forward to trip him. He fell heavily on the deck and saw the rough planking with sudden clarity, as he lay panting and waiting for the next blow.

Instead, Curtis's harsh voice cut across his confused mind. 'That's enough, Steve!' Then as nothing happened, more quietly, 'Fetch the chart, and bring it on deck.'

Jervis stood up, shaking his head to clear the dizziness from his eyes. Curtis regarded him slowly, with something like pity or shame on his set features.

'I'm putting you under arrest. I don't understand what happened to make you act like this, but you were wrong, and stupid!' Then in a louder voice, 'Sergeant Dunwoody, take this officer below, and see that a guard is mounted. An armed guard!'

Dunwoody rubbed his mouth, his eye blinking. 'Yessir. It'll be a pleasure!'

Jervis stumbled towards the gaping hatch, but darted a glance back at the girl. She was staring at him fixedly, but there was more surprise than relief on her face.

Taylor rubbed his bare arms and followed Jervis with his eyes. 'I dunno why you bothered to live!' he said softly.

Below it was quiet and cool, and Jervis was in the girl's cabin, with the door locked behind him, before he really understood what had happened, or what he had done.

He pressed his head against the smooth planking, and closed his eyes. What would his father think when the story became known? Of how he had sacrificed his comrades because of a girl's hidden promise. 'It doesn't matter!' He spoke aloud, as if repeating a lesson. 'This is ridiculous to act like this. I will explain what really happened when it's all over!' He flung himself down on the bunk, wretched and stunned, as the full realization crushed in on him like a crowd of screaming maniacs.

Curtis sat on the rail and watched the bowsprit once more. It was curious how the ship had changed its outline now that the sun was on a different side. He tried not to look back at the twisting wake, as if he was afraid he might see his hopes and his chance of freedom mocking him from the waves, as the ship swung round towards the invisible shore.

Jervis of all people. It was unthinkable, almost obscene.

Duncan sat hunched under the bulwark, his head resting on his chest. An empty bottle rolled unheeded in the scupper, and occasionally Curtis heard him mutter thickly to himself.

Giulio Zecchi appeared at his side, his small hands deep in his jacket pockets. He waited, like a plump bird, until Curtis turned to face him.

'A big disappointment for you, Lieutenant. I am sorry.'

Curtis did not answer, but waited listlessly, his gaze on the man's dark eyes.

'But it is time we had a talk, I think.' He squared his shoulders, and rocked forward on his toes.

He knows that he's soon going to hold the whip hand, Curtis thought, it was amazing how everything had collapsed, and how calmly he was able to view his failure.

'Well? What have you on your mind?'

The mayor pouted his lower lip. 'When we reach the coast, what will you do?'

'Surrender the ship. What else?'

'I will do what I can for you, Lieutenant.' His tone was almost gracious. 'I may be able to help quite considerably where your wounded are concerned. But I am afraid I can do little about you and your three colleagues. You are rather in a different category.' He smiled thinly. 'But who knows? Perhaps you will be kept as prisoners.'

Curtis stared at him coldly. 'Things have certainly changed for you, Signor Zecchi. Now you will be able to return to your fold as a hero, and one who has proved his worth to the Party and to his German friends! Very fortunate for you!'

He smiled. 'Shall we say that the hasty action of your young officer, for whatever reason he might have had, was an act of grace? It is life, Lieutenant.' He shrugged. 'I am afraid you have only yourself to blame, but, nevertheless, I thank you for your treatment of myself and Carla.' He drew a small cigar from his breast pocket and inserted it delicately between his teeth. 'If only one could always foresee the future!' His glance fell on Duncan's still form. He raised an eyebrow. 'And what of the gallant Australian?'

'He'll be all right,' Curtis answered quietly. 'You need have no fear.'

The mayor smiled and lit his cigar. 'I think that fear is now unnecessary for me. It might be unfortunate for the wounded men if anything was to happen to me, eh?' He walked away, humming to himself.

Curtis clenched his fists and stared wildly at the sun, until he could stand the pain no longer and his eyes were running with tears. Every movement and shipboard noise seemed more pronounced, and even the steady beat of the engine filled him with revulsion. Somehow and somewhere, he had allowed his purpose to be blunted and turned aside by his own over-confidence. He beat a slow tattoo on the rail with his palms, his body shaking with uncontrollable despair. To drive away the fear which had first held him in its grip, he had tried to prove his strength and determination in front of the others, and to justify his actions he had endeavoured to produce an unworkable plan, for which he had neither the training nor the stamina to complete.

For a few moments longer he tortured himself with the weapons of self-pity and frustration, and then tried to bring himself to contemplate the future.

It had been a flimsy enough plan, he knew that, yet with any small remaining spark of luck they might have reached safety, and some of the guilt and remorse would have been lost in the fulfilment of the voyage to the south.

The lookout called shrilly from the masthead, and without enthusiasm or interest, in fact with little feeling of any kind, he lifted the telescope and pointed it in the direction indicated by the man's arm.

A small coaster pushed her way northward along the lip of the sea, her squat bridge and funnel changing shape as she altered course laboriously on another leg of her zigzag. Still further distant, a mere shaft of silver in the sunlight, her escort prowled watchfully, no doubt listening for the unlikely presence of a submarine.

The captain coughed discreetly, and Curtis turned with impatience.

'Well? What d'you want?'

Curtis expected him to behave much as the mayor had done, and was surprised to see the intense expression in the man's small eyes.

'*Signore*, I think I have a part of an idea.' He darted a quick glance around the poop and sat down beside Curtis on the rail. '*Permesso*, but as I said, I think we might find a way out of this.'

Curtis eyed him searchingly. 'Why, Captain? Why should you want to help me?'

'Ah well.' He smiled uncomfortably. 'It is also to help myself you understand! But we Italians are not a warlike people, you must know that. And I think that my country will not wait to be stamped into the dust before it feels it necessary to'—he spread his hands with eloquent understanding—'sign an armistice!'

'Go on.' Curtis was suddenly quite sure of the man's eagerness, and felt that he was being as sincere as he knew how.

'I have sailed this coast for many years, *signore*, and I know many people. For months now there have been rumours about what would happen if your armies land in our country.' He shrugged. 'Well, the time is near I think for the dreams to become real, whether some of us like it or not!' He leaned closer. 'We do not like the Germans, that you already know. It was very fine in the beginning, when our leaders gave us great things and promised us more. But when the German army came to the south, and from the desert, things changed for all of us. They did not trust us, and made many regulations and laws to hold us down. Of course, the *Fascisti* thought it was wonderful,' he spat with his usual ease, 'but the rest of us grew to hate the strutting boots and endless orders. It was like,' he paused, trying to find the right words, 'like the barking of dogs! No, *signore,* the Germans will find themselves alone and unwanted!'

Curtis felt his spirits sink even lower. 'I know all this. It was the only thing that could happen.'

The captain laid a fat finger against his nose and watched Curtis sadly. 'Patience! I am trying to tell you what I, Fausto Macchia, would do, if I were in your feet!'

Curtis's strained face melted into a smile in spite of his misery. From the moment he had boarded the schooner this little captain had remained self-contained and yet comical.

'Very well, Captain. Please continue, although I do not think there is any choice left for me!'

'There is always a choice! Did you notice how little interest that ship and the destroyer took of us? And did you not think it strange that there was no signal?' He smiled, as if sharing a deep secret. 'They do not care any more. Why should they?'

'But what has all this——' But the captain silenced him with a frown.

'Please, *signore*, I am arriving at the end soon. It is ver' difficult for me in a foreign language.'

'You speak it well.' Curtis clasped his hands in his lap and tried to mask his impatience.

'Yes, I do,' he beamed. 'But this is what I have in mind. To the south is the Gargano Peninsula, you know of it?'

'Yes. I had hoped to be past that point by tomorrow morning. After that,' he shrugged wearily, 'but what does it matter now?'

The captain's eyes gleamed like black beads. 'We will make for the peninsula, we will not pass it!' He rocked back on his fat buttocks, until the waves seemed to reach up for him.

He was evidently amused by the perplexed expression on Curtis's face, and he gripped his arm with sudden familiarity.

'We are sailors, you and I. We know nothing of the ways of the land, and the people who live there.' He embraced the sea with an excited hand. 'Here, we are safe. *This* we understand. We will go to the Gargano Peninsula! Ask me why, *signore*!' He was unable to conceal the excitement which shone on his round face and made his chins bounce loosely across his crumpled shirt.

'You tell me. Why?' Curtis wondered how much longer he could put up with the man's behaviour.

'Because the Germans are gone from there!' He studied Curtis's face with relish. 'Yes, *signore*, all gone! They have gone to the fighting further south. The peninsula is a good place to be!'

Curtis was fully alert now. 'It's still a long way away. What about the wounded men?'

'Please, *signore*, I have thought of all that. We will drive the ship faster, the engine can give a little more I think.' He dragged his finger across his pendulous lower lip and held it up like a small child. 'The wind, you feel it? It is from the north! We will spread the sails! You give me the idea when you tell me about furling them correctly!' He jumped to his feet and stared down at Curtis. 'We can get there *before* morning! I have friends there, *signore*. Maybe we can get a doctor, and we can certainly get more water! What is there to lose?'

Curtis stood up and began to pace the deck with quick, nervous strides. What is there to *gain*, I wonder? he thought. Aloud he asked, 'Why do you wish to help me?'

The captain sighed and moved his tongue in his cheek. 'If I help you, *signore*, I keep my ship, and no doubt the British will not bother me? On the other hand, if I go back to the Germans, what will happen? They will use the *Ametisa* and her poor captain until they have no further use for us, and then . . . Boom! Finish! They will leave nothing behind in Italy when they go, that I know!'

Curtis halted in his stride and faced him thoughtfully.

'You really believe you can contact your friends?'

'But of course! I was born in Spigno, I know many people!' He dropped his voice. 'What can be lost by it? If I am wrong,' he kissed his fingers, 'boom! But if all goes well, it is a ver' good plan, yes?'

Curtis grinned, his mind made up. He clapped the captain across the shoulder. 'A *very* good plan! I'll get the chart!'

The captain smiled broadly. 'As you wish. For myself, I have little use for such things!'

Curtis reached down and shook Duncan roughly by the arm. 'Steve! Get up! On your feet, you drunken Aussie!'

Duncan stared at him with bleary eyes, unable to understand the boyish elation on Curtis's face.

'Whassup? We arrived yet?'

'I'm going to have one last try, Steve!' He pulled the grinning captain beside him. 'We had a genius in our midst and didn't know it!'

Duncan staggered to his feet and belched grandly. 'You nuts or somethin'? How can things happen like this? Always when I'm asleep!'

The captain chuckled, no longer afraid of Duncan. 'Me. I never sleep! Only my body sleeps!' He punched the big

Australian playfully on the stomach. 'Your captain a good fella!' He beamed at both of them and then hurried to the wheel.

Duncan shook his head and grimaced sourly. 'What in hell's name has got into him?'

'He's given me an idea, Steve. In fact, I'm going to try and break out after all. Whatever the damned consequences!'

Duncan listened unbelievingly, as the little captain screamed out a string of orders at his depleted crew. Taking the wheel, he spun the spokes with deft eagerness and watched anxiously as his men scrambled up the sagging rigging. The ship veered round, and as the first patched sail was unleashed, the captain gasped with pleasure. As he turned briefly towards the two officers, they saw that his eyes were wet.

'For years I have waited to sail my *Ametisa*! Now for the first time since this accursed war begins, she will fly like a bird!'

Soon the thin jibsails crept skywards from the bowsprit, while aft the poop was darkened by the impressive beauty of the swinging spanker, which even the stains and patches could not spoil. The schooner leaned over on her side and stayed there, as the wind thrust steadily at her new power.

Duncan leaned against the tilting rail and whistled with amazement.

'Well, can you beat that! These damned Eye-ties! He makes the flamin' ship move an' now he's cryin'! That really beats everythin'!'

Curtis propelled him to the hatch. 'Get George and tell him the sky's the limit! I want every last bit of power! And you lay off a new course that'll take us to the north-east of the Gargano Peninsula!'

Duncan bit his lip and watched the new light which gleamed from Curtis's eyes.

'Don't bank too much on this, Ralph! It might not come off you know.'

But Curtis lifted his head with complete confidence and calm.

'What is there to lose now?' he asked simply.

Duncan shouted Curtis's instructions to Taylor's incredulous face above the roar of the diesel, and was only sure that he had understood when the little man seized his hand and danced dangerously on the oily catwalk.

He heard a series of disjointed yelps. '... another chance! Show the bleedin' ...' and nodded in agreement.

He ran quickly to the after-hatch ducking his head beneath

the long, unfamiliar boom, and glanced up at the towering sail. His craggy face creased into a reluctant smile.

'Good on yer, you little Eye-tie sea-cook! But I'll believe it all when I see it!'

He was about to step into the cabin when he stiffened, as Jervis called through the opposite door.

'Is that you, Steve? Can I speak to you for a moment?'

Duncan's smile vanished, and he paused uncertainly in the sloping passage-way.

'Please, Steve. I want to try and explain!'

Duncan's eyes met those of the soldier who sat crouched outside the door. He was the one with half his hand missing. Duncan had seen him moving unsurely about the deck gazing dazedly at the fat dressing on the end of his arm. Duncan remembered the water, and his face hardened.

'It's me! Ian!' the voice called again.

Duncan patted the soldier's shoulder vaguely and moved towards the chart. Over his shoulder he called, 'Never heard of him!' He slammed the door behind him and stared down at the chart, his eyes angry. 'Blast the ruddy war!' he said.

True to the captain's promise, the *Ametisa* had taken on new life, and with her frayed rigging thrumming in the wind and her deck beams shuddering to the increased vibration of the engine, she flung herself joyfully across the water.

Curtis stayed with the vigilant captain, the chart folded beneath his arm and an unlit pipe clamped between his strong teeth. Never before, not even on the most hazardous operation, had he felt the agony of passing time. Each unfamiliar movement by one of the soldiers, or a change of expression on the captain's face, made him steel himself in readiness for a change of plans to meet a new crisis. A small fishing fleet, a mere cluster of black dots in the distance, passed with maddening slowness, and he thought it typical of fishermen the world over to carry on with their trade regardless of the world's happenings.

Signor Zecchi came on deck and sniffed the air with obvious satisfaction.

Curtis spoke softly to the plump man at his side. 'Not a word to him about what we're doing. Not yet at any rate.' He was not even sure himself why he felt such uneasiness at the mayor's presence, but something about the man's complete self-confidence and the bland lack of expression on his smooth face, made him cautious.

'We are moving nicely, Lieutenant. It is making a great difference to set the sails so.'

'Yes. With this following wind we are getting another four knots out of her.'

'When do you expect to make a landfall?' The question was light, yet Curtis sensed the strain in his voice.

'It is hard to say exactly. We have drifted quite a bit. And of course the navigation is quite difficult under these circumstances.'

Signor Zecchi's eyes watched him closely. 'Perhaps we shall sight a patrol ship soon. It would be advisable to signal her if so. My daughter and I could transfer to more comfortable quarters, and you would receive better assistance for your charges.'

'Perhaps.' And we would be clapped in irons, he thought. 'I expect that all major war vessels will be congregating in the south.'

'It is a pity we have no radio aboard. It would be good to know what is happening down there.'

Curtis sensed a challenge being offered, and smiled briefly. 'There can be little doubt about the final outcome, surely? Whatever happens to us, nothing can stop the Allied armies now. If your country persists in its resistance, it will suffer much damage and misery.'

'The battle is not over yet, Lieutenant!' His voice was stiff. 'The Germans will not give up without a fight!'

'I see. You mean you've already thought that your people might give up?'

'Never!' The black eyes flashed with sudden anger. 'We are of one mind! One basic principle binds us in a common shield against the invader!'

Curtis grinned. 'Calm yourself, please! You're not addressing a political rally now!'

Behind him the captain chuckled, and the mayor glared fiercely towards him.

'You will do well to mind your manners, Captain! I have a good memory!'

The captain stared calmly at the sails. 'Forgive me, *signore*. I am only an ignorant sailor.'

The mayor snorted, and with his hands bunched into his pockets, he stalked forward towards the fo'c'sle.

The captain watched him go. His eyes were narrow slits when he spoke.

'I think maybe it would be better if he did not reach our destination!'

'No. We cannot blame him for his opinions. Besides,' he smiled wearily, 'we don't know what is going on behind us. He has been missed by his friends, and for all we know, they might have seen through our whole scheme.'

'Hmmm!' He was unconvinced. 'Tell me, *signore*, did you see that dock blow up? The one in Vigoria?'

'No. We were clear by then.'

'It must be a terrible thing to carry out such destruction.' The captain studied Curtis curiously. 'Does it bother you at all?'

'It is war. It is never good to remember things like that.'

The captain laughed with sudden gaiety. 'You are not like the Germans! They would be boasting of their achievements by now, if they were in your position!'

Carla Zecchi walked quickly across the poop from the hold. She stood momentarily by the rail, breathing deeply, her head held upwards against the blue sky.

Curtis saw the dress tighten across her rounded breasts with each breath, and felt his heart beat with excitement which he was unable to control. She's lovely, he thought. So slim and yielding, and yet in some ways harder than all of us.

I wonder what she thinks about me? I practically accused her of sabotaging the water supply. It seemed the only explanation at the time. He walked slowly towards her, and stood just behind her at the rail.

As his shadow fell across her body she turned and looked up at him. He had expected animosity, or open hostility, but her eyes held only a strange sadness.

'How are the wounded, *signorina*?' His voice was almost gruff, and he felt clumsy beside her.

'The same. They are all very strong men fortunately. I think they will survive the journey.'

'I see.'

Curtis stared at the water as it surged and gurgled along the wooden hull. He tried to think of something to say, but her unwavering eyes made thought difficult.

'In England you would talk about the weather?'

He darted a quick glance at her, expecting taunts or sarcasm.

She smiled gravely, her small teeth gleaming. 'What is it you wish to say to me? If it is an apology, I would rather hear about the weather!'

He laughed bitterly. 'Nevertheless, I *am* sorry about all that has happened to you. You have been a tremendous help right from the start. I am sure that had my duty permitted otherwise, things might have been very different.' He paused, again uncertain of how to continue.

She turned her head away from him, and her tanned neck was close to his face. Painfully close it seemed.

'Will you try to escape again when we reach the land?' Her voice was soft. 'You will surely not allow yourself to be taken prisoner now that you have got so far?'

'I don't know yet what I shall do.'

She twisted round again to face him, her eyes puzzled. 'That I find hard to believe. You do not strike me as a man who fails to make preparations.'

Curtis grinned awkwardly. 'You forget. We are enemies.'

'Yes, that is so. I wish it could be otherwise.'

He studied her face with sudden intentness. 'I believe you meant that!'

'Perhaps. I have had much time to think on this ship. And I know you have done what you had to do. Just as my father has acted with devotion and loyalty in the past.' She shook her head angrily and the plait danced down her back. 'The past! It is the future which is so terrifying!' She looked straight into his eyes. 'For all of us!'

She moved as if to leave him, and he knew that he needed her to stay.

'Perhaps after the war we may meet again? Things might be different then.'

'Let us not even talk of the future, please!' Her eyes were filled with concern. 'But I will tell you one thing.' She was facing the sea once more, and he had to bend his head to catch the words. 'I am glad that I have known you.' She moved aside, as he half reached out to touch her. 'Let us leave it at that. For us there may be no future at all, so let us be content.' She almost ran back to the hold, and Curtis was left staring blankly at the empty deck.

It was the final twist of fate. If he had found such a girl before . . . in other circumstances. He halted his racing thoughts. There could be no other girl. But she had tried to tell him that hope was wasted. When the world shuddered in its torment, there was no longer any room for the little people and their desires.

Duncan swayed towards him, his boots thudding on the sloping deck.

'Hey, Ralph! What's into you?' He stood straddle-legged by the lee rail, his eyes squinting against the glare.

Curtis shrugged heavily. How could he even begin to explain?

'I'm tired, that's all. How's everything going?'

'Fair. There's another meal on the way, an' most of the pongoes are tryin' to get some sleep. If only we could give 'em a bit of professional treatment, they'd be fine.' He dropped his voice. 'D'you really think we've got a chance?'

Curtis hid the surprise which welled up inside him. It was odd to see the defeat on Duncan's face. He had always been the driver; the unbreakable rock around which their small team had been built, and now he had changed.

'Well, we've a chance of some sort. That's all I can tell you.'

Duncan smiled grimly. 'It's certainly done wonders for you anyway. You look like a new bloke. At one time I thought you were startin' to throw a fit of tantrums!'

'I was.' Curtis's voice was quiet. 'I think this business has been a real test for all of us.'

'Jesus! It's one I can do without!' He stared morosely at the sea. 'It's like we're not movin'. I wish to God we had a real boat!'

Taylor climbed out of his hatchway and nodded to them. 'Nice day, all!' He sauntered across, wiping his filthy hands on a signal flag. 'Why the glum faces then? I thought we was all fixed up.'

Curtis looked at them and pointed to the horizon. 'When that starts to darken, I'll feel a bit better. In any case, don't breathe a word to anyone about our idea. Not even to the soldiers. No need to raise their hopes unnecessarily.'

Duncan nodded his huge head. 'I was just thinkin'. It's queer without Ian. Sort of busted up the team, I mean.'

'Maybe there was more to it than we know, Steve. He's new to this sort of thing, remember.'

'We was all new once, Skipper!' Taylor's eyes gleamed with sudden fury. 'It was all wrong! I feel all let down like!' He waved the flag vaguely. 'No, 'e didn't 'ave ter do that!'

'We'll talk about it later.'

'Might not be time, Ralph.' Duncan rubbed his chin. 'If we run into trouble, I'm makin' a break for it.'

The others regarded him thoughtfully.

Taylor was the first to speak. 'Wivout us, yer mean?' He sounded incredulous.

Curtis smiled with a calmness he did not feel. 'When the time comes, we'll stay a team. Got that?'

Duncan sighed deeply. 'You're nuts, Ralph. But we'll see.'

Taylor relaxed, his thin face dark with indignation. 'An' I should fink so, too! We ain't in the blessed outback now yer know! This is the Royal bloody Navy, ain't it?'

Curtis strode back to the wheel, his heart pounding. For the first time in his life he knew what it was to feel a leader. They really *did* need him! Before this he had always regarded his position as a mere clause in an act, a signature on a piece of paper.

He looked towards the open hold, hoping to see the girl again, and suddenly began to whistle.

The darkness was so complete that the schooner was enclosed and encircled, a world apart, sharing the night only with the silver crescent of the moon, which hung cold and aloof over the main-truck. The wind had lost its persistent force, and came instead in short, blustery puffs, which whipped the black oily surface of the sea into a shimmering mass of dancing catspaws, and splintered the moon's faint reflection into a broken necklace of silver, whilst above the decks, the limp sails billowed suddenly into shape, the coarse canvas booming and cracking with fury, before falling loose and useless as before.

The beat of the engine had softened into a slow confident rumble, and added to the general feeling of tenseness which hung over the vessel as it crept towards the as yet invisible shore.

Curtis shivered slightly and turned up the collar of his jacket.

'How long now, d'you think?' He spoke with quiet fierceness to the Italian captain, who merely shrugged his shoulders, his face hidden in the darkness.

'Half hour, maybe less. It is a long time since I was here.'

Curtis strained his eyes along the ship's length, as if by so doing he might suddenly see his objective. He was getting jumpy again, and tried to reason calmly with the problem which faced him.

'What sort of place is this anyway?' he asked, and immediately regretted the impulse. He had already examined the chart in great detail with Duncan, and had got a fairly clear picture from the captain, too. But now that supposition and

planning had passed by and the whole operation was budding
into a grim reality, he felt he wanted to be assured once more.

The captain sighed and glanced over the helmsman's stooped
shoulder at the dim binnacle light.

'It is but a tiny place. 'Bout the size of the village where we all
met.' He chuckled to himself. 'Nothing there except a bit of a
jetty and a few fishing boats. Ver' poor place, forgotten, useless.
But I think it will suit our purpose.' He lapsed into silence again.

Duncan padded out of the darkness of the half-deck and
peered down at the compass.

'I've spoken to the pongoes an' told 'em what we're tryin' to
do. Most of 'em seemed to think you're a mug for botherin'
about 'em, but I think that they realize it's the only thing to do
now.'

'How are our prisoners? Keeping quiet?'

'I went along to see that they were O.K. an' had been fed.
That Jerry, Beck, or whatever his name is, kicked up a fuss of
course, but I gave him one of his uniforms to wear, an' think that
cheered him up a bit. The master race didn't take very kindly to
sitting in his underpants in front of his friends!'

Another shadow glided silently along the poop, and Curtis
caught the faint scent of the girl's hair as she crossed to his side.

'Soon now?' she enquired. 'I cannot keep still for wondering
what will happen next.'

They all jumped as the captain grunted and pointed towards
the bows with evident satisfaction. A light stabbed the darkness
half-heartedly three times and then left them in darkness once
more.

Curtis shook his head with admiration. 'That was Vieste
Light? You certainly know this coast very well, Captain!'

'What did I tell you, *signore*? I do not need charts! I can smell
my way!'

'Say, how come we've only just seen that light?' Duncan
sounded irritable.

'Simple, my friend! It has been hid by the headland. Now we
are running into a tiny bay, the one I showed you on the chart.
North-west of Vieste.'

The light stabbed the night again. Three flashes apparently
suspended in the curtain of night.

The old grey-headed seaman scuttled down from the fo'c'sle
and called softly to the captain.

'He can see the coast. He has good eyes, that one!'

He rapped out an order and his men began to shorten sail, the noise of the clattering blocks and stiff canvas against the spars seeming to drown even the note of the engine.

Curtis felt the girl brush against his sleeve, and looked down at the pale oval of her face. When the light flashed its endless signal again, he saw the twin reflections in her dark eyes.

'What do you wish me to do?'

'You will stay aboard when I go ashore with the captain. I hope I shall not be long.' He wondered why he was telling her all this, but he realized that since she had joined him on the poop, he had ceased to worry about what he had to do.

He saw her bared teeth.

'I said that you would be a man to make plans! I was very right, yes?'

'I don't like this, Ralph!' Duncan interrupted hoarsely, as the dark shadow of the land seemed to grow out of the night itself. 'How can this joker know where he's goin'?'

Curtis shrugged. 'Well, it's too late now, Steve. No turning back.'

Duncan grunted and made his way forward to check the mooring lines.

Curtis could almost feel the weight of the land, which grew darker and larger and more menacing with each second that passed. Already he could see the faint arm of the bay reaching out on the port beam, and even the wind had lost them, muffled perhaps by the hidden hills and cliffs ahead.

The captain took over the wheel and peered watchfully over the rail as the ship glided evenly through the calm water. Everyone was silent, and conscious of the lap of water against the hull and the clank of chain as the captain eased the wheel a spoke one way and then back.

The girl gasped and involuntarily gripped Curtis's arm, as without warning, the white hull of an anchored boat loomed out of the night and passed eerily down the *Ametisa*'s side.

The captain spun the wheel and jerked the lever at his side. The engine died away into an uneven neutral, and they heard the swish of water under the stem as the schooner turned slightly in her course and dodged another moored vessel.

He grunted. 'Even less boats here than when I came before!' His tone was almost conversational and showing nothing of the strain of piloting the schooner into an unlighted cove amongst anchored fishing boats.

Curtis smiled, and was conscious of the fact that Carla Zecchi had not removed her hand from his arm. I must be mad, he thought. To think about her now, when at any moment we may be picked up in a searchlight and shot to pieces.

A thin grey finger of jetty loomed up practically under the bowsprit, and as the captain put the engine astern, and a rope fender was dropped between the hull and the crumbling stonework, one of the seamen vanished over the side and could faintly be seen running towards a stone bollard, dragging behind him the huge eye of the ship's head-rope.

Curtis felt a vague sensation of anticlimax, as another man secured the ship by the stern and the captain allowed the engine to shudder into complete silence.

The schooner creaked and groaned against her fenders, and the seamen stood in a group by the rail, staring curiously at their homeland.

'Well, *signore*? Here we are. No soldiers an' no *Fascisti*!' He laughed. 'Now we go ashore, eh?'

Curtis felt Carla's hand slide away, and watched her as she walked to the rail. She was looking up at the dark shapes of the hills, only faintly visible against the starred pattern of the sky.

He drew Duncan aside and tried to see the expression on the man's face. 'You'll stay here as we arranged, Steve,' he began slowly, 'and make sure that nobody gets ashore. I've told the mayor to co-operate with you, so you won't have to use any force.'

'Have you any idea what you hope to do out there?'

'The captain and I will have a scout round and see if we can find a doctor. He says he's got plenty of contacts hereabouts, and I imagine from what he says, that the locals are a pretty independent lot. It's obviously true that the Jerries *have* left here, they'd never allow such a slipshod sort of security!'

'Can't I come with you? I hate the idea of bein' cooped up with all these jokers!'

'Now we've already settled all that.' A slight hardness crept into his voice. 'If anything goes wrong, you'll be in charge, so you must be ready to act accordingly!'

The captain ambled over to them and gestured towards the jetty. One of his men was holding what appeared to be a glistening snake above his head and grinning broadly.

'The fresh water, *signore*! She is connected to the jetty by that hose!'

Curtis sighed with relief. 'Get cracking on that, Steve. Have the tank filled up, and I'll get going for a doctor.'

Sergeant Dunwoody saluted stiffly in the darkness. 'You off, sir?'

'Yes. My Number One's in charge now. Keep all our people off the deck, and see that all the hatchways remain covered. You can take the Schmeisser yourself, Sergeant, and station yourself up by the fo'c'sle.'

He turned back to Duncan, relieved to be moving. 'So long, Steve. I'll try not to hang about!'

There was a sudden disturbance by the aft hatch, and Signor Zecchi ran excitedly across the deck.

'What is the meaning of this, Lieutenant? Where are you going? I insist on going with you!'

Duncan growled warningly, but Curtis raised his hand calmly. 'Please be quiet! I came back to the coast as I promised. For the wounded, not for you, you understand?'

The man swayed and half stepped towards the darkened rail. 'But this is an outrage! I must get ashore now!' He dropped his voice to an unexpected tone of pleading. 'I will not make any trouble.'

His daughter moved to his side. 'It is all right, Papa! You must not get excited.'

Curtis was aware that the captain was waiting impatiently by the rail. 'I must go,' he said shortly. 'No one goes ashore without my permission, and that's final!' He nodded to the girl, and followed the captain on to the jetty.

The feel of the rough stones beneath his feet made him falter and glance back at the indistinct shape of the little schooner, but a hand pulled at his arm and the captain muttered urgently. 'Come! It is nearly two of the clock. We must hurry!'

They stumbled along the jetty's hundred yards and began to climb up a narrow winding roadway, the surface of which was pitted and scarred with wheel-ruts and deep pot-holes.

Overhead they heard the drone of high-flying aircraft, and Curtis glanced up in time to see the shadow of one flit across the moon like an evil bat.

Bombers, he thought breathlessly, as his boots tripped and stumbled across the road. Perhaps they were British planes, and the idea gave him an unreasoning comfort.

They climbed in silence, Curtis keeping his eyes on the road, or on the broad, sweat-stained back of the Italian captain.

The village was even poorer than the one he had already seen, and he was amazed at the flimsy rough-boarded hovels which were hunched on the side of the hills, overlooking the inlet. A dog whined dismally in the distance, and once Curtis thought he heard a child cry out briefly in one of the dwellings. Nets and various oddments of fishing gear, all crude and much repaired, lay heaped between the low rooftops, and they had to climb and duck over several piles, before the captain could find his way on to the main road through the village. There were no motor vehicles of any kind to be seen, and only once did Curtis see any building constructed of concrete.

He stopped dead in his tracks and pulled the captain close. The building was smooth and grey, with small black slits for windows.

'Hold it!' he gasped. 'That's a pillbox, a gun-mounting, or something!'

With something like a swagger the captain walked over to the concrete emplacement and kicked it with his shoe. He chuckled. 'See? Empty, like their promises! They have all left, I tell you!'

They hurried on, and Curtis wondered what the captain might have said if some Germans had come out of the pillbox to see who was knocking at such a late hour.

'Ah! There it is!'

Curtis almost collided with the little man, as he halted and pointed ahead.

'For one second, *signore*, even I was beginning to think I had lost my way!'

The small church was almost invisible against the hillside, and only the small bell-tower broke its dim craggy outline.

They passed around the low side, and the captain pointed at a small extension at the rear.

'I must see the priest, you understand. Only he can help us.' He peered at Curtis with sudden eagerness. 'You trust me, *signore*?'

Curtis nodded wearily. 'Go ahead. But how d'you know it's the same priest who was here before?'

He shrugged. 'I do not. But we will try caution, and if that fails, we will try the revolver!'

He motioned Curtis back into the shadows of the church, and then began to pound gently on the door.

In the stillness of the night it sounded like a gun being fired, and Curtis tore his eye from the captain to look back along the roadway. There was only the pillbox, white in the moonlight, to remind him where he was, and but for the distant murmur of the sea, he could have been anywhere.

A light flickered beneath the heavy door, and Curtis heard the captain speaking softly through a small grille which was suddenly lighted by a lantern from within.

A chain clattered, and the door was opened slowly to reveal a tall, thin figure in the traditional black robe of a priest. His features were thin and yellow against the raised lantern, and the sparse hair on his narrow head stuck out above his ears like little tufts of white feathers.

The captain grinned with obvious relief. 'It is Father Bernucci! We are saved!'

Curtis felt the man's deep-set eyes watching him, as the captain rattled off a lengthy explanation, with many gestures at Curtis and towards the sea.

The old man nodded slowly and beckoned them both inside.

It was cold inside the unlighted porchway, and it was with amazement that Curtis found himself being ushered into a low beamed room, lit by candles and by the cheerful flicker of a dying fire. The walls were lined with old, leather-bound volumes and several faded pictures, and the plain, stone-flagged floor was comfortably decorated by two long woven mats.

The priest continued to question the captain, as he added a log to the fire and then laid cheese, wine and a dark loaf on the carved table.

Curtis sank into the high-backed chair and drank the wine with quiet relish. He was aware of the fatigue which hovered just behind his eyes and the difficulty he had in focussing on the long-stemmed glass in his hand.

The priest sat stiffly on a bench facing him, his bony hands resting in his lap. A large crucifix swung from his neck and glittered in the candlelight.

Curtis felt his eyelids drooping. Another squadron of bombers droned overhead, or perhaps it was the same group going back, their evil work done and their youthful crews returning to their beds.

The priest suddenly spoke, his voice soft and husky, and his English so perfect, that Curtis was startled into attention.

'I have listened to Fausto Macchia, and I think I understand what has happened.' The old eyes rested on Curtis's uniform in a brief appraisal. 'You are an enemy of this country, but,' he lifted a finger as Curtis leaned forward, 'I think it will not be so for long. Be that as it may, I will help you, and at once.'

'That is most kind of you, Father. The wounded soldiers need proper attention, and more than I can give them.'

'If you had not come ashore like this, how many of them might have died?' The eyes were unwavering.

The captain interrupted with a laugh. 'Less than half! Yet the lieutenant here has risked his own life and everyone else's for the sake of those few!'

'I was not prepared to take such a risk, that's all,' Curtis answered simply.

'Quite so, my son. It is strange what war will do to us as individuals. In war, the young often feel they have no real mission, and yet,' he fingered the gold cross thoughtfully, 'perhaps you at least, have been allotted your task to perform.'

He wrote slowly on a sheet of paper, and when he had finished, he glanced at Curtis, his eyes enquiring. 'You would like to see what I have written? It is a message for my friend. He is the doctor.'

'I trust you, Father.' He found that he meant it. 'Will there be any Carabinieri on the roads tonight?'

The priest smiled sadly. 'They have been conscripted into the army. They left this morning!'

He handed the message to the captain. 'Take this to the doctor, Fausto. You know his house.'

The captain tucked it into his shirt. 'Have you still got your old bicycle, Padre?'

The priest nodded. 'Take it, Fausto. It will help to remove some of the signs of good living from you.'

The captain picked up his cap and walked to the door. 'This will not take long, Lieutenant. I shall be back to the ship with the doctor within an hour!'

'Right. I'll find my way back there now, and have the wounded prepared for immediate treatment.'

He took the priest's dry hand. 'And thank you, Father, for everything.'

'For everything?' The priest cocked his head on one side. 'For the help, do you mean? Or for the faith?'

He was still smiling as Curtis stumbled out into the darkness and started to feel his way down the road to the village and the sea.

Chapter 10

DUNCAN SAT UNCOMFORTABLY on the stone bollard opposite the schooner's bows and stared into the shadows at the far end of the jetty. An unlit cheroot hung from one corner of his mouth and his hands lay spread across his knees. Occasionally he looked across at the ship, as an unusual noise or movement caught his attention, but otherwise he remained wrapped in his own concentrated thoughts.

It seemed ages since the skipper had gone up towards the silent village, although he knew that it could not have been more than half an hour or so. At first, he had driven the Italian sailors like mad to get the water tank filled, and he had kept the others occupied with boiling water and preparing the more seriously wounded for inspection. He shifted his buttocks angrily on the cold stone. It was damned unlikely that any such doctor would be available. More likely a couple of platoons of Jerry soldiers.

The corporal, his head wrapped in a balaclava, crossed the jetty, his studded boots clinking on the stones, and halted beside him.

'Give you a break, sir?' The man stared over Duncan's shoulder with practised eye.

'Fair enough.' Duncan stood up and stretched. 'I'll go and give the ship a shake-up!'

He climbed over the gunwale and walked carefully to the hold. Removing the canvas which hid the lights beneath, he lowered himself into the too-familiar place, which to him had become a symbol of suffering and discomfort.

The girl was there he saw, and with Taylor was busy with one of the wounded. It was damned odd, the way that she and the skipper looked at each other.

Taylor glanced up and grimaced. He had washed his hands and arms free of engine filth, and compared to his body, they gleamed with unnatural whiteness under the lamplight.

'Skipper back?' he asked shortly.

Duncan shook his head and took a dirty dressing from the girl. He threw it quickly into a pail, aware of the sickly smell which seemed to pervade the hold.

Carla Zecchi sat back on her haunches and blew a loose strand of hair from her face. 'I'm getting stiff!' She tried to smile, but the tiredness was too strong for her. 'I wish we had just one more helper.'

Duncan grunted. She probably meant Ralph, he decided. 'Well, perhaps the doctor *will* come,' he said. 'But we must be ready for the worst.'

'You're a cheerful one!' Taylor covered the soldier with a blanket and stood up. 'You'll 'ave me in stitches, you will!'

'I am sorry about Ian.' She looked at both of them anxiously. 'It was a strange thing to do.'

Duncan could see that she wanted to ask him something, but his face remained impassive.

'I s'pect he wanted to stretch 'is legs, miss!' Taylor said, and moved across to the next man. He stooped down, his sharp eyes moving despairingly from the bandages on the soldier's legs to the expression of glassy concentration in his eyes. He grinned. ''Ere, mate, let's 'ave a look at yer. Doctor's comin' to fix yer up!'

The soldier moved his white lips and a thin stream of saliva ran down his chin.

'What the hell d'you want to tell the poor joker that for?' Duncan hissed down at him, his eyes hard. 'You'll do him no good if the bloke doesn't arrive!'

Taylor continued to grin at the soldier. "E'll come,' he said softly. 'Skipper'll get somebody.' Under his breath he added, "E's *got* to!'

Duncan stood up and cursed as his head collided with a beam. He was now so much on edge that he felt he had to be doing something.

'I'm goin' on deck to have another prowl round,' he said. 'This hangin' about is drivin' me up the creek!'

As he swung round to leave the girl caught his arm, her eyes steady with resolve. 'I should like to speak to Ian, please. I think it might help. He must be very worried about all this.'

Duncan shrugged. 'Suit yourself. I don't suppose Ralph'd mind. And in any case, I'm in charge at the moment!'

'I'm sure he wouldn't mind anyway,' she answered softly. 'And thank you.'

Taylor watched them go. 'Can't do any more 'ere till we get some more dressin's,' he called, 'so I'll keep an eye on things 'ere!'

'You've been a wonderful help,' she said. 'You understand these men.'

Taylor moved his feet uncomfortably. 'That's right, miss. Proper Florence Nightingale I am!'

It seemed even darker on deck, and the moon had moved behind the hills at the back of the village.

They climbed down the aft hatch and the soldier outside the cabin door yawned and nodded companionably.

'How are you, digger?' Duncan peered at the man's bandaged hand.

'Could do wiv a drink, sir.'

'Nip off an' have one then. We shall be down here for a bit.'

The hatch closed and Duncan reached out for the key which protruded from the lock on the cabin door.

'Want me to come with you?' His tone was gruff, but the uneasiness was clear to her.

'I wish you would. It would make things easier for all of us.'

Duncan swallowed and slammed open the door with unnecessary violence.

Jervis jumped up from the bunk, his eyes startled.

'Carla! And . . . and Steve!' He held out his hands, his mouth quivering. 'Thank God you've come down!'

'Her idea.' Duncan folded his arms and eyed him coolly.

Jervis turned to the girl. 'Where are we? What's happening?

I've been nearly going mad in here!'

'We have arrived at some small place that the captain knows. We have got some water,' she dropped her eyes, 'and perhaps a doctor may be found also.'

Jervis stared at her incredulously. 'But what about the Germans!'

'They are not in this place apparently.'

'So your little bit of stupidity misfired, Ian.' Duncan's face was hard and unyielding.

'Why did you do it, Ian?' she asked gently. 'Why did you not trust your own captain? He is a strange man, but ... but ...' Her lashes dropped with sudden embarrassment. '... he has suffered much for all this.'

Jervis's jaw dropped. 'What are you saying? How can you of all people talk like this?'

'What do you mean, Ian?' She held her slender body erect, her small chin high. 'What are you suggesting?'

Duncan had tensed. 'Yeah, what in hell's name are you babbling now?'

'But I did this for you!' Jervis still stared at her. 'And now everything's changed!' He ran his fingers through his hair desperately. 'I didn't realize we were still going to try to get away!'

Duncan leaned his back against the door as someone moved quietly in the passage. These soldiers don't take long to get a drink, he thought.

'I am only a passenger ... a prisoner, call me what you like.' She tossed her head impatiently. 'But I understand what your captain is trying to do, and I think he is right. My father may think otherwise now, but later on he may be glad all this had happened.' She lowered her voice. 'You were wrong to do what you did!'

Jervis's face collapsed. 'But I did it for you, Carla! I didn't want you to be punished for ... for what you did with the water! But it was all wasted, I——'

She crossed the cabin and seized his hand 'What are you saying? I did not touch the water! I did not even know where it was!'

Duncan breathed out explosively. 'Hold it! D'you mean, Ian, that you just admitted to this, to cover up for her?'

They both turned to him like defiant children.

'I was with the wounded all the time,' she said hotly, 'I could not have done it, even if I had wanted!'

Duncan rubbed his chin, his brain jumping madly. 'Well, if neither of you did it...' He paused, his eyes suddenly anxious.

'Somebody else...' Carla's voice trailed away, and the resistance seemed to drain from her.

They looked at each other. Jervis was the first to speak.

'You think it was your father?'

'Of course she does! Who else?' Duncan jumped for the door, his face wild. He twisted the handle, but nothing happened.

Carla and Jervis stared at Duncan's hand on the door. Neither spoke, and silence in the cabin was complete and menacing.

They all heard the clatter of feet on the ladder and the sound of hurried steps across the deck.

'Here! Open the door!'

Duncan suddenly burst into life, the reality of the new danger making his eyes blaze with fury. He pulled the pistol from his belt, but with a shake of his head he threw his weight against the door.

'Can't risk the sound of a shot!' he gasped, as he drew back and hurled himself once more at the door. There was a splintering crash, and he burst out into the passage.

Followed by the others, but unaware of them, Duncan ran on deck, his eyes wide as he stared round at the silent shadows. He ran wildly along the deck, peering from side to side and over at the deserted jetty.

At that moment Jervis, who had run to the fo'c'sle, called out, his voice shaky.

'Here, Steve! Quick, the sergeant!'

They found Sergeant Dunwoody lying on his side in a crumpled heap, his bandages white against the blackness of the raised fo'c'sle.

'He's still breathing,' commented Duncan briefly as he stood up. 'I think he's had a crack over the head.' Duncan was thinking furiously. 'Call some help from the hold, Ian. I'm goin' to look for somebody!'

He stared at the girl's frightened face, 'I don't know how much you've had to do with this, but I promise you that——' He broke off, as a sudden burst of firing cut across the jetty.

'God! The Schmeisser!' Duncan pulled out the pistol and

vaulted over the bulwark, to land crouching on the jetty.

He dimly heard the girl sob and say, 'He wouldn't, Ian! It *can't* be him!' before he started to inch his way along the lip of the stonework, his shoulders hunched and the pistol unwavering in his hand.

The corporal appeared to be asleep. One hand was beneath his bandaged head, and the balaclava lay unheeded by the stone bollard at his feet. Duncan stepped over him, his teeth bared as he searched the darkness at the end of the jetty. There was nothing he could do for the corporal, the burst of bullets from the automatic pistol had practically decapitated him.

Fired from behind, too, he thought coldly, as he ran on into the sandbank beyond the jetty. He halted, breathing fast. No sound, but for the gentle lap of water against the beach and the barking of a dog, came to his straining ears, although as he listened, his head bent forward, he imagined that he could hear a stone falling on the cliffs, far to his right.

Taylor panted out of the night behind him, his eyes dark blobs on his pale face.

'Get 'im? Where's 'e gone?'

Duncan shrugged. 'God knows!'

Taylor stared round the unfamiliar roadway, his shoulders jerking with pent up sorrow and rage. 'The bastard! The rotten, stinkin' bastard! The poor bloke never 'ad a chance!'

Duncan hissed, 'Steady! Someone's runnin' this way!'

They froze by the roadside and then Duncan stepped forward. 'It's the skipper,' he said quickly.

Curtis loomed up almost at their side before they could actually see his anxious features.

'What's happened? That shooting...' He was breathing fast, and had obviously been running for some time.

They heard the laboured whine of a car engine, and then, as they turned towards the cliff road, an ancient Fiat bounced around the corner and drove recklessly towards the sea.

'It's the doctor, thank God!' muttered Curtis as he caught a glimpse of the Italian captain's fat face through the open window. He turned back to Duncan.

'Come on, man! Spit it out!'

'Zecchi's jumped us! Grabbed the Schmeisser and killed the corporal!' He waved towards the sloping hillside road. 'He's up there somewhere!' He turned to Curtis, his voice unnaturally earnest. 'I couldn't help it, Ralph! I never gave it a thought!'

'What about Carla, the girl?'

'Aboard. I don't think she had anythin' to do with it. He'd not have left her behind.'

The car skidded to a halt, its engine hissing. Curtis reached it in two strides. He saw a small, bird-faced man in a dark suit behind the wheel.

'*Medico!*' began the captain proudly, then catching sight of the others and the drawn guns, 'What 'appens, *signore*? Trouble?'

'Never mind that!' Curtis's voice was terse. 'Get to the ship.' He nodded briefly to the doctor. 'Very pleased to see you, sir. Please do all you can for those men.'

The doctor ducked his head and grinned. 'Pleasure!'

Curtis turned to the captain. 'That road, where does it lead?'

'That one? To Vieste. It is about ten kilometres from here.'

'Are there any police there, d'you think?'

'There could be,' he nodded quickly. 'It is likely.'

Curtis stood back. 'Go to the ship then. We must carry on and catch him before he reaches help.'

The car moved off, the captain obviously eager to know what was happening.

He looked from Duncan to Taylor. 'Right, let's go. We've got to catch him, and that's all there is to it!'

'But, God, it'll be dawn soon! We've gotta get clear!' Duncan stared wildly as Curtis turned as if to go.

'And how far d'you think we'll get, once he's telephoned for assistance! Now come on. Move!'

They started to run along the road, their feet keeping a muffled rhythm in the dust as they turned the corner and pounded up the hill. Curtis's breath was strangely calm, and although he was outwardly alert and watchful, he kept thinking of the girl. She had nothing to do with it, Duncan had said. It was a small light in this terrible darkness.

'Wot's the use?' Taylor spoke between his set teeth. ''E might 'ave cut across the 'ill.'

Curtis shook his head and increased the pace. 'He's not cut out for this sort of thing, and we're supposed to be fit! And don't forget that he's armed!'

They ran on.

The road got narrower, and the countryside was completely

open and windswept. There were no dwellings of any sort, and
even the grass on the slopes was mere stubble and weed. There
was no cover there.

The moon showed itself again as they topped the rise, and
cast a feeble glow over the landscape, leaving the sea dark and
shapeless, like a velvet cloak.

Taylor stumbled and fell, and for a few seconds lay winded
and gasping on the dirt. He was aware of the sharp pain over his
ribs, and remembered the hand grenade inside his blouse. He
saw the other two running on, Curtis merely glancing back to see
that he was all right, and then beckoning sharply with his hand.

He staggered to his feet, cursing breathlessly. For a moment
he was reminded of his rough childhood in the East End, and his
endless search for manhood. Before he could join the gang in his
street, he had been made to fight a boy much bigger than
himself. It had been a terrible and bloody experience for him. He
had found on that occasion that once his blood had become
heated with fury he had fought blindly and viciously, like a
madman, and even when his frightened opponent had run for
home, he had pursued him, his mind blank but for the desire to
destroy his enemy.

He started to run after the others, his rage still as fresh and
compelling as the moment that he had discovered the dead
corporal lying pathetically on the jetty. It was as if something
else had him in its grip, something which he had only briefly
controlled since that fight so many years before. Giulio Zecchi
was no longer a mere enemy, he was the very pivot around which
their lives revolved, and the one person who would bring all their
hopes crashing to the ground.

Taylor was small and wiry, but his body was as hard as nails,
and powered by his new fury, he overtook the others and ran
purposefully down the centre of the road.

Duncan saw him shoot past and for a moment thought that
the man had seen something. He groaned aloud and dashed the
sweat from his eyes, as he half realized what Taylor was doing.

They topped another rise and Curtis called a halt. Duncan
dropped on to one knee, trying to listen in the darkness, but
heard only the savage pounding of his own heart. Taylor
slithered to a stop and looked back impatiently at the others.

Curtis didn't know what had made him halt, but as he stood,
trying to control his laboured breathing, his hands loose at his

sides, he felt that they were very near their quarry. He tried to calculate how long they had been running and how far the other man might have got. It was too difficult, and he stared moodily at the back shoulder of the overhanging hillside. On his left the roadside petered out and after a small rocky fringe, dropped away steeply to the beach below. Nothing there, he decided, and looked back at the road. Perhaps, just a few yards ahead, Zecchi would be waiting. One final burst from the Schmeisser, and he would finish all three of them. He beckoned to Duncan.

'You take the hillside, Steve.' He noticed the listless droop of the man's shoulders and added easily, 'You're the only one who can manage that sort of thing. Try to keep level with us, but watch the road in front.'

Duncan shook himself and nodded. With a sudden burst of energy he jumped the loose rocks at the side of the road and was soon lost on the hillside.

Curtis gave him a few seconds to get started. 'Right, George, you keep on the left of the road and about twenty yards behind me. If anything happens, jump over the edge of the cliff and blaze away for all you're worth!'

Taylor digested this carefully. 'An' wot about you, Skipper?'

'I'm going to walk down the middle of the road,' answered Curtis calmly.

'Bit dodgy, ain't it?'

Curtis raised his hand. 'Listen!' They cocked their heads. 'I heard something! Come on!'

Taylor dropped slightly behind Curtis's tall figure and plodded forward along the edge of the road. He found it difficult to drag his eyes from the skipper's back. Alone, in the middle of the road, striding along as if on parade, he looked vulnerable and completely open for attack.

Curtis stepped briskly round the next curve, his breath momentarily halted as he waited for a shot to smash him down, but nothing happened. Perhaps Zecchi had found another route after all, but he dismissed the thought instantly. He was a stranger here, too, and he knew quite well that his only hope was to reach the nearest village or town.

Chasing a man in his own country, he thought suddenly. It only helped to add to the unreality he now felt. His foot kicked against a small metal object. He scooped it up in one movement and continued walking. He knew without looking at it, that it was Zecchi's cigarette case, and the find gave him a cold sense of relief and loathing together.

His head was beginning to pound with his exertions, and inwardly he told himself to keep with Taylor, near the only available cover. Then it happened. A little above the road to his right there was a savage burst of orange flashes, accompanied by the short, harsh rattle of the Schmeisser.

He flung himself recklessly forward, aware of the bullets singing hotly past his face and snickering amongst the loose stones behind him. As he reached the edge of the road, he rolled over against the rocks and fired two shots indiscriminately into the darkness. Taylor fired, too, and Curtis sighed with relief. He realized that the rocks near him afforded no real cover at all, and should Zecchi have noted his position, another burst would finish him. He bared his teeth savagely. Go on, shoot away! Steve will get you in a minute, you murdering bastard!

Taylor called across the road, his voice hoarse. 'I gotta thirty-six in me pocket, Skipper! Shall I 'eave it at 'im?' He cursed horribly as two shots whined down from the slope and made him duck down the cliff.

'No! Remember Steve!'

He peered round the rocks. Nothing stirred. Zecchi had used only single shot that time. Of course! He almost cried out with excitement. There was only the one magazine with the gun.

His neck ached with concentration and anxiety. The shots might easily be heard a mile away on such a still night. Perhaps that was Zecchi's idea. He jumped, as Duncan's powerful voice shattered the stillness.

'Look out! He's off down the road again!'

Then they were all running again, caution thrown to the wind, like hounds after a stag.

Duncan grunted as he landed in the road and gathered speed towards the next bend, his head hunched in his shoulders.

'Soon now!' he gasped at Curtis. 'He can't manage much more!'

They rounded the curve together, and stopped.

The moon had risen above the hill again, and like part of a carefully dressed stage, the next fifty yards of roadway was bathed in eerie blue light.

Giulio Zecchi had stopped, too. They could just define his round pale face and short grey hair, as he stood in the middle of the road, his square figure heaving from exertion.

Curtis stared past him at the line of figures across the road.
Dark, formless shapes, they might have been of stone, but for
the gleam of moonlight on their levelled rifles. Even as the three
of them watched, another slow-moving line of heads appeared
along the top of the rise, closing the road into a silent arena.

'Well, that's that!' The bitterness in Duncan's voice was
complete.

Giulio Zecchi rested a plump hand on his chest, fighting for
breath. 'Nothing to say, Lieutenant?' He laughed wildly. 'What
about the Australian? Nothing? Such a pity!'

'Oo are they, fer Gawd's sake?' Taylor stood loosely, his hand
inside his blouse. He could feel the rough warmth of the grenade
under his palm. One pull, and I'll blow all of us to hell!

Curtis's voice was cool. 'Some sort of Home Guard, I
imagine. It doesn't matter I suppose, what it is!'

A man stepped slowly from the watching line of figures. He
was small and lithe, his body distorted by the gleaming
bandoliers of ammunition criss-crossed over his shoulders and
the cape loosely hanging from his back.

He stood like a small rock, as Zecchi poured a torrent of
Italian into his attentive ear. His eyes were fixed on the three
figures at the other end of the road, but even across the
moonbathed track, Curtis could see the strange watchfulness of
the man and the evident interest he was showing.

'Shall we make a run for it?' Duncan's voice was a mere
whisper.

Curtis didn't turn his head. 'They're behind us, too. Don't
look round!'

He stiffened, as followed by Zecchi, the man started to walk
slowly towards him.

He halted a few feet away and bowed mockingly. 'I speak
English. Tell me who you are!' His voice was tired, almost
caressing.

'Hasn't he told you? We are British officers.'

'Of course. I just wanted to hear you speak.' His thin face split
into a grin. In the half-light his face looked evil. 'And this is
Giulio Zecchi, I believe? He has told me about your strange
journey, but enough of that.' He jerked angrily, as Zecchi
grabbed his arm and pointed at Curtis.

'Seize them now! We will take the ship easily, there are only a few miserable wounded aboard!' He drew himself up, his composure returned. 'You were foolish to think we Italians could not fight, Lieutenant!' His voice trembled with excitement and contempt. 'I will order these men to take you to the nearest German outpost! They will be very glad to deal with you!'

The little man smiled again. 'I understand you have no radio on your poor ship, Captain?' His voice was even more silky.

'No.' Curtis sensed a slight movement from Taylor's hand, and steeled himself.

'So amusing to speak English again,' he remarked inconsequently. 'I was a law student in London, before the war.' He bowed again, the movement making a beam of moonlight dance along the path of his pistol. 'Allow me to introduce myself, Captain. I am Ludivico Fanali, once a lawyer, now District Commander of the People's Liberation Army!'

Curtis stared at him silently, the words not seeming to penetrate his racing thoughts.

He had turned away from Curtis and was regarding Zecchi with cold enjoyment. 'But for the unfortunate lack of a radio, you would have known that the Italian Government has sued for peace with the Anglo-American armies! There has been a big change here since you were last a lackey of the Germans!' The last words were harsh, like a lash. 'So now, Signor Giulio Zecchi, you are *my* prisoner!'

The mayor seemed to shrink. His mouth opened and shut, but nothing but disjointed sounds emerged.

Curtis saw the armed men begin to close in, as their leader continued. 'It is a fortune of war that you tried to destroy the ship's water supply. But for that, you would have been safe and comfortable in a British prison camp.' He shrugged. 'As it is, I now have in my possession one of the filthiest Fascists our poor country produced!' He laughed. It was a terrible sound. 'You should be honoured, *signore*! Even down here we have heard of your doings and of the people you have condemned to the forced labour camps to please your other Fascist friends!' He stepped back, as if unwilling to be infected by him. 'Say good-bye to the lieutenant! I am sure he has work to do!'

Taylor's hand trembled on the grenade. He could feel the sweat cold on his spine. Another miracle was happening, and he couldn't bring himself to understand it.

'Does that mean we're all right?' He stared incredulously as

Curtis pulled out his pipe and placed it between his teeth. He had seen him do that many times, immediately after an underwater attack. When things had started to improve and the danger was passing them by. To Taylor it was like a sign from heaven.

'You are Partisans?' Curtis had not even realized that he had taken out his pipe, but knew only that he wanted to hug the weird little man who stood so patiently before him.

'I believe that is what we are called.' He laughed shortly. 'We are only just getting accustomed to the idea!' He became suddenly brisk. 'You must get back to your ship. At once! There are German patrols in the area, looking for us!' He smiled apologetically. 'Father Bernucci informed me of your plight. It is as well that I decided to come.'

'Why didn't the Father tell me about the armistice?' Curtis tried to remember the priest's sad face.

'It is as well to be careful. Now please go, Captain.' His voice was quietly commanding and full of authority. 'Time is short for all of us.' He turned to the quivering form of Giulio Zecchi. 'Especially for him!'

Curtis wavered, a feeling of pity in his heart, as he saw the dark, silent figures jostling closer to the mayor. There was a sudden movement from the crowd, and Zecchi whimpered as somebody emptied a can of liquid over his head.

The partisan leader gripped Curtis's wrist, his fingers hard and cold. 'Go now! It is better!'

Curtis wrenched his eyes away and pulled Duncan by the arm. 'Come on, let's go!' He had smelt the tang of petrol and knew what was going to happen.

'We'll run back to the ship,' he said harshly, and kicked viciously at Taylor's boots. He was standing mesmerized by the twisting, gibbering shape of the mayor, as he tried to duck away from the man with the lighted match.

'Forgive them,' said the leader simply. 'They have suffered much, and they have long memories!'

Sickened, the three men started to run down the road. But not before Curtis had seen the writhing figure, wrapped in flames, as it jumped screaming over the edge of the dark cliffs.

Once round the first curve in the road, they halted, and Curtis rubbed his eyes wearily. He heard Taylor retching, and was suddenly aware of the gleaming cigarette case in his bunched fingers. With a feeling of revulsion he hurled it from him and sent it skimming over the cliff edge towards the silent water.

'Ready chaps?' His voice was steady, but he was glad of the darkness.

'Fair enough.' Duncan fell in step beside him and with Taylor plodding silently behind, they started down the empty road towards the cove.

Jervis crossed the schooner's darkened deck in quick, nervous steps and hovered at the side of the coaming over the hold. Every available lantern had been placed there to help the funny little Italian doctor who, with the captain, was organizing the wounded soldiers with all the brisk efficiency one might have expected in a well-equipped field hospital.

Jervis glanced anxiously over his shoulder at the dark bulk of the land. The glare of lights from the hold seemed to welcome attention from every direction, and more than once, his heart chilled as he imagined that he heard the sounds of vehicles from beyond the hills. He tried to laugh off his growing fear, when he discovered that the sounds were those of distant aircraft, but he found only the sick, empty sense of despair, which had kept him company since the skipper had left to look for the girl's father.

He walked stiffly to the rail and forced himself to stare along the deserted jetty. Try as he might, he could not avoid looking at the still shape by the mooring bollard, its head gleaming wetly in the moon's feeble gleam. He swallowed hard and gripped the rail with sudden desperation.

I'm the one, he thought wretchedly. I've caused all this. Just because I wanted to appear the big man in front of her. If I hadn't made such a stupid gesture, the skipper or Steve would soon have discovered the real culprit, and all this might have been avoided. He jerked upright, startled. A faint burst of firing echoed around the invisible cliffs beyond the cove, but before his reeling brain could be brought under control, the silence of the night closed in once more, and he was left listening to his heart.

He felt the sweat trickle across his scalp, and his nostrils quivered like those of a cornered animal. That was automatic fire. Perhaps the skipper was already dead, and Zecchi was on his way to the ship with soldiers. He closed his eyes and saw again the mocking smile of the German officer who had captured him.

'An example must be made!' he had said.

He strained his ears into the darkness, his eyes still pressed shut with concentration. There it was again. Some sharp shots, mingled with the heavy thud of another pistol. He forced himself away from the rail and stared round. If the skipper and the others had run into an ambush, then he, Jervis, was in charge of the whole venture. The ship creaked peacefully against the fenders, and beneath him in the hold, he heard a soldier laugh. It was a high pitched sound, and Jervis had to stop himself from running madly to the safety of the aft cabin. A slow, terrible thought began to penetrate his racing brain. Suppose the Italian captain had arranged all this. Or even the girl, Carla. It was possible, and quite within their power. After all, he thought wretchedly, the skipper had only the word of the captain, and a promise from the local priest, that everything was safe. He felt his hand on the smooth leather of his holster. He must do something. But what?

His legs quivered as he lowered himself into the hold and stood taking in the scene which shone beneath the lanterns like a crude tapestry. The little doctor was in his shirt-sleeves, but still wearing his wide-brimmed black hat. Across his round paunch a huge watch-chain swung and jerked, as he ducked and pranced around the man who lay on a rough table made from odd boxes and covered with blankets. The soldier, naked from the waist down, watched fascinated as the doctor made a few final adjustments to the leg bandages and then sank back on the table, a small smile on his tight lips.

The doctor pulled off his glasses and polished them vigorously with his handkerchief. He frowned briefly, as the Italian seamen who were pouring boiling water into a small dish, allowed some of the steam to billow across the table, and then his eye fell on Jervis. He nodded and waved his hands around the hold.

'Ver' good!' He nodded again, and beamed at the soldiers. 'I think we do ver' well!'

He signalled with his finger to two of the soldiers who were acting as orderlies and, helped by the captain, they removed the man from the table and kicked the dirty dressings into a pail which was overflowing on to the deck.

Jervis watched the girl as she walked out of a darkened corner of the hold, leading the blind soldier by the arm. Her face was pale and strained, and he noticed the streaks of blood on her wrist and on the skirt of her dress, as she moved under the lanterns. She did not appear to see Jervis, and her eyes were dead and dull.

The doctor darted a quick glance at her and rose on tiptoe to speak in Jervis's ear.

'Ver' good girl, eh? She 'as been working like a, like a——' he broke off and shrugged. 'But I do not think she will last much more, eh?' He studied Jervis's taut features with professional interest, and then with a grunt he turned to the young soldier, who was sitting uneasily on the edge of the table.

Sergeant Dunwoody walked shakily across the littered hold, and stared at Jervis suspiciously. He had a further bandage across his forehead, and occasionally his good hand moved gingerly across his face, as if to assure himself that the damage was not more serious. The doctor had been quite angry with him and, aided by the captain, had forced him to sit and rest, but even then he had fidgeted with his pistol and stared round the hold, his eye gleaming with cold rage.

The girl released the soldier's arm and stepped back. Her elbow touched Jervis's tunic and she spun round startled, her eyes black with anxiety.

'Is there no news? Have they come back yet?'

Jervis thought about the shots, but shook his head. 'Nothing yet. Perhaps he got away.'

She studied him, her mouth slack. Jervis thought she was surprised at his remark, but he no longer trusted his judgment about anything.

'He killed that man!' Her voice was low and unsteady, and she spoke slowly, as if repeating a lesson. 'I cannot understand.' She looked searchingly at Jervis. 'All this has unhinged him, perhaps?' She waited, but he could only stare at her. 'I wish I knew what was happening!'

The captain joined them, wiping his fat palms with a piece of cloth. 'That boy is the last.' He glanced curiously at Jervis and then at the girl. 'I think I'll go on deck an' prepare to leave, eh?'

Jervis blinked and then tightened his mouth. 'No! Wait!'

The captain paused, a slight frown creasing the smoothness of his brown, egg-like head. 'For what? Your commander will return soon, an' we must be ready to go.'

Jervis dropped his hand on to his gun, and saw the captain's troubled eyes follow it down.

'What makes you so sure he'll be back?' He had to drop his voice to restrain the tremble which crept into it. 'Suppose you've been lying all the time?' He took a half step forward, and the captain swallowed.

'He will be back. He will do what he has to do!' He darted a quick, unhappy glance at the girl, but she was still watching Jervis. 'Please! Let me prepare the ship, eh?'

Jervis jerked his head towards the hatch. 'I'll come with you then.'

He waited until the captain had started up the ladder, and then turned to the girl. For a long moment they looked at each other, but he could see that she had already excluded him from her own thoughts.

The doctor had removed the bandages from the soldier's eyes, and was staring with bird-like intensity at the man's face.

Carla Zecchi moved automatically to the soldier's side and took his hand firmly between her own, as the man said in a small voice, 'I still can't see, Doctor. There's nothin' at all!'

She pressed his hand still harder, as if to force the rising panic from him, and by so doing, share with him her own private loss and misery.

Jervis blundered after the captain and found him giving orders to two of his men.

'Here! Wait a minute! What the hell are you doing?'

The captain halted and stood patiently waiting for Jervis to catch up. 'The mooring ropes, *signore*. We must slacken off the lines in readiness.' His dark eyes were watchful.

Jervis ran to the rail and listened. Nothing. Not even a gull broke the silence.

They're not coming, he thought wildly. They're dead, or perhaps only wounded, and lying up there helpless. He stared round at the menacing shapes of the sleeping hills. He imagined the stealthy footsteps of the soldiers, as they slowly surrounded the cove and lined up their sights on the pale shape of the small schooner. A nerve jerked in his throat, and he ran his tongue across his dry lips.

'Time? What's the time?' He snapped his fingers urgently, as the captain fumbled for his heavy pocket watch.

'Nearly three.' There was no help in the man's voice.

God, it would be dawn soon. He stared up at the gently

spiralling masts and imagined that he could already see them more clearly. If we left now, we could be well clear, perhaps twenty miles out by first light. He bit his knuckle, as he tried to assemble his ideas in order.

'Well, *signore*? Can I get ready?' The voice was prodding him again.

'Very well. Carry on.' He waited, numbed, as the captain and his two men climbed on to the jetty and began to cast off some of the lines. A figure moved by the bollard, and he almost cried out. He tore at his holster as he saw the dim shapeless form shorten, to kneel beside the dead corporal.

The captain moved with surprising agility. 'It is the priest! Father Bernucci! He will look after the body.'

'What about the soul? Will he look after that?' Jervis laughed crazily, and the man on the jetty looked up, his crucifix shining like a star against his dull robe. The captain shrugged and hurried away.

Jervis walked slowly to the high stern and looked past the bobbing shapes of the two moored fishing boats, to where he knew the open sea lay waiting.

The captain could handle the schooner, and he could navigate the vessel on to some sort of course which would eventually take them to a safe area. But only if they left at once. He stood upright, his arms rigid, as if he had just received an order.

'Start the engine, Captain!' he called sharply, all the pent-up fear released in that one, brief command.

The captain spoke to one of his men and strolled to the wheel. 'We are leaving?'

'Yes.' He wrenched his eyes from the kneeling priest. 'We cannot wait any longer.' His voice rose to a shout. 'Don't just stand there, man! Get ready to leave!'

'I will tell the doctor. He has finished anyway.' The captain loitered, as if to say more, but with a deep sigh he shuffled towards the hold.

The doctor appeared on deck, buttoning his coat. He breathed deeply and walked uncertainly to the rail. He paused, and spoke over his shoulder. 'I go, *Tenente*. They will do well for a day or two. I 'ave left bandages and a few drugs.'

Jervis nodded violently. 'Thank you, Doctor. Thank you very much.'

The little man shook hands with the captain. 'Who knows what the dawn will bring!' He sounded tired and frightened.

The captain darted a glance towards Jervis. 'Yes. The dawn.'

He watched as the doctor crossed the jetty to stand by the priest.

The engine roared into sudden life, racing and spitting under the seaman's careless hand.

The captain grunted and swung the wheel experimentally in his hands.

'We will wait a little longer?' His voice was pleading.

And fall into a trap, thought Jervis, and smiled without humour.

'Ten minutes,' he heard himself say and wondered at his own behaviour.

A muffled thudding rose under the forward deck, and Jervis jerked his hand angrily at the captain.

'What the hell's that?'

'The prisoners! They are fighting, I expect.'

'Go and quieten them!' Then as he imagined he saw the eager light in the man's eyes, 'No, I'll go!'

He strode along the deck, his mind blank but for the ache of fear and anger. He almost collided with Carla Zecchi as she leaned limply against the foremast. He paused nervously. The thudding continued, but the girl seemed dazed and unaware of what was happening.

'Are you all right, Carla?'

She nodded. 'I was hoping they might be back.'

Jervis's nerves jumped as the thudding grew louder, interspersed with shouts. 'I must go!'

'I will come with you.'

She followed him along the deck, her slim shape close behind the pale outline of his uniform.

Jervis climbed down to the storeroom and banged angrily on the stout door. 'Quiet in there! Keep silent!' There was a pause, and then he heard a shrill, frightened voice, and he guessed it was the police officer.

'Please, *signore*! Take this man out of here! He is going mad!'

There was immediately a string of curses in German and more terrified shouts.

'It is Lieutenant Beck,' the girl said distantly. 'He has been quarrelling with the others.' Her voice was almost matter-of-fact.

'I'll fix him!' Jervis was almost glad to be able to release some of his pent-up despair, and he jerked impatiently at the heavy staple, his gun in his hand.

As the door swung back he saw the five policemen cowering at one end under a pile of boxes and crates. The German officer stood straddle-legged before them, a rough piece of timber in his fist. He glared at Jervis, but lowered the club, his chest heaving.

The police officer stepped forward, his dark eyes watchful. 'Please, *signore*! You take us to another place, yes? He will kill us!'

Jervis waved his pistol. 'Tie him up! Use that rope over there!' He gestured with his pistol, and the Italian's teeth gleamed with triumph.

At that moment the girl stiffened and raised her hand. 'What was that? I thought I heard a shout!'

Jervis's heart bounded, and he cocked his head to listen.

The German acted with sudden frenzy. He leapt across the storeroom and kicked the Italian viciously in the groin. With a scream the man fell against Jervis, knocking him into a heap on the deck. As he fell, his head struck against the door-post, and he was only dimly aware of the gun being wrenched from his hand, and the terrified scream of the girl, as the German dragged her up the ladder, the gun covering his retreat.

Jervis staggered weakly to his feet, aware of the stamping feet across the deck, and the captain's excited voice. The police officer moaned softly on the deck, and Jervis slammed the door shut before he dragged himself up the ladder.

The captain shook his arm and peered into his face. 'What 'appen? That German has gone up the jetty! You let him escape?'

Jervis hung weakly to the rail. 'I know! I know! I'm going after them!'

Without waiting for a reply, he broke into a run. He had seen the German's uniform gleam momentarily at the end of the jetty, before disappearing round to the right, towards the village.

His fear was forgotten and he was so overwhelmed by what had happened, that he could only think of it being the final proof of his weakness. He was not even aware that he was unarmed, and as his footsteps thudded along the cobbled jetty, he was filled with the desire to revenge himself on the German, as if by so doing he could drive away some of the shame which was his.

He paused briefly at the foot of the old stone stairway at the end of the jetty and looked up towards the village. The

overhanging hills masked any outline he might have been able to
recognize, but as he watched he heard the girl cry out, her voice
shrill with terror, and all the more chilling because of its
apparent nearness.

'Go back! He is going to shoot!' Then there was a sharper cry,
and silence.

Jervis sucked in his breath and started to climb the steps. For
once, he thought, there was no clear way out, and no one to turn
to. It would only be a gesture, he knew, and any second would
bring the bullet from the darkness which would end everything.
He prayed that it would be quick.

From the cliff road above the cove, Curtis watched the
figures below him, his brain cold and clear in spite of the
unexpectedness of the scene, which was made more unreal by
the pale patches of moonlight and the dark, passive background
of the water.

The German and Jervis, in their identical drill uniforms, were
quite clear, but as he watched the third figure pinned down
behind the low stone wall at the top of the steps, his inside
twisted with unexpected anguish.

Duncan licked his lips. 'What the hell are we goin' to do? Ian's
comin' straight up those steps. He'll never stand a flamin'
chance!'

They heard the girl cry out, and Curtis moved quickly to the
edge of the road. 'Come on!' Then cupping his hands, he yelled,
'Stay where you are, Ian! We're coming down!'

Jervis heard the sudden voice booming and echoing amongst
the rocks, stood still on the steps, his fists clenched to his sides,
and a cold relief flooding through his quivering body. He closed
his eyes but felt the tears wet against his cheek. He was no longer
alone.

Slithering and stumbling down the rock-strewn slope, Curtis
kept his eyes on the German. When he had called out, the man
had swung round involuntarily, shocked by the threat behind
him. He recovered himself in an instant, and without another
glance at Jervis, he pulled the girl to her feet, and before Curtis
had even time to guess his intention, thrust her backwards over
the wall. She gave a short scream and vanished. Curtis
remembered clearly the long steep flight of rough stone steps
and choked back a sob of pain and fury. The German had gained
the lower road and was running strongly and easily towards the
village.

Once Curtis's feet landed on the road he summoned up all his strength and, aided by the overwhelming madness within him, he ran purposefully down the middle of the track, the pistol tight in his hand. The white uniform vanished as if the German had disappeared into thin air, but as Duncan and Taylor panted up behind him, he waved them to a halt and stared narrowly at the pale hump of concrete that he had seen earlier.

'He's in that pillbox,' he said. His voice was flat and devoid of emotion.

Duncan tried to see his face. He guessed what was passing through Curtis's mind. He had known him long enough to appreciate what he was suffering.

'What'll we do?' Taylor dragged his feet uneasily and glanced down at the dark sheen of the cove.

Duncan spoke with soft pleading. 'Come on, Ralph. Let's leave him! We can't force our way in there. He'd pick us all off. Let's get back to the ship an' get the hell outa here!'

'He's in there all right.' Curtis spoke half to himself. 'He knows we can't get in after him, and yet we can't afford to leave him behind. He'd have every damned German he could find after us!'

'But we must go!' Duncan persisted. 'We shall have to chance it!'

Curtis faced him squarely, his eyes gleaming. 'Yes, you *would* chance it, wouldn't you? Bash on, and hope for the best!' He drooped his voice suddenly. 'Well, I'm not like that. I've got so far, and if you think I'm going to let that murdering bastard stand in my way, you'd better get back to the ship and wait for me there!'

Duncan was silent, appalled by the change which had come over Curtis.

'The grenade, George! Give it to me!' Curtis held out his hand and felt the serrated sides of the bomb warm on his palm.

He ran across the road and pressed himself against the tall side of the pillbox. He could faintly hear the German moving about inside, and lifting his head he called out sharply.

'Come out with your hands up!' He did not know if the man understood or not, but he heard him laugh, the sound amplified by the tomb-like interior of the emplacement, and seconds later a shot crashed from one of the narrow weapon-slits and whined angrily across the road.

Curtis pressed his back against the wall, his eyes on the

moon. He knows he's safe, he thought. We can either stay here and wait for him to come out, or go away and leave him to fetch help. Either way we're finished.

He didn't look down at the grenade as he gripped it in his right hand. He removed the pin and threw it from him.

Across the road Duncan heard the metallic rattle of the pin on the roadway and felt suddenly chilled by the finality of the sound. 'He's goin' to do it!' To himself he said, it's because of the girl.

Curtis released the lever on the grenade and seemed to feel it come alive in his hand. With two seconds to spare he spun round and lobbed it through the nearest weapon-slit.

He heard a grunt of surprise change to a spine-chilling scream, before the weapon-slits blossomed into fiery red eyes and the muffled crash of the grenade reverberated around the hills, flinging stone splinters and a choking cloud of dust across to where Taylor and Duncan watched in shocked silence.

Curtis stepped into the road and walked briskly towards the cover. Over his shoulder he said, 'Start the engine, George, we can't hang about here if there are patrols about!' To Duncan he merely remarked, 'Pity about the noise!'

Curtis hardly remembered speaking to either of them, and had to force his legs to remain steady as he approached the edge of the steps.

At once he saw a small group around her body at the bottom of the steps, Jervis's white uniform, the ghoulish shape of the priest, and the short figure of the doctor.

Carla Zecchi's body looked small and child-like, and for once Curtis did not care what the others thought as he dropped on to one knee and felt her cold hand in his.

The doctor smiled unexpectedly. 'Ver' good girl. She safe!'

'I broke some of her fall.' Jervis's voice died away as Curtis slid his arm under her shoulders.

She opened her eyes, as if she had been expecting him. She said one word. 'Father?'

Curtis shook his head, and she sighed heavily and closed her eyes.

Duncan jerked his head at Taylor and Jervis.

'Stand by to shove off! Skipper says we must sail at once!'

They looked down at Curtis's bowed head and the girl's black braid across his arm and moved slowly away.

The doctor smiled. 'She will be O.K. But a bit painful, eh?'

Father Bernucci stood up, and to Curtis appeared gigantic and all-powerful. 'She can stay with me, my son. I will hide her. No one will know about her, or who she is.'

Curtis looked down at the soft, relaxed face, and remembered what had still to be done. Their real danger might still be ahead, and yet the thought of leaving her behind seemed an even greater risk.

There was a distant rattle of gunfire, and the doctor shuddered and ran towards his car.

The priest shrugged. 'That may be many miles distant.' His fine old head was raised to the stars, and Curtis thought he looked like a saint.

'Nevertheless, Father, I think it might be unwise to risk leaving her here.'

As if in answer, the girl's arm moved up slowly like a ghost and hung weakly across his shoulder.

The priest nodded gravely. 'Maybe it is better.' He rested his hands on them for a moment and, as another burst of firing awakened the echoes, he gathered his robe around his thin body and started off along the road. Once he called back, but Curtis could not hear his words.

Gently, and with infinite care, he gathered her up in his arms and walked slowly towards the pale shape of the *Ametisa*. Her hair was warm against his cheek and as he looked at her he saw a tear on her cheek, although she seemed to be smiling.

A tiny silver light caressed the horizon and the moon seemed to shrink away from the dawn's threat, but Curtis was unwilling to notice either as he stepped carefully on to the deck and made his way aft to the cabin.

The lines snaked aboard and with an urgent flurry of foam the huge screw churned the mud and sand from the bottom of the cove, and the little ship tore herself eagerly from the jetty and tacked round smartly towards the sea. The fishing boats bobbed and faded behind her, and the cove was soon lost in the gloom, but above, on the high cliff road beside the smoking pillbox, the priest watched them go. He saw the sails shake out and climb easily into place, and saw the ship heel over, like a sea bird spreading its wings. Then she was gone.

He thrust his hands into the folds of his robe and, with the crucifix swinging against his chest, he plodded towards his church.

Chapter 11

An Italian seaman emerged from the fo'c'sle and walked stiffly to the lee rail, a bucket of scraps dangling from his hand. He sniffed the keen breeze, and without effort emptied the bucket over the side. For a moment he watched the rubbish twist and dance in the eddies of the bow-wave and then turned his lined face to the empty horizon, his lips pursed into a silent whistle.

Duncan stopped his restless pacing across the poop and watched him with dulled eyes. He felt strangely relieved when the man had returned to the fo'c'sle, and by keeping his back to the stooped helmsman, he was able to retain the impression of isolation. A stronger breeze ruffled the water, which in the early morning light had the solid surface of old pewter, and the sails boomed hollowly and made the vessel cant over even more on to her side, so that the hissing water creamed close to the dipping rail.

Duncan noticed none of these things, and merely stared vacantly at the sweeping bowsprit.

His eyes were tired and gummed up with strain and weariness. He no longer relied on his natural resistance to the elements, and it took conscious effort to refrain from shuddering each time a plume of spray spattered across the damp planking and doused his face with stinging salt.

He glared moodily around the ship, taking in the taut rigging and the worn billowing squares of the sails. The schooner had become part of their lives. In fact it had drawn all of them to its own service. They were no longer a team, and it even seemed that each of them was trying to keep away from the other.

He wrinkled his tanned forehead in concentration. It was useless trying to imagine what the future would bring, and the past was so mixed-up and confused, that he found it difficult to space out the events into separate periods. He stared fixedly up at the mastheads and cursed aloud. The skipper had been right about him. His mouth drooped as he recalled Curtis's cold eyes as they stood outside the deserted pillbox. It had been easy before. Routine; an objective; and the savage exhilaration of victory. He flexed his muscles, but it gave him no pleasure.

A sound behind him made him turn, and he saw Jervis walking slowly from the aft hatch, his dark hair rippling in the keen air.

Jervis nodded and stood in silence beside him.

Now that the ship was serenely on her course again, he, too, was aware of the empty feeling of peace with foreboding; a calm spell of unreality, like a ship passing through the storm centre of a typhoon.

He cleared his throat and saw the seaman at the wheel raise his black eyes momentarily from the compass and stare at him, his face empty. 'Everything quiet?' He did not want to speak, and yet the silence was more threatening than the expression of loss on Duncan's face.

'Too damned quiet!' Duncan moved his shoulders beneath his rumpled battledress, and his stubbled chin rasped against the upturned collar.

'I haven't had a chance to speak to you about what happened,' began Jervis suddenly. 'I expect you're all thinking it was my fault?' He waited half-defensively for the other man to attack. Duncan did not answer, but merely grunted.

Jervis hurried on, 'I know I was wrong now! But at the time something made me act as I did. I felt out of place.' He faltered. 'How can I begin to explain? I saw the skipper and you acting as if you'd always been doing this sort of thing, and I just knew there was something lacking in me!'

Duncan sighed. 'I shouldn't give it a thought if I were you. It doesn't matter any more.'

Jervis stared at him and felt vaguely cheated. The reply was flat and indifferent, and he did not know how to continue, although every memory was a torment. 'Can't you understand?'

'Understand? What is there to understand? It wasn't your fault. I thought it was at the time, but now . . . ,' he paused and looked down at his boots, 'I guess it's just the way it panned out!'

'I didn't measure up to my own standards,' Jervis persisted.

Duncan smiled, his eyes strangely sad. 'All men are equal, I'm told. That doesn't have to mean they're all the same!'

Jervis bit his lip. 'Oh damn!' He had seen the round shape of the captain appear above the hatch coaming.

Duncan grinned at the captain but felt the effort almost cracking his face. He was pleased to see the man, if only to shut Jervis up. He felt irritated and ashamed that Jervis still looked up to him in the same stupid, trusting manner. He was too complicated, too stuffed full of tradition and values. What did they count out here in this damned old scow? He watched Jervis leaning on the rail, his face furrowed as if in pain.

'*Buon giorno!*' The captain scratched his stomach and pulled a pair of black cheroots from his shirt. He gave one to Duncan and jammed the other between his thick lips.

'We are making the good time, yes? Soon we shall see a beautiful ship maybe, an' then we will be safe an' treated like heroes!' His paunch shook with merriment. 'Good, eh?'

'What happens if it's a German ship?' Duncan answered sourly.

'I shall tell them you forced me to bring the ship here, an' maybe they give me the Iron Cross!' He laughed loudly, and the lookout in the bow turned his head to watch.

Duncan smiled in spite of the gnawing uncertainty in his bowels. 'A wooden one, more likely!'

The surface of the sea was split into long paths of different hues. The horizon was silver, and the grey pewter had given way to streaks of green and dark blue, whilst above, the sun had lost its first watery pallor and climbed steadily and confidently along its well-tried path towards the blue emptiness of the sky.

Some of the sun's early warmth seemed to penetrate the dirty glass panels of the cabin skylight and give new life to the dingy carpet and the stained, chipped furniture.

Curtis sat crouched on the edge of the bunk, his body swaying mechanically at each roll of the hull, his eyes heavy and sore with fatigue and concentration.

The girl on the bunk lay quite still, and it was some time before he realized that her eyes were open and watching him with quiet tenderness.

His brain summoned his body to life, and he leaned over her, his tired face anxious.

'Feeling better? Would you like something to drink?'

He supported her head in his hand and held a glass of wine to her lips. The warmth of her head coursed through his hand and seemed to give strength to his arm. Her head fell back on the rough pillow and she smiled up at him. He pulled the blanket up to her chin, and thought how strange had been the fate which had thrown them together.

'Tell me about it, please.' Her voice was soft and pitched very low.

'About your fall?' he asked lightly, knowing what she really wished to hear.

'About my father. How he died.' Her voice was without bitterness and her eyes were lacking in accusation, the sadness making them instead dark and strangely still.

'Not now, Carla.' He looked away. 'Later, when all this is over.'

Her hand moved from the blanket and found his.

'Did you do it?'

He squeezed her cold fingers. 'No. We ran into an ambush. Partisans.'

Some of the old fire flashed into her watching eyes. 'The carrion! It is what we can expect now!' But still the tears did not come.

'I am sorry,' he began simply. 'Things moved too fast. We were powerless.' He expected her to remove her hand, but it remained in his, growing warmer with the contact.

'The ship is quiet.' She spoke softly, and Curtis found he was conscious of the water rippling past the hull and the muted beat of the engine. They might have been alone together in the ship. Alone and at peace.

'We might be lucky today,' he said at length. 'We might meet a friendly ship. If only we had a radio! Or if we——' He stopped as she squeezed his hand.

'I shall be sorry to leave the *Ametisa.*'

He looked at her anxiously, but her face was quiet and relaxed.

'The future will be kinder, Carla.'

'There is no future, I think.' She moved restlessly beneath the blanket. 'What will become of us?'

Curtis looked desperately around the cabin. 'Well, we'll get away from all this. Find somewhere we can relax, and try to forget what has happened.'

She struggled up on to her elbows, her eyes pleading. 'Please do not say that! We are together here, and here only! If we get to safety, it will be good for the others, but you and I,' she sank back wearily, her throat trembling, 'we will be lost. We have no place together!'

He tried to speak with confidence. 'The war won't last forever! Why, it might be a matter of months! And then I shall take you away and make you see me as somebody different!' He grinned shakily.

She closed her eyes and moved her head from side to side. 'The war may also last for years. The Germans will go on fighting until they are all destroyed, or they have destroyed you. Then you will have to fight all the others—the Japanese, perhaps the Russians!'

Curtis smiled. 'They're our allies.'

'The Germans were our allies, too,' she answered quietly.

Curtis went cold. 'But suppose you're wrong, Carla? Surely it's not hopeless?'

She opened her eyes and smiled, but her mouth quivered. 'Be content with now!'

He sat in silence as she fell into another exhausted sleep, her hand small inside his own.

She was right, he thought bitterly. All his plans and dedicated self-made suffering seemed unimportant now. Even the nightmare which had robbed him of his courage and changed him into a haunted figure seeking an impossible penance for what he had done. He studied the girl's quiet face. She had once asked him what he was trying to prove. Now, none of that mattered, and he knew that his real atonement would be losing her.

He heard Duncan's hoarse voice above his head, and he gently released her fingers and covered her bare arm with the blanket. He stood up and looked round the cabin once more. The lamp swung peacefully from its bracket and the sunlight moved back and forth in shimmering reflection on the deckhead.

He did not want to leave the place, fearing what he might find outside, where reality could only bring more danger and misgivings.

Duncan was running for the hatch as he emerged, blinking on the warm deck. He saw the man's craggy features lined with something like the anger of one who has been cheated.

'Aircraft!' he shouted. 'Port bow!'

Curtis ran to the rail, his fair hair blowing across his forehead. At first he could see nothing, although the high-pitched whine of the engine cut into his brain like a knife.

It was low down, its thin, wafer-edged shape mingling with the fresh dancing water, as it weaved and curtsied over the wavetops, the silver arc of its propeller seeming to touch the spray which reached up to touch it.

Barely a mile from the schooner, it swerved aside and clawed its way lazily towards the sun, which flashed angrily across the perspex cockpit cover and lighted with fire the dull black cross on the fuselage.

Duncan watched it apprehensively. 'They finally found us!' he said.

Taylor squinted at the aircraft, as with effortless grace it climbed upwards, until it seemed to be pinioned by one of the schooner's tapering masts, and with his jaw set in a tight grimace, he ran lightly to the engine-room hatch. He swung one leg over the coaming and looked questioningly at Curtis.

'Full revs, Skipper?'

Curtis nodded, his eyes still on the enemy.

The old diesel thundered into renewed effort but, in contrast, the breeze suddenly died and the sails, suddenly stripped of their power, hung limp and steaming in the warm sunlight.

'Go to the hold, Steve,' he said quietly, 'and explain the situation to the soldiers. Keep them together and ready to leave the place quickly.'

Duncan ducked his head beneath the boom to follow the plane. 'What d'you reckon he's up to?' He sounded calm, almost relieved that the waiting was over.

'Having a good look at us, and probably wirelessing his base at the same time. We shall soon know.'

Duncan started for the hold, his eyes falling on the Italian captain's face. The man was not looking at the aircraft, but staring round at his ship with sudden fear.

'I'll be in the hold if you want me, Ralph. In case anythin' goes wrong,' he grinned sadly, 'well, it's been nice knowin' you!'

Curtis smiled at him. 'Thanks, Steve.'

Duncan jerked his hand towards the poop. 'What about the girl? Are you gettin' her on deck?'

He shook his head, his eyes clouding. 'No, I'll let her sleep. That doctor gave her some dope. It's better this way.'

Duncan nodded and looked up at the blue sky. The aircraft was a mere silver speck, so high up that it was difficult to recognize its shape. 'If only we had a flamin' gun of some sort! We could at least have a go!' He caught Curtis's eye and ran to the hold.

Curtis turned to Jervis, who stood stock-still in the middle of the poop, his lips moving soundlessly.

'You stand there, Ian. We can try the old deception trick again. It might work.'

Jervis looked down dazedly at his crumpled uniform. 'It's all up, isn't it?' His voice broke. 'We're so helpless!'

'Just keep calm,' answered Curtis patiently, 'and remember that I'm relying on you!'

Curtis stepped into the shadow of the big sail, as with an ear-shattering roar the aircraft plummeted out of the sky, to level off only feet from the sea. It flashed across the surface, so close to the schooner's stern, that they could clearly see the goggled head of the pilot as he turned to study them, as a motorist might glance at a passing signpost. Curtis pressed his back against the mast, and to overcome his trembling limbs, examined the aircraft with professional detachment.

'Messerschmidt fighter,' he said calmly. 'Quite a nice looking plane!'

Jervis raised his hand weakly towards the plane and felt the rush of its passage across his face. He turned desperately to Curtis. 'Do you think he'll go away?'

Curtis did not answer, he had seen the fighter begin its slow turn, its wings fanning over like those of a drifting gull.

'Captain! Take the wheel yourself!' The terrified man gripped the spokes and shouldered the seaman out of the way. 'Ian, get flat on the deck, he's coming in!'

He glanced quickly along the quiet deck. When he looked back to Jervis he saw that the boy was still standing motionless, his pale face turned towards the fighter with disbelief.

'Get down!' he roared. 'He means business!' Then in a quieter voice, 'Plenty of other people have gone through this, Ian. This is the *real* war!'

He saw Jervis throw himself down, and as he turned to find the plane, he saw that it was cutting over the water and coming straight for him.

As he watched the thin edges of the wings, he saw them suddenly come alive in a line of rippling orange flashes. The harsh rattle of the eight machine guns sounded like a giant tearing sheets of steel in half, and before his brain had recovered, the water near the ship's side boiled into a savage frenzy, and as the plane drew nearer, the hull shuddered and splintered under the barrage of bullets. He saw the deck planking clawed and torn, and a section of the bulwark rose into the air, as if detached by an invisible hand. With a deep-throated roar, the fighter pulled out of its attack and zoomed over the masthead. Before its shadow had left the deck, Curtis was across the poop and trying to judge the pilot's next move. The man was in no apparent hurry. He had, after all, all the time he needed.

Jervis swallowed and peered over the edge of the bulwark. He picked gingerly at the torn woodwork and followed the trail of destruction across the ship, over the sea, until he could see the tiny circling shape of the fighter.

Curtis stood close to the captain. He could almost smell the man's fear, and he spoke sharply.

'Alter course when I tell you! Put the wheel hard over, and at once! Hang on to yourself, man! I thought you had nerves of steel?'

The captain's eyes were wide with misery. 'My ship! My *Ametisa*! I am afraid for her!' His body seemed to shrink as the fighter's engine screamed across the sea once more.

He waited, his breath stilled, counting the seconds.

Brrrrr! Brrrrr! The guns rattled and whined. He was getting better at it. This time the bullets clawed across the whole poop like a steel whip.

The seaman at the captain's side spun round, his scream choked short as a heavy bullet smashed into his chest and flung him across the rail like a rag doll. For a moment he hung there, his sightless eyes filled with fear and hatred, and then he toppled slowly over the bulwark into the sea.

Splinters whirred through the air, torn in fantastic shapes from the planking, and Curtis heard the hiss of canvas, as the shots poured through the sails and severed the lamp rigging.

The captain squeaked, as with a clang the brass top to the binnacle, only a foot from his body, jumped from its clasps and rolled across the deck.

The air was full of noise and fear. Curtis shouted above the din of the engine, 'Hard a-port!' and saw the stricken schooner tack round with seconds to spare. The fighter was there again, its wings alive with chattering fury, as it plunged recklessly down, the wing tips seeming to brush the bowsprit.

Curtis realized suddenly that the ship's engine had stopped, and even as he tried to concentrate, he felt the ship slowing down and saw the bow-wave fading and growing more indistinct.

The planks at his feet jumped and shook, and he put his hand to his cheek to feel the warmth of blood where a flying wood splinter had caught him.

Taylor clambered over the coaming, cursing, and trying to tie his handkerchief around his wrist. Blood pumped steadily over his clawed fingers, and Curtis ran quickly to his aid.

Taylor leaned limply against the hatchway, his breath whistling between his teeth, as he watched the plane overhead.

Curtis fixed the bandage. 'Engine finished?'

He shrugged angrily. ''Fraid so. All the fuel pipes gone, and Gawd knows what else!' He watched the fighter with narrowed eyes. 'Nice bastard, ain't 'e?'

Curtis thrust Taylor down with his hand, shouting in his ear. 'Here he is again! Get down!' He felt Taylor's body shudder against his own, as the guns roared deafeningly. The shots seemed to come from all round them, and he winced as a heavy block, cut from the mast, struck him across the shoulders.

He blinked and scrambled to his feet. The fighter was growing smaller and smaller, as it tore towards the invisible mainland.

''E's packed up!' Taylor croaked incredulously.

'He's done what he came to do!' Curtis sounded weary and resigned. 'The ship's stopped and helpless. I expect there'll be a destroyer along soon to pick us all up!'

His searching eyes fell on the captain, and he ran across to where he sat awkwardly on the deck. He had his back against the wheel and one of his short legs was doubled beneath him.

He looked up at Curtis, his face grey. 'As I told you, *signore*! Boom! All finish?' He sagged lower, and Curtis saw the widening stain across his thighs. He knelt at the man's side, feeling helpless.

'Is there anything I can do?'

A bright scarlet thread wound its way from the corner of the captain's mouth and dripped off his chin. He shook his head jerkily. 'My ship! My little *Ametisa*!' He coughed, and a fresh flood ran from his mouth. 'Look what they do to her!'

His eyes were still wide with pathetic anger, as he stared up at the shattered masts and torn sails, when with a deep sigh his head lolled and his braided cap fell to the deck.

Curtis picked it up and gently replaced it on the man's head.

Jervis was shouting wildly. 'He shot us up deliberately! He only shot at the after part of the ship! Just wanted to hold us here to be captured!' He stared vacantly at the dead captain.

Curtis stood up. 'Yes, that's what he had in mind, I expect——' He broke off, suddenly icy cold.

The after part, Jervis had said. All at once he was running, tearing at the cabin hatch cover. He stumbled down the last few steps and wrenched open the cabin door.

'Carla!' He called her name as he burst in, and then found himself staring down at her upturned face. She was lying on the cabin floor, where she had pulled herself from the bunk. A trail of blanket had followed her across the deck, and Curtis's heart surged within him as he saw her eyes open.

As he dropped to his knees a shaft of sunlight hit him in the eyes, and he glanced up in surprise.

Across the side of the cabin was a line of neat round holes.

He stared unbelievingly at the bunk and at the deck. Beneath the blanket he saw the sunlight glitter on the bright red drops which marked the girl's progress towards the door.

With a sob he tried to gather her up, but she shook her head with sudden violence, her eyes dark with pain.

He kept his hand under her shoulders, feeling her life seeping over his wrist.

His eyes were misty, and he had to keep blinking to retain the picture of her pale face as she whispered against his cheek.

'*Sento un dolore—qui!*' She tried to move her hand behind her, but he held her wrist and tried to smile.

'You'll be all right, Carla! You'll be all right!'

She stared up at him, her eyes exploring his face with sudden intentness.

'We are together now!' She smiled as he smoothed her hair from her forehead. 'This is how we wanted it, yes?'

He waited, staring brokenly at her and feeling the warmth fading from her hand.

He bent lower, as her lips moved again.

'Do you remember seeing me on my horse? I saw you striding along the beach, trying to look like a German. You were not ver' good at it!' She bit her lip, and he tightened his hold on her.

'I remember. I thought how lovely you looked. And after you had passed, I turned to look back. I shall never forget!'

She moved her hand flat against his face, her fingers touching his eyebrows.

'Perhaps you will be safe, now that it is night again.'

Curtis glanced fearfully at the bullet holes in the torn planking. The sun was as bright as before.

'You see, we had no future? Only now...'

He nodded blindly. 'Yes.'

She stiffened. 'Hold me! Now!'

But as he gripped her, she relaxed and smiled up at him. When he realized that the smile was fixed and unmoving, he pried her fingers from his hand and kissed her gently on the lips. Her perfume seemed to cling to him as he picked her up and laid her carefully on the bunk.

He closed her eyes and stood back against the bulkhead, unable to leave her. The smile remained, as if she was still holding on to the small moment of happiness.

His limbs were numbed and he stood quite still, staring down at her. Even his breath seemed to have stopped, as if by the slightest movement he might miss something, or if by waiting he might find he was still dreaming.

Duncan lurched into the cabin and stopped dead. His eyes darted from Curtis's stricken face to the still shape on the bunk, and he stepped forward, his hands half raised, as if he expected Curtis to fall.

'What is it?' Curtis's mouth moved slowly, and his voice seemed to come from far away.

'Would you like me to take over, Ralph?' His voice was gruff and very low. 'I didn't realize...' He stared helplessly at the girl's body.

'No. I'll come. There are things we have to do.'

He paused by the door, and Duncan could almost feel the agony in Curtis's eyes as he looked back. There was an expression of complete loss on his drawn features, and something like pleading in his blue eyes. 'I shall come back,' he added.

Duncan was not sure if he was being spoken to, or whether the promise was addressed to the girl. He touched Curtis's elbow, and followed him up the ladder into the bright sunlight.

Curtis stared round the torn decks and only half heard the clank of the hand pumps forward. His glance passed over the soldiers, who were gathering silently amidships, as if they were no longer there, and moved restlessly across the smiling water to where he had last seen the aircraft.

Jervis was about to speak, his streaked face white and strained, but as he opened his mouth he frowned and glanced at Duncan.

Duncan shook his head quickly and turned his eyes away.

Only Taylor spoke. He walked slowly towards Curtis, rubbing his palms against his greased trousers.

For a moment he waited, until the empty eyes were turned towards him, then he cleared his throat, his mouth forced into a smile.

'I'm sorry, Skipper. Bloody sorry.' He waited, his face tense and anxious, but Curtis merely nodded and patted his shoulder.

'Yes, George. Yes.'

He looked quickly over Taylor's shoulder at the khaki figures who stared listlessly at the sea, or were helping their more badly wounded comrades find a little shelter by the bulwark.

'Why are these men on deck?'

Duncan seemed to jerk out of his trance and hurried to his side. 'Hold's makin' water a bit. The pumps are only just about holdin' their own.'

'I see.' Curtis tried to guess what all this could mean, and frowned because he could not bring himself to think of an answer.

'I've ordered a meal and some drink for the lads, Ralph. It may be some time before they get another.' He scanned the horizon in a quick furtive movement. The sea was still empty. But not for long, he thought.

Curtis walked right aft to the worn taffrail and leaned back, so that his body hung suspended over the faded gilt lettering on the stern. The ship was already dead. With each sullen roll, her masts sagged and jerked and the broken rigging swung unheeded across the decks, blocks clattering, and the torn sails casting strange shadows with each uneven movement. The pumps worked steadily and monotonously, theirs the only sound, but for the slosh of trapped water in the hold and in the deep bilges.

He let his head drop on to his chest, and Jervis stepped closer. He saw the movement, but had already dismissed Jervis from his aching mind.

Waiting. We are always waiting. But this time not for me.

The ship lurched and settled deeper.

Some of the soldiers were getting restless, and one was heard to say, 'But there's no life-jackets or anythin'! What'll we do?'

Sergeant Dunwoody looked at the lone figure on the poop and licked his lips. 'This old ship's all right lads! I expect the Jerries'll be soon now. They'll look after you O.K.!' There was no irony or bitterness in his voice. 'I'm almost past carin' meself!'

Curtis looked up suddenly, as a white gull swerved past the stern, and almost level with his face. It hung motionless, one black unwinking eye fixed on him.

He remembered the casual scrutiny he had received from the German pilot. Casual; indifferent; efficient.

He remembered how the floating dock had appeared through the periscope. Had he ever considered what was happening beyond the cold impartiality of the lens? He groaned and Jervis hovered nearer.

'Can't I do something, sir?' He fell back as the eyes followed the gull over the poop, and fixed his face with a flat stare.

'Well, Ian. Have you learned anything by all this? D'you think your father would call it useful experience?'

Jervis stammered, 'I don't know how to answer, sir! I—I'm too shaky to think of anything!' He turned miserably for Duncan, but he was at the other end of the schooner with the soldiers.

'Why are you always running away, Ian?' His voice was mild, and the boy found he could no longer meet those unblinking eyes.

'Why not just sit down like me, and think about it all?' He moved his hand vaguely to take in the ship and the sea. 'This is all experience, if you care to make use of it.'

Jervis shifted uneasily. 'How d'you mean, sir?' He prayed that Duncan would not be long.

'We started off as a well-oiled machine. Look at us now!' He hurried on as if he was afraid that Jervis might not understand. 'Somewhere, somehow, in the middle of all this efficiency, we find something real and precious. I suppose that it could happen to a soldier, too. He might be lying in a shell-hole, waiting for the shot to come which will kill him,' he smiled secretly, 'then he sees, right by his face, a small leaf, or perhaps a flower, which has been overlooked by the efficiency of man. What must he feel at that moment, eh?' He reached out with sudden force and gripped Jervis's tunic in a hand of steel. 'Tell me what he feels!' He was shouting.

Jervis tried to pull away, but he was quite powerless. He swallowed hard. 'Well, I suppose he feels that . . .' He tried to think of an answer, but he was mesmerized.

'He feels that up to that single moment his life has been empty, and wasted, and beyond it there is nothing more!' He stared hard into the boy's eyes. 'Remember that, Ian!'

He unhooked his fingers and jerked the German eagle from the white tunic. He held it for a moment, then dropped it over the rail. When he looked up again, Jervis had gone, and he saw him talking to Duncan by the hold.

The warmth of the smooth rail caressed his hands, and he noticed that there was dried blood on his fingers and on the front of his jacket. He made a last effort to close his mind, to use it like a flood-gate against the torrent which at any moment would finally break him down. He looked up warily as a man shouted.

'There! There it is I tell you!' The voice was cracked and incredulous.

He saw that the others were looking across the rail towards the inviting water.

A muscle twitched in his cheek, but that was the only outward sign to show that he, too, had seen the movement beneath the surface.

A gasp rose from the soldiers, as with a terrifying roar, the submarine heaved itself out of the depths, water cascading from her evil, slime-covered snout and from the squat conning-tower.

Duncan ran aft, his face hard. 'They're here!' He passed his hand over his face and stared at it dully. 'Nice timin', the bastards!'

Sergeant Dunwoody tore his eye away from the surfacing monster and turned briskly to his men.

'Well, come on there! D'you want to show 'em we're licked, eh? Come on there! Fall in! Two ranks, an' pick up yer dressin'!'

The weary men shuffled into line, while their friends who lay on the deck stared unseeingly at the sky, waiting for the inevitable.

Jervis walked to the rail, his limbs suddenly light and without feeling. He watched the water stream from the gun-barrel and dance like diamonds along the jumping wire. It was nearly over. The conning-tower blossomed into a moving flower of heads and white caps, and from behind the gun he saw another group moving briskly under the orders of a man with binoculars. The black gun-muzzle trained round until it was pointing straight at him, and he turned his eyes to Curtis. He was still sitting on the rail, his eyes resting on the submarine with something like disinterest.

A breeze came from nowhere and rippled eagerly across the calm water, making small catspaws dance along the submarine's ugly hull. It fanned across the conning-tower just as a seaman was hoisting a flag on the stumpy staff. It reached into the flag and blew it out stiffly, with sudden pride, over the heads of the men on her bridge.

A soldier started forward from the wavering ranks and pointed, his mouth working with inarticulate excitement.

'Look! Look at the flag!' He broke down, sobbing, as the White Ensign floated in front of their eyes.

The ship was alive with cheering and noise, as the submarine slowly manoeuvred alongside and the gun was trained away.

Before she ground against the wooden hull, seamen were already leaping aboard to take the heaving lines, and from the conning-tower the commander watched the shattered schooner in silent disbelief.

Duncan waved to him. It was the same submarine from which they had disembarked, so very long ago.

A young lieutenant landed on the deck at his side and shook his limp hand.

'It's good to see you! I still can't believe it!'

Jervis was shouting. 'How did you find us?'

The lieutenant grinned, his unshaven face alight with pleasure. 'Too long a story for now. We had a whisper from

Intelligence that something was going on, but we never dreamed it would be you!'

The submarine commander scanned the sky with sudden urgency.

'Look alive there! Get those poor chaps aboard, Brian! And be sharp about it!'

The forward hatch of the submarine was already open, and more seamen were lowering some of the badly wounded men into the boat's bowels strapped like mummies in Neil-Robertson stretchers. As they swung down, many hands reached out for them, and bearded faces grinned encouragingly.

''Ere comes the bleedin' army!' called one. 'Just in time for a tot!'

The schooner's deck was all at once deserted, and the little khaki flood had been completely swallowed up by the hatches, which were closed once more.

The lieutenant walked across to Curtis. 'Are you ready to leave, sir?'

Curtis stooped beside the Italian captain and tied the man's belt through the splintered steering wheel.

The schooner was already much more sluggish, and was no longer answering to the gentle movement of the water.

The lieutenant watched Curtis rise. 'Are you all right, sir?'

Duncan answered gruffly, 'Of course he is! What the hell did you expect?'

'I'm just going below, Steve. You get aboard the submarine.'

Jervis and Taylor clambered over the slippery casing and climbed on to the conning-tower to stand beside the commander and his lookouts. The powerful diesels throbbed impatiently, and the seamen on the casing flicked the lines expertly, ready to cast off.

The lieutenant stared down at the dead Italian. 'It must have been quite a party!' he murmured. 'All those soldiers, the five prisoners, *and* the crew to contend with!'

Duncan was not listening. He was remembering the strange gleam in Curtis's eyes as he had gone back to the cabin.

'S'cuse me! I'm just goin' below. I shan't be long!'

'Well, all right. But for God's sake don't hang about. We'll be in real trouble if the Jerry turns up!'

Duncan walked softly down the ladder, his heart pounding. The ship was quite still, and he was conscious of the eerie silence, which added to the impression of desertion and finality.

The cabin door was partly ajar, and he halted noiselessly outside. He could see the pale shape of the girl's face on the bunk, and framed against the white bulkhead he saw Curtis's tall shadow. He seemed to be saluting, but as Duncan peered around the edge of the door, he saw the pistol in his hand.

He darted across the deck, not daring to call out, and gently prised the gun from his hand.

'No, Ralph.' He spoke quietly. 'Not this way!'

Curtis looked at him momentarily, and then crossed to the bunk. Duncan couldn't see whether or not he was touching or speaking to her, but he saw the stooped shoulders shake violently.

Curtis stood up and walked from the cabin. This time he did not look back, nor did he remember how he came to be with the others on the conning-tower.

The schooner seemed to grow very small as the other vessel drew away, and as if in a dream he watched her slowly heeling on to her torn side.

The submarine commander spoke briskly into the voice-pipe. 'Diving stations! Stand by to take her down, Number One!'

He watched the four figures at the rear of the bridge, staring back at the sinking ship.

Duncan and Taylor stood side by side behind Curtis, and Jervis was gripping the steel plates with obvious emotion.

Duncan stepped forward just as the *Ametisa* dipped her bow under the caressing water and slipped his hand through Curtis's arm.

'You did well, Ralph,' he murmured.

Curtis smiled sadly and craned his head to watch as the white hull began to slide under the waves.

The lonely gull was still circling over the tall masts, and the Italian ensign made a small patch of colour against the torn sails.

He continued to smile, because he was still looking down at her face on the bunk, but as the masts vanished in a small flurry of foam, his flood-gate burst.

For Ralph Curtis the single moment of peace was past.